I0831870

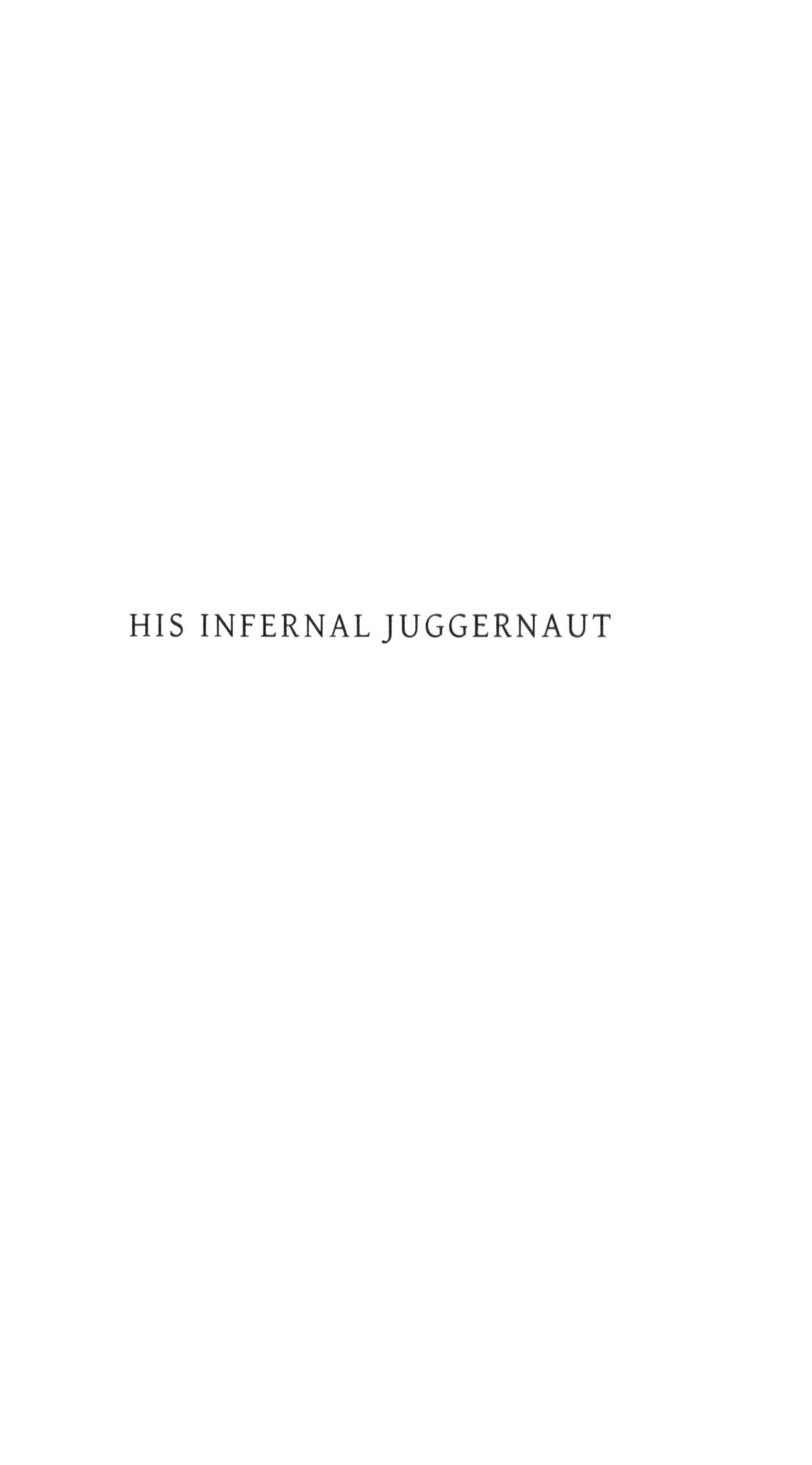

HIS INFERNAL JUGGERNAUT

His Infernal Juggernaut

A Pulp Fiction Space Opera

TOREY RAIN

Stories from Outer Space
Book 1

Cheap Light Books

{IngramSpark Edition.}

Cover design by Aaron Kubacak.

First Printing, 2021

His Infernal Juggernaut

For Jove.
Inescapable, but I become.

-

List of Episodes

The Holy Royal Family—the 25th Dynasty of the Sun Kings
(Capt. Marie Antoinette's Immediate Family)

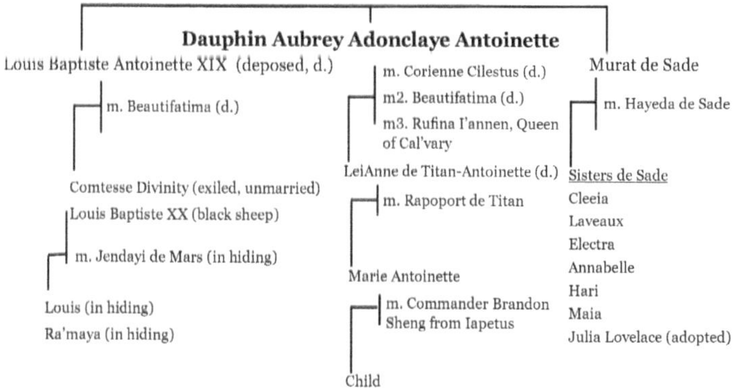

GOLDEN CITY
HOVEL
NEW VOLGEN CITY
NAUGHT
ARAMEN
MECH
WORSHIP
CATACOMBS
LABYRINTH
BEESTJE
MAELSTROM
HOUT
TWEELACH
HALL OF
SAINT
DOVE HOLLAND

PROLOGUE.

INVASION!

Claws dug into her waist and arms, puncturing even through her flight suit breaking skin. She struggled desperately against his gigantic mechanical arms, but they only ratcheted tighter. She felt possessed by him. Her body writhed against his; her legs kicked at his thighs. She was completely smothered in his massiveness; her bosom pressed tightly to his breastplate hewn of cold and ancient steel. The dark signet emblazoned between the screw head nipples on his chest dug sharply into her cheek and neck. The beast reeked of blood and death.

"You recoil in fear...do you not recognize me, Princess?" His voice was an icy whisper of whirring, vibrating transducers. His breath reeked of carrion death rent from defiled tombs. He pressed his freezing lips against her forehead and caressed the top of her head with his cheek. The pallid skin that hung loosely over his mechanical skull felt moist and rancid against her own. This moment of horrible tenderness took her entire breath away. Marie's mind screamed on endlessly, but her voice could not make any sound. Tears filled her eyes. Her terror incited a fierce determination to get away. She attempted to break free, but his taloned robotic hands sought to draw her even closer into his gigantic body. She could feel bones beginning to crack within her chest and shoulders. She feared she would be crushed, smothered, and defiled. A realization crossed her mind—somewhere within this huge contraption of a beast there was, encased, a smaller form. A human heart still beat within this mechanical chest and it was one that Marie was sure she had listened to, once tenderly, before.

"This is revenge dear princess..." he said to her. Hatred clung to every word. A scream finally erupted from the depths of her throat as she felt a rib finally crack in her left side.

Suddenly a barrage of blasts flung the beast into the flaming recesses of the passageway. Marie's teeth clacked together as her face, arm and hip hit the steel grating on the floor of the inferno-ravaged passageway. Hissing metal seared her ears and palm. She flung herself to her feet. Through the smoke and flames the lead man of the crew militia screamed for her to seek safety. At his back stood an army of senturions and more militia members, pulsar cannons in hand. She hesitated. She wanted to help them fight the beast. The lead man sensed this and demanded that she flee. Turning, she made haste down the passageway.

Suddenly there was an explosion at her back. Pieces of fiery hot metal and fireballs erupted all around scattering across the fragmented floor. The beast emerged from the raging fire unscathed. He held in his hands an impromptu battle ax of burning hallway girder affixed with the remains of sharp broken metal wall sheeting. He let out a war howl and thundered toward the army. A barrage of pulsar cannon blasts incinerated the air around him. Now emboldened with rage, the beast hacked through the senturions and militia alike sending guard robot pieces flying amid a carnage of neo-human flesh.

Marie grasped the satchel at her waist containing the chalice as she bolted down the passageway. She was renewed in her efforts to bring the artifact to safety. As she turned the corner of the smoke-filled corridor, she came face to face with Dr. Hannah Krane. The woman stared at her blankly, still, and dumb.

“Run!” Marie screamed at her, “run!”

Another cacophony of eruptions howled at their back. The beast’s cohorts had met him and now their footsteps clanged down the walkway behind them. Marie feared death would not be far gone. Another explosion rocked through the grand passage of the Marie Antoinette...

~ PART I ~

EPISODE 1.

The Dismantlers.

"In these dark sessions,
In this depression,
As sure as the stars shine above,
There is love, there is love..."

Marie's eyes flashed open. The solemn song died on the dank, sulfurous air. It was a tiny voice that sang it. The captain was abandoned. Exposed. The escape pod cockpit was gone, replaced by a churning hellscape. Marie didn't have a chance to figure out the source of the melancholy lines. Suddenly the rhythmic grinding of screeching steel exploded through the somber environ. A crash, then massive gears whirred, lifting up metal again.

Marie's vision adjusted rapidly—a spider-like contraption the size of a space jet eclipsed the air above her. Marie cowered against the screaming, clanking metal. Its spike-studded abdomen thrust the murky, barely breathable air. Its clanging, hook-footed legs thundered the earth at her sides. Red lasers searched her body. Marie jumped free as plunging, metal legs sought to demolish her. The ground exploded at her back. She scampered over rocks and junk pieces of metal. She stumbled down a trench and came to hide in a strangely appointed grotto. Marie peered back. The spider ravenously tore up massive amounts of strange marshy ground where Marie had once lain. A yellow glass headpiece holding sickening rust-colored fluid sloshed to and fro as it did its work. With rhythmic obsession it tore back mounds of mud and abandoned machine fragments searching for something more substantive to disassemble within the marshy terrain.

Marie choked back a gasp not wanting that weak sort of exclamation to betray her location. There were other dismantlers working in the dreary, haze-filled distance. A strange voice filled her mind again, one that she didn't recognize as her own, a strange mechanized human utterance: *six kingdoms of Hout will fall; the rise of the dark code is the death of synthetic ecosystems. The brain of Adelphi Saint must be roused to wake!* It was a desperate plea, a forlorn prophecy, recorded, perhaps, replayed. An alert—or warning. Marie shuddered as the strange voice faded. The small cavern that she crouched within was encrusted with body parts, circuits, and machinery. She attempted to stand. Her mind raced.

What the hell happened here?! What sort of carnage is this!? Her thoughts were cataclysmic as she examined the horrific conglomerations of destroyed humanoid faces dangling on charred wires around her: agape mouths frozen in screams, eye sockets sought to eat her soul with their horrific voids of blackness. Legs, hands, torsos, all intensely hyper-colored, flayed open exposing masses of wires and circuitry impaled on twisted rebar made up the walls of the grotesque hollow.

Marie touched the fingers of a lolling, disembodied hand dangling from a wire—*these are all synthetics...androids. Perhaps one of these has tapped into my mind...* She waited to hear the strange voice again, but nothing. All was dead.

The gargantuan mechanical spider beyond seemed oblivious to her current position. Of that she was grateful. Taking in a breath, she crouched on the ground and took stock of herself: *body—scrapes and bruises, but still alive...* she tried to smudge out the dried blood that was smeared across her yellow flight suit. She realized that there was a gaping wound in her thigh; her arm was on fire and head pounded painfully with every thud of her heart—*alive, relatively, affirmative*; *chalice...*she opened the flap of the satchel that had been lashed to her belt loop. The small vessel still lay inside, glinting dimly in the ruddy light. "There, I have completed your final request—it's here Blake, it's safe with me..." she whispered aloud. *Are you still alive Blake?* She mourned but resolved to find strength. She felt sick. Nauseous. Tearful. *What good would crying do?* She continued her mental status check—*the fetus—hopefully, it lives...*, she held tightly to her abdomen, *I'll say affirmative to that one as well. Weapons—none, zilch, zero—so negative on that one. My escape pod...* "Where's my vessel..." Marie murmured, standing, she peered out across the foreign, dank cavern.

There among the vast conglomerations of artfully sculptural, yet grotesquely composed morgue mounds, she spotted the dismantler that had almost ripped her apart. It now tasked itself with dismantling, hungrily, the hull of her escape pod. It was relentless in its mission, quick and very effective. Now all that was left of the flashing silver lozenge was a few skeletal struts of iron and a couple of sheets of iridium-infused alloy loosely riveted to the remains.

*What I must sacrifice for the sake of art...*Marie thought sarcastically. Her mind raged. *Now, how am I supposed to get out of here?* She wanted to charge the spider, race out in the middle of all kingdom come, shout it down in anger and insult its very need to create shitty sculptures from the remains of her very valuable flight vessel. *However...something tells me that's the wrong tack to take.* She calmed herself. *Very well then,* she straightened her flight jacketed with a frustrated tug. *I suppose I cannot match these gigantic beasts no matter how adept I am at certain forms of Budō.* She sighed. The humor in her mind faded as the incessant, distant, sounds of dismantling fraught the steaming, putrid air.

Marie cursed, sighed, and squatted down. She quieted her mind and realized she was alone and shouldn't have been. *I wasn't in the escape pod alone. Where's Hannah?* Marie stood and scanned the cavernous expanse. In the distance, beyond the enclave of the destructive feast, something gigantic burned—of that, Marie was certain. She thought of her precious starship, the *Marie Antoinette*, her namesake, an inferno upon the raging cosmic winds of the God's Eye Nebula. The reality of this horrible occurrence caused fathoms of sadness to well up inside her. She cleared her throat and pushed the memory away.

Hannah was nowhere to be seen. Marie didn't have to keep up appearances here. *Thank god she's gone.* It was an honest thought. Marie tamed the flare of sickening disheartenment and hatred that often rose up inside her regarding the thought of Dr. Hannah Krane these days.

"What the hell is this tragic place?" Marie said quietly, making her way down the backside of the pile of android bodies to the edges of a grand chasm overlooking a void of steaming, dim crimson light. She peered up into the blackness. Massive riblike structures, ominously arced the air above her. Chills convulsed her spine. The ruddy structures thrust themselves down into the farthest edges of the massive killing field. The earth below her feet was saturated with what smelled like battery acid and bile. More conglomerations of android bodies cumulated here and upon these mounds grew strange flora—vines which choked the android formations with ghastly inky, finger-like creepers. Red veins glowed upon each entangled vine. *Andro-flesh hungry algae...* Marie mused. *No doubt it consumes the remains of whatever goodness is left here—if any existed at all in the first place...*

Marie blew an errant strand of hair out of her eyes and pulled up her sleeve exposing the communi-com device strapped to her wrist. The screen was dark. A nasty crack ran though the center. Marie pressed the crown anyway. The mechanism turned on. Relief flooded through Marie. *Time to tell the Maa'ta Karé where I'm at. If I can figure out how to get a signal to process. Brandon will be furious...he probably won't ever let me hear the end of this—ah, what does it matter anyway?* Commander Brandon Sheng and Marie were barely on speaking terms lately. The complication and headache that was Dr. Hannah Krane...*I wish I could dislodge the memory of her wrapped up in your arms, Brandon... Is forgiveness even possible?* Then there was the baby. Brandon's baby. Too much complication for Marie's tastes, but it was her own fault. She *did* have a history of playing with fire. She cursed at herself. The test came back positive after she left the *Maa'ta Karé Space-port. I'm only a few weeks along—that was the determination of the Antoinette's in-flight medic droid. I don't even want to talk to Sheng about it...but I have to tell him......* The voice in her head annoyed her. She recorded a message to her husband with the news just hours before the invasion, but instead of sending it to him, she pressed delete.

"Come on!" Marie scolded the device which still flashed the message 'loading...' She surveyed her surroundings. All was silent now. Had the dismantlers decided to move on? Suddenly the home screen on her communi-com came into blinding view. She scrolled to the communications icon, and then did a search for the *Maa'ta Karé's* mainframe which responded with the message 'Connection failed,' *Still not working...* She crouched down and clutched her hair wanting to scream. Utter despair crept in and she felt that she might suffocate. She rose, "okay," she said. "You've been in tougher scrapes than this—why do I feel like I'm in a TOMB?!" she screamed, suddenly enraged. Her voice echoed back at her endlessly.

Something in the dark recesses of the killing field seemed to scurry away from her. Footsteps perhaps, or some piece of debris falling. She craned her neck to see. She listened. Nothing. Whatever it was had stopped its movements. "Is someone there?" she called. Nothing. Silence.

In the hazy distance beyond the chasm, orange flares erupted, hypnotic and dancer-like, they illuminated ghastly edifices of city wreckage that seemed to span off into eternity. Demolished gold domes and ash eaten walls still glinting in places with metallic sheets clutched to falling pieces of landscape. Beyond the destroyed structures, a hazy aura of orange created a membrane between the massive horror-filled recess and the blackness of outer space that stretched far beyond. *Was this once a city?* She wondered. *What is this place?*

Hazy recollections of the view outside her escape pod window flashed at the back of her mind: *Space eaten up by massive arms, the nebula eclipsed by planet-dwarfing tentacles sprouting, advancing from churning stardust...*

"*What the hell is that?*" She had said. Marie's voice wavered in her memory. She remembered the chaos in the escape pod cockpit as she gripped the yoke and fought to evade pirate ship fire...

Hannah peered up through the escape pod cockpit window, silent. The churning fuchsia of the nebula outside was consuming by a large black shadow. Her face was plastered with worry, sweat and grime.

A screaming alert sounded, flashing red button cast them crimson. "Hit that for me!" Marie screamed at the doctor. Hannah didn't move. Annoyance flashed through Marie; she shot the woman a death gaze. Hannah finally flicked it. Marie already regretted ushering Dr. Krane into the escape pod. She had done her good deed for the day—of that, she was sure. Invasion. Pirate ship evasion, now the good doctor attached at her hip depending upon Marie for her very survival.

Holographic readouts eclipsed out before them. "...Vessel identity scan doesn't compute...nothing catalogued in our systems," said Marie, flicking on thruster reserves, "looks almost organic...like the bottom of a huge, upturned tree—roots splayed out... a thousand kilometers wide and a thousand kilometers high." Marie was awestruck by the unidentified object's vastness. Hannah craned her neck as well to look beyond the edges of the cockpit window.

Reaching appendages, colossal and threatening, thrust out in every direction. In the middle of all of it—utter blackness. The massive entanglement of arms held asteroid-like formations trapped within them. Marie could just make out passageways threading through the blackness. Strange, haunting portals too. The thrusting, massive thing eclipsed the churning fuchsia clouds of the nebula core and seemed to elicit strobing furies of plasma-fueled lightning strikes.

"What could live out here?" Hannah asked.

"Nothing," said Marie. "This thing is no longer alive...if it was alive in the first place. Obviously derelict...a stealth juggernaut...how could we not know this was out here?" Her question suddenly cut short by pulse fires from ships' cannons and the screaming sound of a horrible squadron at their back. The artful set of maneuvers she'd used to evade

the merciless motley crew of pirate ships had only given them a momentary respite.

"They've found us." Hannah stated, almost defiant. Her tone annoyed Marie.

"Not for long," Marie said, pushing on the throttle, she sent the tiny sliver of a ship into a dive, through the black tangle of the juggernaut's tendril arms. The pirates followed, but not as easily or expertly. The small escape pod had its advantages. It was sexy, sleek, not a lumbering useless cylinder so often found in starships of early manufacture. This pod was on par with an Imperial space jet. It was light and fast, very, very fast.

Hannah clutched her seat handles, white knuckled. "Must you?"

"Do you want to live?!" Marie barked back. Flicking on jet propulsion switches she sent the pod blazing past the edges of the entanglement. Pirate ship cannon blasts ripped through structures just beyond them. The air outside was getting darker, shadows filled the cabin. Marie switched to infrared surveillance.

"Is there a place for us to land?!" Marie yelled at Hannah.

The pirates' relentless pursuit forced Marie to charge the pod deeper into the juggernaut. It was becoming increasingly clear that turning around and leaving this place was not an option. Another barrage of blasts battered the escape pod. Sparks flung out across the control panel.

"We've been hit!" Hannah cried. Marie searched the feedback panels; the fuel line was malfunctioning.

"Problematic...but not impossible..." Marie murmured. Then she saw it, a method of evasion with a possibility for epic failure. She took it. With sudden determination, Marie launched the pod right toward the great wall of blackness at the juggernaut's center. Mere meters before impact, she killed the engines and shut off cockpit lights.

The raging, roaring of their pursuers' speed-hungry engines filled the suddenly silent cabin. Despite Hannah's curses, Marie yanked back on the throttle and kicked down the pedal inciting a reverse rudder. Thrusting downward with whatever propulsion was left in the conveyance, the view from the cockpit window became epic. Pirate ships raced by above.

"Classic," Marie smirked as the cabin erupted with the light of fiery red and orange explosions. Flames of the destroyed pirate ships spewed satisfyingly out into the dark atmosphere. The great black edifice at the juggernaut's center had claimed three of the ships, the other ten in the battalion suddenly turned away.

"What the hell are you doing?!" Hannah screamed.

"Saving your pathetic life!" Marie didn't care that her voice was doused in acrimony. Confident now that the remaining pirates had no visuals, nor any evidence of them on any detection system. Marie turned throttle to propel the nose downward.

"Do you want to turn the pod back on now!?" Hannah cried.

"There's a current, a current..." Marie could feel it. Some sort of cosmic wind surrounded the black interior reaches of the juggernaut. "If I turn on the power the pirates will find us..." Marie bit her tongue. Besides, the pod was totally and utterly devoid of any fuel. That, Marie didn't tell Hannah—however, there was another means of locomotion. "It's drawing us in!" her voice was a celebration. Hannah was annoyed.

"There," Marie said pointing to a ruddy sliver crevasse which erupted from the crook of a great juggernaut arm. "There might be a place to land within that chasm..."

Landing was an optimistic term. Crash was the more appropriate one to use. The magnetic cosmic winds that had been their saving grace had also been their undoing. From what Marie could remember through scant catastrophic memories, the crash had been violent, violent enough to throw Marie and Dr. Krane free into the surrounding carnage piles and leave her unconscious for God knows how long.

Marie was now back up the hill overlooking sleeping dismantlers. They didn't seem as frightening now, though still gargantuan, they slumbered with bowing heads peacefully in a humble, arced posture. *They must be activated by movement,* thought Marie. She sat now upon the torso of a heavily muscled android. She'd used its tattered blue and burgundy shirt for a bandage, finally attending to the wound on her leg which she'd neglected since she'd awoken three hours ago.

"Come on..." Marie shook her communi-com device again and pounded it on her palm. Its power was draining and the status bar still showed that the signal was still too weak. She had spent the past hour collecting android wires, magnets, wire connectors, and galvanized low carbon wire to create a series of signal amplification units. She'd placed these on various piles around the hilltop upon which she now made camp. They seemed to work momentarily, but now Marie was convinced that cosmic winds that surrounded this forlorn place were creating insurmountable interference. She feared communication with the *Maa'ta Karé* was practically impossible. With the battery power draining in her device, it was now becoming increasingly evident that she would have to come up with another plan. *Maybe if I can get around these mists...* Sighing, Marie sat her communi-com device down on the android torso she'd been using as a bench and walked toward the edge of the hilltop, following the amplifier wire that trailed across the wretched ground. Just as she began to fuss with the unit affixed to a metal femur she'd used as a stand; she heard a scuffle at her back. Marie quickly turned to catch a fleeing feminine figure sprint from where she'd just been sitting moments ago. Marie knew immediately what had just occurred.

"Hannah!" Marie screamed. The woman raced into the distance. Marie sped down the hill after her. She knew Hannah now held within her sweaty, cheating grip the precious communi-com device that served as Marie's only lifeline.

The hill of wet stinking earth was steep and slick. Marie thrust herself to the ground, aiming her body in the direction of the wretched woman. Muddy terrain slipped quickly beneath her nomex jumpsuit, cold, damp, and uneven. The momentum of the damp terrain sent her flying down the hillside. Marie, teeth gritted, slammed into the back of Hannah sending the woman pitching forward to the ground. Anger and adrenaline flashed within the captain. Standing, Marie grabbed up the flailing woman's body and took the thief into a guillotine choke hold. Hannah rebounded. Back of cranium cracked full force into Marie's face. Pain exploded in Marie's nose and mouth. Blood seared through her retina. Hannah elbowed Marie's rib cage sending Marie reeling onto the ground. Hate raged in Hannah's eyes and Marie was sure her countenance expressed the same attitude. Marie didn't care anymore. Pleasantries were no longer needed. Here in the middle of nowhere, the gloves could come off.

Hannah let loose a barrage of kicks; she flung her body down on Marie and let out a round of punches. Blood flowed freely from Marie's face. Ignoring the pain, Marie grasped at Hannah's neck and flung her into the muck. Getting two good punches in she was sure the woman was exhausted. This was as far as Marie wanted to take it. The captain stood, wiped her mouth. Backed away. "We're in this together now, Hannah, like it or not," Marie said trying to catch her breath.

Hannah bolted for Marie's waist; Marie responded with a kick across Hannah's' head. The woman evaded. Marie grabbed for nose and chin and cranked Hannah's neck back, slamming the doctor's face with the full force of her palm. The woman howled as Marie thrust Hannah's skittering body over an extended leg.

The woman smashed into the ground. Screaming, Hannah flung her legs out in a round kick from the earth. Marie's smashed into clods of turf. "I will kill you!" Hannah screamed; spittle flung from her bloody lips.

In the distance a dismantler lurched to life. Sensing the melee, it trudged toward the fighting women, red eye beams searching the rubble for whatever it might find to take apart.

Marie's hands caught hold of a plunging spear of rebar Hannah had confiscated from the nearby ground. "I will stab this through your heart..." Hannah said gleefully. Marie, teeth clenched, grasped the rusty surface, knuckles white, palms ripping. Hannah pushed down with the full weight of her body. Marie's arm muscles screamed, her hands shred to bloody ribbons. The unrelenting metal lance punctured the surface of her flight jacket. Marie grunted and thrust her legs up into Hannah's stomach and flung her attacker's body overhead with the very same metal weapon. Hannah crashed through a pile of android bodies nearby. Mechanical limbs exploded into the air around them.

Marie spun back on her knees and leapt to her feet. Hannah was quick to regain footing and charged. With quick movements of hands and arms, fists they met in a barrage of chops and thrusts.

Marie executed a knee to the gut and took Hannah down only to be again overthrown. Hannah slammed her foot squarely on the captain's neck. Marie caught Hannah's ankle with shredded hands, thrust Hannah to the ground. Both women flung out fingers to each other's necks. Each sought to choke the other out of consciousness. Hannah kneeled into Marie's leg wound. Marie cried out and released Hannah. Rolling back, pain searing through her entire body, Marie braced for a killing strike. Despair overcame her. She was only left in momentary waiting before impacts of stone and metal came down with cracking relentless agony. Hannah's weapon of choice was now the chalice of Doña Urraca which she'd wrenched free from Marie's hip satchel during the struggle.

Marie was battered senseless. Miraculously after countless blows, Hannah ceased. Marie watched through blood filled eyes as the form of Dr. Hannah Krane fled off into the ruddy dim landscape, evading dismantler legs, chalice in one hand and Marie's communi-com device in the other. No doubt the doctor was leaving the dirty work of Captain Marie Antoinette's demise to the dismantler that now had its red gaze set upon the captain. Marie sensed the unyielding quality of the advent of her own doom as she struggled against the darkness, but it was no use, unconsciousness soon met her with a sudden horrible finality.

EPISODE 2.

Watcher's Hovel.

"Replacement skin,
I'll take you in
Beyond the land of Naught.
Harsh weather nigh,
She'll wake to find
Forbidden pictures drawn."
-the small voice from before.

Marie dreamt that she was at Versailles again. She was caught somewhere in the dark confusion of her mind, the maelstrom between sleep and dreaming on the precipice between life and death. She felt very small. Maybe herself as a girl of six. She dreamt of that summer on Titan when a thunderstorm lasted a fortnight and she'd come down with a dire case of the Callistan flu. The wild wind whipped treetops outside her bedroom window and cast restless shadows across the rose and ribbon wallpaper of her room. The estate seemed immense to her then. Its grand baroque interior sought to consume her with its endlessly grotesque cumulous forms. The architecture was inspired by fabled structures long lost to time from the revered lands of Ancient Earth. It was a troubling phantasm.

CA(RO)-LYN was her only real friend in those days. The robot chamber maid had a body of gold bones enmeshed in silver and red wires, flesh of tempered glass and glowing innerworkings. Marie always sensed great care housed within CA(RO)-LYN's unblinking eyes of peridot. Marie's small hands often sought to reach out and touch the wiry coif of hair on the robot's head for comfort. It was the color of oxidized copper and shimmered with sparkling filaments.

Marie remembered the calm, timed clicking of CA(RO)-LYN's delicate inner workings. The small tinging sound that emitted from the robot when she walked sounded like a pendulum gently striking steel springs inside an antique mantel clock.

CA(RO)-LYN was made up of endless knowledge. Marie often begged to look at the huge collection of holo-star charts the robot housed. Marie dreamed of starlight and what lay in the farthest reaches in the skies beyond her own back garden.

Marie remembered the first time CA(RO)-LYN showed her the Imperial Constellation Collection 5028th Edition. It comforted her as she lay in sweat-soaked bed, body ravaged by the Callistan fever. CA(RO)-LYN's gentle robotic hands placed endless cold compresses on her fever-ravaged body as Marie searched through the vast catalogues of outer space...

As the dreams born from childhood memories began to fade, consciousness rippled at the edges of Captain Marie Antoinette's sleep. Somewhere beyond, distant thunder roared followed by torrents of rain. Flickering lightning brought her swimming to the fine and languid surface of the membrane that existed between waking and sleep...

Thunder. A feeble structure groaned around the captain and rain raged against a flapping roof. Tinkling droplets spattered the dim cramped room, hitting something metal. Marie awoke. The gut-wrenching horror of the last excoriating hours subsided giving way to somber, quiet, inescapable reality. Her abdomen was in pain, her loins ached, and the back of her head was a raging mess.

Breathe. Marie ordered herself. She wanted to survive. She took in a deep draught of air. It was labored, but she was grateful. *How long have I been here?* She pushed aside a coarse blanket and attempted to rise. Immediately a white searing pain flooded her head; she winced lay back down upon a moss-covered pillow top. Her limbs felt useless.

Two voices spoke to her as she lay there. Both were youthful, but of slightly different quality. They spoke from a hidden recess of the hovel:

"Rest Mam'selle."

"Rest."

"I already said that."

"Hush. You're disturbing her."

"No, I'm not!"

A huffing noise of agitation, a giggle, then silence.

Breathe out. Not so bad. Breathe in, deeply now. Ooof, not a good idea. If I can just keep steady breaths, the more measured, the less painful... Marie told herself.

"Hello?" Marie called out. Her voice was a garble. The cramped hovel captured her utterance and the pounding rain consumed it. Marie touched her mouth, gingerly. A strange, malleable substance covered the edges of her lips. She realized her left eye and cheek and possibly the back of her skull was covered over as well with the substance. Strange sensations, small tingles of electricity pulsed through her body. They seemed to follow her heartbeat.

"Where am I..." Marie murmured to herself, a constant refrain unanswered. She felt captured within the low, rough hewn dome of the ceiling, cupped in the dimness, caught between crevices of burnt-out cables and circuitry. Grotesque formations of wire entangled ceiling and ground. Ramshackle piles of abandoned, rusty conveyance parts and archaic machinery scattered the room. Flickering yellow orbs above created haunting hallucinations on the ceiling. In certain areas where the structure was failing, patched-over expanses of flesh-colored sheets, supple, moist, and porous stuccoed over garish cracks to form healing bands.

Marie took a mental check of herself. *Body—I'm still alive, I guess...if this is not heaven or hell.* She held her palms to her face to examine the deep gashes upon them, but was amazed by what covered them over—"the same substance," she murmured awed by the new skin that bandaged them. It was decidedly more peach in hue than her own, honey-cinnamon-colored skin and it pulsed through with very fine white-light-illuminated filaments. 'Biomechatronic skin...' she mused.

She moved on in her mental check. *Fetus... I suppose it still lives—I can't know for sure...* panic suddenly overwhelmed her. *Breathe*...she advised herself. *Just breathe. No weapons, no communication device, no ship, no way to find my way home. Do I want to go home anyway?* That question, which her mind thrust upon her so suddenly, stopped her breath.

Hannah...I am a constant fool...now I have no means to escape and the chalice...I vowed to the

Queen that I would protect it and deliver it to her home planetoid—I failed. I failed utterly. I suppose Dr. Krane is celebrating a victory. Why not? She has everything. Well, we'll see how clever she is if she really does find a way to escape this hellish place. (Will I be able to find a way to survive this hellish place?)

Another thunderclap shook the hovel.

I must get up, she thought to herself. *I must find a way to get back to the Maa'ta Karé. Maybe then the Queen and I can sort this whole tragic thing out. Send the Imperial Police after Dr. Krane...although everyone's probably in turmoil over what happened to the Antoinette. As am I.* Through clenched teeth she hoisted herself up. Pushing through the pain that existed in almost every part of her body, she righted herself on the makeshift metal cot.

"Rest."

"You must rest Mam'selle."

The voices echoed again from somewhere within the small, dank space. Marie couldn't discover the source; she was too busy fighting waves of nausea anyway. Her head felt as if it might explode and throbbed with every heartbeat.

Marie scanned the junk-filled room. There didn't seem to be anybody there. *Breathe...*

"You there, where are you?" Marie's voice was strained and hoarse. "Was it you that repaired my body? At least someone wishes to bring me back from destruction, instead of destroying me all together," Marie said with a laugh. There was no reply. Marie rose from the cot and took a few furtive, wobbly steps. She stumbled to the fringes of the hovel and steadied herself by placing her hand on a squarish, gear adorned machine. The machine-top, which housed a myriad of jar-like vessels filled with biomechanical flowers, rattled as she regained her balance. Marie squinted to examine the walls of the room. More detail came into focus.

Marie realized that the queer, small hovel was also home to a vast array of drawings. The art decorated almost every expanse of free wall space. Each charcoal rendering was executed upon flattened, dried brown leaves. Careful holes were poked into the tops of each leaf and tied with bits of twine and copper wire, lashed, almost like ornaments, to the vine branches which filled the environ.

"What are these..." Mare said, marveling at the art. She knew the small voice was probably responsible in some way for the sketches. Suddenly Marie felt better. She drank each visual artifact in and realized these were all keys to her location and what this place truly was.

"These are marvelous!" she said merrily, hoping to excite the voice again to speak and possibly coax the being out of hiding. There were many drawings of a vast tree. Marie remembered her first impressions of the gnarled juggernaut hidden within the swirling iridescent clouds of the God's Eye Nebula. Marie enjoyed the whimsicality of drawings' black, toothy lines. *This must be what exists within this place beyond the vast reaching arms and dark black core,* Marie realized, looking more carefully at each art piece. Seemingly within this place was a complex sort of synthetic biosphere. Curling channels and passageways linked by raging rivers, waterfalls, and chasms punctuated by several seemingly inhabited realms. Structures and buildings existed within each of these cells, each kingdom rendered in masterful detail. Marie sensed the quality of these disparate settlements, their unique architectural style and ways of life duplicated in teeny tiny marks. "These are maps—a woody home world..." Marie said.

There were other offerings of details that existed in the tree-world: exotic geometric shaped flowers and robotic looking insects. As Marie advanced down the gallery wall of art, a strange new style seemed to overtake the body of work. It was harsher—more frantic, schizophrenic even. Her excitement was suddenly dowsed. Her smile faded and a sober feeling of fear overtook her. Flowers became the subjects of a blight. Tangled, perverse mosses and killing-fingered creepers. There were larger mechanical bugs—dismantlers—with fire erupting from glowing eyes. There was an image of a tumultuous cataclysm which raged through a foreign city of elegant spires and bridges. Piles of bodies, with expertly drawn anatomy, both humanoid and mechanical became the subject of perhaps twenty leaves. Frozen horrified faces realized, unbearably, their own doomed fate. Their reaching arms and futile hands grasped nothing but the smoke-choked air. The charcoal was dark, black and heavy on these pages.

"You draw what you see. These images are real, not fantasies..." Marie whispered. Still there was no reaction from the voice within the hovel. "What happened here..."

There was another drawing, though, which offered some relief from the terrible subject matter of the previous pages. A drawing of an old man. He had kind eyes, careworn, and wiry brows. A flame-like tuft of hair sprouted from his forehead. He had a moustache that curled at the ends and a loosely buttoned shirt which was rendered with realistic folds in a loving, artistic hand. He was depicted holding a small toy soldier. Marie recognized the style of the soldier's dress—early colonial, imperial. Also, a signature: *'Poppa' by Dove Holland* was scrawled on the leaf in a loopy, childlike hand. "Dove Holland..." Marie read the name out loud. There was a small gasp from somewhere in the dim recesses of the hovel. Marie knew whatever had drawn these images must be hiding out in a small alcove at the top of a ladder just to her back.

"Is that your name...Dove Holland?" she said still engrossed in analyzing the pages. Her eyes scanned over the other folios hanging along the walls. All the remaining sheets were filled with the words 'Dove Holland' written repeatedly and obsessively, sometime largely, sometimes very small. Each sheet was filled edge to edge with the repeated name. Then, at the end of the gallery wall, just as she examined the final few bits of the art installation, her eyes landed upon an image that sent chills through her very core.

It was a drawing of the beast. The mark making on this piece was insanely hurried and violent. Some marks almost broke through the paper in their thrust. Each stroke revealed the portrait of the demon—gnashing hungry spit-covered canines set into a scull of rusty riveted metal covered over with textured bits of rotting flesh. It was a face of a being torn in two. Both human and machine. Marie's gaze transfixed upon the monsters' penetrating, soulless eye lens screwed in above a sharp, blade-like cheekbone. The other eye was just as disturbing. It was seething, almost human, membrane-covered and jet black. Marie felt sick.

"This is the face! This is the face of the monster that invaded my ship!" Marie reeled back and fell to the floor. Something clattered down the ladder behind her, but she was swept up in the horrid feeling of doom as the walls of the hovel suddenly darkened around her—memories seemed to make themselves horribly real as the raging flames of the burning passageway of the starship *Marie Antoinette* suddenly blasted through her memory. She felt the blasting heat, bone jarring eruptions, the suffocation of the monster's ensnaring mechanical arms. His cold breath. His acrid words: "*You recoil in fear...you don't recognize me, dear Princess.*" Marie's vocal cords could barely get out screams. She struggled for breath and balled over in tears for a moment, then looked again to the beast's horrific visage frozen in charcoal on the brown bit of paper clinging to the wall of the small round room. Wide-eyed, she wailed: "He is the one that invaded my ship...he killed everyone..."

A reluctant robot girl, just three-and-a-half feet tall, tip toed out from the shadows into the golden flickering light. "His name is Magnus." The robot said in a voice of the more innocent register. "He is here in Hout and he wants to destroy us all."

EPISODE 3.

Local Unit Contraption Youth; or, Dove Holland, the virus.

"Rest."

"You must rest Mam'selle." This rusty robot child had two voices. One chimed sweetly, like a girl perhaps eight years of age, and the other, was a coarse, low vocalization—like a boy, perhaps of the same age, but Marie couldn't tell. Both types of speech were emitted through petal-lipped speakers situated squarely in the middle of the bot's cherubic hammered steel face. It seemed to be a contrary sort of programming.

"No...no...no. I don't think so..." Marie's words were frantic. "If *he* is here—God help us..." Fatigue filled her limbs as she reached up to grab the ratty ends of her cot. She hoisted herself up into it. The robot girl dove to assist her. "I have to get out of here. My body just won't let me..." stammered Marie.

"I know what it's like to want to run," said the girl voice.

"I know what it's like to hide," said the boy. "Where can we go, Mam'selle?"

"I don't know..." said Marie. "I can't stay here."

"If only you were a spaceship –or a robot that could fly..." said the little girl. Then, shocked by her own speech: "NO! Too

WHIMSICAL—these thoughts—Dove!" The robot pounded her spun glass hair with tiny copper fists in attempt to fling out such errant thoughts.

"You must stay with me," the boy commanded. "You must rest," then to the girl that shared his head, "LUCY..." The robot nodded to itself and clattered up to an alcove above. The robot tasked itself with rummaging. Dishes clanked.

"How long have I been here?"

"Many days of naught," said the girl.

"How many days are many days of naught?" Marie asked as she wiped her sweat-drenched brow. She felt feverish. *It's probably my body attempting to heal itself—increased antibody production induced by this mechanical skin...*

"12.628 days of naught, to be exact...," the girl replied and flitted over to a busted, leaning sideboard. The robot rifled through dented buckets and frayed thatched baskets. Suddenly the LUCY's head spun round backward, and the boy said: "I know you are an Imperial."

"Imperial...funny," said the girl. Then, after a momentary pause, the robot giggled as if she was encoded to respond to the word 'funny' in that way.

"You're right," said Marie. The little bot lurched back to the cot where the captain reclined, its tattered ecru-colored dress rustled softly on the air. The robot girl placed a badly chipped, bone colored plate upon Marie's lap. The plate was heaped with conglomerations of glowing cells loosely formed to resemble fruits and nuts. "Thanks...," the captain said taking up what looked like a deep red plum and bit into it. It was crunchy. Sweet juices erupted upon her tongue. There was a strange effervescence and a curious metallic aftertaste.

"I don't know 'Imperial.'" said the girl, "Dove Holland speaks of strange things."

"Dove Holland. Who's Dove Holland?" Marie asked.

"Not who. What. -(It's a virus)," the girl answered.

"Not a virus, a BOY!" The low voice immediately shouted out.

"Whatever *that* is..." The girl was obviously annoyed.

Marie sighed. This conversation seemed to be too much for the dual personalities inside this robot and perhaps for her as well. Marie questioned whether she wanted to get to the bottom of this conflicted sort of programming. *However, I do owe the thing my life,* she reminded herself. *Where am I going anyway?* She thought. *I'm stuck here. Might as well engage... this strange gizmo might be my only means of figuring out where the hell I am and how to get back to the Maa'ta Karé.*

"So, there are two of you trapped in there..." Marie said at last.

"I am LUCY!" the smaller voice said proudly suddenly realizing Marie was giving her full attention. "...or Local Unit Contraption Youth. I was created to repair everything in the world of Hout."

"Impressive," Marie said tasking herself with peeling a fruit that resembled an orange. She plopped a section of the exposed fruit into her mouth and chewed, thankfully, strength seemed to be returning. The pain in her head was now only a dull ache and the nausea had faded.

"And I'm Dove Holland," said the lower voice. He waited for Marie to comment as if she should know what that meant.

"Yes, and..." Marie prompted through chews.

"A boy. A real live boy. I'm Dove Holland—not a virus. Well, not really."

"Very well," Marie said, only distantly playing along.

"I'm trapped in here. Trapped, Mam'selle." The bot stared at her wide-eyed.

"Well, I'm sure with some re-coding..."

"No! Nooooo!" the bot skittered to its feet. Its spun glass hair, antennae of citrine crystals and eyes that were once an emotive cheerful canary all began to light up an angry red. "That's what the Volgens want to do!" The little girl screamed. Marie skittered back on the bed. She wasn't used to seeing such emotion from a robot of this slight manufacture. "Is...that...part of your programming..." Marie asked, setting the plate aside and bracing herself up on the cot, fearful of the unpredictability emoted in this machine.

"LUCY! LUCY!" Dove Holland sought to calm her—"I'll explain..." he began but was soon cut off by the girl.

"This is all your fault, Dove Holland!" she pouted stomping a metal slipper on the earth. "Once I was a LUCY just like all the other LUCYs in the Garden of Naught. I knew my place, I knew what I was supposed to do, but then I got this voice in my head. *His* voice. Dove's voice...they said I had the dark code, they said that I had the virus that's been killing the whole world of Hout. The same one that killed all the Orzos!"

"I'm not a virus—" Dove interrupted calmly.

LUCY ignored Dove and continued. "I started drawing all these pictures and seeing things like I've never seen them before. My purpose was changing but the Volgens thought I was being zondg."

"She means sinful—immoral," translated Dove matter-of-factly. "It's against the Volgen code for LUCYs to create art. Their purpose is to repair nature. Well, synthetic nature. Everything you see here is mech-organic based."

"All machines..." Marie mused at her surroundings. Her eyes came to rest on what was left of her dinner—a few errant berries and nuts. "So, you created the skin that covered my wounds," she realized.

The robot girl nodded eagerly and proudly.

"The Volgens were afraid of her. She wasn't complying to programming anymore," said Dove.

"Volgens..." Marie said.

"Avian-androids," Dove explained.

"LUCY dizjin xorcime," the girl's voice was plaintive.

"The council was seeking to have her exorcised. Basically, a full system reset. We fled."

Marie suddenly felt bad for suggesting re-programming earlier. Something about Dove's words started to ring true. This was not just some glitch or some mechanical flight of fancy. "So, you made this place your home," Marie concluded.

The bot nodded. "It works—for now." This was spoken in the voice of Dove. "Anyway, I suppose you're wondering what the truth of all this is—that is if you believe us, Mam'selle. Do...you believe us?"

"I do," Marie said at last.

The robot girl clanked over to where Marie sat and took a seat.

"Dove..." LUCY pleaded.

"LUCY, I must tell it."

"I know...it just makes me feel uncomfortable—like all my insides are coming out of me! I just don't feel like myself anymore! I'm not fulfilling my intended purpose!"

"I told you your purpose now is to help me."

"No one is asking me what *I* want!"

"I'm trying to save you—we have to trust Mam'selle. She is from my world—the first person I have found in Hout that is. Please LUCY, trust me."

Dove's words seemed to calm LUCY and they made sense to Marie. The boy was right. If they were indeed from the same world then maybe they could help each other out. The small robot set its gaze more intently on Captain Antoinette. Its eyes were exceedingly round and innocent. They emoted a frozen childlike wonder expertly. “I am a boy named Dove Holland.”

“Yes...go on,” said Marie. Marie could tell by the way Dove began that he had been waiting quite some time to tell someone his story.

“My father and brother were killed in the civil war on Callisto. All I had left of my family was my mom and Poppa.”

“Your grandfather. The man in the drawing,” said Marie.

“Yes,” Dove said. “We found work and a small room to live in aboard a factory ship orbiting Io. Being Callistan refugees we were considered illegals in the Empire.”

Marie felt tense at the mention of Callisto. Bad memories flooded her brain, but she pushed those aside quickly. Marie was adept at compartmentalizing.

“The factory master didn’t request our papers; we didn’t have any to show anyway. We worked day and night making automatons for the children of the Empire. My Poppa was very skilled. I just cleaned up the floors mostly. My mom made clothes for the machines. I only ever had one toy—a soldier. Poppa made it with bits of leftover plastic and metal. He gave it to me. I had to keep it secret. That’s how I learned to keep secrets. The shipmaster was a very mean man. He would’ve had Poppa killed if he knew. So I kept the toy soldier to myself.”

Marie was aware that there were many abusive practices being carried out within these vessels of manufacture orbiting the moon of Io. There were so many of these gargantuan industrial ships churning out massive quantities of product day and night that the skies around the Jovian moon were almost choked full of them.

This poor family, she thought. *His childhood, so unlike my own, yet so similar. I know his type of loneliness.* She was starting to believe Dove. The story was too detailed to be an errant program. Marie felt uneasiness settle in upon her.

"Your Poppa sounds like a kind man," Marie said. She couldn't say the same for her own grandfather, the Dauphin of the Empire, but this was Dove's story, not her own. She listened more intently.

"Poppa disappeared when I was nine," Dove continued. "My mother said he'd gone crazy. He was always talking about an automaton maker named Adelphi Saint."

"I've heard that name before. Wait, I know of him," realized Marie. She searched her memory; some notes she'd taken in a history class at the academy came to mind. "Wasn't he an inventor who lived 100 Imperial Years ago? He was considered a coding da Vinci. He created the core technologies that run all modern androids in the Empire. Many thought he was ingenious. Many say he went insane and was never heard from again."

"Poppa would always speak of Adelphi Saint like he was a god or something. He called himself a disciple of Saint. It was like this Adelphi person could do anything. Poppa said that Adelphi would even be able to save us one day. He said there was a place Adelphi was preparing just for us—a kingdom that he called Hout. Poppa told me one day he had found a way into Hout...a key. Right after that, he was gone."

"How did you become trapped in this robot girl?" asked Marie.

"Right after Poppa vanished, the factory ship was raided by Imperial Police. My mother and I were arrested—charged for being illegals. They shipped us off to the Ophiuchus system—to Omhawk. The court of the overseer. The overseer imprisoned us. A private viro-electric powerhouse. That's where I am right now. Suspended. Sleeping endlessly in a pod full of 'juice'; my brain is attached to the mainframe and my body is being used for electricity..."

Marie had heard of such horrific means of producing power. Poor humans made to be hosts for energy-producing viruses. The specialty germs, conscripted to produce electrodes, were then harvested and utilized. It was doubtful that the overseer was simply using these pods to power his own lights. He was most likely making a mint selling the viral-induced electric energy back to the Empire for a pretty penny.

This was a living death. Marie felt sick. She touched her forehead. It was wet with the sweat of shame. The extent of greed in the Empire knew no bounds. *My grandfather allows things like this to happen—I hate it.* She felt suddenly and horribly useless. Sadness pitted her stomach, "that's horrible." She looked to the robot, "but you are here, inside this bot girl...how?"

"Little by little my conscience was able to explore. I started to remember things, to come back to life. For fifteen years I tried to wake up my mind enough to search out the computer environment that had become linked to my own brain. There was a code I remembered, one that I had discovered written on a sheet of paper hidden beneath my Poppa's pillow just after he disappeared. It was an access point to a system. Once I was able to input it into the network I had taught myself to access mentally, I woke up inside this LUCY."

"So this is where your Poppa is..." Marie felt a certain sad dread overcome her. She realized that this robot, LUCY, was Dove's only lifeline.

"I need to find him, and I need your help—"

"How? I...I can't stay here," said Marie.

"We can help each other..."

Marie was startled; she was unsure. Dove sensed her doubt.

"I know you are a soldier," Dove said.

A pained smile came across her face. "A captain..." she told him. "I am a captain...*was* a captain..." Her voice trailed off. She felt a certain futility in all this talk. A dark depression lingered at the edges of her mind. She thought of the android corpses in the killing field outside. *Was this what the bodies of my crew now looked like too? Are they nothing but ash—or frozen in the depths of space, consumed by the cosmos? Was the starship Marie Antoinette a skeleton in the stardust, listing and smoldering never again to take another voyage? What was Sheng thinking at this moment?* Panic filled her heart. This robot was the only bit of light in an overwhelming sense of darkness and confusion that permeated any thought of what to do beyond the walls of the hovel she now found herself in. Marie's own father and CA(RO)-LYN came to mind. The two who had always loved her and cared for her as best they could. She longed to be back at her father's estate—especially now. "Okay," she said.

Marie realized energy was slowly returning to her body. The mech-organic fruit she'd eaten rapidly healed her cells from the inside out. "I don't know this place, Dove. Where would we even begin?" she asked him.

"Let us begin with your name."

Such a simple question, but the consequences of truth made Marie suddenly feel uneasy. She was fearful to reveal to him her true name and she hated the title of her birth. Experience had taught her to downplay such things. There was no hiding the name of Marie Antoinette. It was a name that held history and power. It harkened back to the glory days of Ancient Earth. It was a name that was a burden and a curse. She looked down to the name patch on her chest. Most of the embroidery was ripped away, now only a scrap of her first initial was left.

"Your name..." Dove prompted.

"Marie..." she responded quickly.

"Marie?" Dove seemed strangely unconvinced.

"What? Just Marie."

The LUCY nodded. Dove didn't inquire further but instead launched into unleashing what information he knew about Poppa.

"A stranger matching Poppa's description came into the Volgen tribe about 12 IY ago. LUCY had footage of him stored in her memory. She healed him...like you. He was in very, very, very bad shape. Almost died, she said. During his time of healing, he asked many questions about Houtan lore, especially the tales surrounding the creator of Hout—Adelphi Saint."

"It's true," LUCY interjected suddenly.

"We need to find Adelphi Saint." Dove was quick to regain the robot voice box, "If we find the automaton maker, I know we will find Poppa too. Once we do, I am sure he can help you find your way back home."

"And then I can find a way to free you too," Marie stated trying to assure the boy. It was obvious Dove didn't want to get too excited about the prospect of being freed from the battery pod.

"Let's find Poppa first," he said.

"Where do we begin?" Marie asked.

"There's a map—" Dove began to cite a drawing hanging on the wall. His words were suddenly cut short by a whirring mechanical twittering sound that erupted into a shrill whistle from somewhere just outside the dwelling.

LUCY screamed. "Oh no! Oh no! Oh no! Oh NO!" Then in electronica, LUCY's internal alert system immediately voiced: "Conscience L77 approaches, alert 25b48."

Trilling in through the open portal of the hovel, a small, black and copper humming-bot zipped in. Its wings tore at the air so quickly it seemed to hover without aid. Outrageous shrill whistles erupted from its golden horn-like beak and tiny searchlights erupted from its eye sockets. Its crystalline breast glowed a bright lime green.

"The Volgens are coming!" Dove shouted. Marie stood. "This way!" the boy told her. They made a run for a small opening in the back of the hovel as a sudden concussion rocketed through the yard outside. It sounded as if a hundred gigantic birds had come to land out in the darkness beyond. Vast wind-chopping wings settled to stillness followed by sloshing, marching boots on the muddy walk outside.

There was no time to escape the hovel. This fact became horribly clear as shadows quickly filled the doorway.

"Tell them nothing!" Dove warned Marie. Suddenly the brightness behind LUCY's eyes dimmed.

"Dove! I hate it when he does this. Dove!" LUCY cried. There was no response in return. "He's hiding again! He's left me to be exorcism-ed!"

Marie had no chance to respond. Within the doorway stood a towering raven-headed figure. He had a black humanoid body of riveted steel. Sinewy ebony plastoid muscles lashed his structure together. Massive wing blades erupted from his back. They were hewn in segmented ebony steel and covered over with spikes. He wore a glinting silver breastplate bolted to his chest emblazoned with codes of power and protection in copper intaglio. Bracers of silver wrapped each wrist and coursed with electric light. His boots were tooled lead and embedded with circuitry. From each boot tip jutted talons of glinting silver. Marie discerned a hilt of a great black sword that was lashed to the raven's back. His oculars whirred—focusing, refocusing, refining, data collecting. He leveled his intense gaze upon the slowly retreating form of Marie. The captain held LUCY close to her. The Volgen general began to speak.

EPISODE 4.

In the Garden of Naught.

"Ve hebben het misje des andromatron. Breng har ter naar het vijhe!" barked the immense anthropomorph raven general in booming electronica. An oscilloscope was lashed around the general's throat which vibrated deep pitched mechanical speech. It displayed within a small black circular screen, pulsing green glowing lines which represented each utterance.

"No!" LUCY screamed "No xorcime! No xorcime!" The robot's tiny rust-colored hands clung to Marie's pant leg and belt. Marie tried to push the small robot behind her body in order to block it from the savage bird man.

The raven-android cawed out a command. Two navy-beaked grackles wearing mercury colored head components and brigandines bombarded the small room. Their phantasmagoric yellow eye orbs shone cold, unfeeling, mechanical. As they crossed the hovel, their ravaging wings sent rusty furnishings toppling and charcoal drawings scattering in every direction. They yanked the robot girl free from Marie's grasp. LUCY screamed and kicked against the grasping, taloned, soldier fingers as they drug her to the door. Her screams would not be silenced. Marie protested and raged against them. The soldiers thrust Marie aside and savagely flung the girl out into the night.

"You can't do this!" Marie screamed from the floor of the hovel. She lifted herself up from the shadows and came to stand starkly before the raven general.

He regarded her carefully, cocking his head to the side. He paused for a moment, then the oscilloscope at his neck switched programing and whirred— "You speak Archaic English," he said. "Are you Orzos?" He strode to where Marie stood. His claw toed boots scratched against rusted tin tiles that paved the uneven ground. His towering body dwarfed Marie. She backed away hitting a small pile of abandoned components. Pieces clattered to the floor. "Only Orzos speak Archaic English."

"I am no Orzos. I am a captain in the Dauphin's army."

"Dauphin. What is Dauphin?" the raven general asked pointedly, jutting his glassy midnight colored eye toward her face. Its black surface reflected Marie's panicked face. She perceived subtle sounds of processors working within the general's ocular orbs as they analyzed her genetic form. "You are mensen then, not mechanishmen," he concluded.

"I am neo-human if that's what you mean. Not an android," she replied through clenched teeth.

"This LUCY has impairment. She must be dealt with."

"I beg you to leave her here."

"You cannot maintain ownership of this LUCY. To commit such an act is a crime in the court of the Volgen council. Do you understand?"

"I was trying to help her –or rather she was helping me. I suppose," Marie stammered. "I lost my ship and everything that is precious to me. I was left for dead in a horrific place—perhaps some distance away. A killing field of android bodies almost eaten by dismantlers...." She paused then locked her gaze again with the andro-bird. "What is going on here?" she asked.

"What happened in the Orzos' kingdom is no longer consequence to the Volgens." The raven replied. "Selfish machines. Jealous, suspicious. They massacred themselves. We did the LUCYs a favor taking them in from that kingdom...we don't talk of the Orzos anymore."

"Your LUCY healed me," Marie said, almost pleading, "she deserves to be saved."

"I doubt if anything containing the 'dark code' can heal."

"General Corvin, the grounds are clear. The LUCY is contained. We are ready to depart," a grackle soldier called from the outside yard.

The raven-general turned to leave.

"Wait! Take me with you!" Marie grabbed the edges of his wing. The feathers were slick unyielding polymer. He paused to listen. "I must speak on her behalf, before your council. Please don't wipe her memory banks before I have a chance to speak to your leader," Marie's voice was low and frantic. *I have no idea how, but I am going to try to talk this LUCY free,* she thought.

"What do you know of the council, or of our leader? Who are *you* to request this?" Corvin screeched out to her over his shoulder.

"I am her friend."

He considered the captain's request for a moment. "You may try. But will not make a difference." Shouting out to a grackle soldier outside thc hovel, Corvin bid him to take the woman within. Then he left.

Marie, sensing she may never see the hovel again, quickly grabbed up the drawings that lay scattered at her feet. The one of Poppa and the one of the map. She thrust them into her flight jacket before she was pushed out by a grackle guard into the steamy red-hued darkness.

The rain had stopped. Only disparate drops fell from somewhere in the cavernous expanse above. Distant lights illuminated the steaming grounds around the hovel with haunting staticky light. The grackle guard led her across the blackened trail to where a strange egg-shaped conveyance hewn of glassy silver energy stood amid the monstrous forms of the other Volgen soldiers. LUCY was already inside. The soldier pushed her toward the egg.

"I can manage!" Marie protested, but soon found herself momentarily awash in static as she was thrust into the interior of the energy egg. The little robot flung herself into Marie, trembling, gears and transistors whirring frantically, her crystal eyes shone bright yellow with fear. The captain steadied herself only to be met again by Corvin's thrusting beak and probing eyes. He peered at the unlikely pair through the silver glass surface for a moment. Seeming satisfied, he turned to his regiment and bid them to fly.

In the concussion of wing thrusts, the egg launched upward into the steaming air. Soon LUCY and Marie were soaring high. The small hovel which lay practically ensnared by inky swells of blight briars just off a dark and twisted trail, was soon eaten up by the ravenous mists. Beyond the entanglement, where the trail disappeared over a hilltop, Marie could again see a vast killing field where the skeletal remains of the Orzos city smoldered and beyond that, a great chasm of space.

The vacuous expanse of the interior world of the juggernaut held a strange churning, steamy atmosphere. The chamber ceiling, massive in scale, seemed to be hewn from copious amounts of petrified circuitry riveted together by ancient hexagonal bolts. From the arching, dank expanse hung ghastly amorphous formations that reached down in threatening, thrusting shapes. Mournful creaks and rhythmic clanking echoed through the enormous derelict body.

The military entourage turned starboard, and they became entrenched in shadows. Below, a snaking silver river reached out through fields of coal-black vegetation strung through with glowing red veins. Amid the choking lichens, ranges of gnarled, stabbing, mountainous jet- black fingers cumulated hungrily along the farthest edges of the cavern wall. They reached high above to the ribbed petrified cavern top.

"All that blackness," Marie said.

"Dark code," LUCY replied.

Marie thought of Hannah lost somewhere down there in the black void. She almost laughed. The hilarity of the prospect of the woman who tried to kill her lost somewhere out in those entangled and thorny arms struggling to survive. Marie felt vindication at the idea of just desserts.

Crazy, greedy Hannah...savage...cheat... Marie wouldn't let herself be cruel enough to celebrate the possibility of her rival's demise. But she did enjoy the prospect of it. *How much does she need to steal?* Marie thought with disdain. *Husbands. Sacred chalices...communi-com devices... So much suffering on the part of my poor crew...and for what? For me to fail. For her to win, again... The fact that Blake died, that my crew died—they sacrificed themselves all in vain.* Marie's eyes stung with tears of lament over that harsh reality. It was truth, she knew it was. She would answer for this failure—that is, if she were able to get herself out of this place alive.

LUCY began to sing softly to herself. It was the same song Marie had heard before, upon the moment she'd woken up, in the field of the dismantlers.

"In these dark sessions, in this depression, as sure as the stars shine above, there is love, there is love..."

"That was you singing..." Marie realized.

"I'm the only LUCY that does," LUCY said. "I'm not like the others at all. I can't help myself," she said sadly.

"To some it's a crime to be different," Marie said, her words were defiant. "I don't think it's a crime."

"Why would I do something that I'm not supposed to do? OH DOVE! It's all his fault. What if Dove is really the dark code, maybe these voices are what the Orzos heard! Maybe the 'dark code' *has* infected me."

"Dove is not the dark code, he's a human boy," Marie said.

"Where is he now?"

"You tell me. God knows. He's left us out to dry." Marie was becoming impatient and troubled by the fact that Dove may have simply lost connection with the LUCY, perhaps for good. *Where would that leave us? Where would that leave Dove?* "Dove. For God's sake," Marie said, she looked into the robot's eyes. "Can you find Dove Holland—somewhere in there?"

The world outside brightened. The choking darkness now gave way to a dim blueish golden atmosphere. Recessed crystals studded the cavern expanse above. Marie realized that their purpose was to provide illumination. *None back where we came from, over the killing fields, they no longer illuminated. Perhaps the energy was drawn out...* Here the crystals glowed with eerie enchantment filling the misty air with twilit glory.

Just up ahead a verdant hyper-green vastness erupted from the creeping blight. Marie sensed the regiment was about to land. Below, housed in the cradling expanse between two rusty canyon walls, an immense valley of glittering generator cooling pools, bio-mechanical luminescent orchards and fields of electromagnetic grasses stood. The atmosphere crystals lit the air here a somber desperate color.

"You spoke of a creature named Magnus," Marie said breaking the forlorn silence.

"Magnus..." LUCY twittered. The name seemed to dive into some processes that strained drives within the girl. "Magnus...the monster."

"Yes, in your drawing. Dove didn't mention anything more about him."

"Dove doesn't know of him. The monster is in *my* memory!" The bot began to quake. "M....my...memory! Killing...kill...kill...killing," then her voice became a whirring shrill, almost a musical hypophonic. 'No one mentioned the dark code before Magnus came!" she shouted.

"LUCY...I," Marie was frantic. The bot girl shook violently. Something was evidently wrong. "Dove..." Marie whispered. "Find Dove." Suddenly the bot stilled, and lights flared and died. LUCY became calm. Marie put a hand to the bot's small shoulder awash in a mix of worry and relief. The robot was still. "It's okay LUCY," she said, patting it. *Whatever this robot knows about Magnus tortures it. It is truth, the beast is here. Where an enemy like this exists, perhaps there will be allies too.* The memory of Magnus' growling voice rampaged in her ear: *"This is revenge, Princess..."* It was a thunderous cursc. *Who are you, really?* Marie thought angrily, hatred and fear swelled in her gut.

Corvin signaled for the regiment to land. The egg conveyance followed the general's order through some unseen mechanical means and dissolved into nothingness. Marie found herself immersed in strange wavering stalks, conglomerations of limber mechanical cilia that held tiny silver staticky orbs on their end. She felt awash in tingly energy. From that energy, an undulating breeze was born. The blades seemed strangely attracted to the black blight forest that erupted at their back. The stocks leaned heavily downward sending a cowering darkness over the reaching veldt around them.

LUCY, animated again, clung to Marie's waist. One of the grackle soldiers, who Marie soon discovered was named Sikula, attempted to snatch hold of the robot girl.

"I've got her," Marie said resisting his taloned reach. "I will take her where you lead."

Sikula harrumphed.

"March then," commanded Corvin following behind Marie and the LUCY. Corvin drew his broadsword and thrust the tip threateningly into their backs.

The journeyers waded through the undulating fields up to the edges of an orchard containing cumulous formations. Each twisted limb hung heavy with translucent ruby and amber orbs. Internal electrical impulses coursed within each gorgeous, bountiful offering. The channels of power pulsed within each tree-like structure and skittered the earth to some distant hidden reservoir close to the base of the cavern wall.

Marie glanced back again at the field through which they had just come. The dark sentinels of the blight that took up residence at the far edges of the garden seemed to clamor at her consciousness. Strange hissing sounds and a vacuous unquenched longing erupted from the massive black structures. Her heart thudded rapidly.

"Move," Corvin commanded.

In the dim orchard orb-light, Marie could make out small figures toiling away amidst the trees. Some of the trees had gone dark and black masses curled upon them. It was at these dark trees that the small robots worked. They were identical to the one Marie now guided through the orchard at her side. Each LUCY removed blotchy black spots which feasted hungrily on the trunks and branches, replacing the blackness with a film of healing, bio-mechanic circuitry.

"They save them," LUCY said. "They work constantly..."

"Quiet!" Corvin cawed.

"If only there were more of them, they might be able to save the whole world of Hout..." said Sikula.

"The last thing we need are more LUCYs to look after," another soldier cawed.

"I should be out there, helping them..." LUCY wailed. She dug her feet into the ground, pulling away from Marie.

"LUCY, wait." Marie grasped at the bot's tiny metal hands, but they quickly slipped from her grasp. Marie was about to run after the bot when talons dug into her arm, preventing her to move. It was Sikula.

Corvin's wings thundered as LUCY fled into the orchard. "This is all Dove's fault! This is all Dove's fault! Monster! MONSTERS!" she screamed.

"You see human! She *is* afflicted!" raged Corvin, who launched out after the bot and snatched her from the ground with taloned fingers.

"LUCY!" Marie cried. Her hopes of getting to Dove again were quickly dwindling. Machine arms swiftly encapsulated Marie and catapulted her up into the air behind Corvin. The ruddy striated edifice of the vast oxidated canyon wall flung up before them and gave way to a massive hidden recess. There, molded geometric forms, columnar towers, egg-shaped vestibules and square hives, massive archways and thoroughfares filled with twisted wire bowers erupted dizzyingly within the mouth of the rock hollow. The windows of each chunky structure danced with strobing amber light. Amid these structures, machine birds with scythe-shaped beaks flitted through the thoroughfares.

Disheartenment swelled within Marie as Corvin commanded Sikula to take her to a chamber far away from the bot.

"You said I could speak before the council!" Marie screamed out. The wind caught her words and thrust them to the ground. Sikula bore her into the darker recesses above the village. *Is there anything I can say or do now to save LUCY from her fate?* Marie's mind raced. "You must let me go with her!" she pleaded to Sikula. Sikula's voice roared back at Marie over the raging air: "You will see the priestess and she will decide what to do with you!"

EPISODE 5.

The Problem with Robot Exorcisms.

Endless depression settled in on Marie. *Just breathe, Marie, just breathe. There must be a way to figure this out.* Claustrophobia clenched her body as two sparrow maids with swooping hats, clad in grey gowns, frantically undressed her. The captain was now in a cramped chamber with walls of dobbed over machinery high in the farthest recesses of Hout, the subject of violent fumbling attempts at a make-over.

"I can manage!" she protested, but the maids were mechanically unrelenting in their task.

"The priestess awaits in the council chamber, you must redress, then you will get your chance to speak. Be thankful that you are of Our Maker's kind. It gives you special privilege by our sacred code, but not total amnesty," said Sikula. These words gave Marie some hope. The maids thrust olive leggings on Marie and a champagne-colored blouse. They secured her into a tawny doublet embroidered with geometric patterns of eggs, leaves and arrows stitched in brown, rust, and green hues. One maid chattered out something in a sputtering Volgen, its silvery sharp beak flashed threateningly in the darkened air as she fastened boots to Marie's feet.

"Pardon?" Marie said. She hated that her voice sounded weak and challenged.

"She said you wear the clothing of a titmouse page," Sikula translated. "Fits you best. They are satisfied." Sikula cackled a statement back at the pair. One of the maids nodded and disappeared momentarily, reappearing with a silver circlet glinting in her hands. She clamped it down onto Marie's head and the other maid quickly braided the captain's hair around it. "Ow," protested Marie. "This is indecent!" she shouted at Sikula.

"A translator," he said. "You will need it to speak and understand the council." Sharp pain suddenly erupted behind Marie's ear as one maid implanted a microchip beneath the captain's skin. Marie heard static, then:

"Good. Looks good." One of the maid's twittering Volgen tongue became Ancient English.

"Now we go," said Sikula.

He led Marie down a passage and across a throughfare that spanned to a courtyard. A massive crowd of Volgens gathered around a tented expanse entrenched in the heart of the village. Sikula shoved Marie through the hulking birds, awash in flickering amber light. Shadowy masses of blade like beaks, strange headdresses and vast unyielding robot wings became a nightmarish canopy above her. The Volgens clamored to know what was going on within the chamber. Sikula thundered orders for the villagers to make way. Bird bodies parted, despite some caws of protest. Quickly Marie discerned a portal leading down into the chamber. "This way," Sikula said. She followed him down into the darkness.

Beyond the twisted steps marking the entrance of the council chamber, a grand round room, scratched into the earth, reinforced with amorphous porphyry revealed itself to Marie. Massive amounts of Volgens filled the shadowy expanse. Sturdy mahogany-colored girders arched branchlike above their heads and tethered to the twisting steel arms, was a tent top of finely woven tapestry. Glowing, flickering light lit the billowing fabric from behind. It was a Dionysian epic painted in thread and depicted all manner of Volgens dancing wild winged and reckless along grotesque tree branches and feasting with greedy beaks within the verdant Garden of Naught.

LUCY, where's LUCY? Marie felt as if she was coming on-line again. Energy coursed through her as she dodged Volgens who haphazardly thrust wings into her path. She descended more steps and neared the center of the expanse, Sikula at her back.

"Behold the possessed! The child of the dark code!" screeched a voice that was a thundering hiss of mechanical pistons and expulsions of trilling electronica. "Behold the dark LUCY..." The crowd gasped. Marie could hear a staticky vibration charge the air in the expanse before the tribunal. "This small bot does vile, indecent things. As we have shown you. Things which deny the Code of Saint. It bows down to an evil that defies the authority of the Volgens!"

Marie caught her breath as she reached the bottom step. There, she glimpsed the little bot girl, suspended midair, head flung back in some sort of frozen ecstasy. LUCY's metal appendages clattered violently in the energized force field that surrounded her. Two conscience drones hovered at her side. *They are the source of her cruel imprisonment,* Marie realized, she found her voice and cried, "Wait!" Sikula gripped Marie's arm to keep her from interfering. She shrugged away his taloned fingers and strode out into the small open expanse beyond.

Marie took in her surroundings. Above her towered a massive tribunal stand where a myriad of mechanical bird faces peered curiously down at her. At the center of the stand, perched an ancient looking owl with gigantic yellow oculars.

Marie could feel a seething gaze train upon her back. "What is the meaning of this," the mechanical voice hissed. It was dripping of acid and disgust. Marie turned. There, very near the LUCY stood a gigantic, hunched figure. The vulture was clad in spiney black robes with iron scythe wings and blood red oculars that sought to take apart and devour. Somewhere in the distance Marie heard Corvin's voice give words of protest and excuse.

"This is the woman I told you about," a trilling melody punctuated the tense air. A tall blue bodied nightingale strode into the light. She had a tawny face and golden beak; a headdress of delicate silvery quills decorated her crown. Her eyes were the shade of a robin's egg and her willowy arms were dusted with ivory feathers and encircled with bracelets of turquoise, silver, and gold.

"She is the kind of Our Maker," hooted the owl magistrate.

"Indeed, Eostrix, but exceedingly less intelligent," snapped the vulture.

"It is not in the Volgen code to launch such insults at guests, Neophron," said the nightingale priestess.

"You are far too kind in your ways, Luscinia, to a fault I'd say, and you only delay the inevitable by this neo-human's presence here. Is this a ploy to undermine the council and the code? Horrible stunt, Priestess! This woman should not interfere with Volgen procedures. What business is it of yours anyway—alien, outlander?" He thrust a gnarled staff at Marie and cowered over her with his massive, crooked beak hewn of rusting steel.

Marie thought for a moment and then proceeded, "Indeed," she said calmly, seeking to appeal to reason. "I do not know your ways. I *am* alien to this world, as you say. But I am here to speak on behalf of this LUCY."

"Speak on behalf!" Neophron said, aghast.

"The trial is long over, the evidence is presented, and the pronouncement has been made," said Eostrix.

"This is sentencing, neo-human. *Sentencing*!" yelled Neophron. "You have come too late to speak on this andromatron's behalf. Far, far too late. The pronouncement is made. The procedure *must* be followed. No errant biological mass can deny the will of our coding! The sacred coding of Saint!"

"Then let me speak on my own behalf," said Marie.

"What do *you* have to do with the LUCY?" asked Eostrix.

"This LUCY is indeed contaminated with an errant code."

Neophron threw up his hands, paced and thrust out his wings. Marie would not be deterred by his grandstanding.

"She contains information that is important to my mission. Valuable information. She is not afflicted with the dark code as you assume."

"Silence! Silence!" Neophron hissed flapping at her and banging the ground with his staff. "You speak vile words. Words that should not be spoken here in front of this sacred council. You may be the kind of the Maker, but you cannot force your will on us! Get her out of here!"

"You are in great danger, danger you cannot even begin to imagine," said Marie quickly. Corvin and Sikula thundered to her side. Corvin's steely grip tightened on her arm.

"Let her speak," Luscinia said. "Who are you, child? What kind of danger?"

"I am here," began Marie, "not by my own will, but by a cruel and horrible fate and an even crueler design, I fear. My starship was invaded, ravaged...destroyed. My crew, slaughtered, mercilessly." Marie's voice was forlorn and anguished. She leveled her gaze at Neophron. "The monster who did this is here. And I fear he seeks to destroy you all."

"And who, pray tell, is this monster?" Neophron asked.

"His name is Magnus."

"Magnus," Neophron was amused.

"Yes...," said Marie.

The crowd erupted into a trilling merriment of twittering sonic expulsions punctuated by the gnashing and clacking of beaks. Eostrix hunched over the small form of the captain and roared with hooting jollity. Marie's ears rang with the deafening clamor of the grotesque sounds of hundreds of machine birds simultaneously rustling and calling. Corvin began to pull her out of the view of the council, anticipating that he would be ordered to do so anyway.

"No, wait, wait!" Neophron said, cackling. "Leave her for a moment."

Marie glared at him.

"Poor misguided neo-human. Your biology has failed you my dear," said the vulture. "Magnus. How dare you speak with such a vile contempt of this being, a perfect union of man and machine, the one who shielded us from the Orzos and brought the Aramen mages under control? He is masterful, my dear. You are nothing but a vile little irritant intent on disrupting our ways and the sacred processes of Adelphi Saint! You may take her away." Neophron flicked his steel blade fingers at Corvin.

Disbelief and anguish arrested Marie's entire being. *How could this be?*

"No! No! This is not right," protested Marie, she yanked herself free from Corvin's grip and grabbed Neophron's hem. "Magnus is not your friend," said Marie, peering up at the vulture. She was met with blazing circles of endless glowing red. *I'm protesting to a soulless machine,* she realized. *My fate lays in the hands of a system I can't control...*

"I am sorry for your suffering," Luscinia said. Her voice calmed the quell around them. She then spoke to Marie and seemed to reach for some careful type of coding. "It is hard. It *is* hard," she said to the captain, trying to relate. Then a program executed, an earnest melody of an epic song which emitted from the tip of her golden, shining beak. It was a plea, a connection, an explanation, a memory. She sang: "But this is truth. Once Hout was alive and rooted in the great nebula moon of Nut. Volgens, then, were truly free. We soared amid the magical breezes and currents of the celestial stardust—we lived among the grandest branches of the exterior world. But then, things changed." Her song became underscored by painful strained vocals. "The Orzos changed. They became greedy. They devoured the moon that once rooted us and kept us safe. They cursed our great home. The great tree was defiled by ravaging storms and set adrift in the dust of dying stars. Insidious blight followed the consumption of the moon. Hout's interior was the only place the Volgens could run..." Her voice trailed off, the Volgen crowd sighed in ghastly remembrance, she continued:

"At first the six tribes tried to cooperate with each other, but the Aramen had always lived inside the tree and were not so willing to share the interior realm with us. At last, we convinced them to let us settle here. Things only worsened after that. The Orzos became sick and mad, obsessed with what little resources were left. They quickly, inexplicably, began their quest of self-extermination. (The Orzos were the ones the Aramen had a quarrel with, not us,) but when their greatest enemy died, we were an easy target."

"But to our great relief, hope came. Part Kind of Saint, part machine. A wonderous mixture of both worlds combined. Magnus. It was Magnus who arrived from the Outerlands. He quelled the last of the Orzos and convinced the Aramen to leave us in peace as well. The red mages so revered him, that he became their leader. That is where he rules to this day, the Aramen kingdom that exists in the darkest, hidden depths of Hout. He is their king; he is their leader."

"There you have it," said Neophron with cold, mechanical finality. He turned to Corvin and Marie, "What a fool you are, what a fool you and Luscinia have brought into this council," he said to the raven general. "Before you take her Corvin, perhaps she should stand and see what foolishness brings." Neophron flung his twisted staff at the contorted, levitating body of the LUCY.

"No..." Marie murmured. She questioned what was real. *Who is this Magnus? LUCY knows. LUCY is the only one who knows! Maybe the only one who could know!* "Wait!" Marie yelled, "WAIT!"

"The council has spoken and so it must be done! The sentence will hold. Commence with the exorcism!" By Neophron's words, his staff began to glow with green electric light. From somewhere in the twisted shadows of the council chamber thirteen small, silvery humming-bots descended around the LUCY, emitting sharp, shrill tweets. Their eyes strobed and the air around the small bot vibrated. They ravaged LUCYs small body with massive sonic blasts. "Dove!" Marie pleaded, her voice was but a small tone calling out over the ringing insanity. Hundreds of Volgen eyes locked hungrily on to the proceeding.

Suddenly LUCY, induced by some inner bolt of programming triggered by the assault, flung erect within the catastrophe of vibrations that surrounded her. Her crystal eyes became searing starlight. A distinct crackling raged within her copper belly. Then a whirring noise, eerie, like the trilling derelict noises of space that reached out through the cosmos, at first faint murmurings, but then a thundering shriek, swelled and became a booming speech: "YOU WILL NOT DESTORY ME!!"

The air around LUCY shattered, sending a pulse blast through the council camber. Marie fought to stand against the detonation but was soon awash in rings of energy that created projectiles out of the humming-bot drones, blowing them through the crowd and tent top above. Volgen citizens and chamber trusses shattered into bits. Suddenly everything was awash in a fiery hot expulsion of pulsing energy. The council took cover behind their bench and a final pulse of energy sent Neophron crashing to the ground.

EPISODE 6.

Quilp, the Rubbish Bin Imp.

Marie's ears felt like they had cotton stuck in them. She rubbed grit from her eyes and peered up through the smoky haze. Shocked Volgens rustled, tweeted, and righted themselves. The council climbed back to the stand; somewhere in the distance Neophron and Luscinia both clambered to their feet. Marie searched the rubble strewn floor and saw the LUCY, unmoving, buried under truss pieces, bits of metal and stone.

"Dove..." Marie murmured, trying to shake away the ringing in her ears. She attempted to stand, but before she could get a foothold again, a small, strange cloaked being crept into their midst. It was the size of a large jackrabbit. It appeared from the ravaged air beyond and stole insensibly into their midst, very near where Marie lay.

"The vile little bot...h...has become a horrible weapon!" Neophron's voice was a ravaged gasp. "Not even the ceremony could expel the evil within her."

"Who knows what it might do next," hooted Eostrix fearfully from above.

Marie flung herself past the small cloaked being and took up the body of LUCY into her arms. "LUCY, can you hear me? LUCY...Dove. LUCY, come on, talk to me," Marie whispered frantically, shaking the small bot hoping to rouse it. Corvin flung himself to her side and protested.

"Turn the bot over to us now," the raven general ordered Marie.

"What do you intend to do with her?" Marie asked.

"That is an excellent question!" a queer gurgling voice interjected. It had a vile and scheming quality. The council was startled by the abrupt utterance and Corvin sought to find its source. Marie soon realized the statement hadn't come from a member of council perched at the bench behind her or even Neophron who leaned heavily on his staff overseeing, with anger, the wreckage of his ceremonial drones, but from the small black cloaked being that had found its way into the middle of the circle, quite close to them all indeed.

"I couldn't help but overhear your dilemma—well, I was in the crowd you see..." small silvery green appendages peeled back a tiny black hood revealing an odd, bass-mouthed, being. It now lumbered into full view from behind Corvin's massive boots. It removed the cloak and flung it aside with clear, dramatic abandon. The small imp was a tiny, armored, conglomeration of disparate wired and bolted together pieces. Oxidized bits of iron were lashed to his hunched back like a shell. The imp possessed very large, round, jaundiced eyes and an antenna of quills sprouted from the middle of his forehead. A curious, silver funnel shaped hat sat upon his pearl-fleshed cranium, cocked to the side. His hands, which he wrung with sweaty fervor, were tiny and attached to stubby little arms. His legs appeared as if they had once belonged to a mechanical goat. He wore a worn brown waistcoat. The pocket bulged full of unseen trinkets.

At first Marie thought the dwarfish machine was extremely displeased, but she quickly surmised that his frozen, furrowed, dog-like brow, made him appear constantly angry.

"Quilp, dear mech beast..." Eostrix chortled uncomfortably.

Quilp bowed before the chief magistrate and said, "I see you've had some trouble with this one." He hopped over to the LUCY cradled in Marie's arms and patted its head with very small steel hands. "Poor, poor thing. My heart simply bleeds for it. I could do wonders for this machine."

"Indeed?!" Eostrix extorted.

Neophron scoffed.

"It pains me to think that you should want her decommissioned..." Quilp said, sighing wistfully. He ground his tiny hoof into the tile and swayed his little round body to and fro feigning innocence, pondering, then: "might I take this LUCY off your hands?" he asked, a patina-colored fish tail tongue lashed his lips.

At first Eostrix seemed aghast. The crowd around them clamored. Marie could sense a certain amount of relief in the rustles and tweets. Eostrix seemed to come to the same conclusion.

"What else can be done?" the owl-bot said at last. "We have tried to do our duty—and failed, miserably, I might add." He glowered at Neophron.

The vulture was about to protest, but Luscinia touched his hunched shoulders with a calming hand.

"This LUCY *is* dangerous," said Luscinia. "We have seen her power and her fury."

"I know you have become fond of the Volgens over these past few years and have proven yourself a friend to us," Eostrix stammered, "I also know of your...talents. However, I should not want this LUCY to be repaired to full capacity, of course. We cannot take that chance. You see what's happened here..."

"But of course," Quilp went on; "I would not think of restoring her—not after what happened here tonight." He peered up at Eostrix with greedy eyes and up turned his lips in a ghastly little smile. "I will take her," he concluded, grabbed hold of a dangling LUCY arm and began to tug. He licked his lips again and examined Marie with his glassy eye. "This one too if you don't mind."

Corvin yanked the captain to her feet and thrust her into the waiting arms of Sikula. "She will not be going with you," Corvin said. "She is to be detained, indefinitely. She has gone against the will of the Volgens. She must be delt with by our codes," the raven general thundered.

"Quite right, quite right!" hooted Eostrix.

"Very well then," cooed Quilp.

Eostrix continued, "So it is settled then. Let us be done with it!"

Before Marie could protest, she was clamped into wrist cuffs and flung across the rubble strewn expanse by Sikula.

Quilp danced and flung the lolling body of LUCY upon his back, singing happily, "she's mine, she's mine, this lovely little LUCY is MINE!"

"Wait! You are making a mistake! You all are in danger!" Marie cried out as she was drug from the chamber. "I'm trying to tell you...listen."

"Yes, yes, tell us all about it at your trial," Neophron screeched dismissing her with a wave of his gnarled staff. As Marie was drug out of the room, she watched helplessly as the small body of the LUCY, in lumbering, lurching movements, was borne on the back of the tiny imp through the smoldering air and out into the darkness.

EPISODE 7.

Remembering Starcourt Tor.

The only thing I knew that day was that I didn't want to feel you again, ever again. But that quickly changed...now there's only endless regret. Marie cowered by a prison cell window in the somber dark awash in fragments of endless twilight. Twisted rusty bars cast sharp shapes upon her body. *I feel pieced together, fragmented, reshaped, shapeless. I don't know, here, but not whole. Just here. It's strange to be caught up in this world, longing to fix it, longing to help Dove, but comforted by not being able to do a single thing about it. I'm okay that you're not here. That I'm not with you.* Marie said to Sheng. *I'm okay with it. Okay? No matter how crazy Hannah is, what she did or what her plans for you were...I'm okay. I have to be, don't I?*

Why didn't I say this to you then? Did you tell her that you loved her? What does it matter? I wanted to feel you, okay? I admit it. I didn't at first, then I did. The pain of what we lost was too much for me. Seeing you...again. One last time. I'm still hurt. The baby. What does it matter? I wanted to feel you one last time that day I came to you at Starcourt Tor.

Marie analyzed the glow from the prison window. *The light here's the same, isn't it?* She contemplated uncomfortably. She glanced around the chamber, small barren and corroded. She was thankful for the light from the window. She turned her gaze back to it again. *Starcourt Tor on the moon of Iapetus—your homeland. The land of your ancestors. I found you there after our fight—after I vowed to myself I didn't want to see you ever again. I went there desperate, lonely afraid—angry. Yes, that was a big emotion for me. So much anger and hurt, but I just wanted to feel something again, maybe take back again what she took from us. I knew it would be painful.*

A divorce would not be easy, especially under my grandfather's rules, the rules of the Holy Galactic Empire that denies such things. Feelings denied, reality denied for the sake of salvation, but I wondered...could we be saved, should we be saved or at least just for a moment, a brief moment, reclaimed?

I came there to ask you for the impossible, a divorce. I was sure excommunication might follow and perhaps the unthinkable—banishment and exile. (My grandfather could be cruel. I didn't want to rule it out.) But it might not be a bad thing. That's what I thought. It might not be a bad thing for someone like me who loved the stars so much and hated the capital city, the iced over moon of Europa, the spotlight. I could just fade away...isn't that what I always wanted, to fade and then to be eaten by space?

Marie was pale and sick. She wiped an annoying tear from her eye and dove into the memory further. It was a desperate act. She wanted to remember it, every detail. She wanted it to hurt. She wanted it to scar over and keloid into a gigantic scar big enough so the entire Empire could see it.

I found you there, just as your mother said you would be. You went out to run among the crags and waterfalls. Your favorite place, Starcourt Tor. You went there for comfort, to escape, to find some sense of peace again after all that had just happened between us. After all the angry words we said. When you saw me there, standing along the relentless cascades, tears came to your eyes. We'd been apart for several

Imperial phases. You were honestly shocked I was there. I had time to think. Too much time to think, now was the time to act.

We locked into each other's gaze for a moment, yours were cautious, regretful, shameful perhaps, tinged with relief and surprise.

"Hi." I was the first to speak, you mouthed the words back to me. Your eyes were dark pools searching my eyes, longing for contrition. I could sense your sorrow. Memories of our past came quick and unexpected. I ached for what had died. I mourned for us and wanted comfort and instead of telling you I wanted us to end. I kissed you.

Gentle at first, then fiercer—passionate. All I could think of in that moment was I wanted to take you back from Hannah's arms. I wanted what she took from me. You were surprised; your body was tense, cold, and unsure. But I was hungry for you then and for your memory and your arms and body. Your mouth. Then you knew. Your arms wrapped around my body and lips channeled longing and repentance. We kissed again. Tentative at first. Our passion was strange. Newborn. Raw and confusing. I felt solace in your arms and at the same time, imprisonment. I didn't care that I was making a mistake.

Then as our lips became raging, feasting explosions of desperation, I gave into what my body wanted. Aroused by your betrayal, I let you into me. I used it, channeled it to feed my passion and my hate. And wanted you. And to let you in, deeper still, a biting hurting fury erupted inside.

We exhausted our bodies amid the wavering crag grasses, exorcising our frustrations on the bruised raw earth. Our lovemaking was frantic, rage-filled and at times, tender. You tried to hold me afterwards. Sudden shame and regret filled me. I closed you off from me—for good I prayed but could not say it. You tried to tell me that you loved me.

I wouldn't let you speak. Instead, I dressed quickly and left.

EPISODE 8.

Fire Flight.

Marie flung off tumultuous dreams filled with silver faced demons. She awoke to fire. *Breathe...I can't breathe.* Acrid smoke choked her cramped cell. Somewhere in the passage beyond, explosions blasted through the expanse. Flames ate hungrily at the doorway; steel groaned, and ground shifted. Marie fumbled to the barred door, screaming for help. *What is happening!* She bowed to the floor hoping to catch disparate lungfuls of what little air might be close to the ground and prayed. Distant clamoring. More explosions. Cries and booming blasts. Suddenly the prison door groaned, clanged, and was torn free. Large talons collected her from the ground. A massive form shoved her into the angry orange passage. "Sikula!" Gratitude washed over her. Smoke choked tears from her eyes.

"We are under attack!"

The passage was a torrent of raging flames. Marie shielded her eyes; steel fell from above. More smoke. "There's no way out!" *This prison tower is a deathtrap!*

Sikula nodded and yanked Marie from the tremoring ground upon which she stood. His massive robotic arms quickly enveloped her and with a caw, he stretched his great black and tan wings and tore through the churning, flaming catastrophe. Ash ridden twilight suddenly surrounded them both.

The atmosphere was filled with heat and fury. Volgens fled in frenzied, screeching swarms. Many flapping forms escaped the village out into the dimness beyond the Garden of Naught. Spires fell, as did dob archways. The swirling turrets of the city ramparts were now bonfires. In the courtyard below, hooded figures robed in vermilion vestments threw out fistfuls of fire and advanced upon the Volgen army.

"They have turned on us! The Aramen!" Sikula's words were barely discernable above the horrendous cataclysmic symphony.

Marie was silent. Too horrified to feel justified. She clung to Sikula's steel arms; they were locked like a cage around her. Volgens who tried to attack the Aramen from the air where quickly shot down in a barrage of red mage fist fire. All seemed hopeless. The mages outnumbered them.

Through billowing clouds of destruction, Marie caught glimpses of Corvin's massive form below. He was consumed by battle. Shielding and thrusting as he fought against the blazing rage of five of these strange mages, he struggled to hold his own against fire blasts. The raven general had successfully mowed down a swath in the mass of red figures leaving a trail of shattered Aramen bodies behind him, but now power drain and fire had taken its toll. He brandished his shield bracers and struggled with his broadsword. His great wings became weapons as he whipped up a barrage of attacks with the massive appendages. The Aramen advanced unfettered with clanging footfalls, their robes whipped violently in the torrents of air. The gusts freed featureless mirrored faces from behind their shrouds. *These are the beings that had invaded my dreams—the Ara-*

men! Marie realized with horror. Corvin was consumed by the fiery onslaught.

"The general needs aid!" Sikula screamed.

"Put me down!" Marie commanded. "I can fend for myself! I can fight!"

Sikula quickly landed. He released the captain from his arms, nodded and then charged off into the war. Marie searched the courtyard frantically. The terra cotta tiled expanse was charred and strewn with remains. Humongous whipping orange and yellow flames spun out around her in a dizzying cyclorama, eating at the tar black wreckage that was once the village of Volgen. Giant warring bodies writhed very near her, silhouetted against the violent tumult. Involuntary swift memories rocketed through her mind. Trauma of the not-so-distant past. The burning decks of the *Antoinette* flashed through the captain's mind. Those horror filled moments—racing through the confusing tilted passageways clogged with smoke and fire; the horrified eyes of her crew; their screams; their burning bodies; all superimposed on top of her current surroundings.

Fight, Marie, fight! Magnus has taken too much. An explosion of Aramen bodies yanked her from her trance. Thunderous cries of battling Volgens quickly punctuated the air. Horror and rage tinged their every utterance. Near Marie lay the smoldering contorted body of a fallen Volgen soldier. She grabbed up his abandoned sword and thrust a steel kneecap on her head as a helmet. Fastening it over her braids, she launched off into the carnage.

Choking flames scorched Marie's throat; she held up her arms against the billowing blasts of ash. Two more mages converged upon the raven general. He was overwhelmed and trapped. *Where is Sikula?* Thought Marie, but there was no time to search out the soldier. Corvin shielded his frame from another barrage of fire. His wings were badly scorched. Rising, he dealt more blows with his broad sword. One mage collapsed in a ring of defeated green smoke and shattering silver metal. Deafening electrical blasts branched out from the suddenly consumed body. Marie dodged the barrage of death and flung herself at Corvin's attackers.

Marie quickly drove her blade into the Aramen's back. Kicking loose the mechanical soothsayer as quick as she'd impaled it, she reclaimed her blade. The lifeless body erupted in swift electrified blasts. Hot green fire consumed its robes.

Corvin shot Marie a surprised glance from under a protective wing. More infernal Aramen attacks erupted around his grand, bowing form. Then, seemingly empowered by the captain's presence at his side, the raven general rose and fought against the fire that ate the air around him. He slashed mortal blows to two more of the mirror-skinned mages.

Marie roused immediate fury within Corvin's last attacker. The red shrouded sorcerer quickly readied its staff, taking a wide legged stance. With a spin of the golden rod, it leapt forward and slashed at Marie with quick angry strokes. Marie braced herself against the barrage of spinning staff thrusts and met each strike with expert precision. She sensed systematic frenzy in its coding. Lurching back on her feet, she paused to let more frantic strikes fall short. Then, seizing her chance, she advanced quickly, catching the sorcerer's weapon with the full force of her blade. Quickly, she flicked the staff free from the mage's grasps. The rod clattered to the ground. Marie immediately spun and struck her attacker's head free from its body with one decisive boot thrust. The Aramen's mirrored cranium shattered on the ground. Newly exposed wires shot sparks from its neck. She shielded her face as its shuddering silver body exploded into a fountain of sharp fragments.

Two more mages quickly met her in attack. They thrust out their hands. Marie was certain they were about to torch her with fiery fingertip flames. Marie immediately raged at them and thrust herself beneath their torching reach of fire, and crashed stiff-legged into the towering attackers. The two toppled. Clattering to the ground, she flung her body on top of them, beating one to death with the butt end of her sword and stabbing the other straight through the throat.

Unbridled exhilaration flooded Marie's senses. These victories were joyously clean, quick and decisive. She surveyed the environment around her. Her lungs were burning sacs. Her labored breath prompted a frantic search for any means to escape the courtyard. The perimeter was clogged with more advancing red robed mages. Many bird bot bodies littered the earth. The Volgen army was now nothing more than piles of rubble beneath the choking air. *The Volgens will not win this battle,* Marie thought solemnly. Then she spotted Sikula. A battalion of Aramen were hacking away at his contorted body. They finished him off with heartless flames. He became a bonfire; they turned and strode towards her; their faces reflected the ravaged expanse.

Marie fled. Sudden nightmarish whispers clamored in her mind. Staticky, clattering, shrieking. She reeled back, losing her footing. Excruciating agony electrified her brain. White hot spasms revealed the formless mirror of an Aramen face. Her body was electrified. She distantly felt the sword slip from her fingers and steely fingers wrapped around her forehead, blasting away her makeshift helmet. She braced for fire. More images flooded her mind. The killing fire stream never came, instead an eerie trilling screech reached a heightened frenzy and suddenly an image flashed full force across her consciousness. A probing red cyborg eye thrust itself into her soul. The stench of death rotted skin flared within her nostrils. A haughty breath still reeking of the grave uttered this word, like a forlorn curse: "Marie..." *Magnus!*

A flash. Marie broke back into consciousness amid the glowing green fire of Aramen death. Corvin thrust taloned fingers about her arm and drug her out and away from the rapidly advancing red mages. His sword blade still steamed with dead mage blood. The air stank of battery acid.

"He knows I'm here! That's the reason they've invaded!" Marie shrieked.

"We need to get out of here, now!" Corvin cawed back at her.

"He's looking for me!" she tried to tell him.

Electronica chattered from Corvin's speakers. "Full systems check engaged. Flight systems damaged but still operational. Power at 40%."

"I think we can make it," he told her. "At least to a safe place beyond the Garden of Naught, someplace where we can find shelter...Luscinia...we must find her. I've lost connection with her!"

"Corvin! She's there!" Marie pointed in the distance.

There, quite near the fiery ruins of the Volgen ceremonial house enclosure, the graceful form of the nightingale priestess parted the masses of Aramen wizards. Hypnotic, drenched in bio-mechanical tears, her pale blue garments clung desperately to her body. Wings arched like reaper tools, arms crooked, eyes pulsing hypnotic fuchsia and green, she advanced through the battlefield. *What strange coding is this?* Marie wondered fearfully. *Their precious priestess, a defense mechanism triggered. Only used as a last resort*, that thought quickly advanced through her mind, almost telepathically, then disappeared.

"She should not be out here! Something is wrong with her!" Corvin exclaimed, "Luscinia!" he raced towards the priestess.

Marie ran after him. Aramen still fell at the fringes of their path. Suddenly Corvin was caught up too as if he struck an invisible wall of electrified energy. Suddenly his oscilloscope sputtered out a dizzying array of coding foreign to Marie. The general fell to his knees, struck immobile by the systems spell.

"Corvin! Corvin!" Marie tugged at the dead-locked arm of the raven general. *Was this Luscinia's method of victory—to render all immobile?* the captain questioned. Aramen bodies fell to the ground one by one around the battle torn courtyard. Somber smoke twirled above the field littered with bodies and wreckage. A momentary stillness washed over the enclave, but that was soon doused by something else.

Nearby, engine sounds fired. Beyond the cliff's edge at the perimeter of the shattered Volgen village, a trio of large angular black and opal ships rose into view. Marie shielded her fear-filled eyes against the glaring head lamps. These were no Volgen conveyances, she realized immediately—these were ships of pirates. Of the same type that had invaded the starship, *Marie Antoinette. These were Magnus' ships!* Marie struggled to rouse Corvin from his trance. It was no use. Fear ripped through her entire consciousness and she chose to hide. Diving beneath the raven's wings, Marie cowered out of sight of the probing lights. She was sure that with the Aramen search party now immobilized, Magnus would be unaware of her whereabouts. Marie soon realized the ships now sought something else entirely.

The prong-bodied jets whipped apart the choking haze and their lamp lights soon discovered the source of the Aramen immobilization. Through a veil of whipping feathers, Marie watched as a crew of pirates disembarked the central hovering ship. The rag tag bunch of humanoid creatures, with disparate pieces of armor salvaged from a varied array of galactic tribes collaged upon their bodies, converged upon the strobing nightingale goddess, apparently unfazed by her hypnotic programing. "This is the source! —It has forbidden codes within it!" Marie heard one of the pirates bellow as they deciphered readouts from a communi-com device. "Bring her then!" another resounded.

They quickly took hold of the priestess. Luscinia entranced, still striding rhythmically, became like a gigantic child's windup toy in their arms as they drug her ambulating form aboard the pirate ship. As quickly as the ships appeared, racing engines propelled the hovering vessel into the air again. As burning structures tumbled and the savage heat of the burning village cracked rock face and sent boulders suddenly tumbling into the square, the trio of pirate ships raced off into the air beyond the cavern mouth and into the dimness beyond the valley of Naught.

Suddenly raven wings came to life around Marie. She gasped.

"Luscinia!" Corvin's strained words echoed mournfully on the quickly incinerating air. Aramen sputtered back to life around them only to be met by more massive falling stones. Pain stricken, Corvin grabbed up Marie in his woeful arms and, dodging calamity, he raced through acrid air and took flight in the direction of the pirate ships.

EPISODE 9.

Mud and Darkness.

Marie frantically smothered Corvin's smoldering, demolished wings with huge fistfuls of muck, leaves and inky, writhing lichens. Plummeting from the sky in his arms had left her with a barrage of bruises and cuts. She denied tending to her own bleeding until the fires ravaging the general's body were smothered and extinguished. Her hair was singed, her fingers blistered, but this was nothing compared to the broken state of the raven general.

Corvin was silent, joints frozen and contorted. *Pain, fear, worry, sorrow, defeat, perhaps—were these the emotions—or something that resembled these emotions, in coding?* Marie wondered what instructions coursed through his components. The captain helped the bird man upright. His long-beaked face hung low on his steel neck. She touched his arm with concern and surveyed his destroyed wings. They were now mangled and twisted steel struts draped with melted jet black plastic.

"You saved me," Marie said to him. A pirate ship's rear cannon, aimed wickedly at them, shot them from the cavernous atmosphere. It was quick, decisive, and catastrophic. Luscinia now seemed hopelessly out of reach.

A survey of damage twittered out a status report from Corvin's oscilloscope. It didn't sound good. His energy reserves were at code red state and his wings were 100% useless. His body frame was a twisted wreck. However, to Marie's relief, he could still manage locomotion. Standing, Corvin tested his limits by lumbering over mounds of black creeper covered porphyry and threw himself against the trunk of a soaring sinter. Corvin peered out into nothingness. His glowing ocular rings emitted sputtering, forlorn flashes of blue.

Marie watched Corvin's stark black silhouette. Suddenly waves of sickness erupted from her gut. She clutched herself. Chills wracked her frame as the silent moment was quickly disrupted by the sound of her own retching. Choking vomit spewed from her throat. She thrust herself face down over a rock and emptied the contents of her stomach. After a few moments of heavy heaves, she regained her breath and then rolled to her back. *The fetus...is not...enjoying this at all...* She gulped in dank air, peering up at intense blackness. As Marie's eyes slowly adjusted to the shadows, she discerned a glowing yellow aura. It came from somewhere beyond the crest of petrified stone monoliths that stood at the farthest reaches of where they now found themselves.

"It's my fault," she said finally, wiping adrenaline laced spit from her lips.

"Yes," Corvin replied in garbled electronica, "Maybe yes...indeterminate at this juncture."

"It was Magnus, he was looking for me."

"It was...Luscinia they took. ...N...not you," Corvin responded, stuttering, staticky.

The mushy wet ground was odd comfort to her. *Here I am lying in a pile of mud and vomit. Is this all there is—endless muck and darkness?* "He wants me dead," said Marie at last. "The Volgens just got in the way. It *is* my fault. I saw him. ...In a mind meld with an Aramen...he won't stop; his anger...his thirst for power and destruction...I saw it in his eyes."

"We...w...were deceived by Magnus..."

Marie nodded. *At least we agree on that*, she thought.

"They were scared of her. Luscinia." Corvin said. "The code...she processed at the last was something...horrific...u...up to this point unseen. Decommission via s...song... It was a powerful spell. Unprecedented." Corvin's straining voice was a mix of awe and horror.

"Whatever disabled you also laid out about forty Aramen. If it was Luscinia that did that, then she *is* a powerful weapon. The pirates may have realized this...collected her to stop her from wreaking further damage—I wonder why they didn't just destroy her?" *Maybe they collected her to destroy her*, Marie didn't say this aloud. Marie finally sat up, she felt mud slide down her back. A wave of disgust followed, maybe nausea again. She choked it back. "...or maybe they're just trying figure out what you and I are trying to figure out as well...how and why...what does it mean?"

"The beings that...piloted those ships?" Corvin said.

Marie nodded. "I've seen their kind before. They are the same ones that invaded and destroyed my starship, at Magnus' orders."

"They're organic, alien...s...scan showed—not Aramen. Outlanders, not Houtan. They don't belong here."

"Magnus doesn't either. We must stop him. Prevent him from doing more damage to your world. Luscinia poses a threat to the Aramen army," Marie said at last. "She can infiltrate their minds and disable them. That's why the pirates captured her," Marie understood suddenly. "It was enough to deter them from going after me...they were just as shocked with her as you and I were. But it's me he's after..."

"Why do you keep saying that?"

"He wants me destroyed, Corvin. He destroyed my entire starship. He killed everyone aboard. He wants me dead. He wants—revenge..." the statement caused her to rise up from the mud. "My family." Horrific confirmation set in.

"Your family—"

"—the Empire..." she stammered, assured. "But why is he here in *this* place? Why Hout?" she continued, "and who is he anyway? I could understand some mad man wanting to damage the Holy Galactic Empire, but this feels personal...the Empire has lots of enemies...it was *my* ship he invaded. It was *me* he was after...still *is* after..." Marie was deeply troubled by her own self-conversation.

"Who *are* you?" Corvin said finally, almost hatefully.

"I'm sorry," she said to the raven general. "For all of this." She hated herself for constantly apologizing, but she didn't know what else to say.

Corvin thought for a moment. "You will help me get her back," he said finally. Rousing himself from his rocky perch, he leapt to the ground. His boots thwacked the earth with a soggy thud. "If Magnus is after you, t...then he will come looking..." Corvin sputtered, even weaker.

"He will." Marie said. This was without a doubt the truth, but she feared this tack. "We can't just wait for him to find us," she was assured. "We must search him out. Secretly. It's the only way we can get the upper hand."

"The lands of the Aramen are...forbidden...uncharted. Who knows...where he...might be...lurking?" Corvin's body convulsed and crumpled. Marie went to him, helped him to stand. Momentarily, he was able to do so on his own again.

"We gotta get you help," she said. "You'll be decommissioned in no time." Then an idea came to her. "Where does that creature live -Quilp?"

Corvin was silent. Transistors and circuitry hemorrhaged within him. "...very near the Mech Mech township...upper banks of the fjord...bottom of the next crest. Quilp lives on the outskirts of the town..."

"Quilp is a mechanist. He can repair you. Restore your batteries—patch you up. This is our only option. He has the LUCY too. The little bot knows of Magnus and she can help us locate the secret city of Aramen."

"Fine." Corvin said at last, the word was like a desperate gasp.

"You think you can make it that far?"

Corvin calculated. "Yes. I...I will lead you there—"

EPISODE 10.

The Dark Code's Disturbing Architecture.

Pale yellow light now gleamed off waters of the black fjord. Marie and Corvin trudged carefully along treacherous slick paths of the cliff face choked full of thorny blight vines. All was eerily still within the dank, vast cavern which stretched into infinity.

"Your family—" Corvin stammered. It was a staticky, forlorn utterance on the dank air. He latched on to pieces of conversation from the recent past. Perhaps he was circulating through their dialogue in his own processor searching for hope. "Who...who are...you?" He was desperate for verbal stimulation. Marie was about to speak when suddenly Corvin posed the curious question... "You know love?"

She was taken aback. "Yes," Marie said at last. "Regrettably, yes."

"Regret." Corvin repeated, he walked more erect. He tuned in to her voice, it helped him ambulate. It was a channel for focus, Marie realized. She decided to use her voice to calm and help him, to tell him what she could about herself.

"Captain first...always. Princess...heir (you know the story), my grandfather's persisting, annoying object...I'm a wife...a daughter..." Marie was about to say mother but didn't.

"Captain..." Corvin responded.

"Of starships. Being a pilot is all I ever really wanted. For as long as I can remember. My grandfather thought I joined the military to be away from the abject gaze of the Imperial populace—it *is* exhausting. He was right. I hate to be looked at and scrutinized constantly, evaluated on their terms for worth, mode, fashion, celebrity, pomp ceremony, adherence to the state religion. Ugh. He found relief though, the Dauphin. He found peace with me searching out the stars...that way I couldn't taint the cabinet with any of my indecent ideas. They wouldn't listen anyway. They like to have a doll. Poseable, malleable, bendable. That's not me. So I fled, as fast as I could. I only go back to Europa when absolutely necessary...otherwise..."

"Europa..." Corvin's oscilloscope buzzed. He must've been curious about the word.

"The capital moon. New City is there, the Imperial City. Its ghastly and frozen. Tundra as far as the eye can see. I prefer Titan. My home moon. That's where my father's estate is. Where I grew up. Along the banks of the Seine..."

Cold black waters flashed in Marie's mindsight. Cold black waters surrounded by warm, bright-lit merry air. The waters were always cold and dark, though. Endless. *Like the waters of this fjord*, she realized. Her earliest memories played out in harsh reality in her head. Wavering treetops, waves lapping against the shore, her mother swimming in the waves, laughing in the merry light, splashing. *She told me to stay on the shore. It was just a day. Swimming splashing then nothing...I waited; I was so small I didn't understand.*

"Y...you know love..." Corvin's voice sputtered indecently.

"I have a husband." Marie was annoyed, wrenched from the errant thought of the day her mother died by the raven general's stutter. *Is that what I'm supposed to say? Talk about him? About our wonderful relationship?* "Love. Hmm." Her mind latched onto her childhood as if the memory of the waters of the Seine would not let her go. She decided to twist the knife that was the memory of her childhood and talk to Corvin defiantly about those painful formative moments instead of what she was supposed to talk about—having knowledge of any sweet love at all. "I don't know really," Marie confessed. "My mother died when I was very, very young. I had an overbearing Catholic governess for a while. Ms. Critch...I used to play out by the river at my father's estate. She hated it. I would come in, sun baked and dirty. Spankings followed—yelling. 'You have rooms and rooms of dolls and you want to go out and make yourself a muddy pirate!' She'd scream at me," Marie's words were threadbare and angry. "She threw my own dolls at my face and would force me to pick them up after. 'Pick these up! You're no princess anyway—out there in the dirt; you act like a servant! You don't even fear the Lord. Did your mother ever teach you anything...'" Marie's voice trailed off. "My mother..." Marie tried to see the face in the shadows, but it was always hidden. There were only portraits. No real woman. The mocha skinned goddess with the haunting gray eyes. Hair done up in some sort of extravagant manner; ears, neck, and wrists, dripping with diamonds; clad in ivory satin holding bouquets of stargazers. That was all Marie knew of her mother—paint on a canvas. "My mother..." Marie stammered again. Her eyes stung. "But I wouldn't give in to Ms. Critch," said Marie, clearing her throat. At last her voice became more resolved. "I stood there, every time; proud faced. I didn't even cry. I never cried. I remained silent. I would never give her the pleasure of my pain, anger or sadness." *I became the portrait of my mother in my mind. Chin held high, steadfast, pure. Seeds of hate and resentment -no, desire manu-*

factured into independence; the need to keep going, to search out the beyond, never stopping. "Then, when she was done with me, I just ran back out to the river..." Marie smiled.

"The...the river..." Corvin stated, almost as if he strove to understand.

"About the time I turned nine, Ms. Critch was let go. My father finally had her replaced with a robot named CA(RO)-LYN, a courtier android for royal operations. She became my best friend. She was a touchstone of knowledge and ideas..." Marie became awash in memories, "CA(RO)-LYN made me feel extraordinary...maybe the only one who ever really did. For the right reasons, not chained to expectation or personal benefit. Just for the joy of igniting something of value within me. Her favorite spot to teach was beneath the reaching arms of the willow by the water's edge—the Seine. Afternoons. Starlit nights. Constellations seeped into my very being. CA(RO)-LYN the conductor of these blossoming new ideas, she made me who I am." The rushing, trilling leaves of the willow tree ignited excitement in Marie's memory and the rushing waters became space jet engines revving. "The stars stretched out before me..."

"That is love," Corvin said. His words were indistinguishable now, awash in sputtering garble.

Marie realized they needed to find Quilp quickly. "Are we nearly there?" Marie said. Corvin flung a shuttering hand in the direction before them. Marie helped the raven circumnavigate a treacherous bend in the rocks, and then, in the near distance Marie could discern odd-shaped city walls erupt from the jet black waters of the fjord. The skyline presented a host of surreal flesh toned shapes lit with amber illumination rods concealed somewhere within the nest of buildings. The structures looked almost organic. Round and oval orbs and some half sphere concave masses grew cumulus from the base of the city, then, from these elements burst forth botanical shapes which reminded Marie of mechanical pistols and stamens. Strung through the structures were silver tracks suspended upon delicate cathedral shaped arches. Small conveyances lumbered along these expanses.

"The Mech Mech city...doesn't look the same," commented Corvin as they came around the bend. He staggered and clutched at the rock that fringed the path. "The light is different...the dark code has intrenched the city walls..."

Corvin was right. The gnarled entangled blight had spouted spider fingered from the dark woods, grown across the waters and now fed red-veined electro-elixir into the amorphous yellow walls turning them the color of bruises. Suddenly the shapes of the city skyline morphed into something different for Marie. Towers and domes seemed to resemble fleshy appendages, like disembodied infant arms and heads. Marie clasped her abdomen. She felt as if she would be sick again.

Corvin nodded. "Q...Quilp's workshop...just ahead, a league." He staggered on. She grabbed his arm to assist him.

"Okay," responded Marie.

They trudged the final measures of rutted stone that led among the ebony petrified pilasters to the base of the trail in silence. For the silence Marie was grateful, relieved to put her personal history and current situation on ice for now. She gave herself fully to the task of helping the raven general down the trail that soon led off across a bleak marshy inlet. In the distance stood a small round stone shack with a funnel-like roof hewn of haphazard sheets of rusty metal. The promise of getting aid for Corvin and hopefully finding Dove drove her forward. As they walked, though, no matter how much she tried to push it away, disheartened hopelessness filtered in. The conversation with Corvin replayed in her head and then a myriad of suppressed thoughts erupted into her consciousness, firing rapidly.

A mother...my mother...cursed child to have a mother die...to have a cursed mother who doesn't know how to be...would be...wanted to be...you there...fetus...I'm not a woman well programmed...there you go, throwing me for a loop—can you hear my thoughts? No, you're just barely even a mass of a few cells...less than a size of a peanut...this is ridiculous. You know your father and I aren't on good terms...we may never be...

The door to Quilp's cottage wavered in Marie's tear stung eyesight. *How am I supposed to feel...you have the worst timing ever...fetus...wrong womb, joke's on you...you asked for this...no, I did...child, shit.* As that thought filtered through her brain, Marie felt the child in her womb stir for the first time.

EPISODE 11.

The Last Time She Saw Him.

"Hey! Hey!...Antoinette!" Commander Brandon Sheng called out over the din in the main docking station of the Maa'ta Karé Space port. Marie didn't look up from the small porter pod in which she had just placed her duffle on top of a myriad of other luggage within.

"Marie! MARIE!" the second call was more abrupt and angry; the captain realized Sheng was nearing the cordoned off area where she now stood prepping for her long journey. Marie braced herself for what was about to come. Dodging ship mechanics and service bots in order to reach her, Brandon bounded down metal stairs and strode toward her.

She sensed his presence close at her side. With a loud sigh, she slammed closed the lid on the porter, realizing ignoring him wouldn't work.

"What are you doing here?" she said expelling her most annoyed tone. Sheng's countenance erupted longing in her. She had missed gazing into his flashing dark eyes; his handsomeness had always melted her heart. He now had very close-cropped hair, different than she remembered. She ached for him to hold her, but she resisted the longing which pained her even more. Marie focused not on her husband's eyes, but instead on the stars and bars that decorated the breast of his

snow-white uniform. Her gaze rested firmly on the medallion bearing the dove of the Order of the Holy Ghost pinned to his chest.

Marie patted the top of the porter pod twice and it rocketed off to dock in a port on the side of the crew's shuttle, a massive lozenge shaped conveyance with an art nouveau frame and encrusted with tiffany glass. The impeccable vessel now took up most of the main docking bay. Its style was late Imperial. It reflected the charm of the immaculate starship, its host, the Marie Antoinette, which was considered a jewel of the galaxy. But the artfulness of Imperial conveyance design was lost upon the pair who stood in momentary silence, then...

Sheng took Marie's hands in his and pulled her close, "Hey, I love you. You don't have to do this." he caressed her face. She was insulted by the statement. It battered her. She still would not give in. He attempted to lift her chin to meet his gaze. She turned her back to him and bit her lip.

"It's too late Sheng. I'm going," she said simply. He did not respond. "You didn't answer my question."

"I'm here to stop you from going, obviously," Sheng told her, "I pulled some strings. I've been reassigned to the Maa'ta Karé for the next 100 cycles. Commandeering a special conquest to do further study within the God's Eye Nebula. Routine really, but to be able to be close to you..."

"The C-Infinity system isn't close."

"So, that's where you're going."

"Queen's Command. Couldn't stay even if I wanted to." She turned back to face him and folded her arms across her chest.

"When will you be back?...After Starcourt Tor, I thought..."

"That was a one-time thing."

"So that's where we're at?" Sheng said. "You know what? I made a mistake, but you're being cruel!"

"We can't keep doing this."

"I'm not like you. I can't turn on and off emotions just like that. Just like a machine! Can't you even try to forgive me?" His pleading eyes searched hers. She did not want to go there right now.

"We'll talk when I get back," she said.

"Maybe I won't be here when you get back," he said. Marie's eyes were alarmed. "That's the thing, Marie, you always expect me to wait...I'm tired of waiting." He backed away from where she stood. Marie would not satisfy him with any tears.

"Well you won't find solace with HER this time, Brandon. She's part of MY crew," Marie said.

"What are you talking about?"

"Dr. Krane. What is it they say—keep your enemies closer?" Marie was indignant.

"It's so laughable," Sheng said. His words were a hurt exhale. He was on the verge of tears. "It was nothing...WE are in the relationship. Hannah Krane will never happen again. It was a mistake, but you wouldn't know what that means, would you Marie?...I guess you've never made a mistake in your life." He flung his hands as if shaking her free from his body, "Run-away, then; enjoy your mission, Antoinette!"

Marie watched him leave.

~ PART II ~

EPISODE 12.

Easter Mystery.

Somewhere within the darkest, most inaccessible depths of Hout existed a city of mysterious indigo. A tall dark tower, ornament shaped, thrust upward from the center of its radiating walls. Each edifice of the city, nested one into the other, resembled thorny arms of an immense century plant, and these, were punctuated with delicate spans rising into the murky, purple-colored atmosphere. Each curling armature held glowing orbs of phosphorescent scapolite. Along the waxy surface of this massive city, veins of silver filament pulsed, and at the farthest edges, structures resembling the mouths of nightshade blossoms, swallowed dark code blight, the killing infection that had taken hold of many of the realms of Hout. This was the city of the Aramen.

Three flashing opal-bodied pirate ships suddenly dipped below churning, midnight clouds. They sliced through the heavy air, screaming toward a yawning portal housed in the tower of the grotesque, exotic metropolis. Quickly the ships landed. The crew made swift work of disembarking. Amid exhaust blasts issuing from the undercarriage of *Soul Reaper I*, a group of pirate henchmen unloaded a small hovering black slab upon which rested a massive silver egg. The grand object was exquisite in its look, filigree covered. No seam was perceived marring its perfect gleaming surface. The pirates immediately took the egg to the throne room.

Magnus was in dark meditation when the pirates came into his chamber, and upon hearing them enter, instant anger an annoyance erupted within him.

"Where's Marie? Where's MARIE!" he shouted and turned toward his chief commanders Kitrank and Faul. "You don't have her with you, do you?" His voice was tinged with desperate sadness. He knew what the report would be, he had seen the frenzied communications scrolling across the visor of his consort Aramen, Red Mage -0- for the past three cycles.

"The Volgen city is destroyed, we deployed the Aramen as you requested..." said Kitrank, a reject Vespa-Mandarinian from Ijiraq who created choppy vocalizations by rubbing mandibles together and expelling the vibrations of speech from a diaphragm embedded in his segmented, humanoid, yellow-black body. Each utterance was underscored by a sputtering of translucent-wing-thrusts. "The princess was nowhere to be found."

"Nowhere to be found...I know she was there. I know it!"

"You are right, Master, the princess *was* there. As you may know, Aramen 6066 located the princess briefly during the battle; the Volgens fought valiantly," said Faul, a Lacer-Is'rondai from the fabled yellow planet Chamomile (famed for its petal-shaped rings of white glittering space rock). She was a voluptuous reptile, clad in an array of patchworked armor gleaned from the warring tribes of Polydeuces. She had lovely arms and legs of green and blue. She wore bracers of gold and chausses of the same hue on each well-formed, scale-covered appendage. A prominent crest of red and green spouted mohawk-like just above her parietal eye. "But as you also may know, records show that Red Mage 6066 was destroyed by General Corvin just after it found Antoinette."

"So, what then? You just left? You left the princess there? You...abandoned your mission? Instead of bringing me Marie Antoinette...YOU BRING ME THIS EGG?" He flung a gargantuan steel boot at the massive silver offering sending it flying off the ebony transport slab. The egg clattered to the floor, rolled in circles, and then sat itself upright again as if something inside induced it to never lay prone for any length of time. This only made Magnus seethe.

Faul was not fettered by Magnus' anger. She never cowered before him. "The Aramen, unfortunately, were incapacitated by the Volgen priestess." Faul spoke in tones which were high-born Chamomilian. She had indeed studied in the finest schools of the pylon city, despite being born humbly into the desert lizard tribes of the Is'rondai. Adopted by neo-humans who lived in the grand tower city, she ran away from her upper-class home when reckless impulses imbued in her DNA got the better of her. She soon learned how to charm the deplorables of the universe, eventually falling in with a band of pirates that hid out in the icy rock rings of the planet dedicated to the god of time. "Besides searching for the princess and razing the Volgen village to the ground, we also had the complete immobilization of our troops to deal with. You should be grateful to us for bringing you this...egg. It holds much power. It *is* the Priestess Luscinia, she slumbers now, but if awakened she can disable armies."

Magnus strode to the great ovular oddity and placed a decomposing hand enmeshed in metal armatures upon it. His nails screeched against its surface. He pondered. "Armies you say..."

"We should have Grand Mech TinWratchet analyze her. The Mech may know how 't crack open her shell and decommission her f'good," offered Kitrank.

"I respectfully disagree," Faul immediately replied. "Decommissioning seems a horrible waste. If we defile her programming and induct her in our ways, she may be of use to us. Perhaps she could even be made to bring the remaining Volgens under our control—the Beestjes and Tweelachs as well. You know as well as I, all the tribes will be thorns in our side for as long as they have a will free of our own design."

"You may be right," said Magnus.

"And as for Marie, there is absolutely no way that the princess could've escaped that village alive. The Aramen were thorough in their destructive tasks," said Faul. "The entire city now lies under a smoldering pile of boulders."

"Is that so?" said Magnus. "Volgens have escaped. A great many of them in fact, according to Red Mage -0-. I knew this even before you returned. You may think you have saved your skins for the moment, but my patience is growing thin. It is possible, Marie still lives."

"I still hold to the idea that the princess may have been killed," said Faul. "The mystic Aramen seers have been scanning the areas outlying the Volgen township—however I must concede that there is difficulty analyzing the terrain around the fjord—that canal masks many dark paths. The fjord's waters emit a strange energy field over the cliffs surrounding them."

"Then go there." Magnus said, his voice was guttural, acidic, and impassioned. "Find her. I know she's out there and don't come back until you have her!"

Faul was about to defend her actions once again, but instead bowed. Kitrank followed suit and the two strode out of the chamber. Magnus paced. Regarding the egg with disgust, he turned toward the massive ceremonial stair leading up to a dais. Upon the dais stood a massive gray throne and beside the throne, an urn-shaped pilaster. A glowing red stone hovered over it. Magnus mounted the steps and went to the red stone beacon which was now encased in a diamond shaped frame. The frame had been retrofitted around the sacred gem as a means to control its power.

"This room used to be sacred to the Aramen..." he whispered.

"It still is...they just don't remember; they have different programming now..." a female voice echoed through the vacuous chamber. Magnus turned in the direction of the voice.

A slender woman with skin the color of pale bone emerged from beyond an arcade of pillars shaped like fluted shimmering gray tentacles. She wore a silver gown crafted by Aramen looms. She had vengeful green eyes and blond hair cropped at a severe angle. Half of her fine-featured face stood in shadow.

"You mourn for her and you pray for her to be alive, don't you?" Dr. Hannah Krane said. "You want Marie so desperately..."

"You don't know what I want," Magnus said.

"I do know. I do know..." she whispered. "You and I are the same." She came toward him in the sick pale light. "First loves...how they do wound us, even to this day." Hannah's voice quaked in the vacuous, yawning space.

Magnus let out a breath and cowered to the earth, cradling his massive legs within the crooks of his metal arms. She was used to seeing many sides of this man. She had known him before and after his transformation. Rage and madness, hurtful contemplation, thirst for power and revenge, sadness—these were all parts of his beautiful mosaic.

"First loves made us what we are," she said stroking his sparse oily strands of hair and kissed the back of his metal studded skull. Carrion masses of grayish flesh protruded between the rivets. "Brandon told me he loved me once. We were only kids then. Then years later, I was nothing but a diversion from his wife. A sick little thing to be used..."

"If Marie lives, she may find a way to destroy us both." Magnus was unguarded in this moment. Hannah was amused at his self-obsessed mind.

"You give her too much credit," Hannah said. "Marie is just a neo-human woman after all. You hold all the cards." Hannah kneeled in front of the beast; she put her forehead against his, and peered deeply into his eye sockets. She had become adept at stroking his concerns and then chastising them. "But...you still love her and that makes you weak."

Magnus stood violently. The doctor reeled back to the ground. Bracing herself with a slender bare arm, she glanced up to him flipping aside her hair. His eyes were bonfires. Magnus' devilish horrific beauty erupted deep carnal passions within her. She had shared his bed many times before. She spoke, her voice was pained and impassioned. "You say you want her dead, but you fear the idea of it and that kills you inside. Even when you clutched her in your very own hands you couldn't go through with killing her. She escaped the carnage you unleased on her starship and she's escaped again. You hate that. I tried to finish the job for you. Clean up the mess. She runs from you, but you love it. It excites you. You don't want her dead; you want her to love you! You want to possess her, but you can't."

Magnus flung his fingers around Hannah's throat and yanked her from the floor. "With one squeeze I could snap your neck, doctor!"

Hannah gurgled a laugh and screeched, defying his grip: "Do it, but then you'll never know Marie's secret!"

Magnus longed to tear her throat flesh with his talons. He stared hatefully at her for a moment and then with an exasperated release of mechanical breath, withdrew his hand. Hannah staggered back, coughing, spasming. She took in desperate heaves of air. She clutched at her own bruised jugular. Despite this she gasped loudly: "Marie carries Sheng's baby." Magnus' immense form trembled. "She carries Sheng's baby...even still she betrays what was promised to you!" There was pleasure in her speech. Her hatred for Marie was great. Magnus turned. Hysterical laughter flung from her throat. "Marie gets what you and I could never have, and she is blessed again and again. Her family took your throne, and her Empire took my womb. What fatal games they play, and they expect peace and harmony in return!"

Indeed, Hannah Krane could never have a child. Not with Magnus. Not even with the man she truly loved—Marie's husband, Brandon Sheng. The horrific fact was she had been sterilized when she entered the Empire as an immigrant orphan. The only reason she avoided becoming property of the state was that she opted to serve in the military instead of becoming a bed-slave to the aristocrats. Hannah's hatred and resentment for the crown was so great that she had made a secret pact to become an insurgent in the military and do whatever she could, to secretly sabotage and bring down the Empire from within.

"You're wrong Hannah. I don't love Marie. I hate her. I want her to suffer. Marie needs to die. That is my only wish." Magnus' voice boomed. "You say I love her, but I don't. How could

I love a woman who has betrayed me time and again, a woman that has turned me from a king into a monster?! I hate Marie Antoinette. I long for her destruction, I lust for her blood. This is truth! This is truth!"

"Yes, yes..." Tears welled in Hannah's eyes as she ran to the beast and caressed him. Looking into his gaze tenderly she said, "it must be done."

EPISODE 13.

Quilp's Entirely Mechanical Ball.

Flickering lights fantastic strobed against the porphyry walls of Quilp's workshop. Electronically created chamber music, synthesized harpsicord, cellos, and violins blasted through the dimness. Marie recognized the haunting and triumphant tune of a Bach concerto often utilized within the salons of the bourgeois. *How strange to hear such a melody here*, she thought. She and Corvin entered the round stone house unannounced, and they now stood at a balustrade just beyond the open doorway which overlooked a cavernous expanse that had been burrowed out of the bedrock.

A myriad of workbenches and piles of machinery had been pushed aside, out of the way, evidently to create room for dancing figures suspended from a grid concealed somewhere in the dark recesses of the workshop's rafters. The mechanical dancers were haphazardly dressed in clothing that loosely reflected the highest Imperial fashions. Ladies and Gentlemen, flat-board heads, startled features hewn in flaking paint, lurched the floor in ratty long coats and tattered lace panniers, turning and jumping on iron dowls that ran through each figure top to groin. Each of their robotic movements, none of which seemed natural of course, was punctuated by the sound of hidden pistons. With each rise and fall, the clunky metal figures' appendages flung out, banging their partner rudely and landed again, harshly slapping back to center against their own rigid bodies. Marie was both enchanted and horrified by these forced manipulations of merriment.

In the middle of the mechanical ball sat a table decked with cracked plates and tarnished silver, a small, crumbled bit of bread sat under a glass dome and a candlestick held a melted taper with a wavering flame. The seats that sat at each end of the table were empty. Stuffing erupted from each dust covered cushion. As Marie and Corvin surveyed the odd cotillion, a small creature dancing with the lolling lifeless figure of LUCY suddenly emerged from behind the chorus of robotic merry makers.

Marie was in the midst of trying to come up with a plan to engage the small imp, but Corvin beat her to it. The raven-general, evidently very annoyed with the whole scene, squawked out a shrill caw utilizing the very last of his power reserves. Its sudden blast alarmed the small creature. Quilp jumped, shrieked, and quickly dropped the little robot girl with a clatter. Upon seeing Marie and Corvin at his doorstep, Quilp stomped his feet and shouted, "Stop the music! Stop the music!" His catfish whiskers bellowed with each word. The synthesizers screeched silent, and the revel makers came to a standstill, bodies hanging precariously still upon each dangling pole. Shop lights immediately came up, dousing everything horrifically fluorescent.

"Are you happy now! Are you HAPPY now? —Everything is ruined!" Quilp fumed; then he saw LUCY on the ground, "BY MY MAKER!" he clasped his tiny hand upon his gigantic mouth and immediately sought to hide the little robot with his own very small oddly appointed body.

"Don't bother hiding her," Corvin said, his voice had regained some strength, but still the oscilloscope at his throat slurred and sputtered with each syllable. "This is highly irregular and blasphemous, Quilp!" Corvin continued as he slowly clanked down the wooden steps that jutted from the earthen wall. "We know you've failed to keep your promise to the council. It is completely evident! You've been dancing with the afflicted robot instead of dismantling her, have you?" His words were raspy and garbled, but booming.

Quilp surveyed the general: the raven droid's trudging steps and tattered body and voice—Marie was sure the next words were meant to deflect the general's accusations. "You don't sound so good, General—what has happened to your wings?!" Quilp was aghast.

"The Volgen city has been destroyed," Marie said following Corvin down to the shop floor, stating the sad truth with a steady, factual voice. "We are lucky to be alive. Corvin was badly damaged as you see. We've come here because we need your help."

That prospect made Quilp laugh. "Me?!?!" He exclaimed, the word sounded high pitched and insane coming from his gurgling mouth. "You need help from Quilp? Quilp the outcast? Quilp the one you must endure and say you like but you really only tolerate—me?!""

"That's enough," Corvin said lumbering over to the antique chair that sat at the head of the table. He did not seem concerned that the table offered more utensils than it did food. Marie assumed that food was more of an idea than a requirement to these robots. She suddenly felt hunger pangs erupt in her stomach, but these were quickly followed by waves of annoying nausea. She took in a quick breath. Corvin slumped down on the damaged chair cushion, stretching his destroyed wings over the back. His big body was a tight fit for such a chair as this.

Quilp wrung his hands and went over to the raven general and looked up to him wide eyed. "You *are* hurt, aren't you? And you *have* lost everything, haven't you? Well...my maker, he made me well and he taught me to create, not to destroy. You see all that I have made," Quilp stated proudly.

"Yes! I see this whole mess!" Corvin blasted.

Marie was quick to make nice. "You created all of this?"

Quilp was pleased at her attempt at admiration. "...with my very own hands, well some things were made by my maker, but mostly this was made by me—this whole mechanical ballet was made by me! Me! Me! Do you like it? Well, I hope that you do!"

"Well I..." Marie stammered.

"It's an entirely mechanical ball, you see for ladies and gents and andromatron-ettes..." Quilp pshaw-ed and went over to a tarp covered mound of machinery and began rummaging through it. Eventually he found what he was looking for and ran back to Corvin, chord trailing behind him like a tortured snake and inserted a plug into an outlet that existed imbedded in the Volgen's wrist. "See I'm helping! I will help! I vow by my maker, Randt von Holland."

"Randt von Holland! You speak blasphemy imp. Adelphi Saint is the creator of all thc creatures of Hout. You know this—not some outlander human." Corvin's words were pained. *Holland*...Marie was intrigued.

"Ha!" Quilp blurted out and swiftly jogged back to the tarp covered machine and then just before flicking a hidden switch, he peered out from beneath the tarp and stated with punctuated constants— "Not. Of. Me."

A whirring sound erupted from beneath the tarp and immediately energy coursed through Corvin's cells. Corvin laid his head back and let the power circulate through him.

"He will be charged within the next hour," Quilp said returning to where Marie stood. He peered up at her expectantly, bubbles gurgled at his lips.

"Thank you, Quilp," Marie said deciding to treat the little creature with the utmost respect. She spoke clearly. "Now about LUCY. She contains important information that we need. Corvin and I have come to see if you can restore her..."

Quilp jumped for joy. "Yes of course!" his cod lips upturned into a grin. Marie watched as the little dwarf skittered on small hooved feet over to where the little bot lay, and he sat down beside her cross legged and began to tinker with screws in the robot girl's abdomen. He produced a set of tools from his small green vest. "You know I was about to restore her myself anyway, but the Volgens, they really seemed serious about the whole dismantling thing. But I couldn't do it. Dismantle her I mean. Not a machine like this. No. No."

"You mentioned a name before," Marie said. "Randt von Holland."

"Yes of course. My maker. He was from the outer worlds."

"A human man."

"Yes—he is a disciple of Adelphi Saint. He often spoke of the far-off places, a fancy world beyond this hollow tree. He was a toymaker and learned to be quite skilled at making automatons and machines—well, I mean, look at me."

"All this. No wonder your mechanical ball seems very familiar to me."

"Randt said there were a great many cotillions in the lands beyond Hout. Parties such as this. Things of fantasy."

"You've done a fine job of replicating a royal ball," Marie admitted to the imp. "It reminds me of parties that I myself have attended—I mean, in a way."

"You're from Randt's world as well..." Quilp mused as he twisted two wires together and shoved them back into a cylindrical housing. He then pushed the element back into LUCY'S chest.

"Randt's stories of the Empire—they have inspired you."

"Yes. He drew hundreds of sketches of the world from which he came—I have a whole folio of them!" Quilp's eyes lit up as if he were about to go off and grab it to show Marie, but then he thought better of it and realized the task at hand was more important.

"Did he ever mention the name Dove?"

"Yes! Quite often."

"Where is Randt now?"

Quilp stopped working. A sad pall came over his membranous eyes. "Gone. For a long time now. He was taken by Magnus..."

"Taken by Magnus..." a sad electronic garbled utterance vibrated out of the LUCY in Quilp's lap. Citrine eyes flickered and lit up and the bot girl raised its copper head.

"She's alive!" Quilp rejoiced, stood, and brought LUCY up with him. "Alive again! Alive again!" he sang and did an awkward jig. "I've done it! Look at me! I'm a wiz!"

"LUCY...Dove..." Marie reached for the small robot which stammered and attempted to walk, almost falling. Marie was able to catch the girl just before she tumbled.

"You will NOT destroy me!" LUCY shouted, replaying horrifically her last moments of consciousness before the council, then garbled electronica and a familiar boy's voice echoed through her speakers. Sounds of recorded explosion burst forth and then became a horrible, frenzied loop. The boy's voice soon interjected and took over, "LUCY! Sleep now, sleep!" more patiently, "sleep." Calming processes. "I can handle this. You don't have to fight any longer...LUCY!...Mam'selle ..." Dove was in control.

"Dove, Dove."

"Mam'selle. I see you and hear you...I can move again!" There was great relief in Dove's voice. He half expected the LUCY to come back at him angrily for hiding and abandoning her to stand trial, but no voice came. He was glad to not have to fight over her this time.

"You know my Poppa," Dove said.

"This is all very curious," Quilp mused analyzing the small bot with wonder. "This is not like any LUCY I have seen. The Volgens may have been right." Corvin made a huffing noise, obviously annoyed at the imp's sudden admittance. "Well, the programming DOES seem off."

"This is no programming," Marie said and quickly explained Dove's tale to both Corvin and Quilp.

"So you're telling me that the grandson of my maker lives in this LUCY." Quilp clutched at his fishy throat in awestruck horror and wonder, then his eyes lightened almost lovingly. "Well, he did speak of you quite often. He missed you terribly. In fact, he spoke often of finding a way to get back to you. He spent many Hout cycles researching the maker of the Houtans and their myths and stories to try to figure out how to locate Adelphi Saint. He said finding Saint was his only means of getting back home. We were in fact about to go looking for Saint when he was captured by Magnus—horrible, horrible day that was.

The bot girl looked sad and bewildered. "Thank you," Dove said. Marie was truly worried now. *What if Randt was dead?* She did not want to speak of such things aloud. Marie decided to back track and get more details.

"You witnessed Magnus capture Randt?"

"I hid while my maker was taken. He told me to hide. So, I did. I trusted him I never thought to fight...anyway it makes me sad. If only I were bigger! If only...I could've done something. The biggest of them all—those evil invaders...Magnus...didn't realize until later what his name was." Quilp turned to Corvin— "You *were* all fools to trust him. I knew. I knew what she knew all along! From the moment he first appeared in the Volgen court with his speeches and grand gestures." He turned back to Marie; "what you said in the council chamber was truth. The Volgens *are* fools!"

Corvin stood, incensed. "Then you should've said something, Imp! You lollygag in the shadows, watching, lurking always so curious to spy but never to tell!"

"Would you have believed me anyway? You took *her* to prison for her dissent!"

"Why would Magnus want my Poppa?" Dove asked.

"They needed him. There was talk among the henchmen of his ability to reprogram the Aramen. See, I knew. I knew Magnus was not the peacekeeper of Hout. Not like the Volgens believed. He wanted Randt in order to gain control the red mages."

Corvin slumped back down in his chair, defeated.

"He obviously succeeded in his task," Marie said.

"We need to find my Poppa." Dove's voice was panicked.

"We must make a plan," Corvin said. He had become somberly resolute.

EPISODE 14.

Wolfsdamsylflies.

"Wolfsdamsylflies." Marie's musing of these horrifically familiar creatures was a mix of both wonder and fear. Her back was now flung up against a rocky embankment leading from the back of Quilp's workshop. Another fiery blast erupted from the silver palm of an Aramen that rode on the back of the gigantic wolf-headed, mayfly-bodied beast. The blast sent flames erupting into an inferno on the roof. This red robed mage was one of an army of twenty. Behind the red wizards, an opal-colored pirate ship hovered like a lethal sting ray. These were no doubt the same bandits that had sought out Marie and captured Luscinia when the Volgen city was destroyed.

"My shop! My shop!" Quilp cried. His eyes were caught up in witnessing the hateful, unprovoked attack. Flashbacks of the moment his master was captured by Magnus rocketed through his processors. This time the demon beast was nowhere to be seen. The tumult of the onslaught had been quick and sudden. They had been in the midst of making a plan to reach the hidden Aramen city when the front wall of the workshop was unexpectedly consumed by magical fire. They narrowly escaped falling mechanical ball guests, trusses and flying stone debris and found refuge in the muddy, bolder strewn terrain outside the shop.

It was then they realized the source of their concern lay once again in Magnus' destructive regiment of doom.

"We must abandon this place! Quick!" Corvin screeched.

"We can't outrun them!" Marie was quick to say.

"We'd better try!" Dove cried, he geared up to try to quickly ambulate the small bot, but soon found that the LUCYs legs were impossibly small indeed. Quilp was glued to the spot.

"They're coming back around Quilp!" Marie screamed. She grabbed hold of the small imp by the arm and drug him away from the sight of his blazing workshop. "No! I! —wait! Wait! Wait!" he suddenly said and stamped his foot. "There's a conveyance! It's hidden. Down there in the marsh. It's rickety but quick."

"You had a speeder all along and you didn't tell us?!" Corvin was incredulous.

"I only just thought of it."

"Show us where—hurry," Marie said.

The small robot girl struggled to move on tiny legs. Dove's attempt to control the steps of the bot were awkward at best. Suddenly LUCY came back online to join him. "Here!" her voice boomed through the mouth speaker. Sudden jets erupted from the bottoms of her tiny slippers and she was soon hovering on the air propelling herself forward. Dove celebrated.

Quilp bounded off ahead along the slick and muddy trail. Marie and Corvin quickly followed, ducking low, as a trio of Aramen on wolfsdamsylfly back swooped down close, blasting the terrain around them with flame thrower palms. The swampy land became a hazy, bright inferno as the land was scorched by flame. Quilp was quicker than Marie gave him credit for, striding along on small hooves almost like a jackrabbit. The quartet of companions raced along the water's edge, reaching a hollow that dove beneath an overcropping of petrified formations.

Soon they were slogging through the last marshy stretch to where a small enclave of water sinters burst forth from the surface of the marsh and soared high into the darkness above. For a moment, the group was protected. Quilp climbed up Corvin's melted wings to avoid high water. He directed Marie and the raven general to quickly uncover a contraption of a conveyance which had lain hidden beneath a tarp of woven vines. It was a sledge hewn in rusty sheets of metal, studded with twisted wires and copper boxes containing some sort of concealed corroded circuitry. Two engines were lashed to the back with chains. It had seats pulled from some other sort of mechanical conveyance and half of it now sat buried in marsh and water plants. Marie hoisted the small robot girl into the vessel.

Quilp immediately leapt into the rusty trapezoidal pod and took a seat upon a precarious bouncing spring with a cushion tied to the end which erupted from the bench seats. Marie supposed Quilp had created this odd-looking chair to accommodate his very small stature. The imp immediately began tinkering with the control panel. The levers of the contraption were retrofitted and enhanced with reaching segmented metal arms.

"Make quick work of this Quilp!" Corvin's voice was urgent. The Aramen army advanced. Marie discerned a sudden whirring of motors within the bird general's body. Corvin's power reserves were now restored fully, he executed a self-defense procedure. Doors opened from beneath his mechanical wrists and machine gun nozzles telescoped out from beneath his palms. Quickly he aimed beyond the slender tree sinters at the leading Aramen-backed wolfsdamsylflies, his eyes glowed a heat-seeking bright green. He blasted a round of sizzling phosphorescent bullets into the air. Three Aramen were struck and flung off the wolf headed flies at once followed by a shrapnel explosion which caused the beasts to flail about on the sulfurous breeze. Amid beast squeals and explosions, flinging figures crashed into the water some distance away. This attack incensed the army of mages. They returned fire. More flames erupted along the marsh's surface; relentlessly, the Aramen advanced followed closely by the hulking pirate ship.

"They won't stop! They'll kill us all!" Marie cried out into the heat of the nearing mage fire.

"Take this!" Quilp yelped, quickly reaching for a button in the sledge's control panel which popped a trap door in the rear. Marie quickly intercepted a chunky-bodied proton gun as it was ejected in her direction. She aimed the weapon and fired. The first round fell short, but the second caught a red mage hovering yards away directly in the chest. It fell. The wolfsdamsylfly, suddenly without pilot to steer it, crashed into the water just beyond the tree circle and then rebounded and flung itself, heavy bodied, into the air again.

"Hurry Quilp!" LUCY cried from the back of the sledge.

After a few awkward tries, the speeder struggled to life. Quilp revved the engine and the sledge rose from the muck. Marie and Corvin quickly jumped in to join LUCY and Quilp as the pirate ship's horrendous hull became a smothering, swirling black and purple opal dome above them. It crashed unreservedly into the circle of sinters which had been their protection. Quilp let out an elated and cathartic exhortation as he launched the skimmer full-blast out across the fjord beyond tumbling, petrified giants. Barraged water churned around them violently.

Marie crouched and steadied herself within the vessel, hair whipping her cheeks as she thrust a glance back over her shoulder. Wolfsdamsylflies studded the dark air behind them like angry locust swarms. The companions were making a quick escape. She was relieved. Turning back to face the helm, she realized they were heading directly for the blight infected walls of the Mech Mech city.

Corvin realized Quilp's intent. "I hope you know what you're doing!" he squawked

"The citizens may offer us protection!" Marie yelled out over the water spray and frenzied air.

Quilp laughed, body pumping up and down merrily on his small spring seat. "The Mech Mech's are as unfriendly as the Aramen! We won't find help from them—but I know a secret entrance! We must find refuge in the catacombs!" His voice was almost singing.

"This is no time to play, Quilp!" Corvin screeched back. He fired another round behind them. The mechanical bullets sent shrapnel explosions into the flying regiment. More Aramen fire fight was returned.

Marie had a sinking feeling. *If the Aramen are this relentless, how will we ever reach Magnus or rescue Randt or Luscinia? How will we ever get the upper hand, constantly running? First things first, Marie*, she said to herself. *Survive this moment.*

Suddenly all became quiet. The darkness of the vast waters of the fjord was consuming. Marie turned away from the gut-wrenching vastness, looking instead to the city. The flesh-colored walls of Mech Mech erupted from the hungry clutches of black, choking blight fingers. The conveyance blasted through the reef. Quilp quickly navigated the sledge through the churning waves and black growth. "Almost there!" he cried.

"What's happening?" Dove's voice was tense.

Marie turned back to their attackers. The massive wolfsdamsylfly-backed army had parted before the pirate ship and ceased fire. Corvin paused his attack as well realizing a proton cannon was quickly being deployed from beneath the sleek hull of the massive chevron-shaped ship. There was no time to react. Marie braced in horror for what was about to come. There was a low thud as a blast erupted from the enormous gun, suddenly everything around her exploded. Her body felt as if it were being torn apart and turned inside out. Her ragdoll limbs caught air, then smashed into liquid surface like a bug hitting a speeding windshield. Dark, salty liquid filled her nostrils. Her lungs burned. Blight coral slashed her skin. She peered through the murky waters; fire danced in slow motion. Her body lolled about in the surf. The shock of the concussion of events made Marie's mind go numb, she let the waters wash over her. Heat seared her face and hair. In the sky above, awash in firelight, the onyx bodies of the wolfsdamsylflies circled in hypnotic flight paths engaged in some slow-motion midair ballet.

He's here. He lives. The realization was cold and chilling. Marie's thoughts were catapulted back to that day. The captain held her breath in her stinging throat and remembered the day Killan de la Mare paid a great price for his betrayal...

"Wolfsdamsylflies," Captain Marie Antoinette murmured to herself as she surveyed with dire sobriety the chaos-consumed Canyon of Bran in the highlands of Callisto from the deck of the massive Imperial war ship 'Crusade'. Imperial space jet squadrons and bombing frigates fended off attacks of the Rovenine beasts, a species bred to defend the well-concealed palace home of the de la Mares. Smoke and fire gushed from the terraced buildings of the palace that jutted from the canyon walls. The terrain was conglomerate frosty citron, rose and amber crystals growing on vast accumulations of jet-black dome-topped meteorite monoliths. The compound had been peaceful only moments ago. The stealth regiment Marie had piloted to the canyon lands had been expert in crafting surprise. Now, explosions and flames erupted into the tumultuous black and blue clouds blasting steel and tempered glass out into

the atmosphere; the once elegant, swooping roofs of the palace, studded with ornamental rib like structures, collapsed with the ever-frequent concussions of bomb blasts. This attack was brutal and relentless.

Marie caught her breath as she surveyed Imperial troops advance through the gardens below. Palace servants and ill weaponed guards scattered across the basalt tiled expanse. Budding fruit trees and flower beds alike were choked with smoke and fire. In mere seconds the Queen's regiment would be invading the palace chamber.

Marie feared for Killan. It was hard to separate the man she once knew from the horrible truths that were now known. She still cared for him, even though she was now sure his hatred for her and her family was great. Marie had once been betrothed to Killan—that was before Sheng won her heart and she had convinced her grandfather Brandon was a better match. She did not want to see death come to the prince of the troubled lands of Callisto, but that was now inevitable. Marie was under the Queen of Cal'vary's command and a captain in the Dauphin's army. This now was her painful duty, and it was evident.

Over the past decade, the de la Mares had become more emboldened and their threats against the Dauphin had escalated. Now they had made their move.

"Word from Dauphin's Pride," Marie heard Second-in-command Blake say. He now received communication via transpondence.

Marie was relieved. Her husband was okay. "What does he say?"

"Commander Sheng reports that the renegade Callistan battalion moving against Io was not deterred by the starship's presence there. Full fire power is now being used against the rebels." Marie knew that Imperial spies had already infiltrated the ring of Callistan sympathizers which attempted to take control of several mining operations on the surface of Io.

"Why would Killan do this to himself? He knows we will slaughter his army," Marie said.

"Perhaps he feels he evokes the full power of God...or the devil himself," said the Queen of Cal'vary striding into the bridge. "The air of righteous rebellion emboldens some. Those who feel they have been horribly wronged, mostly. He did not suspect we would discover his hidden palace—or that we would destroy him at his very heart. Where he lives. Now he knows. Now he will realize the full extent of the Dauphin's wrath."

The Queen of Cal'vary was her grandfather's third wife (he had buried the first two), titian haired, dressed in gold regalia, she was the commander-in-chief of all of the Imperial armies, and she hailed from Cal'vary, a planetoid in the outer reaches of the Dauphin's kingdom where a secret sect of female knights templar governed a tetrarch set of planets. "The Argentine army will soon rally to our aid," the Queen continued. "After a century of struggles they will reclaim the Callistan throne again. This is right and just." The Queen echoed the Dauphin's rhetoric in this moment, and it worked, Marie supposed, if the Queen's aim was to legitimize coming acts of savagery.

Marie felt a certain ridiculous guilt at the moment because perhaps if she'd indeed married Killan there would right now be no invasion of Callisto. The Dauphin blamed Marie for the treacherous track her quest for true love had sent the kingdom on. It was obvious. It underlined their every conversation of late. She knew he resented her. Then, the horrible word came—plans that the Callistan king, was moving to take control of Io by force. Killan de la Mare had amassed weaponry and secret allies within the Empire. Losing control of the Ionian coal rich moon was her grandfather's greatest fear and Killan's bold attempt at starving out the Empire entire. The Dauphin's only hope now was to put the docile and obedient Argentines back on the throne of the nymph-named satellite in order to re-ensure Imperial control over all the moons of Jupiter. (The Argentines had been forced to abdicate Callisto four generations ago and now lived in exile among the red ice caves of Amalthea).

"Yes, Your Majesty," Marie concurred. She was numb.

Suddenly the door to the control room whooshed open. A clamor followed. The Queen turned from the overlook. General Turreau, who had accompanied the Queen onto the deck, was quick to draw a protective sabre. He stood down immediately when he saw that this would not be an attack, but a victory celebration. A throng of blue armored senturions, robot guardians of the crown, led by three ground troops, and four warrior women from the planetoid of Cal'vary erupted through the ovular portal.

"The palace enclave has been liberated. The Argentines are free to reclaim the Callistan capitol," the lead senturion sputtered out in electronica—his wing-decorated visor flashed green, 'all clear' messaging.

There were sonic eruptions from outside as a small squadron of space jets blasted off from the palace roof tops and returned to orbit.

"You have done well," the Queen said to the troops and the warrior women at the robot's side. Each bowed to her in turn.

From behind the victory party two more senturion guards clanged, metal-footed into the chamber. Between them, held fast with robotic vice grip metal fingers, was the lolling-headed form of the once-king of Callisto, Killan de la Mare. His face was bloody and bruised, his braids caked with coagulation. His exquisitely embroidered tunic was now a mess of blood and dirt. He wore no shoes. As the guards reached the center of the control room, they thrust this once-king down on his knees before the Queen.

Marie felt tears sting her eyes. Her sudden raw empathy for the tyrant felt like a betrayal to the Empire. Fear flushed her face. She quickly turned away. Second-in-command Blake was quick to put his hand on her arm. She brushed him away.

"We found this on the Callistan king," Marie heard one of the warrior women say. The captain rubbed away tears with her shoulder and turned again to face the scene. The Queen of Cal'vary held a chalice in her hands. It was small, onyx and encased in a structure of gold and

jewels. Hot anger flared in the Queen of Cal'vary's countenance and projected the gravity of this horrible truth. This was a betrayal of the highest order. This horrible crime—the theft of the sacred artifact long missing from Cal'vary Keep was now evident to her and all aboard.

Beneath pain knitted brows Killan shot his gaze over at Marie. His eyes were seething narrow slits, swollen almost shut with violet contusions. "This is all because of you!" he spat and struggled against his captives. The senturion guards held him fast, arm gears straining against the Callistan king's fight. One of the Knights of Cal'vary quickly pressed her heel into Killan's back. Killan with a grimace, met the Queen's eyes with fearless defiance.

Without even a pronouncement, or even a mere attempt at an utterance, the Queen swiftly wrenched the saber from Turreau's grasp and one-handedly struck Killan's head from his body. Marie yelped, slapping her hand over her mouth. Crimson fluid ran freely as the Callistan king's body fell limp on the steel-grated ground. The Queen nodded to the senturion guards. General Turreau stared on wide eyed.

The Queen of Cal'vary's chest heaved breathily within her corseted dress. Her eyes were wells of troubled anger. She wiped the ruddy blade on her skirt and handed it back to her General-at-Arms. Turreau took the hilt. "Your Majesty..." he said.

"This red mark is a badge of victory!" she said with a horrible sort of triumph. She would not even attempt to wipe away the blood from her garment.

"We should've brought him to trial!" Marie protested suddenly.

"He was no longer the boy you knew." The Queen said referring to Marie's quite evident sympathy. "You are not that young woman either—don't act like it now. You know what the stakes are. The choices he had made." Killan's crimes were great. All the intelligence reports attested to the horrible way in which the paranoid prince had gained the Callistan throne by systematically murdering, over the past decade, all the male rivals in his family including his father and his stepbroth-

ers. He had kept his three stepsisters and adopted mother captive within the palace enclave and took up practicing an ancient religion deemed unholy and forbidden. Furthermore, there was evidence that he had peopled his councils and the government of Callisto alike with pirates, thugs, thieves, dark mystics and enemies of the Empire."

The Queen clasped the chalice to her breast and strode, burdened, to the vast curved window of the bridge. She paused at the railing and then reached over to a glowing green button in the control panel with a dark red painted nail. Pressing it she pronounced to the armada of ships that remained hovering above the canyon:

"You may fire."

All civilization that remained below in the Canyon of Bran was soon a vengeful cacophony of frigate cannon blasts, explosions, and smoke. The palace of the de la Mares was at that moment razed out of existence.

EPISODE 15.

The Chalice of Doña Uracca.

Magnus often had nightmares of his torturous repair. Body separated from face. Images disparate, fleeting, and dark. A mosaic of pain unimaginable, the vacuous feeling of nothingness and a horrible sort of awareness. Attempts at taking breath into lungs that no longer existed—into a body he could no longer control, were seared into his memory. The knowledge that he should be dead, and that death would never come for him, were a maddening sort of consequence. Those furtive, anguished moments following a cold-blooded decapitation erupted back into consciousness: the warp and weave of the fabric satchel exploding into his eyesight, the one in which Dr. Hannah Krane had smuggled out his head from the *Crusade* after the invasion of his home moon, the hushed conversations between her and Magnus' pirate brethren at a secret rendezvous point. After that, much darkness, a limbo, a nightmarish sort of sleep consumed him only to awake again, now, enmeshed in machinery.

In a golden tower surrounded by many Orzos, Mech droids and laying under the lavender gaze of Sefra de la Mare, his birth mother, a witch of ancient origin, who had arrived as a violet-flamed specter from the dark recesses of the galaxy, oversaw the process of his repair. Emoting the unchained demonic, her knowledge of Hout and its capabilities had been his saving grace. She was acquainted with Crysanthia Mesmos the Orzos Queen. Sefra always guided him in moments of dark worship and had held place in his inner council, secretly appearing to him since adolescence when times were most dire, at least, she did, before the Orzos Kingdom fell.

The method the Mech droids employed to reattach his human head to mechanical framed body was arduous. The process to create a mobile frame for him to live in and achieve locomotion, even more. A body cage of gears, apertures and armor took many painful cycles to construct, and each strut had to be riveted down deeply into bone. A new sort of face was constructed for him because rot set in on the flesh of his cheek and brow. Each torturous stage of the process was another moment for Magnus to lean into his unadulterated hatred for the Empire and Marie Antoinette.

"I've found beauty in this pain. Glory in being cursed," said Magnus. He now reposed on a porphyry throne once meant for the Aramen king. Two red mages stood at his side as he underwent the nightly procedure to recharge and drain pus from reservoirs in his armor. His breastplate, bracers and chausses had been removed and now his carrion body lay, naked and small enmeshed in the massive steel framework which housed it, awash in the dim light of the vapor filled environ. Tubes and wires erupted from his sides and neck. The electrostatic collar which re-joined his head to his body pulsed a dim glowing red.

"You had no choice, but to find a certain sort of acceptance of it," said Hannah. She reposed by ecru-colored fire rods suspended in a hearth-like construction just off to the side of the royal dais. She watched as Red Mage 02 and 03 finished administering to Magnus' body. The mages then, almost in unison, came to frozen attention at the beast's side. Pixilated green diagnostic text sputtered into view upon their silver craniums and cycled through in rapid succession.

"But for this..." he told her, eyeing the chalice he now held in his talon-like hands. "Had I any doubt of its power. The curse of everlasting life—I wanted it and now I own immortality. You have delivered it back to me. The artifact that was once my obsession and now has become my curse. This is what happens when you obtain everything you want," he coughed out a sort of laugh. He examined the chalice—"Doña Urraca," he said aloud. "Christ's sacred cup. It was named for an ancient earthly infanta. It held the blood of the savior, traveled the deserts of ancient earth, legendary lands of Egypt and Spain many millennia before the Divine Deliverance. Those were the days of empires and legends.

"Urraca received the chalice as a gift from her father Ferdinand." he smiled as he told the story. "After her father's death, Urraca's power hungry brother sought to destroy her and all his siblings in order to take control of their lands. He viciously attacked her kingdom as well—Zamora. But he failed to seize it. Legends say it was the chalice that held the walls of Zamora against the attack, and it was the guidance of the chalice which led fate to destroy Urraca's brother Sancho who sought to consume so much power...perhaps..." he paused for a moment, then, "Now, the chalice and I are one. I have felt its powers. I have drunk sweet waters from its gilded lip...and now...I am horrific," he said gripping desperately at the cup. "Evidence to something unworldly—disturbing, torturous. I am living proof to what happens when one tries to wield the power of the cup."

"It is precious to you."

"It is precious to many, many who believe in its powers. Even the Dauphin does not know it still exists. The Queen of Cal'vary kept it secret even from her husband the leader of the Holy Galactic Empire. If Aubrey Antoinette knew it existed, if he held it in his grasps, he would drink from its depths too. Just like me."

"It makes me wonder where the warrior queen's loyalties lie. The one who struck your head from your body..." mused Hannah.

"—the one who spouts Imperial dogma like some elegant free flowing fountain...is she so unlike me? In the end? She does what it takes to survive. So did I."

"All Imperial waters are poisoned. Beautiful. Gilded. But poison," said Hannah.

Magnus pondered Hannah's words, as his body became revitalized with electrical charges. He sensed each battery cell 'expanding' with potential energy. His human body, held in situ by expertly crafted spears of machine tech rebar made him feel as if he were endlessly floating, yet caged. He languished in his immobile repose and concentrated upon the chalice. Carbon readouts, chemical make-up and temperatures scrolled within his cyborg vision. But despite this frantic eruption of information regarding the cup, his human gaze drank in the real vision of the cup. The most ancient part of the chalice was a carved cup of agate colored red and brown strewn through with tumultuous marble-like swirls, simply crafted. He pondered the stone, it reminded him of his own decaying flesh. The agate base was caged. Encased in a framework. Magnus' gaze followed the gold ribs outlining, delicately, the curve of the cup and the crook of the base. Those golden elements too were decorated in a layer of gilded filigree which became a thick band around the lip of the cup and wide band around the ancient stem. Those both were encrusted with precious stones of red, blue, and green, enamel inlays and pearls. It was rumored Doña

Urraca herself had the ancient stone chalice adorned in such a way. Beautiful armor, protection, elevation perhaps. But Magnus now saw none of this. "The body of this chalice is trapped," Magnus said finally. Then, "This...is what happens after you get everything that you want...."

"The curse of desire and power, perhaps, but you are singular and magnificent," Hannah said. Then, "There is more to do, Magnus. You and I both know this. You may have obtained immortality, but that is but a means to an end. Our armies are being amassed. The Mechs have done well by us. We have yet to exact full vengeance against the Empire. They must pay dearly for their sins."

"Yes," Magnus said distantly. He was obsessed with swelling hatred and disgust. The chalice became a grotesque and taunting object in his hands. The lines of the gold encasement disgusted him and the cup within reminded him of his own wretched form.

"Blessings from this chalice are prisons!" Tears streamed in his eyes. His grip became a vice and suddenly the gold decoration strained under the pressure of his fingers.

"Magnus..." Hannah stood from the stone sofa upon which she had been sitting. She could only watch in horror as the Chalice of Doña Urraca shattered within Magnus' tightly clenched claw.

He turned his human eye upon her. "No one else will get the pleasure of being blessed by this cup. I alone will know its power. Just me, only me. I own it. Its power ends with me!"

The chalice shards which tumbled to the floor by his throne, only lay there for a moment before some otherworldly force caused them to vanish into thin air.

EPISODE 16.

Into the Catacombs of Mech.

A distant shattering enraptured Marie as she bolted back to consciousness. It had not been the crashing waters of the fjord erupting upon the blight encrusted rocks at the base of the Mech Mech city walls, but the crushing sound of onyx within the grip of a steel claw hand.

Shaking away the daze, she soon realized that Corvin was dragging her quickly through the surf. He had a tight grip around her bicep and her feet flailed about along the skittering waves. She struggled to maintain her legs. Quilp bounded down the skinny stretch of beach, meters ahead, dodging around jagged coral rock and screaming out for them to follow him quickly. LUCY hovered on jet propelled feet just off the coast. She was rapidly gaining on the land.

"They're coming!" the bot girl shouted. "Run Mam'selle!" Dove's voice quickly followed.

"I can handle myself!" Marie squeaked out, water and sand choking her throat. She wrenched free from Corvin and re-grouped with fierce intent, wiping salt and muck from her face. Flinging back wet hair from her eyes she caught her feet and raced after Quilp. The raven general easily met her stride. "They're landing on the beach!" Corvin shouted.

Marie shot a horrified glance over her shoulder. She could make out a battalion of wolfsdamsylflies flapping to the earth behind them. Red mages dismounted and began trudging the sandy terrain, hands stretched out before them, palms facing outward. They prepared to attack.

Marie's weapon was long gone, lost to the waves of the fjord. She felt helpless and useless. She and Corvin were able to immediately duck behind large outcroppings of ebony reef rock just as fire blasts erupted around them. Sand spewed in every direction. Marie shielded her eyes momentarily then scanned the beach frantically for the LUCY. Marie quickly saw the bot girl flitting among the rocks on the beach. Marie cried out. The little bot latched target onto the captain and rocketed to where Corvin and Marie took cover.

A blazing searchlight bombarded them. The pirate ship hovered just meters away in the smoldering air above the raging surf.

"The pirates are trying to scope our location!" said Marie.

"They dare not use cannon blasts on the Mech city!" Quilp screamed from up ahead.

"You better have a way out of this!" Corvin squawked back at the imp over the whipped-up air and sputtering fire. He turned and blasted a round of mechanical bullets at the procession of Aramen at their back. The explosion of shrapnel blasted through the first line of Aramen troops. "Go!" he squawked, thrusting Marie ahead.

Again, they launched off down the coast with great speed. LUCY shot off ahead of them. Tearing up beach, they dodged black jagged rocks and Aramen fire sprays.

"Here! Here!" Quilp's voice cried out just beyond a grand grotto of rock amassed at the base of the city wall. Just above the bending archway, a flesh-covered battlement erupted into strange conglomerations of metal orbs held in situ by massive rusting steel scythe blades. It seemed like a daunting and threatening structure to Marie. Here the sand gave way to an ancient stair carved into the petrified bedrock which thrust downward through a narrow crevice in the blight encrusted coral. LUCY zoomed down the narrow channel, light from slipper jets glittered off the jagged moist surfaces offering an illuminated guide into the darkness. Marie and Corvin dove down the stairs after her. Red mage fire sprays charred the passage mouth behind them flinging off bits of rock and smoke.

"Go!" Corvin screamed out a Marie. He turned on the stairway, thrust arms across his face and executed a rapid defense procedure. A plasma shield suddenly erupted from outputs housed in his bracers. The shield reverberated in a vibrato holding fast against the swift Aramen fire barrage.

Marie raced down the steps gaining on LUCY. She pushed her hand against the small bot's back and thrust the mechanical girl further down into the narrowing crevice. At the bottom of the stair the passage widened again. There, a yawing mass of flesh-colored columns embedded artful with gears and circuitry embraced a portal decorated in geometric glyphs.

Quilp, reached into his waistcoat produced what looked like a small gear box of rotating cylinders, each tumbler contained a series of symbols. An elegant three-pronged access key jutted from one end.

"It'll only be a moment!" the imp called out nervously into the moist dank air. Corvin's curses shrilled over another barrage of mage fist fires as the concussive blasts raged against his plasma shield. Corvin immediately returned fire on the horrible machines. Explosions, shattering steel followed by steaming, sparking Aramen pieces tumbled down the stair past the raven's feet. More mages piled in behind their fallen comrades.

With trembling fingers Quilp spelled out the code on his access bit key. With a celebratory cry, he jumped back from the access point as gears in the walls around them began to turn and the massive door groaned open.

"In you go!" he called out to Marie and LUCY. LUCY quickly complied. Marie hesitated. "*Now* you don't trust me? ...or would being roasted by the Aramen make you happier?" the small imp said. Marie nodded and dove into the darkness behind LUCY.

Corvin blasted at distant reef walls of the chasm sending rocks falling into the chamber; the boulders slammed down upon advancing Aramen. Angry fire was the response. Emitting a high pitched screech through a vice clenched beak jaw, he throttled himself down the stairs and pushed Quilp into the darkness beyond the yawning portal.

"Wait my key!" Quilp protested.

"Forget your key!" Corvin shot back.

Marie stumbled as she peered back through the open portal. Aramen quickly poured in around the massive rubble on the stairs. Ruby cowls cast shadows across ghastly mirrored heads which suddenly erupted into fire light as Corvin blasted the circuitry holding the door open. Sparks and smoke exploded through the vestibule and the door promptly moaned shut across the entryway, barring the mages.

Marie searched for footing in the blinding darkness. A small yellow light in LUCY's belly sputtered into illumination. This was met with the pale blue light which ringed Corvin's ocular sensors.

"Will that door hold?" Marie said.

"Well, we're not staying here. Onward!" Quilp ordered them and marched off into the chamber.

"I know a trick," LUCY said. She quickly produced a plasma from her antenna and melted it around the edges of the door. Laying her palm on the gluey surface she emitted an electrostatic charge into the conglomeration, and it immediately transformed into a hardened steel.

"Good! Now let's get moving!" Quilp demanded. The vestibule was crafted of the same sort of fleshy columns. Delicate, tall spans forested the expanse, rising to the pointed groin-vaulted ceiling above. It was crypt-like, dank, and old. It smelled of copper, electricity, and mold. Marie thought the place seemed strangely holy, like a passageway for souls, an odd sepulcher made of petrified circuitry. Mournful quiet enveloped them.

Up ahead towards the center of the murky expanse, there was an oval shaped mouth. It was an archaic looking portal covered with runes of strange geometry. Awkwardly situated stairs thrust downward beyond the cavernous gateway leading further into the foundation of the city. Two massive effigies guarded the catacomb entrance. They looked to Marie like ancient robotic beings, copper in color, humanoid in appearance. They wore dome shaped hats, and their bodies were made up of a myriad of skinny, tall cylinders. Accordion shaped apparatuses erupted from the backs of their lantern heads. Geometric stained glass glowed in each face. Jutting from each throat, very long tubes sloped down to the slick rock earth in front of them.

"SoulEaters," Quilp explained to Marie with a matter-of-fact tone over his shoulder.

Marie took in each monolithic sculpture as she followed Quilp into the stairwell, the sloping walls cradled each step with a machinery encrusted rib.

LUCY soon flitted down the steps on jet propelled heels and took place beside Quilp. Corvin lingered behind them.

"The catacombs of Mech are a place of internment and reconstitution. The city above, a place of birth—the city below, death."

"This is where all Houtans are constructed," LUCY was quick to say.

"Used to be," Quilp stated.

Corvin scoffed.

"I know. I know, General. You think I deal in all things profane," Quilp lumbered down the steps raising a small pointer finger up in the air back at the general, "but the fact is the Mechs no longer make Houtans. Just as the blight has corrupted the realms, the Mechs too have taken to dark dealings. I have spied on them many a time since the days of my master's kidnapping...the Mechs have busied themselves with making machines of war."

"Magnus..." Marie said. His horrific visage erupted in her memory. The sick realization sent waves of nausea through her gut. She hated that she still felt some sort of sick responsibility for it all—still. *But can this be true? Why are you being so naïve Marie? You know everything Killan did. You know what he's capable of. Cal'vary was right. He's not that boy I once knew. He made his choices. Insane choices. He's a warmonger, a killer, he ravaged my starship and my crew. But I saw Killan die. Am I going crazy now, imagining things? ...How could Killan and Magnus be the same...maybe I'm the lunatic?*

Violent realization suddenly shattered her questioning disbelief. *The sacred cup. Rumored to be the key to everlasting life. It is forbidden by the knights of Cal'vary for anyone to drink from it for this reason. Which is why they held it secret for a millennium and why the Queen reeled in her boots when it went missing and was pushed to an-*

gry vengeance the moment she realized Killan had it in his possession. Killan had it. He knew its power. He used it. That's how...yes, Killan defiled the cup and made it into a tool for his horrific brand of revenge! I should have known. He didn't die the day the Queen of Cal'vary struck his head from his body...he somehow...found a horrible means of resurrection through its powers...that's it. I never believed in the power of the chalice before, but it must be true. Killan and Magnus must be one and the same. I sensed it during the invasion of my starship, but I just couldn't name it.

"I can hear your mind reeling, my dear," Quilp said to Marie. "Out with it! I demand it! No secrets among friends—and we are friends, are we not?"

Marie took in a deep breath. She felt sudden fear of exposure well up within her. She was not used to confiding in others, in fact she trusted no others in the galaxy besides her father and CA(RO)-LYN, and Brandon, once... Then she looked at the LUCY and realized that there was a real human boy in there. A human boy who needed help. Stopping Magnus, yes, but what about that poor lost soul trapped in the robot, desperate to find a way to connect with someone he loves? *We're both lost*, Marie realized. *Dove and I are the same. We're in this together.*

"I have a confession to make, Dove..." she said suddenly.

"Mam'selle?" Dove's voice echoed from within the LUCY.

"I am Marie Antoinette, the Imperial Princess, granddaughter of the Dauphin. I was afraid to admit this to you at first because of the horrible things that happened to you and your family. The tragedy that the Empire enacted against you is a crime. I feel somehow responsible for it, ashamed that it was my grandfather's policies that caused you such irreparable harm. It may have been cowardly, I know, but I must tell you that what happened to your family pains me. I don't think it's fair. I vow to make it right. I must make it right. I will do everything in my power to help you find your Poppa."

The robot pondered this for a moment, then nodded. "It's alright Mam'selle, I knew, at least, that you were a soldier for the Empire, did I not? When I first met you, you wore the flight suit of an Imperial soldier. Do not fear. It is good that we met. We need each other." The LUCY puffed up its chest, "We will find a way to get you home too!"

Marie smiled. This was the first time in a long time that she felt comfort and joy. Just by Dove's optimism. The mere words. Funny, it was just for a moment, but then more dire thoughts filled her soul. She took a deep breath. "Magnus, I fear, is an old enemy of mine..." Marie began and then suddenly the whole story fell from her lips. How Killan de la Mare had become a tyrant and tried to undermine the crown in revenge for her rejection of his betrothal as a young man. She told them about what happened the day the Empire invaded Callisto and about her suspicions regarding the chalice and Killan's possible resurrection as the horrible beast, Magnus. She told them of the invasion of her starship, only days ago, and about the mission to deliver the chalice back to the safety of a keep on Cal'vary in the system of C-Infinity beyond the fringes of the God's Eye Nebula. And finally, how she thought Hout was now being used as a means to create weaponry to employ against the Empire itself all for the sake of revenge. "How Magnus discovered Hout and came to take control of it is still a bit of a mystery to me," Marie admitted at last.

"The fact is, it happened." Quilp said bluntly.

Corvin cleared his throat "This powerful cup which grants everlasting life to humans—where is it now?" They were all startled by his voice.

"Stolen again. I'm afraid," Marie told him, "Taken by the *Antoinette's* ship's doctor. We fled the ravaged starship in an escape pod and crash landed near where you found LUCY and I, just outside the Orzos Village. Dr. Krane beat the living daylights out of me and ran off with the cup and any hope of contacting a base stationed outside the nebula. I was lucky to have survived thanks to LUCY here," Marie said.

The little bot's eyes twinkled happily.

By then they had reached the end of the long and winding stair leading down into the bowels of the Mech city. Before them, an elevated steel throughfare suspended on trusses hovered above a great chasm. The broad steel pathway ran along through a vaporous atmosphere of pulsing, blue electrical light and connected a series of massive, jagged, reaching towers lit up with cycling and flashing circuitry.

"Here we are!" Quilp announced triumphantly.

"Where are we?" Dove whispered to Marie.

"The only way to reach the Aramen city is by the air. We should be going up, not down, Imp!" Corvin bellowed.

"Shows how much you know, Grand General of the Volgens. You obviously don't know the geography of your own realm. Aramen can also be reached from below. It is treacherous. But doable."

"How do you know this?"

"Randt von Holland taught me many things. The Catacombs of Mech are the entry point to a secret path which leads to the temple of Adelphi Saint. The path is an ancient byway long forgotten by many in Hout. It also connects Houtan cities as well along the way. Aramen is but a stop on this hidden byway."

"Then we must go," said Dove. "We must," LUCY parroted right after. She did not seem as enthusiastic.

"Right in to Aramen? After what happened in the Volgen village?" said Marie. "We'll need more than just the four of us if we want to get into that city, don't you think? The Aramen mages have pursued us relentlessly and have left us running again and again. Magnus has sent out two attack armies already. They are too strong for the four of us alone."

"The Beestjes," said Corvin.

"The what?" said Marie.

"You said this byway connects all cities. The Volgens have allies in the City of Beestje. We will go there first. They will help us with the Aramen, perhaps even lend us weapons. We can raise an army," said Corvin.

"The path is dangerous, there are hidden foes, but, with my knowledge of Hout—which is much greater than yours Corvin, I might add, we will be able to make it through using smarts, honor and comradeship," said Quilp happily.

"We better get a move on then," said Marie. "Who knows how long LUCY's door brace will hold the Aramen invading from the beach. They have a lot of fire power. They could be coming down those stairs behind us any minute."

"Lead the way, Imp," ordered Corvin.

EPISODE 17.

SoulEater.

Thirteen grim robots suddenly appeared as the companions neared the first mechanical tower. These Mechs descended slow and mournful from the dark upper environs of the vast catacomb.

"MechWraiths," Quilp said. He motioned for the companions to slow their gait. Marie sensed a solemnity in his tone. The wraiths were black, sleek-bodied scythe-shaped Mech Mechs who's primary means of locomotion were a pair of bat-like wings flapping in methodical time to one another. Spidery legs, sharp and steely, jutted from their segmented thoraxes carrying the broken bodies of Houtan decommissioned.

"The wraiths are bearers of the irreparable—the decommissioned. They are a part of the sacred cycle," said Quilp.

Marie wiped a tendril of hair from her brow and felt her soul cease moving. She stilled her feet. Corvin, LUCY and Quilp all rustled to a stop, pausing their journey along the twisting suspended causeway to let the machines do their work. Corvin let out a hushed exhortation in electronica which startled Marie. Each wraith laid bodies of the decommissioned out in careful timing before the mechanical tower's main portal. It was then they could see the identity of the machines the wraiths had carried.

"They must have scavenged the destroyed Volgen village," Corvin said soberly. "...Sikula..."

Marie realized Corvin's soldier, the one who had valiantly rescued her from the burning prison tower, was among the delivered dead. As soon as the bodies were deposited at the mouth of the tower, the wraiths ascended again into the sulfurous electrified dimness on plodding, chugging wings.

The permanently broken Volgen citizenry lay in mangled messy piles before them. Marie could barely make out one machine bird from another among twisted necks, crooked wings and beaks akimbo splayed out along the path. Steam escaped from some broken frames. Marie smelled electricity and fire. The horrific events in the Volgen Village flared back to life in her memory of catastrophe and war. She was quick to quiet the images by settling her attention on the towering figure of the raven general. She realized Corvin knew sadness.

"Look!" LUCY's voice was shrill and abrupt upon the tomb like silence. Marie turned her attention back to the pile of carrion ironmongery which now was immediately swarmed by very small spider-like robots. Red pinpoint eyes scavenged the jumble, and Marie tracked each frantic movement by the glowing orbs riveted to the tops of their heads which resembled small amber marbles. These small robots immediately began to dismantle each Volgen with rapid and expert precision. Each separated piece, the dismantler hoisted above their head on miniature arms and skittered back toward the tower, disappearing into the yawning, green-lit portal.

"Dismantlers...but less massive than the ones outside Orzos..." Marie recognized the species of robot which had made every attempt to kill her upon her emergency crash landing in Hout. "But no less intent in their work. We better stay clear."

Corvin would not hear of it. Marie sensed processors firing off within him—emotional ones, coping ones. "Leave him alone!" the general cried and bolted toward the destructive little beasts, incensed by the sudden and irreverent dismantling of his comrade. With a thundering caw and a thud of his boot, Corvin sent dismantlers scattering away. He fell to his knees and began picking up abandoned pieces. "This is all that's left!" He was in anguish.

"He's to be interred now—it is his noble path," Quilp said.

"You speak of *our* religion, Imp! You, who call Randt his maker!" Corvin's words were acid. "My village is gone, and you say this is procedure...you abhorrent creature!"

Marie was struck silent, by Corvin's tone. LUCY cowered behind Marie.

"What do *you* know of me?!" Quilp raged "—*You* who were programmed to constantly bellow and shriek?! Disparage! Constantly disparage!" Quilp's chest puffed up and his face and eyes illuminated a bright red. "I am not like you, Volgen general! That I can assure you. And for that I am proud. Maybe I wasn't born up there in the gilded factories of Mech like you Volgens—constructed alongside the Beestjes and Aramen...Tweelachs as well—all the 'higher' Houtan life forms! But Randt *thought* to bring me to life. I am a *masterpiece*!" Quilp let out a shrill scream of frustration and then continued, more quietly then, "Randt loved me. Randt held me in esteem. You might see me as an ugly little patchwork thing made from the rubbish bins of this place, but I hold knowledge. *Know-how.* Learning that Randt taught me—and I am *more* learned than you *Corvin*! I am the one who will get you through the underbelly of

Hout and help you on your quest to rescue Luscinia. Don't forget—it is *Quilp* who helps you! It is *Quilp* who you need!!"

Even as Quilp spoke the Houtan death process had rebooted. One defiant little dismantler had pried open the membrane just at the base of Sikula's skull and expelled a small, intensely glow ing orb from within. It rejoiced and with a sputtering signal rallying the others who had fled; it called them back to their work. Three times as many dismantlers flooded out into the causeway and began taking to their destructive tasks, now with super-rapid expert fervor.

Limbs, nuts, bolts, tubes, wires, bio-mech panels, circuits and beaks were all hoisted and carried away back into the tower. Poly feathers and even clothing bits as well. Volgen wings were kept whole and carried on the backs of hundreds of the little beasts working together to complete the job—so complete it they did. Mechanical bodies dissolved into pieces right before Marie and her companion's very eyes. Soon nothing was left on the causeway except for the astonished company who still lingered behind the kneeling, mournful Corvin. The raven general stared numbly at the two bits of his deceased friend which he held with talon-tipped trembling fingers.

"Quilp is right." Dove was now emboldened to speak. "We all have suffered loss."

Marie nodded and went to Corvin and offered her his hand. He released the pieces of Sikula he held. They clattered to the ground. He took hold of the captain's outstretched hand. He stood, resolute. "We continue, then."

"Very well," said Quilp. Marie sensed that Quilp recognized Corvin's pain, if only for a moment. The small creature led them down the causeway and into the yawning mouth of the first mechanical tower.

Beneath a phosphorescent canopy, a rib-walled vestibule fed down into an interior well. The mechanical walls of the well were buttressed by a vast network of pointed arches. Each delicate, cathedral like expanse radiated cross the interior in a complex arrangement all of which, when viewed from beneath in conglomerate, created the impression of a starburst progressing upward to a brilliant and haunting shaft of light. The quality of illumination emanating from above reminded Marie of Jupiter-lit puddles glinting off the surface of Europan ice sheets in the late second-sun light. Marie felt an unsettling ache. The expansive dizzying architecture made her feel frantic and helpless. She quieted these emotions. She realized she was a living being enmeshed, almost suffocatingly, in the immense mechanism that continued the Houtan death process within the interior of the tower expanse.

The last pieces of the dead, carried on dismantler backs were deposited into artful piles along the causeway's balustrade. Marie discerned that a hidden track existed, edging the machinery enmeshed walls. Columns of small compartments punctuated the ancient Mech enclosure. Yellow bodied beings running on these tracks rolled to and fro on slender but massive flashing twenty spoked wheels. Hydraulic arms, whooshed out and in from yellow breastplates, extending and retracting, as pincher ends grabbed up parts from the piles, scanned each piece and ushered the fragments into a corresponding compartment in the wall. Once the correct number of pieces were stowed in each cell, a mechanism triggered. Amid steam pumps and screeching rusty chains clanging from a hidden recess, the filled compartment cycled up one notch, advancing the parts to be recycled cell by cell ever closer towards the bright, phantom oculus above.

"Come along." Quilp trudged out into the middle of the expanse, rounding an altar studded with glowing cells. The soulbits collected from the craniums of each of the Volgens had been placed atop the steel catafalque in ceremonial indentations. Ancient symbols and sacred numerical codes decorated the top. LUCY seemed uncomfortable and quickly bustled past Quilp, headed swiftly towards the portal at the other end.

"Let these processes be." Quilp admonished Marie and Corvin for lingering among the Mech stowers. "We best be quick and not dally. The SoulEaters—" Quilp's messaging was cut short.

A clanging noise and an unhinging screech foreshadowed a morphing rearrangement which occurred in the mechanical edifice close to the far door. LUCY leapt back on jet propelled heels as a towering form of emaciated steel lumbered into their midst from the dim recess of the iron works. Marie recognized the shape immediately. It resembled the monolithic guardian statues which decorated the entrance the catacombs. The skeleton of slender copper cylinders trudged toward the center of the enclave where the altar stood, a pair of red demon eyes, set in stained glass emanated pulsing vibration from under a dome hat. The Mech angel seemed to not regard them at all. Sparks flew before half-moon feet as the long pipe that jutted from its throat scraped along the ground. Once reaching the sacred table, the copper angel took up its throat pipe in hand, lifting the fluted end from the ground and placed the tip atop the surface of the platform. Sucking wind emanated from the end piece. Slurping up each Volgen soulbit in turn, the giant consumed all the little glowing orbs. Wing apparatuses, acting as some sort of bellows, jutting from the back of its neck, expanded, retracted, and pulsed bright, amber-illuminated, accordion skin.

Marie slowly backed away from the monster and pulled Corvin with her. She nodded to LUCY with an intent eye. The door was not too far away. The path leading out the other end seemed to be their saving grace. Before she could illicit her feet to move, the massive creature's sucking pipe silenced. Then a vibrating, irritated "WAIT!" clamored out from some unseen mouth. The companions froze. "You who have consciousness should not be here!" The SoulEater's voice was a cacophony of electrical vibrations.

"We are merely passing through, SoulEater," said Quilp wringing his hands feverishly.

"I do not recognize your kind—" It said regarding Quilp. "Nor yours for that matter," he must have meant Marie. "Though that does not mean much these days," it admitted. It went on, seeming to relish the fact that it now had company and could express these matters openly, perhaps thoughts it had been stewing on for quite some time. "Times in Hout have become very strange indeed," the SoulEater said, "...more dead now than ever before ...so many poor decommissioned machines to process... so many soulbits to store. I fear there shall be no citizenry left, not with the Mechs taking to building cold, unconscious machines—inventing weaponry most foul." Marie noted that this statement was in keeping with Quilp's appraisal of what was going on up in the Mech Mech city above. The SoulEater continued: "But it is not my place to speak against these things, is it Corvin?" the great copper angel now spoke to the raven general. Corvin cocked his head to the side. "Yes, I know your name. I know the names of all who are born of Hout and run the code of Saint." His voice seemed to sadden, "You are lucky to still be in operation. I fear one day soon Hout will be cold, barren and in permanent slumber. Every soulbit stored...no more soul eating processes to execute..."

"Our quest is to stop the one who has incited these changes in your realm," said Marie.

"Can such things be stopped?" the SoulEater mused. It clasped two tiny hands resolutely in front of its slender torso. "Our sacred code is under attack. The DNA of our existence. The blight now consumes architecture, sinters, electrodes, piezo and water...perhaps, soon, though, I fear it will continue to burrow its way into every Houtan, down into our very souls."

"The Orzos..." LUCY's voice resounded in the chamber, her brave interjection immediately made her glass bowl abdomen blush red.

"You are right LUCY 260.02-13b," said the SoulEater. Marie thought it kind of the angel to reassure the timid bot. "The Orzos nor the Aramen for that matter—they are no longer brought into this chamber to be consumed—the source instruction of Saint has deemed their kind tainted. Consuming them may lead to further malicious entrenchment of the blight. Even Adelphi Saint has begun to shut down processes. Such a troubling time..."

"Not to worry, SoulEater, we will journey the Core Path and rouse the Beestjes to our cause. The Aramen will turn or fall," said Corvin. Marie was heartened by the raven general's more optimistic tone.

"The Core Path," the SoulEater scoffed.

"I know the way," Quilp assured the angel.

"Cypher gate guardians exist within these channels," the SoulEater said quickly. "Dangerous beings which you could not hope to overcome. They are the mega giants, the originbots of Hout. Now they station themselves along the Core Path to guard the way to Saint's temple. You'll need more than bravery and a vague idea of direction to survive that."

Corvin squawked a laugh. Quilp did not seem to take the comment as an insult, he was about to respond, but the SoulEater continued: "Even the distance from here to the Beestje city is fraught with treachery, a labyrinth and a portal guarded by the gate guardian, ThaltechMega, a behemoth..."

"So, we arm ourselves," said Marie.

"Weapons are of no use against ThaltechMega, she becomes more powerful the more one tries to destroy her. She reshapes, reforms, grows new limbs...she makes earthquakes. She has claws and teeth of massive clanging blades. Her blood is scorching hot liquid mercury."

"She must have a weakness."

"There are ancient writings of ThaltechMega in Saint's Apocrypha —which I am sure you've all read..." said SoulEater, eyeing Quilp.

Marie quickly dissolved the jab, "Please, tell us what you know, SoulEater."

The SoulEater recited:

"ThaltechMega, once disparate parts of stardust "and wind
"Forged in galaxian fires by thy maker
"to protect the Path of Saint
"With fierce tremors she shatters the earth
"All who seek her mysteries will know death
"In her mouth she holds the key
"Only to be unmade by the sphere of heaven."

"I may have read something of that." Quilp thrust his arms across his chest. "The path is long; we best get going—I know the way!"

"Yes, but perhaps first I could gift you something, dear ones," the SoulEater said.

"What would that be?" asked Quilp, annoyed.

"I noticed this Volgen has lost use of his wings. As you see, we have lots to spare," the SoulEater motioned to the piles of

Volgen parts being processed by the stowers. Corvin cocked his head. His lens eyes reeled in an out in thought. Marie scanned the room around her. There were wings of all sizes strewn in among the pieces, but one set seemed to attract Corvin's attention.

"Very well, SoulEater," Corvin said motioning over to where a very grand and powerful pair lay disembodied on the floor. "I wish to wear Sikula's as an honor and remembrance to him. They should fit...." then sadly, "they should fit."

EPISODE 18.

Corvin's Carrion Wings.

"Who will we get to attach them?" Quilp asked regarding Sikula's wings. Marie could not tell if Quilp was being serious or coy.

"Why not you, small droid?" the SoulEater suggested, "I sense a bold and artful programming in you."

"Well," Quilp paused, "Only if you insist."

"Proceed with care," Corvin admonished.

"You, hush," Quilp said. Marie helped Corvin retrieve the majestic and powerful set of wings from the pile. She was amazed that they had been practically untouched by the Aramen fires. Some miracle, perhaps... The polyethylene feathers covering each graceful appendage shone an iridescent jet black, deep purple and blue. Corvin beamed with admiration as he and Marie laid them on the ground before Quilp. The little creature took out his tool kit and immediately set to work unfastening Corvin's melted and mangled wings and replacing them with the practically perfect pair once belonging to the valiant Volgen soldier. When the repair had been made, and movement tested Corvin, put a hand upon the imp's small head and spoke. "Thank you, my friend."

"Indeed. See?! Appreciation." Quilp stuck his fishy tongue out between two crooked teeth, then, apparently liking the taste of his upper lip, he licked more heartily as he deposited his small tool kit back into his waistcoat. "Randt made me well. You see this now? Forgive and help is what Quilp does you're welcome, Corvin. See? Was that so hard—to appreciate? You do have more manners and care in your programming than I once thought, I must say...well, wonders never cease..."

As Quilp went on, the yawning portal and the path that lay beyond caught Marie's attention. Somewhere outside the tower room there was a distant ringing. She strode toward the opening and listened.

"I hear it too," LUCY said from somewhere behind her. Abruptly a loud siren call echoed through the tower chamber. Red and amber lights flashed on from the archways above, dousing them in frantic strobing light. Marie shot her gaze back at the SoulEater.

"The Mech's don't want you here," the SoulEater announced. "There's been an alert within the city. That's not all—an invasion. At the catacomb entrance. Aramen mages led by two outlanders—pirates, I think. All at the behest of Magnus." Marie realized the SoulEater was reporting on some internal messaging relayed from a central source within the Mech city.

"I was hoping the door would hold..." LUCY lamented.

"Thank you SoulEater," Marie said quickly.

"Follow me, we must reach the end of the causeway—" Quilp shouted leaping around Marie. "Past the twelve towers—not a short distance to be sure..."

"Take this!" Corvin quickly tossed Marie a Volgen sidearm, perhaps once belonging to Sikula which he retrieved from the rubbish pile before the stowers could process it. It was large and unwieldy, made for Volgen hands, but it had a holster. She fastened the thick vinyl strap around her waist and another over her shoulder. She nodded to him.

"They're coming!" the SoulEater gasped. Its eyes were trained on the tower room entrance, then backing away from some unseen enemy, the portal suddenly erupted into pulsing infernos. Hooded red robed figures emerged through the smoke.

Amid a confusing cacophony of blasts, Marie brandished her weapon and shot off a bevy of rounds into the advancing army before racing toward the door. Explosions and fire raged at her back. Dodging return fire, she leapt through the black choking smoke quickly flooding the tower room, tumbling out onto the vast causeway beyond.

The massive cavern outside offered fresher air, but it was no longer a solemn and quiet expanse. Shrill alarms deafened Marie's ears as she struggled to see through the orange dimness. Electrified stitching impulses now leapt across the vast canyon, twisting, and turning angrily across the yawning stretch. Marie fled out into the melee. She felt exposed and small. Tower two was a tall, jagged shadow in the distance. Marie wasted no time and raced for it. Quilp and LUCY were meters ahead. Corvin shot off mechanical bullets into the unrelenting Aramen as he exited out onto the causeway to meet Marie's rapid strides.

"Get to the tower!" Dove screamed.

Marie gripped her jostling firearm to her side and ran with all her might.

Behind them tower one groaned. Marie braced as a barrage of debris rained down upon them from where the tower top had once touched the cavern ceiling. The entire causeway shook and swayed. The violence flung Marie forward, front-planting her on chest and arms. She struggled to regain breath as the momentum of the tumult shot her out farther along the path.

Suddenly a battalion of black and yellow orbs descended from the blackness above. Marie flung hair out of her eyes and hoisted herself back up to her feet. Steadying herself on the groaning causeway, she sprinted onward; the ground around her erupted into a barrage of gunner blasts.

"MechGunner drones!" Quilp shrieked from up ahead. "We can't outrun them!"

Marie dodged flying bullets and responded with gunshots. Exploding drone pieces rained down peppering the causeway with shrapnel. Her firepower did little to dampen the gigantic swarm. Marie felt suddenly helpless as the causeway lurched and gave way beneath them and tower two seemed too far away to reach.

Marie braced for a tumultuous and painful death, but gigantic arms soon took hold of her body as she was hoisted up into the catastrophic air. She heard Quilp squeal with glee and discerned his tiny face peering out from behind Corvin's grand neck. Massive flapping wings silhouetted in gallant splendor against the amber-illuminated steam.

Up ahead LUCY's foot jets propelled her full blast past tower two. Marie gave quiet thanks for the rescue. Corvin, clinging to her one-armed, reached back to return a bevy of blasts into the gunner drones advancing quickly upon them with the wrist gun of his other hand. The raven general, successful at blasting a sizzling hole in the swarm, picked up speed and dove through twisting electric currents.

Marie surveyed the dizzying kaleidoscope from the safety of Corvin's arms: red robed figures advancing on the catwalk below, Aramen charging forward, evading the tumultuous tower one collapse. The causeway quaked. Sputtering electrical blasts churned through the incendiary atmosphere. Tower three quickly approached. It was a tumbling jagged rampart, and up ahead more gunner drones descended in a horrible buzzing mass.

"Hold on!" Corvin squawked and thrust them downward into the darkness below the causeway. "LUCY!" he cried up to the small bot. The robot girl realized the raven general's plan and quickly shot herself around tower three and down into the sheltered recesses below the causeway.

Marie, focusing her weapon above Corvin's head, began picking off gunner drones who quickly found and targeted them. Corvin followed her lead sending shrapnel explosions blasting through the angry defense machines in a catastrophic display of fire and destruction.

Up ahead LUCY celebrated the companion's winning fire fight, but her rejoicing was short lived as a gunner drone rapidly appeared nearby and fired. Marie and company watched helplessly as the small bot was consumed by a ricocheting of sparks and stunned electrical pulses, her small frame sputtering in reaction to each impulse, then stillness and falling.

"Corvin!" Marie cried up at the bird. The raven's eyes grew bright blue as they focused laser-intent upon their plummeting comrade. Marie clutched at Corvin's massive arms and held steady despite the incredible speed whipped up by the powerful flapping of his carrion wings. Soaring past electric light and rock formations jutting from the steaming cavern floor, Corvin dove and snatched up the lifeless little bot, then he quickly bore the crew up again, flinging them all into cataclysmic buzzing space.

Somewhere inside the little LUCY, Dove swam through the bot's unconsciousness. Her internal code still processed, he sensed, realizing that an important cell was destroyed. LUCY's interior code was like a wonderful visual puzzle to him. He patched through, feeling out another channel expertly, he worked around the electric gap and connected again, suddenly vision sputtered back across his mind's eye. The LUCY was awake.

"Mam'selle!" Dove cried out thankful for life and consciousness.

"We got you!" Marie called back to the small bot, who's heels again shot flames and the LUCY pried itself free from Corvin's grasp.

"I got her! I've really got her!" Dove cried out in cathartic joy and rocketed the small bot body into the expanse beyond. The imprisoned boy rejoiced, sensing the air and excitement around him was more tangible than ever before. He found a new awesome level of wakefulness.

Soaring past more towers, Corvin rocketed Marie and Quilp into the vast stitching cavity. The electrical impulses lurching across the crevasse became even more frequent and frantic. Corvin evaded the lightning charges with finesse, but the blasts soon became a hinderance to the slower, less maneuverable gunners who succumbed to the charges and exploded in a massive and thankful chain reaction.

Tower twelve came rapidly into view and Marie tracked the causeway that threaded its center leading up to a vast impenetrable wall. She felt Corvin's arm tighten around her, bracing against the unexpected betrayal of their escape which now presented itself. LUCY landed before the massive edifice and searched the petrified surface with dim citrine ocular lights.

Corvin landed beside her. "What is this, Imp?" he demanded.

"Not to worry," Quilp said nervously leaping down from the place he had been perched among the raven general's neck feathers.

"There's an access point, a portal key," said Dove, who quickly discovered a small, recessed socket secreted among the stony surface of the wall. The bot placed its hand against the socket and a small access bit injected itself into the port from a cavity within its palm.

"I can see!" Dove's voice was an awed sigh as codes fantastic flooded across his brain. He guarded himself against the vastness that attempted to consume him.

"Dove what is it?" Marie asked, she was concerned. The LUCY's eyes pulsed vibrant and intensely.

"I...I got it Mam'selle...so much information, but I can decipher it. If I can find the right path, it's dancing imagery...but I found a way..." suddenly a myriad of chugging electronica sputtered out from LUCY's voice box and then an access-granted ding, emitted. LUCY's eyes dimmed and as the bot retracted its palm from the access point, a great heave thundered the air around them. The massive edifice rose a mere meter and a half from the causeway surface creating a low yawning gash that spanned the cavern width entire.

"In we go," Quilp said skittering out into the endless cramped environ.

"Are you kidding me?!" Marie ducked down to see into blackness. The weight of the megaton monolith doorway hanging above all their heads was horrific to her. "Who knows how long it will stay open, how far do we have to go? It could crush us all."

"There's only one way to find out!" Dove shouted gallantly as LUCY fired foot jets and rocketed itself into the darkness within.

Corvin nodded to her. Beyond his towering form Marie observed red robed figures amass just outside the doorway to tower twelve. "We have no choice," said the raven general. He realized the Aramen would soon be within firing distance.

Pushing away panic, Marie thrust herself beneath the lip of the monolith and crawled belly to the earth onward. Speed was hard to attain. But she dug in foot and forearm and pulled herself steadily forward. Corvin had difficulty fitting his massive body within the confines of the gap, but somehow, he was able to maneuver it and he was soon scooting along at her side. Marie traversed with impressive speed for a distance, then exhaustion set in.

"I see it! There's the exit!" Quilp yelled out ahead.

"Thank God," Marie gasped. "How much further?"

"100 meters," Dove's voice cried out from the darkness ahead.

"100 meters," Marie sighed, exhausted. She felt the insanity of the task ahead. She paused.

"Move!" Corvin's voice suddenly thundered at her side. Marie didn't even have the chance to react before she felt Corvin push her ahead of him. At their back, fire erupted out into the yawning stretch. Tongues of flame leapt out at Corvin's heels and intense heat suddenly encased Marie's body. Marie screamed. Flames died. She quickly expelled a barrage of expletives as she grabbed at slick rock, bloody nailed, and hurled herself farther and farther along the ground.

Red robes fanned out around them. The Aramen were swift at crawling and took to the environment like crimson arachnids, spreading around Marie and Corvin in a horrible infestation.

"They will choke us off at the exit, and from behind as well," Corvin squawked. "Brace yourself!"

Fire spray erupted around Marie. The Aramen at their heels were getting too close. Corvin shoved himself around her and pulled her along with him from behind.

"Let me go!" Marie screeched, she flipped over to her back and slid the nozzle of her gun from beneath her, aiming into the advancing mass of red. She braced herself and gripped the trigger and fired. Machine gun blasts shattered the darkness. Through grimaced teeth, Marie locked her finger unrelentingly on the trigger. The rapid fire propelled her small frame backwards along the ground even closer to where Quilp had yelled out that the exit existed. Aramen bodies exploded in the distance.

Corvin's talons gripped into Marie's arm again as the toothy ground ripped through her back flesh, neck, and scalp as well. Pain exploded in her shoulder as she was pulled unrelentingly along the ground. Above them the monolith groaned. Marie could feel its massiveness begin to grind steadily down upon them.

More fire rent from Aramen palms lapped at Marie's legs. She grunted and screamed as ceiling stone weighed down against her side and cheek. Just as she was sure the advancing tonnage would expel the life from her body forthwith, Corvin tugged her struggling body free from the vice press, birthing her out into vacuous dimness beyond.

Startled, Marie reeled back on awkward legs. The lapping Aramen flame thrower spray flung out beneath the portal gap and was pressed out, quickly extinguished by the massive wall crushing all that lay beneath it with a humongous and echoing thud.

Marie collapsed on the ground and fell back against the now-closed doorway. Just above the din of her deafened sense of hearing, Marie discerned the muffled *thut, thut, thut* of Corvin firing off rounds, killing off the few Aramen that had seeped out into the chamber from beneath the closing wall.

Marie stared blankly ahead, pulling rapid shallow breaths into her lungs as LUCY pressed a small cool palm to her forehead saying, "Mam'selle, you're alright."

It was then Marie realized there were definite drawbacks to being a neo-human in Hout.

EPISODE 19.

The Tomb of the Robot Behemoth.

Marie hoisted herself up to her feet and kicked the char off her boots. Her body was exhausted, and she was torn up; blood ran freely on her arms and side. "I'm not a machine, you know?" she spat angrily at Corvin, wiping dirt and sweat from her mouth. Her saliva tasted coppery. "I feel like I've been hit by a meteor least half a million times," she laughed and steadied herself against the rock edifice at her back. She was both elated and angered by all that had just occurred.

The raven general eyed her suspiciously. He was not used to such displays of emotion. "You'd be dead without my actions."

"That is without a doubt the truth...where are we anyway?" Marie attempted to look around. Pain exploded in her head. She felt as if the space around her did endless cartwheels, nauseatingly. She plopped back down on the ground. She bathed in darkness. "Trapped, somewhere deep within this infernal juggernaut..." Her voice echoed out in the dead still quiet of the place. She felt as if her words invaded something ancient and sacred.

Dove could sense what the captain needed, "Mam'selle," Dove said, taking Marie's hand "....LUCY," he called to the girl who lived inside with him. "Yes Dove," the robot girl replied. LUCY immediately took charge and went to work. Expelling bio-mech skin from extruders in her antennae, LUCY applied the healing substance carefully to Marie's wounds. "This will safeguard you against further injury."

Marie immediately felt a calming charge tingle through her skin. Thankful relief ignited within her. She was able to breathe deeply again. The air was musty and dank. She made mental check of herself, as was her process; *still alive*, was all she could now come up with.

She peered around the solemn environment that surrounded them. Marie realized the companions now stood at the edge of a precipice, a circular ledge which ran a long distance around the perimeter of the chamber off into the shadows. A stale putrid wind blew up from the chasm nearby.

"What is this place?" she asked eyeing huge ribs of petrified circuitry that jutted from the rocky lip ring marking the perimeter of the space. The spans arced the bottom of a gargantuan domed ceiling up to a recessed point.

"Someplace hallowed perhaps," mused Corvin. "Whatever it is, the Mech's didn't want anyone to get in. It's protected by a 100-meter-thick wall."

"Some sort of tomb..." Quilp said. "There are writings here." Quilp pointed to the great dome and indeed there where strange numerals and hieroglyphs etched into the stone.

"What do they mean?" Marie pondered, wincing as LUCY applied skin to the deepest gash on her back where course rock had torn through her finely woven doublet and shirt.

"Incantations perhaps. Mech Mech...I recognize some characters...they are words of warning," said Quilp.

"That's encouraging," Marie said sarcastically. She eyed humongous lengths of ruddy wires and cables which ran the underside of the dome sprouting from somewhere deep in the chasm at their feet. The bundles of thick tubes choked together into a mass within a circular recess at the center of the ceiling. Hovering just below the wire-filled oculus, suspended on vibrating cables, was a grand orb of exquisite molten mercury. It glinted in the dim light emitting from the circuitry above and hummed, surface undulating, particles attempted to break free and then rejoin again by some electromagnetic force at its center. Marie was entranced by its strange beauty.

"Ah yes," Quilp said, reaching some sort of internal conclusion, "See there?" He pointed through the darkness. Marie's eyes had adjusted to the tiny pin lights that dotted the dome above allowing sickly yellow light to filter into the chamber. It was as if they were standing under a field of cursed stars. Marie felt strange eyes upon her, something stirred toward the center of the room. A cold electricity coursed through her spine, her whole body shivered. She tried harder to make out what was in the distance.

There, laying upon the middle of a dark colored circular expanse, was the slumbering pile of a behemoth. Each piece of the giant lay in separate forms, all monolithic blocks of steel molded into cubist-like hands, feet, legs, abdomen, chest, arms, neck, and head.

"ThaltechMega," Dove said. LUCY had completed her task and now the small bot was inching toward the chasm. Just across the yawning gash lay the levitating circular catafalque upon which the monster slept. "It all makes sense now," Dove told them. "The codes in the port key, they warned of what the wall protected. There is no way out of this tomb—no way out without defeating the behemoth."

Marie slid to standing. She pressed her back up against the wall, clutching her weapon across her chest. She sensed the behemoth stirring. Surely their voices and their rustling movement broke the spell of sleep. "Are you sure about that Dove?"

"Well, I'm not going to stand here wondering!" Corvin cawed and jumped into the air, aiming his weapon at the mass of monster.

"Corvin!" Marie shrieked back. She readied her weapon but was unsure this was the tack to take.

Quilp rolled his eyes.

A screaming sound like a million rockets firing off resounded in the room. ThaltechMega's disembodied head rose from the ground, eyes clicking on like bright stars cutting through the darkness in blinding flares of illumination. Marie shielded her face with her arm. The sudden exposure made her heart thud in her throat. She was unsure if she should flee. Instead, she froze in place. ThaltechMega's head levitated high above the platform and then as if some secret spell had been cast upon the body parts that surrounded it, its massive limbs gouged across the rocky expanse and drug themselves into position, stacking to form the body of the gargantuan beast.

Corvin quickly fired off rounds into the behemoth. Mechanical bullets exploded against Mega's metal body. Fragments of the barrage exploded back into the air. Corvin retreated, wings flapping wildly in the darkness above, dodging the reflected bullets. Delayed detonations erupted along the dome. A fountain of shrapnel followed flinging pieces of metal into the ground and walls. Marie cowered. Quilp took cover by the leg of a ceiling rib.

"Wait!" LUCY cried out, but her voice was lost in another barrage of bullets from Corvin. The little bot had journeyed over the chasm and was crossing the massive center platform.

"LUCY!" Marie screamed after the bot, but her voice too was lost in the sudden thudding of Mega's feet. Tremors erupted across the chamber. Teeth jarring, bone breaking tremors. Marie felt her weapon slip from her fingertips; she grabbed for rock wall. The ledge beneath her feet disintegrated. She flailed wildly over the widening chasm, fingers digging in deeply to cracks in the wall. Her arms strained taking her full body weight. She let out a gurgled screech.

Quilp bounded over falling rock and found a pathway on the stone face. He grasped at Marie's hands. The small imp tried desperately to keep hold of her. Marie felt her feet catch some stone beneath her and slip. Her sweaty fingertips would soon no longer be of use. Somewhere above Corvin screeched chants of war.

ThaltechMega screamed back, its body clamored horrifically, steel grinding against steel, moaning leg blocks finding more locomotion and then another earth-shattering tantrum.

"Mam'selle!" Dove, realizing the captain's peril, propelled the small bot to where Marie dangled. Marie felt small hands take hold of her waist and attempt to pull her to safety. She cringed as the stone around her erupted into a fountain of rubble and the three were caught up in a landslide. The momentum of the crashing tumult flooded the chasm space near where Marie had fought for footing. Marie plummeted over pouring rocks and was thrown clear of the yawning expanse only to be rocketed across the levitating platform in the shower of debris, tumbling to rest before the shaking feet of ThaltechMega.

LUCY and Quilp clamored to Marie's side. Both had handled the cataclysmic discharge with more agility than she. Nearby she discovered her abandoned weapon. They pulled her to her feet. Marie grabbed up her firearm. The trio fled gigantic crashing feet as Mega banged out more seismic upheavals in a violent ceremony of destruction.

Corvin was just as enraged as ThaltechMega. His eye disks flared a vengeful crimson. Undeterred in his task, he punched an access code into his forearm keypad, bracer compartments whooshed open, tilting out an armory of small rockets. The raven general expelled a tirade of shrilling caws followed by an onslaught of buzzing ThaltechMega-seeking missiles.

Marie raced the expanse of the platform, watching in horror over her shoulder as the screaming battery of missiles crashed into Thaltech's abdomen. Behind her, Thaltech detonated; Marie flung herself forward, rolling and ducking as Mega's thousand-ton body parts flung far out across the ground, their horrible tumbling inertia reaching the far distances of the tomb. Then, as if some electromagnetic trance took hold of the disparate monolithic parts, they slowed to a standstill, only to fling themselves back together again with a horrific force.

Marie flattened herself to the earth, shielding her head with her gun as Mega's fisted left hand shot back to situ narrowly missing a total plow-through of her body.

Through gritted teeth, she pulled herself up to stand yet again; Marie turned to face the monster. She sensed a great anger humming within the reconstructed body of Mega. A chain reaction of mighty clangs rattled throughout the jumbled form of the behemoth. Marie feared what was about to come.

"No firepower will work against the beast," she told Quilp and LUCY who now rallied at her side. "Hold on!" Marie cried out thrusting herself back down to her abdomen as Mega's furious humming reached an ear shattering pitch, then with unreserved expulsion of power, Mega flung its gargantuan body into the air and thrust its massive feet back down into the earth again sending out a concussion of fault lines coursing through the platform.

Marie became a tumbling mass of flesh caught up in violently rising and falling tectonic plates. Everything around her clashed and crumbled. She held fast to a quickly rising edifice. She hoisted herself on top of the ledge determined to be heard. To her angered annoyance, Corvin shot off more mechanical bullet blasts into the beast. Marie quickly responded by firing a warning shot at the raven general with her own weapon. Corvin reeled back, his wings beating the air against the betrayal. He shrieked an angry cry at her and flung his body down to where she stood. LUCY and Quilp had managed to meet the captain on the swaying, jagged platform piece erupting from the once flat plain.

"Be still!" Marie screamed over Mega tremors still resounding through the tomb. She braced herself. "Be still!" she yelled again.

Corvin touched down in front of her and raged against her. "You can't kill a foe by not attacking it!"

"Be still, Corvin. That's not what the SoulEater said, be still—your shots are only making it stronger!" Marie told him.

In the distance Mega prepared to bang out more tremors. Marie could suddenly hear her own rapid breath on the stilling electricity-charged air. Her heart pounded in her ears. Then, thankfully, the giant lumbered clankingly to a halt. The aftermath of Mega's anger vibrated the platform, but then, after a moment, aftershocks grumbled to quiet. The colossus settled and stared, unmoving, into the far reaches of the chamber dome with eyes blazing. Marie was encouraged by this.

"Is it your plan to get us all killed?" Marie whispered angrily at the raven general. "You'll never get to Luscinia at this rate! And I doubt we will find Randt either!"

Corvin was about to respond, but LUCY's small voice began to sing:

"ThaltechMega, once disparate parts of stardust "and wind
"Forged in galaxian fires by thy maker
"to protect the Path of Saint
"With fierce tremors she shatters the earth
"All who seek her mysteries will know death
"In her mouth she holds the key
"Only to be unmade by the sphere of heaven."

Marie gazed upward and nodded. "If you want to shoot something, shoot the orb."

"The what?" Corvin asked.

Marie pointed to the hovering molten sphere of mercury. "The sphere of heaven. It must draw its energy from that source point."

Corvin's oculars buzzed into focus. He nodded, resolute. "We aim at the sphere then." He hesitated to wait for Marie to aim her gun as well.

"No matter what happens, keep shooting at it," Marie said, "hold steady," she told LUCY and Quilp. Quilp took hold of Marie's leg for assurance. LUCY ignited her foot jets and hovered just above the ground.

Marie and Corvin wasted no more time and emptied quick, pulsing rounds into the sphere. It whirled and sputtered. The cataclysmic sound of the onslaught incited a rumbling again within the belly of the behemoth. Marie ignored the beast's minor agitation and squeezed the trigger of her weapon with finger-numbing vigor. Rapidly the orb began to spin wildly, a blue hot glow erupted within it. Marie erupted into a celebration of delight. A chain reaction began.

"Duck and cover!" Marie cried out sliding along the uneven surface to find shelter along with Quilp, LUCY and Corvin beneath an overcropping of ravaged stone.

In a churning whirring fury, the sphere imploded and then expelled a fountain of silver rain. The companions were doused and dusted with sparkling fragments. Somewhere beyond where the beast still stood there was a mechanical groan and a shrilling charge that warbled to a quiet. Then the behemoth tumbled, legs thudded to the earth followed by a plummeting, clanging torso. Its hands plunged into throat piece, all of which crashed into arms, and finally, the head thundered down, toppling over the massive pile of itself. The entire platform took one last mighty shake and an earth-jumping lurch as the massive face of the beast rolled to a stop just beyond where the companions had taken cover.

The beast's eyes flickered to darkness and from its massive grinning mouth, smoke poured between razor teeth. Relief flooded Marie's entire body as she and her companions stood shakily. The platform rumbled with final protest and then all was quiet.

"In her mouth she holds the key!" Dove called out and propelled LUCY toward the beast's head. Marie was about to protest, but then felt confident in their work. The bot would be safe as it navigated into the yawning gap. There was a metallic clanking noise inside. "Here!" Marie heard Dove's muffled rejoices followed by a faint click and then the entire ravaged platform rumbled into motion as it began to descend slowly into the darkness below.

EPISODE 20.

Labyrinth Heart.

Weariness crept in upon Marie as she watched the walls of the chasm roll by. The porphyry-like stone was now dusted with the quicksilver remnants of the destroyed orb. The companions were flocked with the silver, glimmering sheen as well. As the platform that they descended upon was swallowed up by the darkness that lay below, shadows crept in and the glinting silver vanished. A cool dankness came upon the vast war-torn platform. Mega was nothing but a massive mound of permanently slumbering parts. A sense of peace overcame Marie as she crouched down and let LUCY and Quilp settle in beside her.

"Where is this taking us?" Corvin asked. His blue ringed eyes were now the only source of light besides the small yellow glow of LUCY's belly.

"Down of course," Quilp said.

"I know that, Imp—but where?" Corvin was annoyed.

Quilp remained silent.

Marie let herself be consumed. She relished the stillness. LUCY hummed a simple tune and momentarily Marie thought she heard quiet words but could not make them out. Dove's voice suddenly superimposed the background music.

"When I find Poppa, I might punch him instead of hug him," Dove said suddenly.

Marie unhinged her gun from her hip and laid it on the ground. "Why's that?" Marie said.

"For leaving me and mom like that. For promising to rescue us and then disappearing like that. He was supposed to help us find freedom, but instead we got the toil of the factory and after that, the punishment of the overseer's battery fields..."

"Your Poppa loves you, Dove. Something happened to him..." Marie said. It felt awkward to reassure without facts to back it up. She was disheartened by the knowledge of harsh realities of her past. Peacefulness drained out of her body giving way to unsettling thoughts that lay beneath: *How can I ever be sure enough to be consoling? I feel like I'm lying all the time—to everyone. How could I lie to innocence? How could I ever think to bring innocence into the world just to bear the harsh truths of life?* She thought of the child within her. She thought of Commander Brandon Sheng. *This baby wasn't supposed to happen,* Marie's mind suddenly became a dark vortex. *I was reckless. Now I possess something Sheng had wanted for so many years and something that I told him I may never want. How could Hannah not have happened? How could I expect this attitude to make my husband happy...that moment at Starcourt Tor will leave its mark forever—maybe subconsciously I was begging to possess a piece of him—something more pure and loving.* She spoke then to the baby growing within her—*My child you are becoming more real to me every moment.*

"Quite right," Quilp piped up. Marie was called back from the fathoms of her mind by his voice. She was relieved and pushed doubtful thoughts of becoming a mother to the farthest reaches of her brain. The dwarf bounded over to LUCY on skittering hooves and took the robot girl's hand. "Randt spoke of you often, Dove. He regretted leaving you. The truth is he didn't have a choice. He told me that if he stayed with you, you and your mother both would surely have been killed."

Now they suffer a fate worse than death, Marie thought sarcastically. She kept her mouth shut and opted to listen instead. She could not take any more pessimism from herself right now anyway.

"By who?" Dove asked, the little bot lifted its chin challenging Quilp's explanation.

"He was being pursued by Disciples of Saint," Quilp said, "Vigilantes. Assassins. Randt wanted so much to be a learned follower of Saint. He didn't know of the Disciples' true dark work—he thought he could become a follower among their ranks, but that soon proved to be impossible. The fact was, he had discovered an ancient artifact—a Hout key, an access port leading directly to this realm. He thought that he could bring you and your mother here to escape the harsh factory in which you all worked. But when the Disciples learned he had the key in his possession, they pursued him savagely—finally he had no choice but to run—he narrowly escaped being killed by the Disciples and used the key in order to evade their wrath."

"That's how he arrived here," realized Marie. She was heartened that at least there was some sort of explanation. At least there was proof that Dove's abandonment was somehow justified. She hoped Dove found peace with Quilp's words as well. The little bot did not say anything. Quilp continued: "He longed to return to you. The Hout key was destroyed when he entered this realm. He had a horrible run in with blight monsters outside the Volgen city."

"I remember, I helped to heal him," LUCY said. "He came to the Volgen village badly damaged..."

"So, we're trapped," Dove said. "If he no longer has the key..."

“There are many ways to get to Hout,” Marie said— “and to leave it. I crash landed here. You were able to hack in. Magnus was able to arrive here as well in some way...there’s a way out. I know that Magnus has pirated vessels here—ones he used to invade my starship. Once we rescue Randt and Luscinia we will find a way to get to you Dove.”

“Won’t people be looking for you as well, Mam’selle?” Dove asked.

The last conversation she had with Sheng flashed through her mind. “I suppose,” she said—"they would know something horrific happened...”

“You are the princess of your people, of course they will be looking for you,” said Quilp.

Marie nodded. “But I fear no one will be able to find me. Hout never appeared on my starship radar. Your kingdom is swathed in cloaking mists and no doubt created an un-navigable nebula storm around it. It is up to me to find a way back...”

The platform reached the floor of the chasm; it groaned to a steady stop.

“Looks like we reached our destination,” Quilp said.

“Looks like the middle of nowhere to me.” Corvin eyed the little dwarf then turned to scan their surroundings. “...In a deep hole with no way out. What was ThaltechMega protecting—a well with no escape?” The oppressive chasm wall surrounded them.

“There is a path, we must just find it,” Quilp replied.

“There,” LUCY said pointing to a glow in the distance.

Marie looked beyond the uneven field around them. There, practically hidden behind a disembodied Mega hand was an oval portal bordered with an ornate type of circuitry. It had a silvery white luminescence and was inviting and ethereal.

“Let’s go,” said Marie; gathering her weapon, she stood.

They came to a stop at the portal entrance. Beyond the mouth was a winding passage advancing off into eternity. Above the door, a carving on the keystone caught Marie's attention. "Wait," she said to the companions. "Look." She pointed to the decoration. It was a circle filled in with traveling serpentine lines leading to a center point, a round void edged with six petals.

"Mere decoration...or more Mech hieroglyphs of warning..." Corvin said.

"A sigil," Quilp said.

"I've seen this before, LUCY...you have too! Look, I saved these from your hovel. I totally forgot I had them." Marie produced battered sheets of paper from an inside pocket in her doublet. She laid them out before the robot girl.

"Drawings Dove and I made together," LUCY said. Dove's voice rapidly followed excited by the fact that Marie had saved them: "LUCY had all these images floating around in her system—I just had to get them out on paper!" The robot girl touched each leaf with enthusiastic fingers.

"Yes, a map of Hout indeed and vague ideas of underground terrain..." Quilp glanced over them with interest. "Our path perhaps. There's a jumble here and a symbol," he pointed to an expertly drawn illumination that showed the grand outline of Hout and depicted all the kingdoms within it.

"I've not seen these places before—" said LUCY. "The idea of them frightened me. Dove pulled them out from inside me and drew them on leaves of paper."

"All beings Saint created have complete knowledge of Hout whether they know it or not—Dove must have been able to access deep reservoirs of information in order to draw these," said Quilp.

"When I drew, LUCY and I both became calmer," Dove offered, hoping that this statement would settle what he perceived from LUCY as an attack.

Marie nodded. "Look here, there's a symbol. It's the same."

"A sigil," Quilp corrected her. "It's a sign of what's to come and a spell that conjures angels or demons and allows one to control them."

"Is there such a thing in your world?" Marie asked.

"All programming has an inner will whether it be used for good or for evil. So says Saint. He strove for balance and peace in this particular passage which is why this sigil conjures the concept of the labyrinth."

"So, it's a maze," Marie said peering into the yawning doorway. "How will we know the way?"

"Not a maze, this is about a journey—not a method of trapping and retracing. There is one path through this doorway and that path leads to the middle—of that, I am sure. Look here just in the midst of this jumble of lines..." Quilp said pointing back to Dove's drawings.

"There's a fork, a two-pronged path," said Corvin.

"One leads to the Aramen city from beneath, the other, back out again across a great expanse and then to the city of the Beestje," Quilp interpreted the lines.

"So we are on the right track," said Marie.

"Indeed, we best get moving." Quilp marched ahead leading them on into the vestibule.

The passageway led slowly downward. The floor, enshrouded in vapor, felt strange, slick, and curved beneath Marie's feet. The waxy, sallow walls seemed like they belonged to the chambers of a mummified aorta. Somewhere beneath their membranous surface glowed a network of undulating lights. Marie found herself often reaching out to the walls for support. Their smooth quality lulled her into soothing meditation. Marie soon became used to navigating the oscillating oval passage.

The companions traveled a great length in silence before LUCY began to sing. It was the same quiet tune Marie had heard the robot girl humming on the platform during the descent, the words were this:

"Hout bows down in shivering winds,
"Leaves rustle in branches frantically
"Unrooted from the diadem
"Of time at the birth of the galaxies."

As the little robot repeated the song again and again, Marie found a curious drowsiness had overcome her. The vapors seemed to caress her body and somewhere, distantly, a timed thudding beat pounded out along the chamber walls. Marie felt her own heart match each vibration. Her ears were consumed with the sound. Images crept into her mind. Marie realized that as her feet shuffled relentlessly along the passage, a lucid place in a subconscious realm overtook her body and mind:

The burning decks of the Marie Antoinette stretched out endlessly before her eyes. Its expansive damage was all consuming. It felt like her body, helpless and paralyzed, drifting horrifically just beyond the cockpit window of an Imperial space jet. The familiar sounds of beeping electronica from the space jet control deck was a peaceful soundtrack to the carnage raging outside.

Her hands felt bigger, stronger, more masculine. Looking down to her fingers she saw that she held a small filigree framed miniature of herself. It was soon awash in tears. –Sheng's hands, these are Sheng's hands, she realized. In a voice that was a mixture of elation and horri-

ble realization Sheng shouted out: "We found it! We found it!" Over the space jet transpondence a crackling reply: "This is not good Commander." There was a squadron hovering out the cockpit window. "Scanning," another voice rang out via communi-com in the cockpit.

Time seemed to overlay here. She heard her name said a million times in a million ways in tones loving, desperate, angry, tearful, despairing, destroyed. Then a dead silence as the Marie Antoinette exploded before her very eyes sending a ring of fiery destruction far out into outer space.

"The core! It was the core!" "Move Commander!" Distantly she felt large fingers fumble for a space jet throttle and the straining of engines to evade the destructive aftermath followed by a long and mournful scream...

Wind like the memories of rustling leaves once thriving and alive, howled against the window frame in her childhood bedroom at Versailles. Marie was entranced by her own reflection in a mirrored wall. She realized her hair was longer and a different style. Shadows fell upon her cinnamon skin; her eyes did not recognize who she was. There were no memories, she realized, not even Sheng was familiar to the woman in the mirror. Perhaps a trespassing spirit sparked a glimmer of recognition in the dark eyes of this Marie. Perhaps it was a spirit of an invading consciousness.

The woman reached out to touch the glassy surface before her. Suddenly she found herself shattering into fragments. A million Antoinettes stared back from each jagged piece. Each face was trapped and made into a horrific mosaic. Wide aching eyes, nose, forehead furrowed with worry, lustrous curls and lips that were frozen and contorted in fear.

Marie reeled. She was afraid she could no longer find herself. "I'm here!" she screamed out into the darkness. "Sheng I'm here!" She watched helplessly from the broken glass as her husband's figure sim-

ply passed her by...feet crunching upon the shattered bits and retreating off into nothingness.

She wanted to run after him; she wanted to make him see—and just as she struggled against weighty mists that choked her into stillness and silence, she was called back to the steady pace of her own feet trudging along the passageway of the labyrinth...

"Mam'selle, you were sleepwalking!" Dove admonished the captain. Marie blinked as reality surfaced around her.

"Dove... "Marie stammered, her voice was low and sedated.

"The vapors of this place have a strange effect on you," commented Corvin.

"Indeed," Quilp agreed.

"How long have we been going?" she asked them.

"A very long time Mam'selle—you were probably tired...but we didn't think to stop, we just kept going."

"That's alright Dove." Wakefulness had charged her body again. Peering at their surroundings she could just make out a yawning end to the labyrinth and a dim ruddy light pulsing from within the room beyond. "Almost there," she said pushing ahead of them. Her pace quickened, but abruptly her feet came upon a strange obstruction. Marie stumbled and steadied herself against the wall. "Something..." she voiced quizzically. Looking down to the floor she saw what she had tripped over. There, amid wavering mists, she could make out a carefully woven crimson garment clinging to the form of a ravaged splayed-out figure. Scorch marks darkened the fabric. "Red robes..." Marie said soberly. She looked to Corvin and Quilp.

"What's this!" Quilp bounded through the steam and ahead of Marie, dodging hidden figures that lay buried by the haze. "Aramen! All of them decommissioned!"

Cautiously Marie and Corvin forged ahead, followed by the hovering form of LUCY. The companions followed the carnage into the chamber beyond which was a vast circular room giving host to six radiating apses. They stumbled over more Aramen bodies (for a vast multitude littered the expanse choking the floor wall to wall). In the middle of the arrangement of bodies, one Aramen figure stood erect and stone still, its left hand outstretched to the companions in a prepared stance for battle. In the low light Marie could just make out a smooth, glinting mirror face concealed just beneath the hood of its red robe. Her own contorted features reflected back at her horrifically in the dimness.

EPISODE 21.

The Renegade Aramen.

Corvin quickly pushed ahead of Marie and raised his arm blaster at the Aramen mage. Suddenly the smooth silver face erupted into a display of cycling green binary code followed by a burst of blue static. "Quilp...Q..Q...Quilp," it sputtered. Corvin cocked his weapon.

"Wait!" Marie shouted.

"It spoke," Quilp trotted over to the robotic magician's flowing crimson hem. He gazed up at it in wonder, "it knows my name..."

"Back away Quilp—" Corvin cawed.

"Aramen never vocalize. They run on a silent telepathic processing language that they broadcast between themselves. This is highly unusual," said the small dwarf.

"Quilp...Q..Q...Quilp," the Aramen sputtered out again.

"If it meant to kill us it would have done it already. Lower your weapon, Corvin," Quilp told the raven general.

Corvin did not comply.

Marie boldly pushed her way in front of the general's weapon and strode to the frozen soothsayer. She was entranced by its cycling face static and wondered what secrets lay within the machine. She reached out to touch its looking glass face.

The Aramen stuttered to life and reeled back on its heels almost tripping. It's flailing arms balanced itself, then, recompiling, it stood erect and sputtered out: "Q..Q...Quilp, I've been w...waiting for you."

"For me, you say?" Quilp tapped his lip with a small finger thoughtfully.

"Explain yourself Aramen!" Corvin cawed angrily.

"I...I wasn't sure if you'd come, but I was told to wait. Randt told me to, so I did."

"Randt told you to?!" Marie exclaimed. LUCY, now unafraid of the robot in their midst, emerged from behind Corvin and came closer to the red mage. Shutting off her shoe jets, she touched gingerly to the ground, looking on quizzically.

"Who killed all these Aramen? You?" Corvin asked. He stalked a circle around the companions and the renegade, stepping over broken and burnt bodies of the wizard's brethren. In the middle of the room, amid the radiating forms of the dead, a collapsed structure of stone and steel glistened under pelting rivulets of water pouring into the center of the expanse.

"Who are you?" Quilp asked.

"...999..." said the red mage.

"Nine nine nine...Nines, may I call you Nines?" –Quilp went on not waiting for a response, "This is all very curious indeed. You speak of Randt here among a vast killing field of your own race. I must admit it's very strange, but we are glad to have an ally in the midst of an army that would've most surely killed us," said Quilp.

"...I...I...had no choice. I had to do it," Nines was pained.

"A confession," said Corvin.

"Indeed," said Quilp.

"I was protecting Randt. He is Hout's last hope," Nines told them.

"We are looking for him," Marie said. "We expected you to blast us apart when we came into this chamber...the Aramen have not been friendly to us. In fact, up until this point, you have all wanted us dead."

Nines pondered Marie's words and then spoke, turning his attention to the imp: "Q...Quilp...you are a child of Randt von Holland. I too have been touched by the code maker. He spared me from horrible bondage."

"Magnus kidnapped him. His intent was to force my maker to enslave your people," Quilp replied.

"M...My brother's minds are no longer their own—they are enchanted by a horrible sort of programing. Once quiet seekers of meditation and enlightenment, they have now turned savage. I...I however was one of the ones spared from this dark sort of control," Nines told them.

"The Aramen were never friends of any Houtan," Corvin squawked sternly, "Even before there was a Magnus. The Aramen tribe was responsible for standing against us when we tried to flee to the great interior in the days of the cataclysm—when the tree fell."

"P...perhaps distrustful at first, but eventually we came around," Nines' electronic speech was hypnotically soothing; "Aramen have always sought the illumination and solitude of the internal. You must realize your invasion into the inner realms of Hout came as quite a shock to my people who had always known the quiet darkness."

"Your people destroyed my village!" Corvin was incensed. "Only days ago!"

"Magnus has caused this, remember that Corvin," Marie was quick to point out. "It is this beast that has exploited your old quarrels." She then turned to Nines, "Randt...you've spoken of Randt...we are looking for him."

"He is my Poppa," Dove's voice rang out sweetly on the murky air.

"Another child of Randt..." Nines mused.

"He's my grandfather, Quilp said that he was kidnapped and is being held in the Aramen city. You must help us find him," Dove was hopeful.

"S...small one," Nines crouched down to the little copper bot, "Randt is no longer imprisoned at Aramen."

"Where is he then?" Corvin demanded.

The red mage slowly pointed upward with a graceful silver hand. Marie turned her gaze to where the magician gestured. She felt vertigo overtake her as she peered up at the broken spiral stair that hovered impossibly far above them. Its serpentine vortex reached up into forever amid spattering drops of rain.

"That's the way to the surface," remarked Quilp.

"Yes, remember the map," said Dove. "This is where the trail forked. My Poppa must be on the way to the city Beestje.

"Which is where we are headed," said Marie. "How long ago did Randt take his leave of you?"

"A phase," said Nines

"Ten Houtan cycles..." Quilp pondered. "Randt could be anywhere by now..."

"You said Randt spared you," Marie prompted Nines.

"Y...yes," the red mage replied, "Randt indeed was forced by Magnus to reprogram the Aramen. To bend them to the warlord's will, but Randt created a secret exception in the code."

"An exception," Corvin scoffed.

"Every Aramen repdigit 9, including 09, escaped the reencoding. In return we helped Randt escape the city. Randt then promised to find a way to save the world of Hout from Magnus and from the blight. He's on his way to Adelphi Saint. The creator will know how to stop this."

"Where are the other nines?" Quilp asked.

"They remained in Aramen—awaiting Randt's return. Your Poppa is our final hope." Nines caressed the robot girl's cheek then turned to the rest of the companions. "I will go with you to find him."

"Oh no...we don't need help from your kind," said Corvin.

"Corvin," Marie admonished.

"How can we ever trust him?"

"I...I sacrificed a battalion of my own people to save the man who will bring about a rebirth in Hout. I...I barred the path to the Aramen city leading from this very chamber extinguishing all hope of returning. I...I think I have proven myself already as a valuable member to your quest," Nines said.

Corvin looked to Marie. "Trust him if you want to," he said at last. "Things have changed for us anyway. Randt is no longer at Aramen, but Luscinia is. At Beestje we will split paths. You will go on the Path of Saint to find Randt and I will gather an army to fly to Aramen to rescue the nightingale priestess."

Marie was immediately somber. His words made sense to her, but Corvin had helped them through many narrow scrapes. Him leaving the company would be a horrible loss.

"You seek to invade the city then?" asked Nines.

Corvin nodded.

"Then you will need my help."

"How so?" asked the raven general.

Nines pulled back his cowl exposing his perfectly faceless oval cranium. Processing a series of programmed chants, the silver and blue static that now pulsed out upon the mirrored surface conglomerated into a wavering view finder. "Look..." Nines motioned for the companions to come nearer and gaze upon his features. Marie and Corvin approached the red mage. Marie was startled to witness the figure of Magnus caught up in mid speech. "Magnus' throne room," Nines said. "I've connected with 09 who resides within the Aramen palace. You will be able to now see and hear everything that happens within..."

EPISODE 22.

Into His Infernal Chamber.

Marie discerned amid wavering lines of static, the hulking form of Magnus de la Mare pacing the length of a cavernous and hauntingly lit expanse. The image of the beast brought back horror filled memories of carnage and fear aboard her ill-fated starship. Catastrophic images spiraled within her head. "Tell me what you see," Magnus' voice echoed out, tinged with electronic garble. Marie was startled by the cyborg's voice; it seemed as if he were talking directly to her. Despite being reviled by Magnus' image glowing upon Nines' display-face, she drew nearer, horrifically entranced, to take in more glimpses of detail. The companions crowded in around her to look as well.

"This elegance has an artful sort of consciousness even in this state..." replied a sputtering feminine robotic voice. It crackled out of a levitating starburst shaped Mech. "...of course this Volgen was made by the expert hands of the early Mechs many centuries ago..." Marie realized the gyroscope robot was referring to a very large egg that stood upon a platform towards the center of the forlorn space.

"We believe the nightingale priestess who slumbers within this egg has great power. Power to control armies. We must make sure she can be turned to advance our cause," a woman spoke, striding into the frame. She was dressed in long robes and her hair was pulled back severely; she wore a dark circlet. Marie's face flushed hotly with horrific realization. "Dr. Hannah Krane," she murmured aloud in sick disbelief.

"The one who tried to kill you?" Quilp asked.

Marie nodded. "...Is...this truth?" she was incredulous. Her mind spun off in a million directions. "She was in communion with Magnus all along..." this was more of a statement than a question.

"This egg has many fantastic abilities. Physical. Transformative. Powers belonging to a sorceress—SirenSong, a spell that entrances, disarms," TinWratchet said.

"All of which can surely be used for our purpose?" Magnus prompted.

TinWratchet's eye-orb pupil lurched to and fro as it analyzed the egg with a sensual tenderness, a horrible realization suddenly set in. A small tone, one that only TinWratchet could hear, perhaps, sounded within her processing unit. A tear pooled within its very large eye. TinWratchet blinked, gears strained with the expression of sadness. "No," the Grand Mech told them. "No...I..." There was a sputtering of sounds and then a rhythmic glitch— "My tribe and the Aramen..." It was a forlorn expelling of speech. A revelation. "My tribe...slave...process. Code. Slave code."

"There's something wrong," Hannah said. Then suddenly the straining gears within TinWratchet snapped to focus. Its dilated pupil lasered in on Magnus. Something had come over this robot, Marie realized, it seemed as if a trance had been broken.

"TinWratchet." Magnus was stern. "Need I remind you that you still exist because I have given you my grace?"

"You want relief and salvation, my Lord...from *us*..." TinWratchet's voice became an incredulously tinged, acrid-charged burbling. Magnus stopped his pacing and turned to face the bot full-attention, shocked by the outburst. “Indeed, the nightingale priestess does slumber, of that I am sure.” TinWratchet proclaimed, “But in time she will make slaves of you just as you have done to the Aramen and the Mech Mechs! I can neither console you, nor can I help you!”

“You are on thin ice Wratchet!” Magnus bellowed. “What sort of programming protocol is this—Randt...”

“Oh yes, Randt von Holland, your precious coder. I suspect things will be increasingly harder to control now that Randt has escaped the palace,” TinWratchet clamored.

“Remember, you hold the fate of your tribe in your hands, Grand Mech,” said Magnus.

“You threaten me?” The Grand Mech was now a sputtering enraged conglomeration of mechanisms. “I mourn! I mourn and I am ashamed for being your compliant token! Suddenly now I see. Everything is clear to me!” The Mech spoke in quick gasps. “It was by Randt that you were able to ensnare me and harness the tainting power of the blight! You turned my people from life-givers to makers of war! I am horrified! I was lulled by you and your temptation—promises that became lies and then your coder-magician took my own mind from me—and my own will!” TinWratchet’s voice cried out on the somber air. Marie was struck through with sadness for this robot. “I beg you to free my tribe—for you to leave the Mech Mechs out of your plans. The war you wage is not our war anyway!”

“That is enough TinWratchet!” Magnus screamed.

TinWratchet knew her pleas could not sway the beast; she then set to cursing: “This system you created, one of dark spells and lies is contaminated! I pray it will be your undoing! What more can you do to us?” The Grand Mech’s whirring speech reached an incensed shrill.

Magnus paced away from the droid, murmuring in pondering tones, "what more can I do...what more...what more, let's see," raising a finger in the air as if an idea just dawned on him, the beast leveled his gauntlet at the Mech leader unleashing a barrage of flashing shurikens into the body of TinWratchet. The Mech exploded into hundreds of steaming parts, sparks and one last expelling vocalization of terror. Marie was startled and enraged.

"What good are you!?" Magnus raged, "What good are ANY of you!?"

"The destruction of this robot for the best," Hannah said quickly and coldly. "We will overcome the result of TinWratchet's resistance," she attempted to soothe the savage, brewing rage within Magnus. "Besides, the Mech leader was right. We *do* hold complete and total power over the Mech Mechs and Aramen—no matter what torments TinWratchet has uttered upon us. You know as well as I do the weaponry the Mechs create for us is in the final stages of production. Within a short time, our planned invasion of the capital city on Europa will occur. Then the Holy Royal Family will finally see what it's like to have all hope gutted and their kingdom fall before their very eyes."

"...I must stop this..." Tears stung Marie's eyes. She felt her throat tighten as if Dr. Krane herself were tightening a noose around her neck. She feared for her family and she feared for the Empire.

A pinging noise erupted within the chamber. It was then Marie realized that a circle of Aramen stood in statue-like stillness around the platform enclosure which the egg rested. Magnus and Hannah both turned to Aramen 01. There was a flashing message signaling upon its visor. "A transpondence," Hannah said aloud interpreting the staticky green characters, "from Kitrank and Faul."

"Very well, put them through," Magnus instructed Aramen 01. Immediately a holographic image of the pirates sputtered to life within the center of the expanse.

"What is it?" Magnus demanded.

"We bring news, my Lord," Faul said.

"Have you found the princess?" Magnus asked.

"Yes, my Lord, we had found her."

"*Had* found her?"

"On the upper banks of the fjord, however she evaded our cannons and army. She's escaped into the catacombs beneath the Mech Mech city with three other Houtans," Faul went on calmly.

"I see," Magnus said. He fingered a battle ax sheathed at his hip. Marie could sense more palpable rage seething within the body of the hulking cyborg.

"She's accompanied by Local Unit Contraption Youth, the Volgen raven general and a small imp that once lived on the outskirts of the Mech village." Kitrank's choppy speech offered details to the report.

"Did she?" Magnus stated simply.

"They evaded our Aramen armies and have gone into the bowels of the forbidden pathway of Saint," Faul rejoined.

"On the way to where?" asked Magnus.

"We suspect to the city of Beestje and beyond—to the sacred Hall of Saint at the very center of Hout."

"I wonder what her plan is..." Hannah mused.

"I have grown weary of being patient, dear Faul and Kitrank. I am no longer interested in subtle methods of control. I realize now that such artful manipulation is lost upon everyone here and perhaps was never the right tack to take in the first place!"

He turned to face the pirate duo and jabbed a gigantic robotic finger at them. “Fly now to the city of Beestje with our other ships and exact all your firepower against them—oh, and while you are at it, BRING ME THE HEAD OF MARIE ANTOINETTE!”

“Yes, Sire,” Faul stammered. The pirates bowed very, very lowly and vanished.

“The armies of the Houtans may rally against us. Beestjes and Tweelachs have defense capabilities.” Hannah clutched her arms across her chest as if a cold wind had just issued through the chamber entire.

“Are they really all that powerful? Such small armies—all these divided tribes longing for better days, days when Hout grew fierce and strong... now they fumble in the darkness of this awful place like blind and lost children...trying to cling to civilization they once knew. We did them a favor—we gave the Aramen and Mechs a greater purpose. The other tribes will bend, or they will fall. Destruction is the only thing these bio-mechs respond to.” Marie watched in horror as Magnus unsheathed his battle ax and strode up the perfect ecru egg enmeshed in silver filigree. He caressed it, metal fingernails screeching along the surface.

“You broke the spell on TinWratchet, dear Priestess...” Magnus murmured at the egg. “What wonderful powers you possess... This is where it ends,” heaving the ax above his head he grunted out a guttural sound of vengeance.

“No!!!” Corvin shouted, pushing Marie aside he grabbed hold of Nines. He shook the red mage in a frantic attempt to save his beloved. Marie grabbed at Corvin’s arms. “No!!” Corvin screeched.

“Corvin!” Marie grunted through clenched teeth. His shaking was so violent, Marie was thrown to the ground. Nines was a flinging mass of lifeless limbs in Corvin’s talons.

Magnus, shocked into stillness by the noise of a shuttering frame clattering into a nearby pilaster, lowered his weapon. He glanced to Hannah who pointed out the source of the commotion. Magnus went to the steadying body of the Aramen.

Marie, finally able to calm Corvin, pulled Nines back to standing. Suddenly the face of Nines shone with the ghastly countenance of the beast.

"Cease transmission Nines!" Marie shrieked. "Cease transmission!"

"See, Hannah, the nightingale priestess has already begun her work of turning our Aramen against us. She must be destroyed." Magnus then, with one fatal movement, struck through Aramen 09 with the blade of his battle ax.

Nines sputtered back into motion. The throne room vision disappeared amid a flurry of staticky snow which now filled his display. "T...Transmission has ceased," he said.

"Good," Marie said, catching breath. "Don't do that again. We need to go," Marie said.

"We need to get to the Aramen city!" Corvin squawked. "Luscinia!"

LUCY looked frantically to the faces of each of her comrades.

"The Beestjes! We must warn the Beestjes!" Quilp said. "A whole city will be destroyed! Before it's too late—we must get to them. A war has surely begun!"

EPISODE 23.

Symptom of the Twisted Stair.

Marie's mind was a raging storm. Corvin lifted her in his arms and soared toward the ravaged stair hovering high above the labyrinth heart. The city Beestje was the farthest thing from her mind now. Her body was an awkward mess. "What did *she* do? What have *they* done?" Marie's voice sounded tortured.

"Take the stair!" Corvin cawed at her, ignoring her sickened words.

Marie grabbed at rain drenched steps. They were uneven, impossible, and dangerous. She fought to gain a foot hold. She was reckless and uncommitted. Corvin thrust himself ahead of her and lodged himself in the upward passage. Bracing with wing and arm, he helped hoist Marie to her feet. Nines clattered up the walls like an arachnid from the floor below. His movements were quick and unnatural. He was soon clattering up the stairs behind them.

"We must hurry!" Quilp leapt down from Corvin's back and skittered up the stairs sending spatters of moisture down upon them with his boots. LUCY wailed from below. Nines helped the tiny bot up the first dangerous rungs. The compromised steps trembled and fell. Nines quickly yanked the robot girl to safety and pushed Marie up the stairs as well. Marie was a confused, desperate, despairing angry mess.

I let Brandon die within me! Her mind screamed. *I already had this resolved—I decided!* But now all those resolutions exploded. *I let him go!* What she had witnessed in Nincs' display-face, ripped the lid off every neat compartment she had ever created within her own psyche around her husband and the affair. *Hannah doesn't love him. I loved him...then I let him go! She was using us all along!*

Marie grabbed at more drenched rungs. Her hair was a wet mess. Blight vines choked the passage above. She grabbed at each creeper expelling vast amounts of anger and sadness. *But does that even matter? He fell for it! He desired her...*this roused some semblance of angry focus in Marie. She grabbed at more vines and paused; breath ceased in her lungs. She remembered it—that horrible moment when she caught a glimpse of the doctor, swathed in bed sheets, naked. The unintended reflection in Sheng's bedroom mirror—the communique that bore a hole through her brain. *I thought about that every day! It was torture!* She now screamed at Sheng. It made her sick. It was a well-watered seed of anger. An infernal system. She feasted upon it and let it grow perverse within her until it became an infernal juggernaut.

But you were wronged too, weren't you Brandon? Played—you're a fool! She wanted to scream this out loud. *I'm a fool*—this thought was a dose of sobriety. *Can I forgive him now? This knowledge must mean something to me. Does it?* She remembered the vision from the labyrinth. *Sheng thinks I'm dead.* A horrible nausea filled her stomach. *I heard your torturous cries, my darling—even from the depths of this place... Those visions must've been a window into truth...he loves me still...do I love him?*

She paused upon the stair. Nines regarded her with surprise. "Be wary, the stair Mam'selle," Dove called from behind him. Now Marie felt reckless. So *what if it falls?...we all have fallen...*

"We must continue up," Nines' soft electronic voice called Marie back from insanity. She nodded and returned to climbing.

*...And the baby. Why now? I didn't want...*Marie swallowed hard. Her mind was a maelstrom of babble. Her feet rampaged the twisting dark stairs with every processing thought. *An impossible miracle...why this? I could just fly away—keep flying...scot free—nothing binding me...we told our mistruths, didn't we, Sheng? —For protection...*

The medic droid aboard the Marie Antoinette called it a defective subdermal birth control implant. *Who knows how long I was walking around with a defective implant in me? The symptoms of the malfunction had never truly surfaced...except for the pregnancy, which is the ultimate symptom,* Marie thought sarcastically. *This wasn't supposed to happen.* Such a thing was extremely rare. *1 in a million, but it happened...* She was quick to bury the remembrance of receiving the illegal implant at all. It was forbidden for heirs of the Holy Empire to deny nature in such a way. To do so carried strict penalties under the governing laws of the Empire. *No one knew...no one... It had to be that way for my own survival...* Marie stumbled and struggled to regain footing. Nines hoisted her back to her feet.

God's plan, Marie was awash in disdain. She was not sure if she believed in such things, but here it was. *God always seemed to be against me.* She pulled herself forward with the help from more black vines. They were disgusting twisted arms and she hated them. She spoke to some spirit hidden in the darkness: *God, you finally caught up with me—clever. Is this a lesson for trying to evade you? 'You don't even fear the Lord!'* Her governess' voice rang out in Marie's memory. It resounded within her soul and the weight of such cruelty on all sides made her numb and weary.

Marie wiped her sopping wet face. *I have to tell him, I guess. I have to get back to Sheng somehow and let him know.* She regretted deleting the communique to him with the news of the child. *Sheng would love this child with all his heart...he would be brilliant. I don't know if I would be. I miss him...I hate to admit it, but I do...maybe I got what I wanted for way too long...I just wish we could just find peace again...love...*

Marie's ankles buckled. Violent shaking launched rocks and debris down on them from above.

"The stairway will surely give way!" LUCY cried.

Marie grabbed at Corvin's feathers; she had become enmeshed in them as he lumbered up the steps just ahead of her. Brittle treads came off in chunks and pieces beneath his gigantic feet. Marie stumbled over them and pushed Quilp up the steep rise. Nines and LUCY clattered up just behind her.

"Be wary! The steps have already been compromised!" Quilp yelled.

Marie let out a frenzied breath. She caught a dizzying glimpse of the labyrinth heart far below. Red swathed bodies of Armen dead scattered the pavement around the mound of rubble. They were horrible harbingers to Marie. *I can't let this child die. It's depending on me. I have to get us out of this!* This idea again roused a greater sense of duty within her. Purpose. Marie's heart leapt as an entire step collapsed before her. The porphyry rained down upon the rubble pile below—

"Hold tight!" Marie called back, coming back to sense. Determination flared within her. She grabbed at more vines and navigated the catastrophe, pulling up Nines with LUCY in tow.

"Not much farther, I see surface!" Corvin called from ahead.

Heavy rain poured in freely from above. The steps were increasingly slick. Nines lost footing and jarred his head against a rung behind Marie. Marie and LUCY helped him to his feet again. At a longer distance the vines they used for handholds became sharp and riddled with thorns.

"Horrible disease—this unrelenting blight!" Quilp commented at the blood which poured freely from Marie's hands.

She nodded, a little annoyed, "Don't worry about me." Ripping the shirtsleeves from her blouse she wrapped her hands and was able to navigate with more comfort. She continued up; her mind roared: *This child needs me. What's done is done. The Empire needs me. Everything is in jeopardy now. Magnus showed his strength by invading my ship—he will not stop until he's destroyed the capital entirely. I may be the only hope to save His Holy Galactic Empire.*

'Get your head out of your own concerns for once'—that's what Sheng had told me. 'Life is not all space jets and missions.' Maybe he's right, at least in that. There is a bigger duty here and it's not out in the stars. It's back home. It's saving Hout. Marie felt strength erupt from within her gut as she and her companions emerged into a tangled burning forest above.

All Marie heard before explosions thundered the ground sending the exhausted stairwell falling to labyrinth innards behind them, was Quilp's small voice screaming: "We're too late!" Suddenly dismay buried Marie's recent hopeful ideals. She pushed the maelstrom of her mind to the farthest corner of her brain and prepared for the battle that now presented itself to them.

~ PART III ~

EPISODE 24.

Attack in the Field of Thorns.

Marie wrestled twisting sharp brambles choking the portal to the surface. She stumbled along the ground, falling to her knees. Nines quickly produced a scimitar from his robes and chopped through the hungry creepers that still grabbed at Marie's legs. LUCY helped Marie to her feet. The princess stood and searched the environment around them. It was a horrific cataclysm to be sure. The air was rank with smoke and venom. Marie wiped annoying tears that readily poured from her eyes with shredded and bloody arms. She only succeeded in smearing her face with coagulation.

Some distance ahead, beyond the entanglement of thick and thorny creepers, four pirate ships rained down doomsday upon the Beestje City. The cavern canopy above collected smoke and embers and then produced rain. Thickets of sinter columns punctuated the vacuous and devastated expanse. The proud city of domes, blunt topped turrets and mound shaped bridges baring glowing orbs of enchanting bioluminescent elixir, shuddered and tumbled beneath proton cannon blasts. Fires raged within the city walls.

"Oh no! Oh NO!" Quilp screamed in a forlorn wail. He bound through the tangled blight quickly behind the raven general.

Acidic rain stung Marie's face and hands hatefully as Nines pulled her through the tangled terrain. Another explosion thundered through the cavern expanse.

"T...The pirates made quick work of navigating the outer ring—this is a true horror!" said Nines. He dove ahead and slashed through another choking thorny thicket. Black blood spewed from the severed vines.

"Had we any hope of warning them anyway?" Quilp's voice was tinged in mourning.

"We may still be of some use," Corvin shouted.

"Such optimism!" Marie's words were choking and garbled. Eyes rendered useless by scorching air, Marie stumbled and searched her surroundings with trembling hands. Her lungs quickly tightened, and throat became a spewing pit of fire. Coughs wracked her body. The little robot girl, realizing the princess was in jeopardy, thrust her small body toward Marie who was contorted with seizures. "Mam'selle!"

"This air—poison, I think!" Marie choked out.

LUCY quickly extruded more clear skin and placed a membrane of it over Marie's eyes nose and mouth. Her burning skin, now awash in a tingling mechanism was revived. Clean filtered air filled her nostrils and lungs. She regained breath. Marie gave LUCY a thankful squeeze on the shoulder. *My throat is aflame, but at least I can breathe*, Marie thought.

"We must hurry!" LUCY shouted.

"Rushing towards our own doom again, no doubt," Corvin said.

Over the din of destruction, a thunderous buzzing echoed through the cave. Marie looked ahead. Erupting from the flames of the city, a battalion of glowing-tailed Beestjes blasted through the fire and smoke. They were small by wolfsdamsylfly standards and had beetle-like bodies and very large wings. They quickly swarmed the Aramen armada, spraying the mages with large swaths of molten plasma. Wolfsdamsylflies, enraged by the attack, reared, and plunged headlong into the thicket below, flinging massive amounts of red robes into the far reaches of the cavern. The crimson wizards that remained on beast back, spurred their animals and dove after the squadron. Fountains of fire erupted from their hands, consuming attacking Beestje lantern flies, sending the mechanical bugs tumbling and exploding.

"Valor and courage over your knowledge any day!" Corvin quickly told the imp, thrusting himself airward toward the dogfight on gallant wings. Brandishing gauntlet guns he fired in rapid succession, disappearing into the madness.

"Corvin!" Marie screamed, but her words were muffled by LUCY's plasma mask. She paused in mid gait. Searching the torrent in the skies for him, she could not help but despair.

Corvin switched to wireframe vision and navigated the savage Aramen squadron searching out the nearest pirate ship cannon. He spotted something ahead through the mess of smoke. A gigantic light-ringed nozzle emerged quickly. Corvin slowed flapping. He soared, riding air currents just beyond the cannon opening. The light ring became a whirring circle of blazing energy; protons ignited within the barrel. Through grimaced beak, the raven general fired off rounds of ammunition into the spinning gun. Fire erupted in the belly, sending a chain reaction rocketing through the cannon. Immediately the pirate ship that housed the weapon erupted into a blinding inferno.

Steaming debris pounded the air as Corvin fought to regain flight in the concussion that rocketed him through space. He dodged stalactites and oncoming Beestje lantern flies. Grabbing hold of the trunk of a slick sinter, he flung his body around and thrust himself back toward the fight.

Just beyond the falling body of the pirate ship, two more opal-bodied vessels advanced through the war-torn air. Portals opened along each side and spewed out thousands of MechGunner drones. The yellow and silver orbs spread out in a massive circle. Machine gun nozzles telescoped out. Immediately they sprayed the sky with bullets. Corvin kicked wildly against the attack. His wings faltered upon the angry air. Red alerts resounded within his sensors as ammunition clanked through his machine skin. Corvin flung his body downward toward the twisted brambles. The swarm of drones quickly followed.

The burning plunging underbelly of the crashing pirate ship rumbled through forest columns and kicked up vine covered earth. Marie grabbed hold of Quilp and LUCY as they tumbled through the hateful brush. Everything around them was quickly consumed by fire. Explosions of screaming rubble ricocheted along the ground.

"This way!" Quilp broke free from Marie's grasp. She and LUCY raced with him through the thunderous inferno. Just as they reached the edges of the fire, Nines' voice rose above the din somewhere at her back. He screamed something repeatedly. Marie turned momentarily as LUCY on rocket feet, snapped her back to attention, dragging her rapidly along. The air exploded at her back. The sky and ground became a dizzying confusion. Marie was launched airborne, all around her explosive arms of fire sent pirate ship pieces flying off into vaporized fragments.

Robot arms roused Marie from a biting bed of thorns. Nines and LUCY grabbed her up. Marie could barely hear their frenzied words above the thunderous ringing in her ears. Her limbs were useless. Her side was a torturous cacophony of pain. The air smelt of burning flesh. *Another wound to add to my collection,* Marie thought through grimaced teeth. Nines pulled her back up to her feet and by some miracle she stood. The two were momentarily caught up in each other's arms. Nines' visor was a churning orange ball of reflected catastrophic light marbled through with black veins of billowing smoke. "T...They know you're here!" he said. Marie discerned ruddy movement reflected in his mirror face. She thrust her gaze to where he stared. There, emerging from the tangled brush, thirteen Aramen mages advanced through the flaming forest led by the barbaric figures of Kitrank and Faul.

The air above the city Beestje was teaming with static and rain. More lantern flies exploded somewhere in the distance, victims to Aramen fire sprays and drone blasts. The drone machine gun rages were unrelenting. The ground churned a furious raging bright red. Corvin's internal processors sputtered with arrays of flight plans and trajectories. Damage alerts flashed in his ocular lenses. Taking on more damage would not be an option for him. He quickly evaded machine gun blasts from one annoying, undeterred drone. Swiftly Corvin contorted his body and returned fire. The annoying orb rocketed back through the atmosphere, a spinnaker of sparks. Corvin soared out beyond the trio of pirate ships hovering just beyond the city walls. They stood strangely quiet. *Perhaps they are awaiting more orders,* Corvin thought. *Perhaps we crashed their lead ship.* Corvin spotted more wolfsdamsylfly-backed Aramen spiraling just above the tangled forest below. A clearing was not far away.

Two small silhouettes quickly sped across the expanse. They were soon overtaken by a mass of striding red figures. Analysis of the ground showed Marie and Nines to be at the center of the mess.

I must stop the Aramen, Corvin realized. The red wizards flying just above were about to land and rally to the aid of those who marched upon his companions. Machine gun fire erupted at Corvin's back. Drones had spotted him. Synapsis clicked. His processors roared. *What a clever command operation!* This electrical connection had turned up a shining token, a plan. His whole being submitted to the idea and he dove headlong into the squadron of descending red mages. The raven general evaded oncoming fistfuls of fire and swooped below wolfsdamsylfly legs. He fired back at the drones who bared down on his fleeing form. The ensuing confusion elicited lethal rapid drone machine gun fire directly into the landing wizards. Magicians and wolfsdamsylflies exploded at his back. He cawed in victory and flung himself on flashing wings back into the air. The handful of Aramen who survived the attack, turned rein, and launched upward, full throttle after him. The army of Mech drones followed closely behind.

Marie quickly found herself wielding Nines' double-edged scimitar. She had lost her gun somewhere along the tumultuous path. Adrenaline fired through her body—her desperate order to LUCY and Quilp, "RUN!" still screamed in her ears. She hoped they had both found a safe place to hide. The blade of her fine weapon met the thunderous momentum of Faul's broadsword. *I must not bend!* Marie strained under the weight of the downward thrust. Faul didn't remove the blade. *She is a beast of sheer power*; Marie's mind was a myriad of curses. Veins bulged angrily within the lizard woman's sinuous muscles. Each movement sought to dominate Marie with brute strength. Marie thrust her leg back, bracing herself. The scimitar was her only defense, her only shield. Marie grabbed her sword blade. The lizard woman pressed down in heavy rage. Her fists where masses of straining fingers gripping the hilt. Marie held her breath. She denied the wrath of the Is'rondaian broadsword. Her palm soon was a crimson mess. Marie cried out, holding on a moment longer. Marie and Faul locked eyes in a flash of hateful stillness. The Lacer Is'rondaian's gaze was a blazing yellow. A hissing noise erupted from within her throat. Crying out, Marie buckled and tumbled free of the crashing blade.

Marie rallied with a low roundhouse kick. Faul tumbled to her back, then quickly rebounded, slashing at Marie repeatedly with her sword. Marie met each crushing blow expertly. Clattering sword steel shattered the crackling air. Somewhere at Marie's back clanging metal and static blasts joined the sound of swordfight.

Nines utilized palm blasts and kicks, fending himself against Kitrank's electric mace. Voltage shattered the earth around them, and searing heat engulfed the clearing. Nines retaliated with a barrage of flaming sprays. The Vespa-Mandarinian took flight and Nines grabbed hold of the mace-end. With super strength he flung the wasp man back to the earth and pummeled him with fire. Kitrank defected the onslaught with his shield.

Marie and Faul locked blades. Marie's neck and shoulder skin sweltered under the pirate woman's haughty breath. "Such a pretty thing..." Faul hissed at Marie. Her gigantic roving eyes oscillated with pleasure. Marie held on to this respite. *I must find calm*, she told herself, *I must plan my next move carefully*. Firelight glinted in her periphery. The flames raged upon the face shields of the thirteen mages who gathered around the fight. They stood frozen in the clearing.

Faul's words echoed out on the charred air, "Stand down, dear Aramen the princess is ours to destroy." The mages thankfully obliged, but Marie was not sure how long the command would last. Taking in a final breath, Marie flung herself into a spin, sliding under the returning broadsword blade. Marie rejoiced as her simitar caught lizard woman belly flesh. Green blood flowed freely. The Is'rondai let out an ear shattering scream followed by an intense clattering rage. Marie soon regretted the attack. She was bombarded with savage thrusts and hacks. Rolling out from underneath the broadsword barrage, Marie found her feet again. She took a defensive stance. Suddenly she realized she was standing back to back with Nines.

"We are done for!" Quilp wailed as LUCY pulled the imp to safety. They took cover behind a piece of steaming pirate ship near a burned-out gunner drone. "There must be a way to help!" Dove's voice echoed beneath within the steel shell. It was once an engine housing. The small bot could no longer see Marie or Nines. The two were now at some distance from the clearing and the burning thicket. Quilp soon pointed out the soaring figure of Corvin in the far recess of the smoldering cavern above.

"There are still three ships," Dove said.

"And a whole lot of gunner drones..." Quilp assessed.

"Too many." Dove said. Even though Corvin had fallen back behind another fleet of charging glow beetles, the angry Mech drones had arced back and now were following closely behind him. The raven general evaded their blasts, but Dove could tell, their friend was losing steam.

"He'll be hit from behind!" Quilp shouted, biting his fingertips in fear.

"Not if I can help it," Dove said. The small robot girl skittered over to the downed gunner drone and extended a palm towards an access point on the charred surface.

"What are you doing?" Quilp hissed.

"If I can give it some power from LUCY's reserves..." Dove said. "Yes, Dove," LUCY quickly replied. "I can..." Suddenly Dove felt a relay of electrical charges coarse throughout the small bot's frame and the drone's search light flickered on.

"Be careful with that!"

Dove did not respond. Instead, the boy let the machine's codes wash through his consciousness. The world within became abstract images, but these images when interlaced with gunner drone language, began to make sense to Dove. With resolution, Dove soon knew the answer and with glee he accessed a secret procedure hidden deep within the machine. He could see other access points to nearby drones and the possibility of infiltration. "Yes," Dove said entranced. "This is it. This procedure will execute!"

Corvin flapped among charging glow beetles, dodging amber spray and machine gun bullets. Beetle bodies exploded in the mechanical spray. He flung back and extended his gun gauntlets, but only a disheartening clicking sound was heard. His ocular display was correct. All ammo *had* been exhausted. His wings flapped desperately treading the air. His energy was at 5%. An overwhelming amount of gunner drones amassed all around him.

Which program should I execute, thought Corvin, *the one that keeps me flying or the one that crashes me to the ground?* The coding for survival within him was primary. *If I am decommissioned, what will become of you?* The image of Magnus charging Luscinia's egg with a battle ax ravaged through his mind. Something like despair rocketed through his circuits. *There is another option Corvin, do nothing and be riddled with bullets by the oncoming drones*, he processed that idea with a sarcastic bit of code. It horrified him.

The drones were now a thick mass all around him. The steel orbs seemed to savor cornering him in thin air. Hundreds of machine gun nozzles focused their sights. Corvin moved to shut off his oculars, but a flashing light sent his vision sensors into high alert.

A massive spiderweb of glittering electricity rocketed through the air around him. Focusing vision again, drone after drone around him erupted into blasts of sparks and flames. Somewhere down below, Dove looked on in wonder and pride as his self-destruct code invaded each Mech.

The princess and the renegade Aramen were cornered back-to-back. Faul and Kitrank paced angrily around them.

"It won't end like this," Marie growled, and nodded resolutely at Nines. Courage and resolve roared within the princess' eyes. Marie charged Faul as Nines took hold of the flinging chain of Kitrank's mace. The Aramen channeled the weapon's electric charge. Impulses fired off deep within his body and the renegade expelled it back, savagely, into the pirate. Blue lightning ravaged Kitrank's body. He collapsed to the earth in a pile of steaming armor. His wasp legs and arms splayed out at impossibly awkward angles. Nines then turned, stood wide legged and outstretched his arms before him. He stared down the faces of all his Aramen brethren. They stared back at him, unmoved.

Marie again parried against savage sword thrusts. She realized Faul was not tiring, Marie feared her defenses were losing pace. Any moment a misstep would have her losing her head. Suddenly flames erupted at the lizard woman's back and the pirate fell to her knees in pain. Fire quickly blackened her green skin. She lunged forward, thrust aside her sword, and raced toward the woods. Nines quickly grabbed Marie by the arm and drug her away from the circle of stoic mages. Rapidly, he thrust the princess back into the forest of thorns.

At length, Marie's pace slowed. Her attention was caught by a blinding display of electrified explosions which laced across the heavens. Mech drones became fireballs and screamed to the ground pummeling the forest around them.

"Keep running!" Nines yelled.

Marie evaded barrages of blazing metal and charged through tangled vines. A horrendous noise rocketed through the cavern expanse. Marie craned her head upward toward the sky. She could clearly see the underbellies of the three remaining pirate ships. Marie and Nines watched helplessly as their furious whirring cannons raged back to life.

"They will be firing soon!" Marie shouted. "The city will be done for!"

Abrupt and horrific cannon blasts thundered through the cavern expanse. Marie cowered as more structures within the city tumbled. Amid the smoke and flame, a black figure, wings dead to the air, plummeted to the earth beyond the walls of the burning city.

"It's Corvin!" said Nines.

"We must go after him!" Marie cried.

EPISODE 25.

Holdout at the City Beestje.

Marie feared her raging heartbeat might never find serenity again as she raced through the noxious mix of green colored mists and smoke. The churning haze enshrouded everything. The tangled brambles made any meaningful progress nearly impossible. The princess felt assurance, though, in Nines who said he had a lock on their destination.

Quilp and LUCY followed them with eager speed. Thankfully, the pair had rejoined Marie and Nines just beyond the clearing. Now their only goal was to make it to the city and somehow find Corvin.

"These fumes are melting my circuits!" LUCY screamed.

"Major off-gassing from the defensive venom spray," Nines called back. "Once we make it into the city, we will be protected. Not much farther!"

His words were drowned out by thunderous explosions. The heavens churned with ferocious electricity. Marie doubted they would find safety ahead, but what choice did they have? The city Beestje was now in full defense mode. Turrets in the city walls let loose massive sprays of vermillion acid which doused the pirate ships unrelentingly. The invaders were in range to receive the caustic blasts and the venom was making an impact. The foremost ship listed. Thick black smoke poured heavily from the hull as metal melted and broke apart. Suddenly a chain reaction of explosions erupted from the underside of the ship and it fell, crashing through sinter columns and plunging headfirst into the vast catastrophe on the ground.

Another cannon blast ravaged the shaking earth. Sinters vibrated and fell; city domes crashed inward, and more detonations and flames churned within Beestje. Marie and her companions fled the rushing debris.

"There won't be a city left at this rate!" Marie screamed out into the smoke. "They won't stop until they have me. I am the cause of all of this." She ceased running.

"You'll be killed!" Quilp admonished her, he appeared at her feet and tugged on her pant leg.

"T...they advance upon us..." Nines' voice was a gasp. Marie rushed toward his voice. Suddenly the dark brambles cleared to a swath several meters wide.

"A path!" LUCY said.

Marie was thankful. It was a relief to see such a trail. She was about to launch headlong after Nines, but a sudden hissing flared at their back. Marie looked to where they had come. There, an army of red wizards trudged through the blight, flinging lashing tongues of fire through the smoke and embers with silver hands. Their faces glinted in the fire spray and turned crimson robes a horrible shade of red. Metal feet clanged quickly along the ground.

"Aramen!" LUCY screamed. She turned up jet boots and shot ahead grabbing Marie's hand. They both plowed in the direction of the city through the dense gray green haze. Quilp jackrabbited behind.

Marie fought to keep pace with LUCY's jets. Thankfully, Aramen receded into the distance, but this respite was soon thwarted by a horrific symphony of trilling howls which pierced the air.

Marie sprinted full throttle. She would not allow herself to look back, but it was no use, they were easily overtaken by the furious pounding of animal feet and the sound of hungry growling and gnashing teeth.

"Horrible beasts!" Quilp shrieked as wolf jowls plunked him from the trail. A wolfsdamsylfly reared him up on its haunches and chewed gleefully at Quilp's writhing body. Marie leapt at the animal, thrusting scimitar against the villainous monster. She plunged the curved sharp blade through the beasts' thorax. Blood wretched out onto the slick black earth. The monster fell into a steaming pile. Quilp's body tumbled along the ground. LUCY rushed to the imp.

"I'm alright, I think I'm alright," he told her breathlessly.

"We better go!" LUCY said. She looked to find Marie and Nines. The little bot was quickly disheartened to see that the pair was surrounded by four of the wolf-headed flies. The beasts paced the ground around the princess and the renegade. Their tongues lolled from between razor sharp teeth and translucent wings fluttered in frenzied anticipation.

Quilp shrieked and threw stones. LUCY followed his lead, but the rocks bounced uselessly off the thick-skinned bodies of the beasts.

Nines quickly blasted a protective ring of fire from his fingertips. Marie raised her sword. These actions only seemed to ignite the wolfsdamsylfly's anger. With a raging cry, the beasts pounced through the flames. Marie fought off fangs with her blade alongside Nines who wrestled another wolfsdamsylfly to the ground. Arm gears groaning, Nines tried to suffocate it with a choke hold.

Wolf lips gnashed at Marie's face hungrily. She was awash in hot breath and saliva. She punched the monster in the mouth. It squealed and retaliated. As she fought against its angry mouth, more teeth chomped at her heels. Suddenly, she was entangled in a mass of writhing beast bug bodies. Hungry canines pierced her flesh. Her rapid scimitar slashes caught some flesh, but it was soon evidence that it was a hopeless attempt.

LUCY quickly pulled Quilp to the protection of the brambles as more monsters thundered down the path followed by a procession of Aramen. Quilp would not be deterred. The imp launched from the brambles and charged towards damsylfy tails.

Suddenly the ground rumbled, and a massive tumult of turf and rock sent wolfsdamsylfly and Aramen both tumbling. From beneath the earth, pinchers and brown blunt heads emerged, erupting through the ground followed by horse-sized segmented bodies and a lashing blade like tail. Wolfsdamsylflies shrieked as they were taken apart by hungry mandibles. Marie scrambled from beneath the feasting field and came to rest at a pair of silver feet peeking from beneath a mud-spattered red robe. She peered up through the damp air and braced herself for an Aramen fire blast. But the Aramen grabbed her up and hugged her to him.

"M...mole crickets—Beestje conveyance machines of war," Nines said of the monsters that had just plowed up through the ground. Marie clung to Nines' arms and thrust her eyes back to the battle. Fire blasts rocketed through the mess. Aramen amassed around the melee. They quickly recognized that the princess was near and advanced undeterred through the mists.

Nines and Marie raced the path kicking up slogging earth followed by LUCY and Quilp. Wind wailed and torrents doused the fiery terrain as they fled out toward the city. Somewhere up the path a fitful tremor vibrated the ravaged earth.

"Make way!" Nines screamed suddenly. Then Marie saw it: two massive forms rumbled toward them. Marie thrust herself aside as a pair of Beestje soldiers on mole cricket back raged by. They charged the advancing Aramen, devastating the invaders with plasma gunfire. Marie turned away from exploding mages and wolfsdamsylfly squeals that wrecked the savage air. The companions raced the path with greater intent, ducking low as five lantern flies rocketed overhead, very near the ground. The glow flies joined the skirmish, dousing the remaining Aramen army with massive amounts of amber goo.

"There!" Marie screamed. A towering pair of earthen doors, recessed in a vast wall appeared through the fog. Marie charged ahead. She denied herself celebration. She feared too what lay within. *Nines said it would be safer. Out here we suffer the ravages of war. But within we may find...Corvin...* The thought of reaching the raven general fueled her legs, but the sound of her own footfalls was quickly overtaken by many pounding bug feet.

"Nines!" Marie cried out as the companions were accosted by frantic and angry consonants. The sputtering and gnashing language doused them with forbidding sounds.

Having defeated the Aramen and wolfsdamsylfly army, the Beestje soldiers overtook the companions and quickly barred the path. Marie slid to a stop suddenly finding herself nose to nozzle with the Beestje soldier's long gun. She braced for a shot through the head, but to her relief and surprise, Quilp faced down the soldiers himself. He sputtered off the same language at them. The soldiers paused momentarily to consider Quilp's plea. Swiveling their small, black diamond shaped heads towards each other, they began speaking at a frenzied pace. Yellow oculars glowed and pulsed in time with their words while their spidery antennae lashed the air wildly. Marie struggled to understand their words. Something was wrong with her translator.

An immense conflagration of buzzing and rumbling exploded in the skies above. Marie yelled out frantically over the melee—"Quilp, hurry!" The Beestje soldiers then sputtered something to the imp.

"Quickly now. Climb up." Quilp told the companions. "Renardii and Zelus will take us to a safe place within the city—there is an underground bunker."

Renardii offered Marie one of his four hands. She hoisted herself up behind the soldier and reached down to pull LUCY up too. Nines leapt behind Zelus. Marie held tight to Renardii's exoskeleton as the mole crickets lurched to life, bucking down the path with amazing speed.

Overhead, a massive pirate ship, overcome with enormous amounts of defensive amber and venom, shuddered and quickly tumbled toward them. Renardii sputtered out a message into his wrist communicator. The massive city doors parted. The envoy raced through. Marie shot a glance backward and witnessed the raging pirate ship hull meet the earth as the doors whooshed closed. A gigantic and horrific smash reverberated the passage followed by a horrendous groan of tumbling metal. All seemed quiet for one terrifying beat, then, suddenly, the portal exploded, and rocks and debris rampaged down the passage after them. Marie braced to be buried as thunderous tremors reverberated violently throughout her body. Darkness swallowed them hungrily. The mole cricket lurched into full steam. Tumbling debris clamored against Marie's flesh; smoke choked the air as the crash ravaged the passageway; suddenly a ruddy light broke through the darkness. Erupting into a greater expanse, a main agora within the city walls, the mole cricket they rode, skittered out quickly amid fleeting Beestjes, swung around and slammed to a stop. They watched in terror as the portal in the city wall disintegrated into an avalanche of boulders, steam, and fire.

Marie cleared grit from her eyes and mouth and searched the octagonal expanse that surrounded them. Columns, rocks, and boulders had smashed through canopies and wares. Dim firelight filtered in from somewhere in the upper reaches of the city Beestje. Walls of the inner dome had collapsed revealing suspended avenues and chambers which reached endlessly into the dimness beyond the cracked roof, leading to a massive nest of hives. Beestjes fled out everywhere. This inner sanctum roared with lamenting Beestje voices. Clicks, shutters and electronic wails. Almost every surface writhed with the panicked bodies of the beetle mech droids. Marie frantically scoured the skittering and horrified citizens that crowded the main square. Corvin was nowhere to be seen.

Renardii kicked mole cricket with a thwapping of long spindly legs. Marie barely had time to cling fast as they charged through the crowd and toward a passageway concealed some distance beyond the main square. The mole cricket plunged down a long and winding passage. It was narrow; its slick walls shone with the lamp light issuing from the soldiers' yellow oculars. Soon they gained access to a grand chamber that stood behind thick amber doors. Soaring archways housed an immense treasury of glowing containers of crystalline liquid. Narrow thoroughfares twisted through the sparkling rock. Renardii charged ahead and came to a stop in an enclave deep within the bunker which featured a raised dais housed under a massive, twisting columned, baldachin. Several figures conversed underneath. Two of them were very familiar. Marie looked to LUCY in surprise. "Volgens..." she whispered. The small girl shuddered.

There, on the platform, the grand round form of Eostrix stood near the horrible hunched, long necked Neophron. They hovered over something which lay concealed on the floor between them. They were joined by two gold and red oval-bodied Beestjes with headdresses of jet black dangling bells, a long bodied, lilac throated mantis with pink glowing eyes and an fuzzy tawny bristle bodied asp with soaring blade antennae. Marie slid off the back of the mole cricket and helped LUCY down. She was soon joined by Quilp and Nines.

"What are they doing here?" Dove's voice spontaneously erupted from LUCY. The boy's voice startled Marie and prompted the princess to analyze their surroundings even further. Marie struggled to make out the conversation. The translator in her hair was a tangled mess of slender silver wires. She fumbled with the connector behind her ear. There was a staticky click and the audio implant made a connection again.

"Your Majesties," Renardii regarded the group on the dais and bowed. Marie could not readily tell who in the group were of the ruling class. "One pirate ship remains, but it will be handled swiftly by our airborne legions. Troops have swept the fields—no more Aramen are left...and the beasts..."

"What is the meaning of this!" Neophron's thundering voice rocketed through the chamber, realizing their presence. He quickly strode in front of the group and brandished his staff. It crackled with green electricity. "Aramen in our midst! Have you lost your mind! And you—you there. The prisoner..." he spoke to Marie. "I should have guessed. With you, destruction surely follows!"

"The imp has requested sanctuary for all," said Renardii. "It is our honor to save those who seek asylum in Beestje."

"Ah yes, Quilp..." Neophron's voice was acid.

LUCY trembled and hid behind Marie.

"...and the possessed machine..."

"We mean you no harm—we are on a mission," said Marie.

"Do not trust them," Neophron told Renardii and Zelus.

Eostrix's forlorn voice followed. "We have lost everything...due to trust..."

"Horrible, horrible," lamented the two Beestjes with dangling bell headdresses.

"Yes, Your Majesties," the mantis soothed the small oval Beestjes. Marie gathered he was a minister of some sort.

"The Royal Globulares have spoken," the fuzzy asp announced to the room.

Neophron regarded the words and turned again. "How can you think to bring this abhorrent group into our midst, Lieutenant Renardii?"

"You are not my Lords, I bow down only to the Royal Globulares and the code imbued by the will of Saint," the soldier replied. "Need I remind you that we gave you asylum here as well?"

Neophron thought for a moment. "Perhaps you are tainted by the blight—as are the Aramen. Their kind has turned a killing hand against all of us."

Renardii scoffed at the ridiculous charge.

"Horrible, horrible," the Bell-Bearers chorused.

"the Royal Globulares have spoken," said the asp.

"And to think such outlanders have come to exist in Hout." He strode to Marie, "Strange, pure, organic life...this one. I used to think the Kind of Saint had some divinity over us, now I know they are an evil sort—not like the maker at all," He pushed his staff beneath her chin and brought her eyes up to meet his. Marie resisted his searching, circle-eyed, unemotional gaze. "Need I remined you of the wolf headed beasts and the pirates that invaded our cities? They share this same quality of make—the one hundred percent biological. Strange, ghastly, abominations...this one has questioned our practices and indeed gone against Volgen rule of law. She must leave this court; she must be punished; her presence here defiles the authority of the Volgens and the sovereignty of the Globulare Court!"

Marie pulled away from Neophron. "You didn't mention Magnus. Did you forget about him? He is the one that wrought this destruction upon us, not this LUCY, not me. It is in your best interest to help us in our quest," she told them.

"Are you sure?" Neophron screeched. "Magnus was looking for you. He destroyed our village because of you! You are to blame for all of this!"

Marie was struck silent. She paused for a moment. "It is not just me. Magnus wants to destroy your world," she said at last. "Your world is dying. It is being turned against itself and fleeced for resources by Magnus! You have seen the truth. And I attempted to warn you. Don't you see that Neophron? I am on your side. You are all victims of Magnus and it will only become worse. If you stand against us, if you deny us what we are seeking, then you will destroy yourselves."

"Let her continue Neophron," one of the Globulares said timidly.

"The Royal Globulares have—"

The asp was interrupted by a beeping rejoicing erupting from the crowd on the dais. A small Beestje skittered out in front of them. "Ah ha! Ah ha!" it proclaimed. "Outta the way, outta the way!!!" sputtered a trilobite with large green goggle oculars. It pushed through Volgen legs and came out into the open space.

"HE has been restored!" it announced as if some miracle had been produced by its tiny oscillating limbs.

"Corvin!" Marie cried. The raven general rose to standing from the dais. His body shuddered and wings undulated mechanically. He seemed entranced. The general had lain concealed until now, and Marie realized his body must have been the object of the group's attention just before their arrival. Marie pushed through the crowd to embrace the towering raven droid. Neophron rustled his feathers in protest.

"You're alright! You're alright!" Marie said, holding on to him for dear life. She felt his hands tremble. Nines, Quilp and LUCY, all joined her in the reunion.

"He's still scrolling through updates to his system. He will be fully functional momentarily," said the trilobite. The trilobite then began to rattle off a litany of repairs and improvements he had made, up to and including imbuing Corvin with a miraculous, ultra-charged piezo apophyllite crystal battery, which held vast amounts of energy, far beyond anything the raven had been imbued with at manufacture. The piezo battery glowed with pulsing icy blue light within Corvin's breastplate. Something clicked in the avian-droid and sputtering electronic gibberish gushed from Corvin's beak followed by the words: "my friends."

"Don't go getting soft on me..." Quilp hugged the raven's boot, wiping away a tear. "Sorry, my maker programmed me to express intense sentimentality...sometimes..."

Suddenly Renardii's wrist communicator erupted into a ruckus. A Beestje on the front lines reported: "The pirates are turning around! They are fleeing!" There seemed to be a chorus of beeping celebration chiming out in the background. "The final ship has turned. We have victory!"

"It is as I predicted. You have done well commandant. The Royal Globulares are pleased," Renardii radioed back.

"Victory, victory," the royals sputtered. "Yes, very pleased!"

"The Royal Globulares have spoken."

"They'll be back," Corvin said.

"N...no doubt that is true," said Nines. "This may only enrage Magnus further."

Neophron's oculars narrowed at the Aramen. "What recourse have we, then, Red Wizard?" he asked.

"We fight. We must take on the city of Aramen ourselves," Corvin said. "We must direct our armies there and decommission this threat once and for all. They have Luscinia and they will use her to control us all. We know their plan. Renardii, Zelus, we must conference."

"The Beestjes have claimed victory, but the cost to our city has been great. Do we stand a chance against this threat?" said the mantis minister.

"Y...yes," said Nines, "and I...I will tell you how..."

EPISODE 26.

A Plan.

Marie at first was unsure of the plan, but as Nines spoke the idea of it became ever more plausible. She sensed that his words were quickly winning over Beestje and Volgen alike; both longed desperately to rid themselves of the recent threats born from the foreign despot that now ruled over the Aramen and the Mechs. The thirst for long lasting freedom was palpable. The only issue was that the plan hinged on everything going perfectly right. *Nothing ever goes perfectly right*, Marie thought sardonically.

"Your plan is a grand one Aramen, with little probability of success or survival," said Renardii, then after a moment's thought, "But I want to see this foreign enemy crushed and he must be. I like a challenge. If we win, there will be glory for us all."

"And a promise of a bright new day," said the Bell Bearers hopefully.

"The Royal Globulares have spoken," said the asp.

"How can we trust that what the Aramen says is true? How can we trust this is not a trap?" said Neophron.

"I...I want to free my people just as much as you do," said Nines. "My fellow Aramen, the ones who escaped the horrific mind control code, have been awaiting a time to act. Now is that time. It is our only chance..."

The renegade Aramen's plan was to use the mind-meld with his small crew of Nines to assist the rebel army to first gain access to the city Aramen. Then the idea was to direct one of the Nines to reprogram the Aramen's sacred red crystal to release the rest of the Aramen from Magnus' controlling spell –the only issue was Randt was the only one who knew how to hack that code. They needed to find him.

"We don't even know where Randt is," Marie said.

"But we know he came through here only a few Houtan cycles ago," Dove said excitedly. "He must not be far off."

"The LUCY is right. The master coder stayed with our people only a few cycles ago. It is our only chance," said the minister. "The code master was searching for the Trail of Saint leading to the sacred temple at Hout's core. Our ministers directed him to the entrance to the trail. It is concealed near the city of Tweelach."

"The city of the AmphibioMechs...it lies across the apophyllite swamps," said Quilp.

"We must take the Royal Globulares there for safety while the city Beestje is restored," said the asp. "We will show you the way..."

Marie nodded. "Quilp, Nines, the LUCY and I will go with you."

"And I will lead the army to Aramen," said Corvin.

"So, it's settled then. Corvin, Renardii and Zelus will lead what Volgen fighters are left and the valiant lycorma squadron—as your majesties have so generously pledged," said Eostrix, nodding to the Royal Globulares who in turn sputtered bug bodies in agreement, "and head to the city of Aramen."

"We must be stealth at first, the Aramen firepower is great," said Zelus.

"Agreed. Once you reach the outskirts of the city, the greater part of the army should stay hidden within the blight forest...you will signal back to us on the communication device the trilobite mechanist has given us..." said Nines.

"Renardii, Zelus and I will rendezvous with your people in secret and they will lead us to Magnus' throne room," Corvin said.

"By then we will have found Poppa..." said Dove hopefully. "And he will assist Nines in relaying the recoding information to his crew in Aramen."

"I...I will use our mind-meld to re-write the SenStone code and my brethren will turn against Magnus and free us from this curse," concluded Nines.

"And if we fail..." said Zelus.

"Then the valiant lycorma and courageous Volgen armies move in and unleash all the firepower we have," said Renardii.

Marie was relieved there was a backup plan. She was scared for what lay ahead. "We can't fail," she said.

"Indeed, neo-human," said Renardii.

"And what of the war machines the Mechs are constructing?" Marie asked.

"The machine gun drones, and the pirate ships are but two examples of the Mech's new handiwork," said Quilp.

"All the more reason to remain stealth with our armies until all other avenues are exhausted," said Corvin.

"Who knows what Mech firepower lurks even now within the Aramen city itself?" said Eostrix.

"T...the Mechs have yet to deliver upon the vast armory of conveyances and drones, Magnus has but a few, as was the case just before Randt and I escaped. But time does grow short," said Nines.

"We must make haste," said Renardii. Then to Marie, "Perhaps the most important part of this mission lies in your hands."

"Yes," she said. "we must be quick to depart. Who even knows how far Randt has got?"

Renardii regarded her tattered clothes and bloody body. "First though, the Beestje Lieutenant said, "We best get you some clean clothes and armor."

EPISODE 27.

The Armor of Crysanthia Mesmos.

"Crysanthia Mesmos...such a thing of beauty. Magenta skinned, ice blue eyes, a poetic type of programming to be sure, an andro-mech of the most exquisite quality, by the standards of Saint, of course. She was a valiant and entrancing sort of being, I can see why Renardii would suggest these garments for you." The mantis minister's half-orb eyes pulsed with deep purple and fuchsia illumination as it spoke. "This armor was a queen's desperate attempt to save her own people from their horrific selves."

Marie peered into a mechanical cask that sat before her. Tre, the mantis minister had led her to the armory to retrieve this sacred vestment of war as the others prepared the troops for battle. Within the cask, a neatly folded trio of white silken undergarments: mantle, blouse, and pants, were lain over with glinting silver and gold chain mail. Beside them lay a cuirass, pairs of nested gauntlets, grieves, and a helmet with boots to match—all hewn in exquisitely polished ice blue steel. Each piece was inlaid with computer chips arranged in a geometric, floral mosaic; gold decorated the edges in circuit filigree. Marie ran her fingers over the well-made surface of the cuirass in admiration of the quality.

"They should fit you nicely. The cloth is the finest quality, extruded by the wormery, crafted together by our arachnid weavers and the armor was forged in the flames of the fire bees, imbued with electronic intelligence by the mantid priests, my own brethren," said Tre proudly. "Our guilds were renowned and revered by the Orzos—back when such things of beauty mattered to them; Crysanthia was perhaps the last of the andromechs to request such a thing of impeccable quality from the ministers."

"This armor has never been used," Marie pondered.

"Alas, it was an elaborate creation, unfortunately left un-delivered and never to be worn. The Golden City of the Orzos fell, just as the last circuit was put into place."

"You must be parched. Great care must be taken for the neo-human." Tre gathered up an abandoned scoop shaped piece of metal from the floor of the armory and collected water in it from a quiet spring concealed near the wall and offered it to Marie. Marie thanked him and, wiping the last remaining bits of LUCY-made flesh from her mouth, eagerly drank the water. It was ice-crystal cold and refreshed her fatigued and injured body. She washed her face and ran a little bit through her hair, readjusting her translator circlet.

"You've been chipped," Tre realized.

"Yes, the Volgens. They said it was necessary for me to communicate."

"Very good. We can interlace Crysanthia's armor with that existing micro-processor. With some practice, you may be able to control the suit with mental stimulation. It houses several systems of self-defense weaponry. I will get you the ammunition required. The trilobite will assist us." Mantis called for the mechanist.

The mantis plucked up the silk base garments from the trunk and presented it to Marie. The princess accepted the gift from his crooked, ivory hands. She was curious about the Orzos queen and how this strange new character played into the history of this place.

"Luscinia told me of the jealousy, passions and rage that overtook the Orzos. She said the Volgens wanted nothing to do with them," then regarding the gift, "I am forever in your debt." She swiftly began to change. The mantle and underclothes were easy to maneuver, the chain mail and armor proved more difficult. Tre helped with the mail fastenings and armor attachments. "Renardii was correct in his assessment, this armor is a perfect fit."

Marie regarded herself in a mirror that was attached to the underside of the lid of the mechanical cask. She was a flashing warrior goddess in molten silver and blue. She felt valiant, powerful, but a sullenness soon overtook her countenance. She felt the presence of the being for which this armor was intended. Sadness of an unrealized hope flooded her emotions and the horrific reality of a final cataclysmic destiny.

"Magnus..." she whispered. "This armor was made to battle Magnus."

"It is as I calculated. Here is proof. In your very words. The Aramen are not the first Houtans to have been made soldiers of this beast." Tre said. "The Orzos too, of that I am now convinced."

Marie remembered how blind the Volgens had been regarding Magnus during LUCY's trial. "The Volgens once thought Magnus a savior," she said.

"I have no doubt Crysanthia did too, at one time. I knew of a man who had come into their kingdom from the outlands. A realm called Callisto. Records of Saint showed that it was her tribe and the Mechs who both sought to heal this man with sacred methods of the Grand Mechanist—after that, the records cease and the breaking of Hout ensued, the blight began, and all became dark."

"But the Orzos queen contacted you to make this armor."

"Requested via Renardii. Renardii relayed to me that the Orzos queen seemed in a desperate state. He said Crysanthia told him that horrible knowledge had come into her tribe. She admitted to secret crimes herself— helping an outlander initiate code to redirect the Mechs to make war machines, which in turn, disrupted the Mech Mech system of Houtan birth—now we see, irrevocably. She was fearful of the other tribes' retaliation, but she said she would make things right again—if only we would craft armor for her—battle armor to defy all other armor. She asked this in strict confidence and with strictest confidence it was made. Renardii valued Crysanthia dearly."

"But the armor was never delivered," Marie pondered. "The Orzos city fell...Magnus failed in his task to turn the Orzos into his personal warriors. They turned on each other instead. Magnus moved on to the Aramen then...what really happened in Orzos? Whatever it was, it caused the breaking of Hout and the birth of the blight..." Marie was curious as to the nature of the events that befell Magnus in the final days of Orzos. But that curiosity was soon thrust to the back of her mind as the trilobite scurried into the armory followed closely by Quilp and the LUCY.

"What has been taking you so long?!...My, my!" Quilp shouted as he came into the room and was at once struck in awe by the now gleaming armored form of Marie.

"I see now. Quite a transformation..."

"How may I help?" the small mechanist said in buzzing speech. The mantis explained his intent to interlace Marie's chip with her armor.

"Okey, dokey," said the mechanist and he immediately set to work, grabbing Marie's arm with its tiny legs, he inserted a cable into the bracer and started sputtering out trilling songs of computation.

"The army is nearing ready. Corvin and the Beestje Lieutenant will be departing shortly."

"And we must be going, Mam'selle. Soon. Poppa...I feel it in my bones. He is close," said Dove.

Marie felt the need to leave immediately to go to Corvin, to see him off. The trilobite sensed her anxiousness, and he sputtered a protest. She decided instead to sit back and let him work. The mantis watched quiet and motionless. Marie felt uncomfortable with the knowledge of what she and Tre had just spoken of. It seemed sacred and sad.

"Stand," the trilobite ordered Marie at last. Marie did. "Speak to it."

"The armor?" Marie questioned. The trilobite nodded. Then with uncertainty, she uttered the word, "Hello?" Suddenly her retinas flared brightly, and a rocket injection pulsed through her nervous system. The circuitry in her arms, chest and legs glowed and coursed with piezo power. Her vision became overlaced with green lined screens and data coursed along the bottom of her vision, fuel reserves, weapons status and more rotated along the x axis. "I see it!" she exclaimed. "I feel it..." the was an utterance of wonder.

"The connection is made!" the mantis rejoiced.

"Now to get you weaponized," the trilobite said rubbing its small hands together in pleasure and excitement.

EPISODE 28.

Goodbye from the Ramparts of Beestje.

Marie found Corvin on the broken turret of the Beestje city. He was standing beside Renardii in deep conversation. His towering sleek black body eclipsed even the tall and slender Beestje lieutenant. She admired Corvin's sleek ebony feathers, they looked velvet-like in the murky yellow light that hovered over the vast war-torn field that stretched off into the still distance. She rounded a crumbling column and jolted out along the rampart.

"Corvin!" she yelled and sprinted toward the raven droid. "Corvin!"

Corvin cocked his head to the side at her second shout and then turned. His oculars now shone a shocking color of vibrant yellow and contrasted, almost breathtakingly, with his jet-black raven features. He seemed renewed. Resurrected. Marie realized she must have appeared the same to him, rushing out before him, her body now gleaming adorned with silver and gold mechanical armor. He analyzed her appearance and let out a cawing welcome. Marie slowed her gait and paused before him. She felt suddenly unable to speak. Corvin motioned for Renardii to leave them. The lieutenant bowed and strode along the bulwark to give them privacy, he paused a distance away and peered down to the lycorma army which filled the ravaged courtyard below. Undulating wings glinted silvery cascades along the squadron bodies which lined the platforms and thoroughfares of the fallen levels of the city Beestje. Their sound sent an eerie trilling out into the darkened air, the army was ready to fly.

Corvin regarded the princess for a moment, her new look seemed to please, if not amuse him. "You are becoming one of us now," the raven general said at last pointing to her mechanical breastplate. "I recognize within you a heroic sort of code."

"The trilobite mechanist is to blame, I'm afraid." Marie smiled.

"He does artful work. Very admirable."

"Yes, he does. If it weren't for him...well..." she changed her speech track, "...not even Neophron can say I'm one hundred percent biological anymore. Just some enhanced circuitry really...nothing—"

Corvin would not allow her to play off her initial thought, he interrupted, "If it weren't for *him* what?"

"The mechanist? What? You would be decommissioned, obviously," she said. She felt strangely exposed now by her worry, but she felt somehow emboldened by it.

"And that scared you?" he said. Marie sensed an amused tone to his words.

"Yes! Why wouldn't it?"

Corvin said nothing to this. Instead, his oculars zoomed in and out emitting a quiet whirring. *Does he not know what to say*, she wondered—or *was there something he just won't say?* This uncertainty frustrated her. "I'm glad we found you," she said at last. "—I'm glad the Beestjes found you," said Marie.

"I wouldn't say found. They had no choice, really...I was hard to miss. The minister told me that I crashed headlong into the royal entourage fleeing from the pirates," Corvin said matter-of-factly, but the seriousness of his tone mixed with the image of the falling bird raining down upon the unsuspecting royal retinue caused Marie to laugh. Corvin seemed to not understand her reaction, he continued, mistaking the display for confusion, "He said I fell right through the processional canopy. It caused a great fright."

Marie giggled harder.

"What are you doing? What is that? What is this display, Princess?" she waved at him and hid her face. "—oh yes," he calculated. "Funny. You take this as a joke? I could've killed the Globulares!"

"The Globulares!" Marie laughed more heartily, she felt sudden relief.

"Good thing I didn't," Corvin ruffled his feathers and stood taller, "...or else I would have been decommissioned totally for committing such a crime."

"I could only imagine the look on the Royal Globulares' faces!" Marie took in a breath and sighed, calming. "The Globulares. Well, I'm glad you weren't killed! I wouldn't be able to stand it if you left me now. But here I am, aren't I? Saying goodbye to you, nonetheless. At least you're alive. Good thing Renardii will be there to look out for you."

"Is that any way to speak to me? I've been a general in the Volgen army for one million and fifteen Hout cycles. I think I can handle myself, Princess."

"Yes, to a certain point, perhaps. That is until your batteries run out or something tries to blow a hole through your central processing unit. Seems to me like you are the one needing to be rescued lately."

"I've done my fair share of rescuing," Corvin cawed, "Need I remind you of the catacombs of Mech? You'd be blasted to bits if it weren't for my quick processing and eloquent handling of the situation. –or flawless flying, I might add."

Marie was amused. "Yes, I suppose that's true. But I won't go into you almost getting us killed by ThaltechMega. More firepower than brains..."

"It is my duty to defend, Princess. I can't help it. It is my programming. But more than that, I do so willingly."

"Just don't let your need to defend erase any and all sense. You're lucky you weren't decommissioned long ago," said Marie.

"Luck?" He paused then. His oculars cycled.

"Corvin?" Marie felt a sudden tingling in the chip just behind her ear. She felt strangely analyzed. Corvin immediately dropped his gaze. The raven general's sudden silence disturbed her. "What is it?" she asked him.

"I'm sorry," he said. "Your new coding allows me to see things I haven't...or perhaps shouldn't."

"Tell me," Marie said.

"I sense something."

"What? Are you realizing what it means to be cared for, General?"

He shook his head. "No," he told her, his tone seemed strangely reverent. "I sense another essence about you." Marie felt her throat tighten and she swallowed hard as he continued to speak. "Another being yet unnamed, nothing more than a spark of life really...the word mother..."

"You sense that too," Marie laughed again, but this time it was mirthless. She felt strangely embarrassed. Uncertainty crossed her face, then resolve. "It's all new to me, I must admit. Unexpected. Lots of confused feelings. I've only known a few weeks; the child can't be much of anything right now. Anyway..." She couldn't continue. She hoped that statement would be the last of it.

Corvin seemed to still be processing. "Ah yes, I sense in your features something now that is not at all contentment."

Marie sighed. "I'm unsettled as a matter fact. The future seems somehow less bright, sadly. You live for protecting. I live for captaining starships. I lived for a man once—well, he would tell you he lived for me and I was the one who was always running away and using him. Things don't always go like they are supposed to Corvin. No matter how well planned, how well programmed." She bowed her head. "This doesn't have to make sense." He had an impulse to inquire further.

Marie felt frustration overcome her. The silence between them was unnerving. She almost felt as if she were conversing with Commander Brandon Sheng himself for all the uncomfortable pauses. The need to push reality away again flooded her entire being. "Don't worry about me, Corvin—or my features," Marie said pulling him out of his processing loop. "We need to save Hout and Luscinia. Magnus must be destroyed once and for all." She pulled his giant hand to her cheek and laid his cool steel palm against her flesh. "Please be careful, General" she said looking to his eyes, but no matter how hard she searched for the raven being that she thought might lay within, she saw only her own reflection peer back at her from the depths of the yellow-illuminated glass. "I care about you," she said, the words came out strangely hollow with the realization that he may be nothing more than a machine. This made her tremble.

"Care," Corvin said, almost entranced. He seemed to cling to the words of the statement with gratitude and for that Marie was relieved. The raven general then stuttered back to a more conscious state. "Yes, then I must," he said, resolved.

"Take this." Marie was relieved to change the subject. She placed a communicator bracelet on his wrist. Four buttons decorated the top. "Illuminate amber when you reach the city Aramen," Marie instructed. "I will illuminate blue when Randt is found. Green means proceed. Red means attack forthwith with the full force of the lycorma army...that all other plans have failed. The last resort." She latched the clasp and released his hand.

Corvin touched the bracelet gently and nodded. He seemed reluctant suddenly. Marie sensed this was about the baby, but she would not hear of any more talk regarding the matter. She already felt horribly exposed and perhaps proven inhuman.

Corvin only stood and stared at her. "Hurry now," Marie gasped harshly at him, feigning anger. Quick hot tears stung the corners of her eyes. "I will lead the others to find Randt as fast as I can," she said quickly hoping the raven general would not discern any more errant emotion from her. "We must follow the plan." Not waiting any longer for a response, she turned away from Corvin and fled down the heavily damaged turret stairs. She heard the raven general let out a readying caw, thankfully, and braced against the earthen wall of the stairwell as the lycormas launched their frenzied bodies into the churning, sallow atmosphere above. Clutching her fist to her abdomen, she watched as the army disappeared into the troubled darkness beyond.

EPISODE 29.

Smuggler's Crossing.

The secret passage leading out of the City Beestje was a tin roof-covered trench which the bug bots used to bring in refined piezo apophyllite crystals to the city from the Tweelach village. The AmphibioMechs mined and processed the crystals. It was not long before Marie learned more illicit details of the Orzos in the days following the fall of the Golden City and the breaking of Hout. Eumasta, a talkative kings' guard, was all too happy to share with Marie how expertly his soldiers smuggled in and hid the energy substance, keeping it safe from the greedy hands of a dying race of machines scrambling to get their fix. The Orzos, in their final days, would commonly attempt to ambush the Beestjes who delivered the life-giving piezo to the city.

Eumasta had left the side of the Globulares to ride by Marie. The mole cricket the princess rode kept up a plodding pace behind the royal entourage which included the Globulares, asp, the mantis minister, Tre, and quartet of pages who held the remnants of the ceremonial canopy, the one which Corvin had crashed through during the battle. Marie could not help but find merriment in watching the tattered fabric and crooked sticks swing awkwardly, almost bending to collapse, with each step. Still the royal pages held to their task with honor, and no one mentioned the obvious damage.

Eumasta whispered to Marie behind a small, crooked hand: "the reason the Orzos were so thirsty for piezo was that they had taken to the nasty habit of infusing their andro-blood port with massive amounts of crystalline liquid...of course such a horrific gluttonous thing is strictly forbidden by the laws of Saint, but they ignored such edicts and look what happened."

All Houtans, Marie discovered, could run on piezo batteries. Even her electronic armor had a sacred port that stored the precious material. But to inject such a substance directly into a system, according to Eumasta had monstrous effects. "These vile processes eventually infected the Orzos' internal coding. They soon became angry and had an unquenched desire for killing and destruction—pity how beautiful ones, once so peaceful, loving, and joyous could be turned into lawless fiends of chaos."

"Forbidden knowledge..." Marie mused, she looked over to Tre. The mantis minister nodded to her, but he would not chime in on the conversation. He held to his story with strict confidence. Was this method of piezo infusion what Magnus taught the androids? Marie surmised his intent was to use their thirst for pure piezo and its effects to turn the Orzos into his personal machines of war. She remembered the vast killing fields upon her arrival. Strewn with body parts and andro-blood. At the time it seemed nothing more than a mass of cold, anonymous, robot wreckage, but now, wearing Crysanthia's armor and knowing the horrific story, Marie's heart ached for the beings who were involved in their own mass extermination. The weight of Crysanthia's conscious weighed heavily on Marie, almost as if the armor she wore somehow invoked Mesmos herself—or, perhaps, it was the events aboard her own starship, the memories of the carnage that Magnus leveled against her own crew, that held an accord with the Orzos queen. In any case, the wellspring of dark and depressing emotions of regret and sadness sought in this moment to overwhelm her.

"Detestable. Detestable," bobbled the noble, Bell Bearers.

"The Royal Globulares have spoken," the asp called out into the cramped darkened passage.

Marie looked to Nines who followed closely behind. Quilp was seated on the head of the mole cricket he rode. LUCY floated beside them on foot jet feet. The little bot seemed strangely quiet. Marie had told Nines about the history of Crysanthia Mesmos, just before they left the city Beestje. In the secret conference she had detailed all of what Tre had told her regarding Magnus and the Orzos queen. Nines corroborated Tre's claims by what he knew: "M...Magnus was angered endlessly by what happened in the Golden City. Losing control of the Orzos clan drove him in his angry pursuit to take over the Aramen, even to the point of desperation."

"He was afraid." Marie said.

"P...Perhaps yes, of losing control. Acquiring Randt was an obvious boon for him. His saving grace and the beginning of our misery. To finally gain control of the Aramen clan and to re-solidify his hold over the Mechs via more mind-control coding emboldened him even further. Mesmos had been the one to initially initiate the Mechs into Magnus' schemes before Randt's abilities solidified his power."

"Crysanthia later regretted helping Magnus," Marie lamented.

"It...it led to her destruction. Of that we can now be sure," said Nines.

"And Magnus spun the whole thing in his favor to the rest of Hout to the point of making it seem that he was a savior: 'taking care of the Orzos threat'—a menace he created I might add—'reigning in the Aramen' (by reprograming them to do his bidding) and making it seem as if he took control of the Mechs whom he, in reality, is using to create more war machines..." Marie remembered how much the Volgens had been bamboozled by the cyborg, for good reason, she supposed now.

"He was nothing but complete in his perversion of events," said Nines.

"A master false truth spinner and manipulator. The Volgens believed him whole heartedly. Possibly the Beestjes and the Tweelachs as well..."

Marie's mind let go of the memory of the conversation with Nines as she realized she was becoming increasingly content in the confines of the darkened passage. The plodding straight ahead gave her some comfort. Who knew what would lie ahead? What dangers, what trials? She could only pray Magnus had not rallied more troops and ships to meet them in the hours ahead. She was sure, though, Magnus knew nothing of the smugglers passage through which they now traveled.

Eumasta had spoken earlier briefly of what lay beyond, of the apophyllite swamps where raw energy crystals grew plentiful just beyond the passage exit. Marie tried to discern a distant glow of the power gems but could make out nothing but blackness ahead.

"Several leagues yet, Mistress," Eumasta told her, predicting the manner of her posture. Just as the guard spoke, a green wireframe wavered into view, augmenting Marie's vision in response to her own inquiry of the passage. Crysanthia's armor had awoken another process. She scanned the length of the walls buttressed with lead pilasters which held back the earth from falling. Her vision sensed the metal columns up ahead up until the last. The readout showed the length: *4.759 leagues to be exact,* she realized.

"Nothing but darkness," she heard Quilp mutter. He clung to the large smooth brown head of the lurching mole cricket he rode awash in a dramatic air. Peering deeply into the cricket's dark, unflinching eye he posed the question: "Any sign of my maker, yet?" He seemed forlorn and tired, these last words he flung on the air carelessly as if their utterance might materialize the master before them. "A foolhardy wish..."

"Why such despair?" Marie asked him.

"Careful, Quilp, you may run your charge out with your constant emotional processes," said Eumasta. Quilp had just received a fresh power-up in Beestje.

"We will find Randt," Marie said, then looking to the LUCY for some response to her encouragement. The small girl bot stared straight ahead. No acknowledgement.

"By the time we reach Tweelach, of that I am certain. If not within the city itself. If the Beestjes said he came through only a few Houtan cycles ago..." Nines said.

The LUCY remained silent. This worried Marie. She knew the small bot had grown fearful since leaving the city and Dove had done a lot to comfort her. The boy had confided to the princess that LUCY's intense fear caused him to lose connection with the bot. That it was a constant struggle for him. And since the battle in the field of thorns outside Beestje, these bouts were becoming more frequent. "Dove..." Marie spoke to the small bot. Nothing, for a moment, then quietly, an eerie song emanated from the mouth hole of the robot, in the voice of the little girl:

"In the last days of the golden palace,
"I was the handmaiden of Mesmos,
"I brushed her hair, I held her hand,
"As the walls fell down around us,

"The monster was in the bedroom,
"The horror already inside,
"The Queen tried to rescue her people,
"But saved them instead with the blight."

Marie was startled by the song. The Beestjes too, all around they ruffled and sputtered with discomfort. "LUCY, your song," Marie whispered. Behind her, where the remaining Volgen tribe traversed the passageway, Marie sensed the seething eyes of Neophron train upon them from the darkness. She could sense a palpable hatred course within his processors. Perhaps it was Crysanthia's suit that allowed the princess such insights. Right now, Marie was only concerned for Dove and the bot which housed him. The little girl was about to repeat the refrain, but fear caught swift hold of Marie. She could not let LUCY continue. "LUCY," Marie said again to the bot, her tone was hushed and frantic.

"It just came out of me!" LUCY wailed in a frightened, plaintive tone. "I remember what I forgot..." –then Dove's voice: "Mam'selle, she has memories of the queen of the Orzos. I see them now—memories, horrific imagery; they fill her processors...but her hold on them makes...me... lose you..." static filled LUCY's mouth.

"Silence! Enough of this!" Neophron's voice suddenly screeched out, echoing horrifically through the chamber. "Evil falls from this robot's mouth, even still. Cursed thing. She will bring destruction upon us all!"

Eostrix moved to quiet the chancellor, but the vulture launched itself toward the bot.

"You *will* find destruction because all you believe in are lies!" Dove shouted back at the vulture gaining control, but then his voice was eclipsed by LUCY screaming.

Neophron, incensed, raised its staff against the small droid; the gnarled rod sputtered to life with pulsing green electrical energy. Marie flung herself between the vulture and the robot girl. The princess' eyes pierced him with their ferocity.

"This robot is your saving grace!" Marie shouted at him. "You will not harm it, or I will stand against you!" In her rage, her armor began glowing a threatening color of cerulean. Electrical pulses coursed between the gladiolus-shaped circuits on her arms and legs and lit up the bay tree emblem decorating her cuirass.

Neophron's oculars became narrowed slits of hate, he recognized within her a Houtan's intent to strike. Neophron lowered his staff and spat back at her through his contorted beak, "If this vile thing is our saving grace, then for certain we are all doomed."

"No! No! No!" LUCY cried.

Marie turned. "LUCY...Dove..."

The small bot flung herself out from behind Marie and screeched, "You will NOT destroy me!" Fear and flight impulses sent cycles of insane procedure throughout the body of the machine and then, to Marie's horror, LUCY's foot jets became raging infernos and the small bot rocketed down the length of the passage, quickly out of sight.

"LUCY!" Marie screamed and without a second thought, charged out in the direction that LUCY had fled.

EPISODE 30.

Swamp Monsters that the Blight Created.

"Dove!! LUCY!! LUCY!! DOVE!" The bot's heat signature had vanished into the murky swamp lands outside the smugglers crossing; no scan Marie could conjure within her enhanced vision could figure out where the robot girl had fled to. All around, Marie was met with nothing but rolling fog, slogging silver ground and the curling forms of blackened, ailing tree-like structures. And strewn throughout this forlorn landscape, tors of glowing lattice aggregate, iridescent raw piezo apophyllite. These glass-like crystals created labyrinthine walls and mounds stretching out far beyond the murky gray-yellow dimness of what was visible. A slight buzzing sound pulsed the quiet air.

Sloshing footsteps soon stole upon Marie. She turned. Nines and Quilp on mole cricket back, Eumasta on his bug steed came with them as well.

"She's gone," Marie said.

"Beautiful little creature. Wayward wandering soul, troubled to the last..." Quilp lamented.

"You're not helping," Marie admonished the imp and looked to Nines and the royal guard. "We *must* find her."

"Never fear, the Royal Globulares have headed out toward Tweelach, they are being cared for by my comrades. I will help you find the Contraption Youth," said Eumasta.

"W...we will branch out. Quilp and I will head Tweelach-ward, Perhaps, Eumasta will look to the left mists," Nines suggested.

"I will continue on to the right," said Marie.

"Very well," Eumasta replied. The companions were quick to launch off in their respective directions. Lonely stillness soon embraced Marie as she trudged onward through the swamp.

"Dove....LUCY...LUCY!!!" Marie yelled. She was uncertain if the bot would even respond to her cries. If Dove still had any consciousness or control, perhaps he could persuade the girl. But if not, hope may be lost. *There must be some signature, some sort of evidence of where she went off to*, Marie thought. Her armor's Mesmo-vision only radiated with the blinding auras of the piezo all around. "I can't see past these energy fields..." she said aloud, dismayed. Marie picked up pace and raced ahead through the haze. *Perhaps if I can get past these crystal mounds.* She frantically tried other means of detection. All wireframe showed were more outlines of crystal mounds ahead. "Dove! Dove please, if you can hear me, say something..."

A quick splash reverberated in Marie's enhanced hearing. Telemetry analysis displayed something moving along the concealed shallow waters just to her right. "Dove!" Marie ran out into the swirling mist enshrouded expanse. She could see nothing with her human vision. The atmosphere was chokingly thick. "Dove!" she shouted again. Then, without warning, Marie felt a flashing explosion thunder against the back of her armor. The force of the blast pitched her forward into the swamp. Water and muck filled her eyes and mouth as she tore up turf and water with her skidding armored body. Gaining upright stance,

Marie snatched her sabre from the scabbard at her side and frantically scanned the mists around her.

Rapidly narrowed ocular and caruncle of ruddy hammered steel, electrified into being, followed by a thrusting, coarse crooked beak and the hulking hunched-over black form of a vulture. It stood against her unmoving. It bore a gnarled staff it its taloned fingertips which it thrust across his body. The walking-implement-turned-weapon now raged with green static voltage and electrified the air all around them.

"Neophron." Marie's voice was a frantic gasp. Mesmo-vision analyzed him. Scrolling systems scanned the vulture's advancing form. Red alerts, plans of attack, and readouts regarding her assailant scrolled across her vision. Then she saw it, there was a ravaged cell within Neophron's system. Its source time stamp, pre-dated even Marie's arrival to Hout. The vulture had been damaged all along.

"Neophron, you don't have to do this..." Marie said, readying her sabre. She knew the trilobite could heal him if only she could convince him to put down his weapon. But even with this need to save him, she imagined LUCY slipping further and further away into the swamp. She became desperate, "please, put down your staff..."

Neophron didn't speak, the only sound that came from the avian-droid was a garbled sort of raptor screech. Marie feared language had left him and now he was nothing more than a robot with the clear intent to kill. Neophron thrust back his weapon with a clattering bolt, propelling it with agile robotic fingers, shoulder over arm, it became a rapid spinning disk. Neophron advanced. Marie anticipated methods to engage the dizzying force field of electricity. Perhaps recklessly she charged forward.

Neophron lurched at her, wings thrust back, neck crooked horrifically. He smashed his staff to the ground. Electricity erupted into a fountain of green fiery fingers. Marie was electrocuted by the charge. Despite the fires' energy that coursed through her armor, she slashed her sword at the vulture's neck. Neophron's fire stick clamored against her blade, blocking the attack. The air smelled of burned metal. Weapons stitched together with green lightning. Through gritted teeth, Marie slashed back. There might be no saving Neophron, she realized. Static, steel and charged explosions rang out in the atmosphere between them. Neophron flung the pulsing stick around; Marie jumped, somersaulted back, and met up the spinnaker staff, clattering electricity against steel. Their weapons became a mighty conflagration which served only to wrench her saber from her hands. The steel blade rocketed the air and splashed down, unseen in the mists beyond.

"Neophron!" Marie shouted. Whipping his staff back, Neophron took air on vengeful wings and flung his body at her with full force, his staff raged. Marie's armor took hold of her body. Defense mechanism executed. Arms slammed together, electromagnetic metal bracer blasting against bracer in an ear shattering clang. The fury of the expulsion forced her to her knees. Marie's body became an earthquake. Neophron was suddenly slung off into the distance on exploding waves of energy. His arms reeled and wings searched frantically for balance before he smashed down into the distant surface of the murky swamp. His staff let out faint gasps as its electricity was extinguished by the fountain of water.

Marie stood. She was confident. "I will take you to the trilobite, he will repair your damage," she told the bird aloud.

"Damage...d...damage..." the vulture's head was an epileptic surge of impulses. He seemed pathetic to her, a lump of crumpled robotics, fumbling in the murky waters for his staff.

Marie neared the bird. "Neophron, give me your hand." As she came upon him, a rumble issued from deep beneath the swamp. The surface of the silver waters vibrated frantically. Then as their raging reached frenzied crescendo, three hulking figures were vomited up from the swamp. Marie, wide eyed, stumbled back through the waters. Android body parts entangled in shapes of blight growth that had found means of locomotion and had reached monstrous proportions now lumbered towards her and the vulture. Her Mesmo-vision went haywire. With the new and present threat of the swamp-born Orzo-zombies, Neophron's processors also went into defense mode. His head whirred round to backward, oculars suddenly flared. His panicked screech was a siren on the mists. He propelled himself upright, grabbed up his staff and raged at the beasts.

Marie was sure these monsters only sought to devour. They now appropriated Orzo pieces for the last energy stores of piezo within their android veins to fuel blight that wanted to take shape and live. This couldn't be a good thing. Marie initiated a code. A compartment opened in her bracer and a photon gun nozzle telescoped out beneath her wrist. She backed away.

Neophron's staff was again an electric whirring of green lightning kaleidoscopic. He repeatedly flung the gnarled stick down, lopping up frenzied and desperate sprays of swamp water. He was a wreck of a robot just executing some broken desperate system to survive. The eruption of static danced along the beast bodies and only served to further enrage them. One of the beasts grabbed up Neophron's staff and devoured it within its own churning form. It seemed to grow larger. With new-formed black fists, it smashed the vulture and flung him back into the swamp. The monsters now turned to Marie.

Marie did not hesitate. She fired off a round of proton bullets into the monsters. Blackened fungus flung off in every direction along with Orzos legs and arms which had been held in situ within the dark material. But even still, the beasts advanced. Two beasts, coming close to one another, sought out the opposing forms and accumulated, merging into one. The large lumbering mass then slogged toward Marie. Many staring oculars from half hidden faces of long dead Orzos locked on to Marie with ghastly intent. Bullets only seemed to enrage.

Time to try another tack, she thought. Kneeling, she belted out another Mesmo-earthquake. Rings of energy blasted from smashed-together Mesmo-bracers, flung the massive monsters back into the waters. Rallying herself up with brute confidence she strode up to the mounds of waterlogged zombies and unloaded a rage of bullets into the beasts, disintegrating the zombie mass in fists full of fire. Her vengeful screams still rang out upon the air even after the last bullet rocketed apart a final bit of monster flesh.

In the aftermath, catharsis flooded her mind. She caught her breath and scanned the mists around her. Neophron was gone. Surely, she had lost valuable time in this pursuit.

"Dove!" she screamed and ran off into the mists.

At length, just as Marie assumed a safe distance from the battle site was obtained, taloned fingers suddenly found her body. Marie let out a cry as she was helplessly flung about, like a marionette on the end of a string. The puppeteer was a rapacious vulture, and its wings made a horrific controller. Steely, rust covered nails bit through mail and armor. Hands found their way to her neck and soon blackness eclipsed her vision as she was engulfed in Neophron's suffocating body. His joint gears moaned and hydraulic tendons strained. Her armor sighed under the crushing force. A loud Mesmo-alert rang out in Marie's mind. Searching all process, Marie found a pathway in the code and executed the saving process. Suddenly her body became a sonic boom. Rings of power and raging waves flung mists and water for leagues around. She was struck upright by Mesmo-force and through the rain and churning air she watched as Neophron rocketed back into the swamp, losing an arm, fistfuls of feathers and a foot as he splashed down and then was still.

The swamp settled around them. Marie's heart was a thudding battalion of beats. She felt her blood course through every cell. Her breath was deep gasps, she stilled the adrenaline-induced panic. All became still. She gave thanks for her own survival. Her armor scanned its resources as she was about to turn to continue her quest to find LUCY, but Neophron's twisted figure sputtered and rose slowly in the distant mists. *How much more could this ravaged avian-droid take*, she wondered. She readied to defend, when suddenly from behind Neophron, a gigantic zombie beast, one which easily eclipsed the three that had attacked them only moments ago, rumbled out of the gray air and engulfed Neophron's body. Momentary terror cycled through the vulture's oculars, a quick dilation of the lens, as the villain bird was folded inside the conglomeration of horror, followed by shrieks and electrified explosions as the gargantuan beast crushed the vulture within it. Neophron's disparate pieces, Marie assumed, would now become a part of the beast's nasty collection of decommissioned Houtans. He would be feasted on for what was left of his piezo charge.

The monster was not satiated, even as it consumed, it raged toward Marie. Marie did not have time to defend or run as the monster tripled in size and became a wave of hungry carnage. The carrion beast was eager to feast, and Marie braced for the churning promise of decommission. But just as the blight monstrosity thundered to overwhelm her body and take it, the beast was yanked midair by a force that awed Marie to her core.

The massive body, entangled in the mists above, hovered for a moment and then, immense vibrations expelled through each cell and induced a raging detonation. The explosion was massive, ear shattering and breath taking. Pieces of diseased Orzos and blight particles rained down in a great circle around her. And through the far-reaching debris field, smoke and electrified haze, Marie discerned a figure standing at some distance in the fog.

It was a man, of that Marie was certain. His stride was a prideful swagger. He wore a black duster and a flat cap. One hand was stretched out before him. An orb hovered just in front of his fingertips, surrounded by gyroscopic rings. The element hummed and he spoke to Marie as he came upon her.

"Peace then, my friend..."

Features came into view. A merry set of twinkling eyes peered out from beneath the dark half-moon shaped brim of his hat. Long dark hair tinged with grey framed his face and even grayer hair feathered the edges of an ample beard. Marie knew these eyes. Flashes of LUCY'S hovel and the artwork that decorated its walls came into her mind. The eyes were so familiar. Then she knew, she had seen them before. In the bot's drawings.

"You're human," the man said, his tone was mirthful and pleased.

"You are too—" Marie gasped.

"Curious," he said; then, "You wish to know who I am; I assume? Well then, you shall. Randt von Holland's my name."

EPISODE 31.

His Haunted System.

Magnus laid his weary head against Luscinia's egg. His body was exhausted from trying to break it. He could sense the form within the shell—perfect, unyielding and then he imagined the time he held Marie Antoinette's body close to his own, tenderly. "I knew how much you hated debutante balls," he said at last. "Satin ribbons...chiffon, the way ladies and lords of the court spoke politely to your face, then cut you to shreds behind your back all for their own pleasure—or perhaps to feel superior...."

"The Beestjes have downed our ships, only one remains. It has just arrived back to us. Our Aramen army was devastated, and they turned back, however we did strike a mortal blow to the city of Beestje itself. Still...no Marie." Hannah gave the report from a distant corner of the room.

Magnus did not respond to her, instead he continued the dialogue with the ghost of his tormentor. "Let's give them something to talk about—that's what you said to me, Marie. That sly smile, a woman on the verge of blossoming. You wanted to feel it all with me, didn't you?"

"Pull yourself out of this Magnus!" Hannah said. "We cannot lose another fight. Your mother has abandoned the cause; the failure to turn the Orzos to our will was the final straw for her—of that, I am sure! Such failures. And now the entire plan to rid ourselves of the Empire for good may be in dangerous jeopardy. You need to focus."

"I need. I need." He murmured.

"We are too close to getting everything we want. Magnus, darling." Hannah went to him and laid her hand against his steel shoulder. He did not seem to notice her. "How will I break you of her?" Hannah said.

"Break..." Magnus' interlaced processors where a hurricane of memories, feelings, and phantoms. "In those days of forced courtship, I knew you weren't ready to commit. So, I said let's have fun instead, hoping that one day you would choose me, like your grandfather wanted you to do. In a way...I suppose you did. At least for a moment. You plucked me up from the wild vines of youth and brought me into your arms. You *did* want to feel me once...I'm not crazy. You *did* want to feel me... We escaped the royal chaperones and the party in the grand hall of my father's house. I knew you were never the marrying type anyway. You were a caged bird of prey, perhaps now you would call me the same, are we the same, now, Marie?"

"We took my laser red speeder out into the Callistan night. Free from the confines of court. You left your party dress flying on the raging winds of the shattered black porphyry fields that led out to the wilderness from my father's estate. You were there, the girl beside me, ravishing, black-underwear-clad. The moonlight held your body like I wanted to hold your body. I allowed you to take the wheel and you piloted the conveyance faster and more daring than I ever tried..."

"Magnus," Hannah attempted to call him from his remembrance. He ignored her.

"This scared me at first, then excited me. I cheered and then bid you to pull over. You eventually complied and I was soon met with the dark depths of your eyes. They made me fear. I could not see what lay within those depths. They were almost soulless. They erupted desire within me. For what I could not discover in your eyes, Marie, I discovered in your sweet cinnamon-colored lips instead.

"It was a sweet, inexperienced kiss that soon grew into a garden of forbidden touches. Fitful and frenzied, our hands explored each other's bodies and with breathless gasps you bid me to thrust past any limits. For a moment both divine and torturous you were mine..." He languished on the memory of Marie's pleasure filled body, writhing on top of his as the starlight blazed around her hair and the fragments of Metis, a small moon which had left its once safe orbit for a closer dance with the gas giant, was pulled apart in a fiery cast across the night sky by the immense forces of Jupiter.

"You found what you wanted for a moment, Marie." A slight hurt smile flashed across his decaying lips. "For a moment she wanted me, then she never wanted me again. I never stopped loving her after that night..."

"Magnus..." Hannah stroked his hair and took his hand in hers. "You must forget her. The Mechs have created enough of an army to begin moving our warships into place. We will enact everything as planned and fly quickly toward Europa. The inter-dimensional warp cloaking technology of Adelphi Saint will keep our ships hidden until we launch the attack upon the capital city. The Empire will fall, and no one will know who pulled the trigger. Chaos, then we take control. You and me. Emperor and Empress..."

Magnus did not engage, he was too lost in the memory of her wedding day...

Magnus could still feel the cold steel of the proton gun concealed within his tux jacket as he mounted the stairs of the Chapel of the Immaculate Heart, the Dauphin's private chapel within the Imperial Enclave in the capital city on Europa. Getting past the guards had been easy, with a stolen invitation, lifted from his cousin who declined to attend. As he entered the church, Marie and Sheng were exchanging vows on the dais. Pope Innocent was just about to give them blessing when Killan yelled out across the aristocrat-packed nave.

"Marie!" His voice was thunderous and immense. Marie appeared before him a glowing slender ethereal goddess, her dress was form fitting, fit and flare, with an endless train of pure white which spilled out along the red carpet in bountiful excess.

"So, this is how promises are kept!" Killan's voice rang out against the court in defiance. Marie's eyes were fearful; Sheng pushed himself in front of her and senturions surrounded the royal box where the Dauphin sat, others ran to surround the altar and the bride and groom. Weapons were soon trained upon him. He expected this. "She was meant for me, Your Majesty! You made promises to me and my father! This is a disgrace!"

"Killan!" Marie shouted. "Don't!"

"Apprehend him!" the Dauphin shouted to his guards.

Killan imagined taking out his pistol and raging toward the apse, killing all who got in his way, including and especially Marie. Their blood-soaked bodies piled at his feet. Their horrified faces agape and startled, but his hand faltered. Instead of unleashing terror, he let it fall to his side, limp, numb and impotent. He hated himself for not acting.

"Of course I won't," he said at last. "You win, Your Highness. It always is about you, dear sweet Marie... your wants and your needs. Doesn't matter what you take or what you lie about...our what you break. You're all the same, you Antoinettes. My father was right about you. Our people suffer for this, I suffer for this..."

Senturions soon surrounded him, and he wrangled out of their grasp. "No need, no need!" he flung up his hands and strode back toward the door. "Your virtue died with me Marie!" he screamed. There was a clamor among the crowd.

"Killan!" his name was a curse on Marie's lips. That last word from the princess reverberated in his mind, even still to this moment.

"I couldn't do it then; I couldn't do it now..." Magnus said. Hannah hushed him and held him close. "I couldn't do it then; I couldn't do it now—I COULD NEVER DO IT!" His fists pounded against his chest and anguish filled his features, tears fell, and Hannah hushed and wiped away each one.

"It is over...hear me, Magnus? It. Is. over. Her family *will* pay. We will make them pay."

"She won't get away! Not this time!" Magnus screamed.

"Hush, hush my darling," Hannah kissed his lips and stroked his hair; she pulled his angry hands to her body and bid them to explore her breasts, her waist, her neck, her cheek. She kissed him more passionately, all efforts to soothe his savagery. What worked in the past would work again. Now her sex would pull him out of his misery. He finally looked her in the eye and returned her kiss with cold raw lips. His icy breath dove deep into her throat and she relished it.

"Yes," she said to him as he pulled her bodice away from her heaving flesh.

And as he drew her body close to his he spoke this tortured phrase: "Marie, yes, Marie....one last time."

EPISODE 32.

Arrival at the Tweelach Ruins.

Tweelach was a massive, gnarled cone, an ancient stalactite reaching down from the hazy atmosphere. Its gnarled tip thrust itself down into the silver body of the swamp waters. Only a small portal and some crumbling steps leading up from the glassy gray surface served as access. Massive black creepers spilled out in terrible, thick inky sprays choking the surface of the structure. Dark portals peeked out here and there from beneath the diseased curtain. Lozenge shaped terraces jutted in all directions, spiraling along the sides of the formation, and housed more ample black forests of blight. This was once a proud city, of that Marie was sure. Now, however, it was only a cold specter hanging before them trapped and suffocated. Randt was correct, the city of Tweelach *was* dead.

Inside, a myriad of still-dark chambers honeycombed the domain. These were connected through with twisted labyrinthine staircases. The blight growth seemed to have left the interior untouched; however, the effect of the blight on the inhabitants of Hout was horrifically seen. Frozen bodies of Tweelach citizenry peopled each chamber. Among them, stone-still frog-headed beings with staring blank black eyes, armored in rust and ochre machinery and tall, deep-purple, salamanders wearing long chest plates studded with tarnished buttons, dark CRT screens, and spent electrical ports. These beings were all posed where the extent of their power had left them. Some in mid-conversation, some at their worktables and others manning the refinery mechanism—a huge pulley and cart piezo delivery system and distillery that existed within the hollow core of the city.

"We're too late, had we known this..." lamented Tre. The royal entourage was now taking up residence within a vacuous chamber just beyond the main portal. Marie assumed this room was a gathering hall of some sort.

"The vile swamp monsters must have sucked out all their reserves and the blight choked them off from the outside. They simply ran out of energy..." said Quilp. "I'm surprised they haven't been collected by MechWraiths."

"Barely anything can get through with this troubling blight," Eumasta told them. "We barely made it through."

"Good thing too...they may yet still be revived," said Tre.

Marie looked to Randt; the scruffy, mud caked man said nothing. Quite a contrast to the reunion in the swamp where the imp and Nines had rejoined them in their quest to find the LUCY. The meeting was still fresh in Marie's memory: how Quilp leapt joyously from head of mole cricket to come to cling around Randt's neck in an uncomfortably long embrace along with exclamations of "My maker! My maker!" squealing from his fishy lips. He would not let go from Randt. "Very well, my little one, good to see you again," was Randt's calm response. "So good to see you all." Randt then looked to Nines; the renegade Aramen nodded toward the rapscallion code master.

"We need your help," Marie told him.

"We best discuss this from within the safety of the city walls," suggested Randt. "It has housed me for several days...but I fear what you seek in the city will only serve to disappoint."

Marie was not sure what to say, but a bucking figure on mole cricket back appearing quickly through the fog saved her from commenting at the moment, anyway. It was Eumasta and he was carrying in his arms the small body of the andromatron that had caused them so much stress.

"LUCY..." (Marie remembered her worry.)

"Hi yo! Eumasta called, galloping toward them, his voice was panicked. "Get into the city, NOW!" behind him, an army of blight monsters raged ahead through the dark waters.

"Quickly now!" (Randt obviously thought it better to run and flee than stand and fight). There was no time to ready themselves for battle—and why risk losing? Marie's memory was a flash of flight here—fleeing through mist, only to be met by deep waters where the bottom of the swamp gave way abruptly to an unseen abyss. Marie and Randt rapidly took to swimming; the mole crickets fluttered a flight; the city steps loomed just ahead. Though challenging, Marie navigated the waters and felt utterly relieved once boot bottom touch the first slippery step of the city. She was even more relieved once she realized that the swamp monsters' flailing bodies where soon consumed up by the deep silvery fathoms. (Evidently swimming was not one of their abilities.)

The owl magistrate's voice called Marie out of the remembrance.

"Our own reserves have limited capacity..." Eostrix said nodding to the Globulares, almost as if on their behalf. Neophron's demise was a subject that had yet to be broached and Marie was not in any hurry to speak of the fight in the swamp. In truth, Neophron was not the only one consumed by the blight zombies. The asp and several other Volgens had been consumed as well.

"We have the means to begin the enrichment of piezo. I believe that should be our task. The knowledge exists within the mind banks of the citizenry. We need only access it and continue where they left off. Perhaps we can revive a few of them and then begin to restore their city as well as our own..." said Tre.

"A hopeful thought; these plans will take time. The monsters will not relent; if Tweelach themselves could not keep up mining the crystals without being starved out—what makes you think we could for any length of time?" Eumasta told them.

"Is this place any safer than Beestje?" The Royal Globulares chimed in unison. Four pages still held the royal canopy over the twittering little bots. It was now nothing more than tattered strings of tapestry, hanging low on fully bent and splintered sticks. Two guards were stationed close to the portal of the room. "How many Hout cycles has it been since we've heard from them? —we should've known something horrible occurred," the royals put small hands in front of mouths to display fright.

"But if Magnus and his pirates think that the city is overrun and no longer functions, then perhaps Tweelach is the safest place of all," said Tre.

"We must fight our way back to Beestje, there is no other way...Hout is dying, Tweelach is evidence to this. We have no recourse if we stay here, but to wait to be extinguished," Eumasta was adamant. "At least we may stand a chance back at Beestje."

"Our only hope now lies with Corvin and the destruction of Magnus...how will Hout ever be set right again?" said Tre.

Randt bowed his head and moved away from the conversation circle. Marie watched as he took a seat in the shadows by the lifeless body of LUCY. The andromatron was piled up by the feet of Nines at the spot where the renegade Aramen had taken to the darkest corner of the room. Quilp followed Randt into the dimness.

There was a momentary conversation and then all agreed. They would be ready to leave Tweelach within the next few Houtan cycles. Probabilities of a successful return far outweighed the possibility of a complete and total slaughter.

Marie glanced at her communication bracelet. All the lights upon it were still dark. Corvin was not in place. *How much longer*, she wondered. She thought to light up the blue button to signal that Randt had been found. Something stopped her; Marie wanted to talk to the master coder first. She was curious as to what thoughts lay behind his enigmatic, leather clad exterior.

"You need my help," he said as she approached him. "I suppose the Beestjes do as well. I have gotten adept at exploding swamp monsters," he said with a laugh. "That's about all I've become good at—that and running..."

At least he was an honest man, Marie thought. A look of turmoil crossed his muck-plastered face. He would not look Marie in the eye. Then he said, "Why are you here?" Who are you?"

"A woman Magnus hates above all others. He invaded my starship. I crash landed here. My name is Marie Antoinette..."

"Marie Antoinette, the princess of the Imperial Colonies?" Randt looked alarmed. But he seemed to know of the plot. "So, the beast succeeded in his task—his attempt to test Mech war machines on your poor ship... he knew of your sacred mission to Cal'vary. He received intel from an insurgent in your ranks. You are the princess...I should show respect..." He took off his hat, muddy steel colored hair erupted around a dingy bald spot.

"You saved my life. For that I will be forever in your debt; Hout and the Imperial Colonies need your help."

"The Empire!" Randt scoffed. "I have such power? I am cursed, Marie Antoinette. Cursed by the stars, by ability and fate. I'm no good to you. Besides, the Empire can save itself; I am no friend of your kingdom. They are not a friend of mine either." Marie was disheartened by his unwillingness, but she was not surprised. She was sure Randt probably resented the crown just as much as she did.

"The Empire is not perfect," Marie admitted. "But there are innocents within the colonies that must be protected."

"Sounds like the job of a princess, not a criminal and a refugee like me," Randt said as if that was to be the end of the matter. "You should be wary of the company you keep."

"There are great evils in this universe Randt," Marie persisted. "I don't think you're one of them. You may have others fooled, but not me. You may think a woman in my position might have all the power in the world, but I too am powerless. All my life I've only been a hand for something else, an unwilling agent...a prop. I ran—just like you." She could see his eyes lighten. He was about to respond, but she continued. "And maybe I'm still running. But if I run away forever, I will never have a voice. I will never be seen. I must turn around and face the ugliness before it's too late for me and for the Empire. I must, for the future. I need your help Randt. We need you to undo your programming of the Aramen in order to overthrow Magnus and his war machines..."

"I'm not sure...Killan." Randt wrung his gloved hands. Marie was surprised to hear that name come from the coder's lips. "The beast is persistent. He even overcame death."

"I am aware of that too," said Marie.

"He won't stop until I am destroyed. Of that, I am sure. He captured me and my family during the Callistan civil war. My grandson and daughter were put in an Argentine encampment. My son and another grandchild killed by Killan's soldiers. Killan wanted me for my ability to analyze and manufacture exquisite types of codes—Saint level codes."

"But you escaped," said Marie.

"Yes, I was able to save my family from the camp and we became refugees in the colonies. We took a new name, and I became a simple automaton maker at a robot factory orbiting Io. It was the company started by Adelphi Saint over two centuries ago. Advanced Adelphi Robotics—you might know it as Robotolux. 'Machines created for everyday life'. I could program hundreds of automatons an hour. I was good at my work. I knew my place and my family was safe, but there were abusive practices. I knew we couldn't stay. I wanted to save my grandson and my daughter. I stole an artifact from AAR's secret vaults. It was a key, a special key—"

"It's how you came here. Quilp told me the tale. The Hout key, how you were pursued by Disciples of Saint."

"Evil guardians, horribly possessive of Saint-knowledge. They shot me," Randt laughed. "Just before I opened the portal to escape. I wanted my family and I to live here happily. I thought this place was a Shangri-La. It was once—before Killan came here in order to be resurrected and morphed into the monster cyborg, Magnus. He's turned this place out, fleeced Hout for all of its resources and inherent beauty and joy. All the things that Adelphi imbued in it to become his 'perfect place'—where machines worked in a sacred ecosystem fueled by his patented nano-tech cells..."

"You couldn't escape Magnus."

"No. What a horrible coincidence that he had taken up residence in the one place where I fled...and I became his pawn yet again. –I've tried, Princess, I've tried to save people before, but apparently, I can only save myself. It's really best if I don't interfere."

These words seemed to affect Nines, who bowed his head in dismay. Randt looked over to the Aramen nervously. Marie didn't need to defend Nines' position. It was obvious. The fact that the Aramen had valiantly helped Randt escape, killing his own kind in the process for the promise of one day helping his fellow people escape the mind control of Magnus. She could see it in Randt's face, he felt detestable. The horrible thing about it though, Marie sensed, was that the master coder had become used to feeling that way. He did not want to change. He was caught up in depression. He had only given the Aramen hope in order to use the renegade in his personal effort to escape the cyborg monster.

"Isn't it too late for that? To turn your back on Hout?" Marie said. "What if I told you that we have your grandson here with us right now?"

"My grandson?" Randt's eyes trained on the princess. They were a mix of hope, fear and hurt.

Marie nodded to the imp. "Quilp...re-activate the LUCY."

Quilp looked to her astonished, but he seemed to realize the importance of the task. "Alright, but be prepared," he warned. "Nines," he said to the renegade. "I may need you to hold her."

The Aramen nodded and grabbed hold of the little girl by the shoulders. Quilp took in a whirring mechanical deep breath of preparation and flipped the switch housed in LUCY's neck ring.

LUCY's crystal citrine eyes flared bright. Her whole body became rigid, then horrific screams issued from her mouth hole. She tried to ignite her boot jet feet, but Quilp ordered her to be calm. She was a clunking writhing mess of panic.

Marie went to the bot girl and stared at her directly in the eye. "LUCY you're alright, you're safe here. We are in Tweelach now and Neophron can no longer harm you. You are safe...I need to speak to Dove...Please, let me speak to Dove, allow him to come forward..."

Randt turned pale, the name. "You know him..." he said in awe. "How else could you know my grandson's name?" The master coder said this almost as if he was trying to convince himself of the truth.

"I've circumvented her jet feet. She won't be able to run," said Quilp, having turned a hidden dial in the girl's hair.

"LUCY, LUCY, listen to me. There's someone here who needs to speak to Dove. His grandfather, Randt."

With that name the andromatron sputtered, the eyes flared even brighter, and the LUCY let out a horrible gasp.

"Dove, I, no...Dove, I won't be destroyed!" cried LUCY, then "Mam'selle! I see! ...I see you! Poppa!" Sparks flung from her chest plates and from beneath her copper hair. Inside, great processes whirred. "I'm sorry LUCY, I'm so sorry, I have to see—" the boy cried out, then the girl: "Dove...I..." these last, sad words faded on the air. "Poppa!" the little bot's citrine oculars sparkled, and the body animated and clamored across the floor to jump into the master coder's arm.

"Dove! Dove!" Tears sprang from Randt's eyes. "I can hardly believe it my boy. But how?"

"I hacked in, I wanted to find you so much."

"Where are you Dove?"

"Trapped far away...being held. Prisoners; Momma and I—the Empire..." Dove looked to Marie she nodded back to him. "We were captured. I found the code under your pillow..."

"The synch cypher from the Hout key," said Randt.

"Me and Momma are here..."

"They are being kept in a coma, in a viro-electric power plant..."

"Oh my God, oh my God my poor boy," tears sprang to Randt's eyes. "What a horrible mess, what a horror you endure! It's all my fault. My boy, my poor, poor boy. I thought I was doing you a favor by leaving you behind. The Disciples of Saint wanted me dead, and I was sure they would kill you too. I had to lead them away from you. But now I see, I only did you the greatest harm. Had I known, I would have never stolen the Hout key from AAR. You reap horrifically what I've sewn."

This seemed to satisfy Dove. Marie at first had been afraid that this reunion might be filled with more pain for Dove, but gladly Randt knew the results of his actions. She also knew Randt's understanding, now, of what happened to Dove, would be the impetus for which they would get the master coder to re-program the Aramen and help in the process to overthrow Magnus.

"You have to help us now, Randt. Your grandson needs you. Hout needs you...and I do as well." Suddenly the amber light in Marie's communication bracelet illuminated. "Corvin has made it to Aramen. We must act," she said and replied back to the raven general by illuminating blue and then green.

EPISODE 33.

Corvin at the Gates.

The cavernous expanse surrounding the Aramen city was the darkest realm Corvin had ever seen. He was sure he never wanted to see it in the first place and thought he never would. It was a marvel to be sure—to commune with those the Volgens thought mysterious, strange, and untrustworthy. The vile and repugnant act of destruction and terror that the Aramen had exacted upon the Volgen city, no matter the true cause of their behavior, enacted harsh programming to cycle rapidly within him.

As Corvin and Renardii neared the crest beyond the forest which overlooked the city and the downward path towards it, three Aramen appeared through the ultra- violet-lit fog. The quality of light here doused their ruddy cloaks the deep shade of dried human blood. Corvin was tense, his gears and joints locked in heavy consideration of the red mages. He fought every process within him—subroutines that bid him to fight. Each mage came before him and Renardii honorably. True to Nines' word, these Aramen did not melt them down with fire sprays, but instead they held up silver hands of peace. The wizards identified themselves: 99, 9,999 and 99,999.

The Aramen sought to connect with the Volgen and the Beestje via internal means. This type of communication was strange and unnatural for Corvin. These were indeed dark magicians. Corvin at first resisted the Nines' infusion into his system. They were searching out his orders and they verified that the Volgen and Beestje were here to help, not to harm. *At least we are on the same page with their mutual concern*, Corvin mused.

"[...O...Our brethren have b...bid us to come and so we have. W...we...enact 999's orders. We p...pray this will lead to restoration and the...S...senStone will once again be our solace and host, again completing our one m...mind...]" Codes of deep hurt and fracturing followed these words. Corvin found accord with his own feelings regarding the destruction of the Volgen city.

The raven general was desperate for news of Luscinia. "Magnus has imprisoned our priestess within his throne room, we ask that you take us to her. Our comrades have found the master coder. He will help to break the spell Magnus has placed on your people in return for your assistance."

"[The n...nightingale priestess... she rests soundly; even still against Magnus' attempt to break her. She is w...well.]"

Renardii peered cautiously back into the dark wood behind him. The army rested beyond this place, deeper within the wood, beyond Aramen detection. There, thousands of lycorma quietly nestled in among black bramble and vine to await an order of attack. All now lay under the command of Zelus.

"[...T...The blight here thinks to consume, but it has yet to make the leap from object to being as it has in other realms of H...Hout. You and your army should be safe in this environ...for now...]" the Aramen told them. Then a cacophonous trilling of three voices: "[f...follow us/follow u...us/follow us...]"

The trio provided a scrambling shield so that the small envoy could pass under their possessed brethren's Aramen SenSight undetected. Renardii and Corvin were led down the jet-black porphyry trench into another thicket. There the blight vines became arbors of far-reaching fingers, woven together in strange grotesque ways. Slender lines of the indigo city glimmered hauntingly through spaces between the enmeshed creepers. Down they went into a hollow. Here the shadows were deep.

Corvin peered down at his closed-circuit communication bracelet. Three lights glowed: amber, blue, and green in the darkness. Zelus and Renardii had also been given tokens of similar design and function. Red remained unlit and he wondered at the probability of having to use it. Calculations progressed involuntarily with the initiation of the idea. Then, just as quickly, a number spat out annoyingly across his vision. It was indeed a dour percentage. He chose to thoroughly ignore it. Instead, he initiated a vid remembrance of Marie—their last conversation on the ramparts of Beestje. This program execution soothed his processors immensely. He hoped to see the princess again and mused at the fact that they were once enemies. Marie's fiery words in the council chamber; they grated upon all his processes. Luscinia tried to change his mind about the human woman, though, just before the horrific attack on the Volgen city. She said things which both confused and angered him. The nightingale priestess had been right, though. The human woman had proven trustworthy, valiant and was indeed a powerful ally. Luscinia could see things he could not, Corvin realized. He needed her. He joyfully anticipated once again being in the calming company of the wise priestess. Something resembling deep desire and love swelled in each cell of his robot body.

The black trail snaked out into a bridge which cast itself precipitously from the mouth of the briar entanglement along a chasm wall and across a lake of molten violet strewn with a floating lattice of ebony blight. Up ahead a doorway was concealed, a long unused entrance to the city and one which gave the comrades safe passage into the city. In the yawning amorphous mouth, Aramen 999,999 awaited them behind an iron gate appointed with archaic and odd filigree. He was linked to 999 back in the realm of Tweelach.

"[T...there you are. Honored to see you again my friend.]"

"Nines..." Corvin recognized the signature of the voice. Just beneath the shadows of the Aramen's cowl, encased within the ocular cranium of the mage, Corvin could make out several figures: the green-lined, staticky image of a bearded man in a strange hat and just behind him, peering over his shoulder, the beautiful and thankful visage of the princess. Corvin detected relief wash across the woman's face. "Marie..." Corvin whispered.

"[This is Randt, Corvin. We have found the master coder,]" she told him.

"[W...we must move ahead to the throne room, quickly now,]" said Nines.

Corvin and Renardii bid them to proceed. The dark passage ahead led to an indigo stairwell. The crew traversed the twisted stair quickly and passed through a portal into the city. Inside, slick-walled passages, shimmering and opalescent, branched out in labyrinthine and confusing avenues. The repdigit nines were sure in their task. They led the soldiers quickly through the strange and twisted pathways without hesitation. Chambers, still and quiet, studded the way. These spaces seemed sacred and hidden. One, Corvin guessed, was used for some sort of prayerful ceremony, another for piezo battery storage—here columnar containers lined a waxy gray wall etched with Aramen hieroglyphics. Another long passage followed, and then, a grand hall opened up before them. It had soaring ceilings of darkest opal and dangling geometric chandeliers with tapers lashed to each black arm. The candles glowed low-wave ultraviolet. Beyond this space, in an antechamber, was a gallery of Aramen paintings. These heroic frescoes depicted the red wizard's secret history. Extreme discomfort emitted from the repdigits. Corvin realized then these places were not meant for outsider eyes. He realized too these secretive Houtans were also betraying long-held traditions for the greater cause.

More passageways and stairs lay beyond, and finally, another yawning mouth led to a vast, wide open expanse. Corvin paused momentarily. He was cautious. In the grand courtyard, throngs of red cloaked necromancers took to mysterious and silent constitutionals. The quartet of repdigits bid the Volgen and the Beestje to follow still. Thankfully, they simply walked right past the hundreds of Aramen that crisscrossed the massive yard in a bold parade shielded by the magical forcefield the nines held over the intruders.

What lay in the center of the expanse awed Corvin and Renardii. There, a massive tower of glowing pale green and violet soared upward, past a dark oculus created from the vast fluted walls which rose from each side of the massive courtyard. Both the raven general and the Beestje lieutenant stopped, struck in startled silence, analyzing the sight with whirring wonder-filled oculars. The repdigit nines took hold of the foreigners and led them quickly along the shimmering pavers toward a bridge.

Corvin was at first alarmed by the sudden ushering, but his fears were dulled by the words: "[D...Do not pause. C...continue. W...we must always continue,]" they spoke in Aramen, directly into his CPU.

They rushed out along the catwalk that fed into a massive deep purple portal within the tower's edifice. Corvin determined that there were dangers below the causeway. At the bottom of the trench that surrounded the base of the tower was a glowing circuit board of charging stations. At this very moment, thousands of Aramen were being refueled at each power-pod. Among them thousands more wolfsdamsylflies sputtered and paced. *They will be ready to fight if it comes to it*, he determined, *their number well outnumbers our own.* He doubled down in his resolve. *Luscinia must be rescued without incident and the Aramen, reprogramed. Magnus must fall, and with a swift and undetected execution of plan.*

With a flick of a programmed repdigit wrist, the soaring slender doors of the tower swung quietly open. An octagonal chamber met them. Beyond, another doorway led to the central part of the tower, but the envoy went swiftly right. Behind a small, unassuming onyx door lay a dark and narrow stair ascending upward. Excitement, fear, anticipation warred within Corvin as they traversed the dizzying space. At length, they emerged into a long hallway with fluted walls marching on to eternity. The Aramen quickly led them to a smooth unexceptional portion of the passageway wall. The wizards placed their hands upon the shimmering opalescent surface.

"[Curious...analysis shows...the chamber is devoid of inhabitants.]" Then a swelling trill from all four, "[This is f...fortuitous/ this is fortuitous/T...this is fortuitious/Th..this...is fortuitous.]" Enacting a secret cypher, an internal mechanism clicked within the wall and a hidden portal into the chamber eclipsed open.

There, amid archways and amorphous stepped platforms and hollows, partially hidden in an alcove behind a grand fireplace roaring with ecru fires, shimmered a filigree encrusted object—Luscinia's egg. Corvin rushed over to it.

The egg stood silent. Corvin could feel the priestess within. Her processes were quietly executing. She was changing, morphing, he realized. He felt a sense a peace, a stillness in his own processing. Her influence only extended out a few meters beyond the pearlescent surface of the egg. It seemed all that would come into the egg's aura would be undeniably healed.

"We cannot move it. Can she be roused to wake and become herself again?" asked Renardii. As Corvin and the Beestje general quietly discussed, the quartet of Aramen went to the dais where the throne sat. Machinery now hung about the monolithic stone chair for the purposes of administering to the cyborg who now took up illegal residence here. Beside it stood the SenStone pedestal, itself enmeshed in sacrilegious mechanisms created by TinWratchet and programmed by Randt. Behind this arrangement of strange elements stood a now open window that overlooked the city and the dark void beyond.

"[There it is.]" said Rant, voice echoing telepathically from within 999,999. Nines bid his comrade to mount the platform stair and immediately the Aramen began unhooking and unhinging pieces around the glowing red SenStone. A terminal sat beside the column; Randt instructed the method of cable hookup and immediately fed verbal coding instructions via Nines to 999,999. The process seemed to proceed smoothly.

Corvin and Renardii meanwhile searched the egg and called for Luscinia to emerge. Corvin's words were hurried and longing. He suddenly felt more desperation descend upon his inner network the longer the egg stood still and silent. Then, from the catwalk outside the window, something swiftly moved into place.

Corvin turned to the commotion in the window just to see a swift swath of red pour into the room from the balcony beyond. Suddenly a concussion of static violent vibrations radiated out across the room. His body slammed into the wall beyond the egg. Renardii was apprehended, frozen against the floor in the same way. The repdigits where soon overtaken by a dozen of their red robed brethren, eight with silver sabers, and behind them strode the hulking cyborg awash in pious hate.

Corvin thought he heard Marie cry out in protest and Randt cursing at the same time.

Then Magnus spoke, striding down the steps from the window leading to the throne dais. He was pleased. "The Aramen veil can work both ways."

Hannah appeared from behind him in a clinging gown of sickly pale peach, it was as if her own skin had been flayed and rearranged back on her slender frame in a grotesque couture arrangement. Her eyes were seething sparks of emerald.

"I see you there Marie." Magnus flung a static charge from his fingertips and 999,999 lurched to attention before him, contorted and frozen upon the air. The cyborg coaxed imagery from the Aramen's cranium and caused it to spill out into the middle of the chamber. Marie and Randt came into holographic view, their forms made up of undulating green lines.

"-0- here found an anomaly, an anomaly which troubled it greatly. A disruption in the canvas of code which cascades over all his brethren. Dr. Krane and I discovered what you were up to. How feeble you must now feel. Your little plan is no more than a blip, a dying gasp for breath. It is a time for this to end, my dear Marie, once and for all."

EPISODE 34.

Her Death Vision.

Nines was also horrifically caught up in an imprisoned contortion. Marie staggered back as an image just as large projected out into the darkened hall at Tweelach from the face shield of Nines. Magnus' horrible countenance loomed in front of her in a ghastly epic proportion. The Beestjes who had made comfortable places to pause in the farther reaches of the space, stopped their quiet chattering conversations. Randt stumbled and fell to the ground. The cyborg's sight trained closely on Marie. His one human eye was a seething bit of hellscape and the mechanical ocular—a vacuous void which sought to dismantle and then consume her. Quilp shuddered at Marie's feet. LUCY's citrine eyes dimmed, and the small bot stepped back cautiously on clinking copper heels.

"There you are, Princess," Magnus said. He seemed to breathe her in perversely. Marie felt sickened. "You're a survivor, aren't you? You always seem to land on your feet, always get the upper hand." His icy words were choking velvet; his hoarse, guttural voice now seemed to purr like a hellacious engine that might never be quelled.

Marie prepared to speak, but Randt shot her an adamant look. Her eyes darted to him and he put a finger to his cracked lips and slipped his fallen body over to the Nines. A plan was brewing in the master coder's brain. Marie decided to let the madman speak. She prepared to take the entire brunt of his focus.

"I'm a survivor too. If you couldn't tell." Magnus bowed to her feigning pleasantry. "No applause for me? Well your hatred matches mine evidently. You're a heartless lecherous little fiend. How could you ever love anyone but yourself?"

"You're right, Magnus," Marie's voice was leveled and calm, but her eyes filled with intense disdain. "Only myself, right?" her voice sounded sickened. She simply could not resist speaking. Randt shot Marie an alarmed glance. He was in the process of accessing a port in Nines' back panel. Quickly he unzipped a seam in the center back of the Aramen's robe, opened a compartment and connected a cord from his coding bracer into the wizard's circuitry.

Magnus laughed. "Indeed. The fact is—all I ever did was love. I am an unending fount of everlasting LOVE!" his words blasted through the air, screeching insanely. "I was the bastard child of my father's mistress. I longed for him to love me. Did he? I loved him. I did nothing else but try to please him! I TRIED to please my stepmother as well. Ha! She showed me the back of her hand *repeatedly* in payment for my childish wants...." his voice became a whisper. "I showed her my heart and she showed me what the price of love was!" he screeched. Then rage, "I learned! But I still loved! You remind me so much of her, Marie. You too were my teacher, a teacher of what love can bring—you showed me so many things, Marie. From the first moment I laid eyes on you, I knew love...I showed you love, DID I NOT!?"

Marie fought to stand silent against his words, like Randt wanted, but the torture of standing there, saying nothing, was too great—finally: "You have suffered then," she said at last. "Only *you* I suppose. Bludgeon me then! Bludgeon me to death beyond recognition with your words!" Randt franticly typed codes into his bracer, he cast worried glances her way. She didn't care. "You suffocate those around you with your ideas. Your wants! I suppose you expect me to placate you. I suppose you expect me to apologize," said Marie, "...you want me to pay for every woman that's hurt you—that's what you expect...BUT I WON'T DO IT, KILLAN!"

The word made the monster cower. His own name superimposed over top of his stepmother screaming '*Imbecile!*' The word rent repeatedly from his stepmother's lips rang just as loud as his own name now uttered by the princess. It pierced through Magnus' brain. Again, he felt the hot flare of a hand, one hundred strikes, perhaps, but then on into thousands. The sharp edges of jeweled rings cutting into his flesh—including the massive diamond one which stood out above all others on her monstrous hands. He remembered it with agonized reverence, its unyielding, biting settings. How he hated that precious item, the token of his father's love. Magnus was certain his stepmother wore jeweled rings as elements of torture and these beatings were only the beginning. Sixteen years of abuse encapsulated in a moment, in an act where one crime became just like the others for they were plentiful and numbing to him and these ignited his soul into an endless inferno. He was that boy again, sobbing in the darkness, locked in the cellar of his father's palace, a secret servant of torture.

"You think I should not marry whom I choose," said Marie calling Magnus from his psychosis "...that I should've made you my husband...that I should not think to do as I want to do. Just because I let you have me once, doesn't mean you could have me forever!"

"And what did you do with that husband of yours?" Magnus erupted back at her. "Brandon Sheng. I pity him. You lied Marie. You lied to me and you lied to him. Is that your brand of love, careless duplicity? You carry his child, but he doesn't even know it. I doubt you even want him to know. Will you ever tell him? Do you really love him? Do you even love the child you carry? What kind of mother would you be anyway? A horrible one. Of that, I am sure."

His words became an insane echo. Marie's rage turned to rain. Endless, fathomless depths caught hold of her very soul. She moved to speak, but uncertainty crept in, sadness even. Was this *the* horrible and inconvenient truth?

"Look here Princess," Magnus continued. Suddenly the face of Hannah Krane filled the air, gnarled, claws choked with wire ligaments encircled the doctor's slender throat. Wide eyed, complete and utter fear rocketed through the woman's face. Hannah struggled to speak. Her own pale hands flailed out at her assailant, but these attempts were useless.

"Is this what you want Marie? You hate Hannah Krane, don't you? You hate her with all your precious little heart. Why don't I do what you don't have the courage to?" With groaning gears, he tightened his grip. Bones cracked and a fatal gasp expelled from the horror-stricken woman. In this awful moment, eyes of the past haunted Magnus in a cacophony of hate and fear and betrayal. His father, his stepbrothers, Crysanthia Mesmos...all flared out in his memory, but he brushed the images from his mind like bits of inconvenient ember. This was his cursed power—to exact forbidden vengeance and then seek more with relentless hunger. He felt his loins stir excruciatingly. Hannah's lifeless body slipped from the warlord's hands and now only the cyborg's contorted and rage-filled face filled the air in front of Marie.

"I'm coming for you Marie; of that you can be sure! No God, no lie or pompous righteousness will save you from that now!!"

Randt cursed in relief as he hit the 'enter' key on his coding bracer. A hastily patched together program executed. Suddenly the image of the murderer that hovered in front of them extinguished into darkness as Nines clattered to the ground in a pile of lifeless silver and red cloth.

EPISODE 35.

Fight in the Throne Room.

The electromagnetic air around Magnus short-circuited. Repdigits collapsed into sizzling, decommissioned piles. Randt's code executed; they now were sacrificed innocents. Corvin clattered to the porphyry floor, released from his supercharged imprisonment. A surge of elated freedom coursed through his processors. Immediately the raven general caught boots and charged full force toward the beast, letting off a barrage of mechanical bullets. Exploding fragments shattered around the warlord. The air sizzled then died. Magnus stood unscarred and flicked his battle ax from his left hip, a broad sword from his right.

"Your feeble world has ended Houtan. There is no hope for you."

Corvin bellowed a war cry. He flung his body at red robes who strode afront the beast. Silver hands sizzled. Flames exploded. His oculars flared. Bracers crossed, Corvin met the fire flash. His arm gears groaned against the fire force. The charged metal wrist plates glowed an angry red, collecting the energy blast and flung it. The blaze ignited wizards. Crackling red mage bodies tumbled away. Ferocious explosions scourged their bodies and then fizzled.

Corvin immediately fired another bombardment of mechanical bullets at the beast who stood mountainous behind the carnage. Magnus' cuirass ate the metal charges hungrily, each bullet landing cold and un-ignited.

Magnus cried out in rage, taunted the general, then readied stance and then leapt. Corvin flung his body, wide arced, grunting. He evaded Magnus' forceful broadsword sling, and met the back end of the body- shattering edge of Magnus' axe. Corvin yelped, bird tongue lashing out a shocked shriek. Parts of arm, leg and shoulder flung off. Sparking metal shell and circuitry clattered across the ground. *I must survive, I must overcome this offense*! Cowering down, wings became his shield. Unrelentingly Magnus thrust downward with broad sword, the carrion wings held, but plastid feathers sheared off in copious amounts. Sparks rained down along the black pavement.

Just beyond Corvin's struts of wing, the general focused ocular lenses on Renardii, his comrade, warring with red mages. The lieutenant clanged at the wizards ferociously with his electrified saber pistol. Fire sprays scattered out along the entire expense, setting the room a violet fit of orange. Renardii shielded and then rejoined in the battle, clattering weapon against silver arms and bodies. Glinting mage pieces shod off in a satisfying manner, several fell in piles, but more sages descended from the recesses of the chamber. The lieutenant met this new battalion with full force of sword. These new mages carried slender sabers. A cacophony of clashing metal and electrified hisses filled the air.

Corvin was emboldened. He desperately wanted to unleash a rain of terror and destruction upon the beast. The kernel idea of the beast's decommission imbued within him hateful pleasure. Vengeful processes took hold. This was final war. Corvin realized there was no turning back. Flicking the red button on his bracelet, he signaled to the lycorma army to attack. He plucked his black-flame-shaped-blade from where it had been lashed between his shoulder blades. Thrusting body and wings, Corvin became a powerful and dizzying carnage ballet. His weapon clattered with the beasts' furious two. The combatants tore up floor and column, the throne room eaten by blade and body. He found courage in his rage and, grunting, thrust every ounce of power to feed his fighting arms. Finally, the raven general wrenched the battle ax free from Magnus' taloned hand. Corvin's immense satisfaction was fleeting.

Magnus bellowed. The sacred throne room trembled. A seething grimace etched across the cyborg's visage. Corvin met the monster's gaze. The beast sought to devour the general with their fury filled gaze. Cawing, the raven general warred again, steel rent against steel, the two combatants became a hurricane of clashing weaponry.

Shattering steel, shots fired, sizzling electrified sword thrusts and screeching metal of Renardii's grunting mandibles caught focus in Corvin's ear. The general faltered and became victim. Humongous Magnus arms suddenly enveloped the raven. Corvin sought to fling out wings forcefully against the suffocating beast, but decaying-machine-ridden-vice-grip-arms only crushed into him relentlessly.

Shots shattered the air. Renardii blasted silver bodies. The Aramen fighters fell, but these were soon followed by more clanging foot falls and hissing fire sprays. These sounds were insanely ample. Corvin heard a death cry from the lieutenant and to the raven general's terror, a shod off orange and black arm still holding the valiant weapon of his comrade, clattered across his steaming black boots. Angry red alerts clamored within

Corvin's eyesight. Shooting gaze across the fiery throne room, Corvin witnessed writhing red mages hammering down with fire and steel horrifically upon the flailing body of the lieutenant. Then, finished with their task, the devils turned faceless silver masks towards their warlord leader who clutched onto Corvin with wicked mercilessness.

The beast, straining fingers, nails grasping raven chest plate seams, tore metal compartment open. Corvin let out a suffocated cry. His batteries were exposed. The precious blue glowing elements were now revealed to be defiled. Corvin grunted, ferociously flinging legs against his attacker, but they were useless weak things as claws wrenched loose the life-giving piezo cells. Corvin fainted to the floor. The drain was shockingly immediate. Only lingering piezo-electrons coursed lightly through his system and allowed him feeble consciousness. Helplessness, fear, and the concept of nothingness for eternity computed like an apocalypse across his senses.

EPISODE 36.

Story of Adelphi Saint.

Marie was shattered. Her heart was awash in numbness as if she had just been beaten until dead. Hannah's murder sickened her, and the beast's gloating memory made her want to vomit even more. She felt directionless. She clutched her abdomen. She wished to see the child within her. To prove to herself that it was real. She expected to feel something, a spark maybe—a wondering consciousness, perhaps. She wanted to feel awash in love and joy but was only awash in fear.

Magnus' words gutted her. *Aren't I allowed? I don't know the answers! I don't know. Damn this. This child...is the only thing. It lives but can I accept it? Will I know how to love it, do I know how to love it? Do I destroy everything I touch? Do I destroy? Like he does? Is it me? Sheng...turn and face it, another thing I must turn and face.* That proposition was daunting and mountainous. *But for right now compartmentalize, push it off for another moment. I must survive! Corvin...all is ending...I just must survive Hout and maybe make it out...with this child...will we survive? Can I do any good at all?*

Randt touched her arm. A distant and concerned "Mam'selle" fell from the LUCY's lips in the voice of Dove. Quilp peered up at her. "Are you okay?"

Marie wiped a tear from her eye and nodded. The room was silent. Then, "What are we to do now?" clamored out from somewhere in the refugee circle.

"The lycorma army is set to attack," Marie announced realizing the red lamp had lighted on her bracelet. "All other options have failed. Corvin..."

"He has a fighting chance. I released the electromagnetic chains Magnus held upon him and Renardii, but the repdigits..."

"Nines..." Quilp lamented the pile of decommissioned Aramen in their midst.

"We will have the trilobite repair him," said Tre, coming over to the group. He motioned for the tiny bot who had rolled up amidst the entourage in the corner of the grand dark room. The twittering thing clamored over and began immediately inspecting the silver pile.

"Doable....doable," it said.

"Our only hope is the army, Corvin and Renardii," said Tre.

"Magnus will not go down without an epic fight."

"There's something else we can do," said Randt. Marie turned her gaze upon him. "Adelphi Saint."

"You were on your way to find him," said Quilp. "Their God Who Lives in the Root of Hout. Where the Trail of Saint ends. He will help us?"

"In a way. The man is not here—that I must be clear about, but his mind exists... A mind. Well, a synthetic receptacle of a brain-like central processing unit that is an approximation or imitation of the brain of Adelphi Saint," said Randt.

Marie listened, mirthless.

"These Houtans have told you the myth of this tree, what has been programmed for them to understand, but to you and me, Princess, Hout in reality is an interdimensional space station that was designed by Saint, a whimsical experiment to some perhaps, but for him it was a desperate attempt to create beauty in a galaxy that only gifted him betrayal and pain," Randt told Marie. "Adelphi was indeed a man of great knowledge and he was *the* inventor of our millennia. Some say he was able to access Zero Point knowledge and was trained in secret by Janid priests."

(Janids were elusive ethereal beings awash in the complete knowledge of the universe. They made their appearance in apocalyptic times and most notably rescued the humans of Ancient Earth upon its destruction. They played a part in ushering in the neo-human race that could withstand, much better, harsher environments of planets and moons in space).

Randt continued: "Adelphi *did* begin robotics companies; he was revered, but eventually he was betrayed by those around him. He was more of an artist than a businessman. I doubt if he ever really wanted to be a trillionaire ten times over. After his companies were stolen away from him, he went into hiding—perhaps he hides still."

"He lived over a hundred years ago," said Marie.

"When one has complete understanding of synthetics, does one truly ever die?" Randt posed the question, pausing for delicious effect, then continued, "This knowledge is well hidden. The disciples of Saint make sure it is so. Anyway, in my research of Saint, I have discovered Adelphi came up with the idea to populate space interdimensional with synthetic tree-like worlds. These were complete ecosystems created and perpetuated by the elements found in stardust." Randt became obviously enchanted by the words he spoke. "Adelphi sent out palm sized probes into the galaxy and their mission was to seek out host time/space bodies. Once found, the probes implanted themselves, fed on heavenly elementals, gestated, grew, and became entire worlds. The primary architecture of all this—this is the genius of Saint—an atom-sized machine called a MechElemental. This is the basic building block of all that makes up Hout. And what controls his whole synthetic world, you may ask? —The palm sized probe sent out by Magnus' own hands. It still exists, the seed, an Adelphi 'brain' which acts as the CPU of this place. It is through this object that all of Hout is fed and controlled."

"So, we find the brain and we control Hout," said Marie.

"Right now, it no longer operates, it is broken I'm afraid. Through my investigation of this place, I have discovered a horrible truth...an errant code was placed into the system, a code that created the blight and decommissioned the brain of Saint," said Randt.

"Crysanthia Mesmos..." this was Dove's voice emitting from the LUCY.

Randt appeared pleased at hearing his grandson speak. "My boy..."

"LUCY was the handmaiden to Crysanthia—" said Dove slowly. "LUCY only just remembered it. Just before the swamp. LUCY witnessed the last days of the Golden City. She was very afraid of Magnus. She knew Crysanthia was afraid too and was planning to overthrow him. Mam'selle, the armor you wear was made for the Orzos queen—to complete that task...Magnus turned against the queen before she could prepare to fight. There are horrible memories inside." Dove's voice became a shudder, then, "He killed her, but before she died Crysanthia executed a defensive code—the code that created the blight and turned off Adelphi's brain. She sacrificed her world. She knew she must do this if Hout was ever compromised by man. It was in her coding to do this..."

"Finding the brain is the only way to gain the upper hand now," Randt's words were quick and true. "We must reset

Hout...restore what's left of its people. Once Magnus no longer has control of the Mechs or the Aramen—he will fall."

Marie nodded. "We best get moving then, quickly."

EPISODE 37.

Last Song of the Nightingale.

Corvin interpreted fleeting visions. Staticky, rolling pictures of the world beyond his body. The shape of the window past the crumbling Aramen throne wavered and then faded. Some darkness and then rolling frames. He caught vision of the SenStone pedestal that stood practically untouched despite the war in the throne room. The red stone softly glowed in the dying fires of destruction that littered the room. Then again, the window, his oculars focusing, repeatedly attempting to grasp hold on the world beyond the casement. Flashing, dizzying lights seared into elements of the frame. Armies of bright-lit bodies. Lycorma filled the darkened air. Amber sprays doused distant portions of the city. Flames erupted. Wolfsdamsylflies soared up from beneath the tower and out into the air carrying red mages who flung flames out into the atmosphere to meet the attack. The war was distant. Another crackle...and darkness.

Audio lingered in Corvin's memory banks. There were only small elements of energy lingering along the wires. The voice of the hellacious beast echoed, guttural unmistakable amid crackling fires and explosions. Corvin realized Magnus was engaged in a communique. It was once sided, perhaps the cyborg was wired to receive voice correspondence directly into his processors. "You are only making communication with me now!" The tone was incredulous fury "...you, who were responsible for such failures!!...You'd better be right about this...yes...keep the princess in your sights. Ping me your location. I want her for myself!" then he barked out across the room, perhaps to an Aramen servant. "Ready my speeder!" Retreating thunderous footfalls. Then silence.

Darkness. Corvin didn't know for how long. Music roused him from decommission. Then, he saw her. She looked markedly different, a silver-blue goddess of shimmering steel. Her face was immaculate—bright white, silver filigree decorated, studded with gleaming, deep fuchsia oculars. Her glorious sharp beak was long and slender, tipped in precious alloys. Her body was more viciously aerodynamic and highly decorated than ever before. Enormous silver wings erupted from her back. Corvin was sure he had never before seen such an expansive wingspan in any Volgen since his consciousness began. The nightingale priestess was indeed now a striking, humongous war bird.

Warm energy coursed through him from the battery well in his chest. It was an unusual sort of super charged thing. A beautiful gift from the goddess. It was mysterious and regenerative. He was awash in her. He looked deeply into the nightingale priestesses' eyes. "I fear I come too late..." she lamented. "Change only happens so fast, I fear." A melodious song of feathery graces emitted from within the priestess' body promising rousing elixirs of salvation. Corvin was enveloped by the song. He looked around. He was startled by what he saw. All around them, kneeling in reverence, were Aramen wizards, including roused repdigits, which had once been short-circuited by Randt's rescuing program.

"I can only rescue a few of these poor machines at a time, I fear. I must try to rouse more—out there." She motioned to the battle raging beyond the window.

"You may be destroyed, priestess, I cannot allow—"

The priestess hushed him. "You must do as *I* say now. I must fight the war even though it may be a losing prospect. But you cannot stay here. Pursue Magnus. Destroy him. If he survives, Hout will surely be lost for good."

Corvin was silent.

"Take these Aramen with you." Corvin looked to the red mages. They numbered twelve. It would be enough to have an upper hand of sorts, at least against the relentless lone monster. Corvin nodded. Luscinia caressed him tenderly and stretched her immense wings. Corvin was shook by her thunderous beauty. She cried out, war-like, and trilling songs burst from the tips of her shining wings. She launched herself, a flashing blue quicksilver beauty, out into the raging war.

EPISODE 38.

Temple of the 1000-Wing Scarab.

"There are two more cypher gates—guarded, I would imagine; then the core leading down to the root and the temple housing the brain of Adelphi Saint!" shouted Quilp as he scurried along the path ahead. It was a slick-stepped passage which spiraled upward suspended in arms of petrified stalactite formations high above the swamplands below. They had been quick to travel the interior of the decommissioned city of Tweelach leaving it for the upper chambers of the cavern. Heaps of black blight entangled the pathway here, each choking mass glowed amply with angry red feasting veins.

"You're sure it's this way?" Marie asked.

"I've committed the LUCY's map to my memory banks. Yes, I'm sure!" The imp shouted back. His words were tinged with indignance.

"My good fellow," Randt smiled. The LUCY rocketed by. "What clues do we have about this cypher?" asked Dove.

"I jotted some important information down," said Randt slowing his quick gait. He pulled a battered leather-bound book from his duster. The spine was lashed with frayed wire. He clicked on the brim-light of his hat and began leafing through yellowed crispy pages.

Marie paused to let him look, wiping sweat from her brow. A glowing crystalline substance came away upon her glove. Marie regarded the substance carefully. *Perhaps a byproduct of the bio-Mech fruit I ate back at the LUCY's hovel—or the infusion of Crysanthia's armor into my own skin?* She pondered. The armor seemed one with her flesh now. She breathed deeply for a moment and stood proudly, comforted by the metal plates of the suit that hugged her body. She enjoyed being gilded, electrified, transmogrified, blessed by robotic powers she had yet to discover. She was impatient and ready. Her thoughts went to Corvin. Stuck here in the darkness, she longed to do something—anything to try to get the upper hand on Magnus.

As Randt fingered through his book, above the rifling parchment, Marie discerned distant shuffling—footfalls perhaps—not their own, obviously. The skittering noises resounded with hi-fidelity resolution within her transponder, then became still. She scoured their surroundings. Trudging out along the path along which they had just come, she readied her arm blaster. Mesmo-vision showed nothing but blight veins. She walked further. The silence in the distance became immense. Somewhere up ahead, a bit of rock fell free, blight arms coiled and retreated away from the bit of stone as it tumbled across the path and out into the atmosphere below where it was quickly swallowed by the fog. A distant splash resounded back.

"What is it Mam'selle?" asked Dove.

"Nothing." Marie said at last, then, "blight...rousing to life...possibly... It must sense us." She turned back to the group. "We best be moving on."

Finally, Randt announced in the voice of a grand orator:

"Khephri-Dio, scaraboid warrior with 1,000 "wings
"Protect the sacred gravitational vortex

"With eye-lit disk and rays and wind;

"Turning over day to darkness unlatches
"The Sabre of Destiny in your gut;
"Open up the heavens to reveal the horror
"Of another cypher enigma;

"Caught between the wriggling Serpent of Ba'al
"And the maelstrom that surrounds the door;
"No mariner or angel or devil could solve
"What the force of destiny could swiftly cure;

"To open up, to destroy, access and acquire,
"Strike with blessed energy
"The lead eye of the beast,
"Channeling the lines between sacrifice and "crime
'To access the core of Hout..."

A mixture of intrigue and wonder cast across Marie and Quilp's faces. The LUCY's citrine eyes cycled brighter, then dimmed, as if Dove was deep in thought regarding the lines. "W...well," Randt stammered, he had been caught up in the moment of recitation, deciphering the ancient text with gusto. "...From Saint's Apocrypha," he explained, citing the source, "I divined this information from the heart of a MechElemental. There's an encrypted codex in every particle of Hout," he said.

"So, there's three challenges," said Quilp posing the question, tapping his fishy mouth with a tiny scaled finger.

"Saint didn't want his core processor easily accessed, of that, I am sure," said Randt

"It's almost as if he made these challenges for humans to discover," said Marie. "If this code lay all along in the inner working of Houtans and they never thought to seek out their source...he put it there for someone to find..."

"Was there ever any need before this?" the imp pondered.

"I think he wanted Hout to be found by his own kind," Dove offered matter-of-factly, "He wanted his world to be researched, discovered and traveled by humans—he wanted his realm celebrated."

"It may never have been discovered by humans at all. A strange place created on a futile hope," said Quilp.

"I doubt he ever thought it would be subjugated to make war machines..." Marie murmured.

"But there were safeguards in place. The blight for one. If left un-checked it will surely devour everything in sight. He knew the power of his invention and if it were to be defiled, then no one was to have it," said Randt.

"This is no simple invention or game," said Marie. "Quite frankly it's life and death. We'd better get moving."

The pathway led off in meandering ways, but Quilp was sure in his navigation of the path. This was more than just LUCY's map, it was almost as if the imp knew the way now, as if he was tapping into the soul of this place for guidance. *More MechElemental knowledge?* Marie wondered. It verged on the spiritual.

The trail was treacherous at places; they climbed up lengths of steep-stepped expanses. Vines clung at them hungrily. Then, as the companions reached the dizzying heights at the very tip top of the cavern, they came to a slippery ledge at a wall where the waterfall of dark vegetation cascaded over a precipice. The only thing left bare was a smooth oval piece of lighter porphyry. It was the color of bone, with faint cracks crisscrossing the surface. The formation appeared to Marie to be the top of a humanoid skull emerging from the black entanglement.

"Help me clear away the infestation," Randt said. They quickly took to pulling blight vines away. Dove slashed happily at each appendage. He had been given a slender sword by Eumastus. It was delicate, but sharp. He was content and gleeful in his work. The handle was a jade steel dragonfly. Quilp attempted to pull the blight away with only his tiny teeth and hands.

They soon realized the smooth exposed piece was in fact the tip of a massive stone-hewn nose. Marie was eager to uncover the rest. She clutched at fistfuls of the inky writhing masses. Climbing up further into the blight growth to grab more pieces away, a thick arm slipped quickly around Marie's waist. It clutched hold and bore her up into the air, squeezing and coiling. "Horrific pests!" Randt screamed, beating the vine arm with rapid-fire fists; Quilp latched on to it with tiny piranha teeth and Dove unleased a fury of Beestje sword slashes. It coiled tighter still.

"Stand clear!" Marie screeched. Wrenching her arms free, she hammered the writhing enemy with two rounds of wrist gun bullets. Released, she skittered the ground. A fountain of black blood doused her silver clad body. Each black dot suddenly became a writhing black tentacle of its own. Before Marie could react, the Mesmo-suit, sensing a penetration into its elemental makeup, electrified and toasted the small writhing vines, turning them to ash.

"Best be careful with these. Looks like they have awareness, and they want to procreate and appropriate," said Randt. He grimaced and clutched his brow. Marie stood and regarded the man's strange behavior. Rant suddenly beat on his head. The display alarmed Marie. "Wait, what, what? No! Silly, silly stupid me!" Randt suddenly yelled. It seemed like a complete over reaction to Marie. "Everyone, get away! Get, get away stand back...clear. Yes, the orb. I cannot believe I forgot... Stand back way clear, once it catches hold of MechElementals within, it can be hard to release again."

Marie shook her head, sighed, backed away. Randt thrust his stubby finger upon a strangely shaped button embedded in his wrist bracer. Suddenly a whirring commotion erupted from his duster patch pocket. Randt's orb soared out from the pocket and just beyond Randt's palm. With a flick of the coder's wrist, the rotating ringed spheroid danced out toward the blight cascade. "This will be much easier," he said to Marie over his shoulder.

The strange field of energy the orb created quickly cleared away of the curtain of blight, easily folding back arms of protesting creepers to reveal more of the proud nose they had only just began to discover. Then lips, round cheeks and eye sockets holding closed heavy lids, a brow ridge then a massive forehead appeared. Then ears with gilded oblong earrings and a diadem of gold and green. It was a slumbering stone giant, male humanoid face frozen and encased within the surrounding wall.

"What now?" Quilp said impatiently gesturing to the monolith face.

It was if the imp had been heard. The eyelids on the face slid open. Rays of gold darted out along the ground casting the black stone an odd gray-green. Marie braced herself. A distant rumbling followed. Soon the noise became gigantic and thundering. The wall around the massive head clattered, telescoping back revealing an ancient turquoise beetle body. Black steely arms ejected from the sides of its body as well as grand translucent blade like wings. These slid apart multiplying in an array, undulating, fluttering, vibrating. The enormous wings soon numbered thousands and whipped up massive amounts of air. They sent the bug flying overhead, shooting up, buzzing off into the ever-expanding room. Gold panels descended around the company; the ground they stood on transformed into an octagonal expanse. The entire chamber rose steadily upward, and a great dome appeared overhead.

Hurricane force winds battered their bodies. Marie ducked low; Mesmo boots attached themselves to the earth. Randt cowered too, grabbing hold of the crevices between pavers on the platform they stood upon. Fingertips digging in hard. "Hang tight!" grimaced Randt, who clutched tightly to his hat. Quilp ducked beneath the master coder's coat tails and the LUCY's foot jets strained to keep the small bot afloat amid the ravaging gusts rent from the wings of the mammoth scarab, Khephri-Dio.

Suddenly the room was doused in immense light. The illumination rivaled that of the sun star, the center of Marie's Jovian solar system back home. A massive disk appeared above the scarab, held within crooked forearms. A strange ocular appeared on its surface. The disk glowed brighter still.

"Shoot it? Yes? No?" Quilp screamed out.

Marie leveled wavering arm. "I'd say yes!" she screamed and fired off wrist gun bullets at the beast. The beetle cried out an echoing alert and blazing light beams shot from the disk, raining sparks, and blasted out yellow lightning down upon the group. A Mesmo shield of plasmoid MechElementals clattered out from Marie's armor to shield her from the blast. She bowed low against the raining tumult.

Randt tumbled and yanked out two homemade pistols from holsters at his waist. He fired. The beetle lurched. The levitating beast tumbled back and flung itself directly overhead. Then Marie saw it—a glowing blue element housed within the scarab's belly. Dove screamed out, seeing it too: "The Sabre of Destiny!" The little bot grunted electronica, shielding itself from more lightning blasts with the tip of its Beestje blade. The electrified charge collected by the LUCY's sword became powerful ammunition. The little andromatron flung back the lightning, gleefully dousing the beetle with its own power emission. The massive bug stuttered and clamored back. Sizzling electricity blazed along its abdomen, legs, and face.

"'Turning over day to night, releases the Sabre of Destiny in your gut,'" Dove paraphrased the cypher.

"Day to darkness..." Randt pondered, as another hurricane blast, followed by relentless electrified explosions, created catastrophe upon the octagonal platform. Marie bent down against the wind; body held almost parallel to the ground. She dug in, bowed her head. The light around them became blinding.

"The sun disk!" Marie called out; her voice practically eaten by the torrential air. She flung more bullets its way. An electrified blast clamored back; Marie blocked; Randt retreated and fired more shots as the wind pummeled his body.

"Turn the beetle over, shoot it out!" Quilp screamed, flapping wildly in the air, clutching to the hem of Randt's coat. The little imp suddenly hatched an idea. "The oculus of the scarab follows movement!" Quilp shouted. "Its body follows!" The wind quickly died down. Marie fired at the disk. It grew with electrified impulses. Quilp immediately skittered out along the platform and scurried, dodging sun disk rays with rocket launch speed. He leapt full force toward the massive attacker. Amid fistfuls of fire power from Randt's side pistols, Quilp shot through the air and landed squarely on the back of the beetle. Cries of jubilation shot from the little imp's throat. The beetle's sun disk oculus, prepping to send out another barrage of terror upon the company, paused in mid charge, now concerned with what threat now lay upon its own body. The eye frantically searched out the source. It lumbered sideways and flicked metal feet against the ground. It shook and bucked and Quilp held tight, gleefully riding the beast. In startled confusion and frustration, the beetle crashed itself into the ground. Thunderous tremors erupted across the platform. Marie and Randt flung their bodies across the earth to evade the humongous scarab. The LUCY scampered, fire-booted, back toward the edge of the platform as the beetle's steely legs clamored across the ground. Its movements were an awkward dance. Quilp pounded the beetle's humongous back with his tiny fists and yelled tauntingly at it.

Suddenly the beetle's wings spattered out commotion and the entire thing tumbled over onto its back. Quilp screamed as he was thrown from the back of the beast. The sun disk shattered. Shards flickered across the earth, then died. They were all doused in darkness. Only the glowing pale blue light of the Sabre of Destiny entrenched in the belly of the scarab illuminated the floating chamber. With the bug unable to move, legs turned skyward struggling to find ground it would never attain, the LUCY leapt into action.

"Grab it! Quickly now!" Randt shrieked, rising from the ground. Marie was wide eyed. She prepared herself to shoot off more rounds at the beetle if needed. Quilp joyously leapt up onto the beetle stomach along with the little bot and both pulled at the hilt of the sabre. Finally, the imp wriggled the elegant weapon free. Marie breathed a sigh of relief as the churning engines inside the scarab sputtered and became silent; its legs and wings trembled and then all became still.

Victorious, Quilp thrust the Sabre of Destiny above his head; he looked mighty and valiant for a moment. He shot Marie and Randt a proud glance and was about to speak when from somewhere within the chamber, a thunderous clap rang out. Quilp's eyes became disks of horror as his body catapulted, a fiery wreck, out across the platform. The imp became a clattering mass of sparking wires and exploding pieces. The Sabre of Destiny soared through the air, hit the pavement, and skidded to a sizzling stand still just before Marie's feet.

Horror erupted within Marie. The decommissioned imp lay in a steaming pile before them. Randt let loose a horrified exhale. Then, from the depths of the chamber strode two pirates, massive guns drawn. Both wore evil sneers plastered across their murderous faces.

EPISODE 39.

Darkness Surely Comes.

Marie's heart shattered. The darkness of the chamber devoured her. Kitrank and Faul's monstrous features glowed horrendously in the low blue light of the Sabre of Destiny's aura. The valiant weapon lay abandoned on the ground.

"Donnot, dare t'move," Kitrank grunted. Marie wasn't sure she wanted to anyway. She felt bound to the earth by immediate, suffocating sorrow.

"I suppose you thought you got the best of us Princess," rejoined Faul. Marie could sense distinct pleasure within the woman pirate's voice. It made her sick.

"I could add to your collection of wounds, gladly," Marie said, immediately mustering strength and resolve. She welcomed hatred now.

"They're only slight impairments," said Faul. "You will never truly stop us, Princess. Even now our leader approaches. Rest assured, Magnus will be here soon. Then you will pay dearly."

Marie sensed Randt seething behind her. The LUCY landed near where Marie stood. Dove was silent inside the body of the robot girl. The Beestje sword now hung loosely in the little bot's slight grasp, lolling dishearteningly at its side.

"This mistake will be your last," said Marie.

"Ahhh...such brave words from a woman who has two proton launchers leveled against her. You'll be obliterated at a single tap of my finger, Princess. Disintegrated to ash..." said Faul. "You've seen the power..."

Marie couldn't look at the wreckage of Quilp, instead her eyes searched the vacuous dark that surrounded them. *A way out...anything?* Faul strode to stand dead center. She hoped her movements would attract Marie's attention. Marie did not accept the lizard woman's wanting eyes, but instead latched her vision on to gigantic carved symbols that decorated the gilded panels surrounding the room. Strange formations, archaic looking—foreign. She did not understand their meaning. She was sure they had something to do with the guardian of the next gate.

"I sense great fear in you Antoinette, not so brave now that you don't have your precious Aramen slave here to guard you."

"You're mistaken Is'rondai," said Marie. Faul turned, fingered her proton cannon, and stepped with slow, knife turning purpose.

"And what of your poor dwarf here?" Faul toed Quilp's crumpled body with a probing boot toe. "Sad?" The lizard woman was caught up in the sight of the mangled pile. She smiled, taking pleasure at her work and then turned gaze to Marie. Immediately and with swift force, Marie smashed a fist through Faul's proud chin. The lizard woman let out a throaty gurgle, mouth filled full of her own green blood. Faul's proton cannon clattered across the ground. She flung her body full force at Marie.

Shots exploded the air somewhere beyond where Marie and Faul clashed. Randt's pistol bullets ricocheted off Kitrank's body armor. *Ka-thoom* flashes of proton energy exploded back in the dark air. Randt and the LUCY, seizing the opportunity, fled across the platform. Randt fired back and would not be deterred as more protons ate up the ground at their heels.

Marie, with full Mesmo-force, took down Faul with a dizzying roundhouse kick. Red hot anger flashed within the princess. She hungered for swift vengeance. Marie leapt upon Faul and battered the pirate with lightning hot fist smashes. The lizard woman wrapped legs around Marie and flung the princess back to the earth. Back smacking paving stones, thunderous concussive explosions rocketed through Marie's vision as her visor shattered to pieces around her head. Marie quickly rebounded and fired wrist guns. Screams erupted in her throat as she relentlessly emptied round after round at Faul. Clanking bullets flicked off Faul's bracers and cuirass. The lizard woman raged toward the princess.

Randt bee-lined for a saving option in darkness. Kitrank's heavy footfalls clamored the ground behind him. The pirate leveled his cannon; the LUCY, boot jets flaring, rocketed, flipped, and grabbed hold of the nozzle and squealed. Kitrank reeled back and misfired a barrage of blasts into the blackness above. The LUCY clattered free. Kitrank angrily smashed the bot with his boot and ran after Randt.

Randt was laser focused on the wall panel at the perimeter of the chamber inscribed with the name of the leviathan, Ba'al. Proton blasts shattered the earth around him. Randt evaded exploding earth and with one mighty leap, flung his body at the panel. His shoulder and hip clashed the hovering stone pediment. The LUCY, rejoining, rocketed into the panel at the master coder's side. They thrust fists against the wall and the massive stone heaved. Randt took in a gasp of air. Steely clattering echoed through the chamber; hidden mechanisms activated. Randt slid to the ground only to see Kitrank rail towards him, feet first. Randt's head met the full force of the wasp-man's boots. Somewhere up above, the dome ceiling clattered open. Randt revolted against the pirate, returning Kitrank's attack with streetfighter kicks and pummeling fists as screaming maelstrom heavens revealed themselves.

The raging howl, unlike anything Marie had ever heard before, rang ear-shattering through the expanse. Fighting paused. An immense catastrophic miasma was lain open above them. Ferocious winds sought to collapse their bodies as if they were made of nothing but feeble sticks. Marie swallowed hard; she felt her soul leap. Mesmo-boots dug in deep. A massive swirling whirlpool of white-lit waters hovered in the darkness above their heads.

It was a strange formation, a thundering swirling nebula of water spinning in a gargantuan expanse of space—and through these crashing waves, the body of a steel snake monster wove. Upon its back, glinting sails, stories high, sliced both wind and wave. It had a humongous mouth of razor teeth—five rings deep, each line rotated independently and consumed water and light. A giant protruding eye orb emitted rays of starlight. Its massive body tore through the fathoms with silent reverence, bound to its own task of endless swimming. Marie was mesmerized by the horrific beast's elegant movements. At length, its belly glowed, and fire leapt from the rotating tooth mouth. Waves erupted into sparkling aquamarine. Glittering elements, particles of seafoam ignited, undulated, and then died.

Faul shot Marie a horrified gaze. Marie punched the lizard woman square in the face. The pirate clattered across the ground. Marie readied for the woman to retaliate, but then suddenly felt a strange force overtake her body. Tingling sensations rippled along her armored form. Even the gigantic body of Khephri-Dio was affected. The lifeless juggernaut guardian, shuddered then leapt, hauled into the air, quite easily, by some magnetic field. Marie struggled to maintain her footing and too was carried up. *This is the core of Hout's gravitational force*, Marie realized. Electromagnetic energy captured everything around. They were being delivered into the body of maelstrom.

Clutching fingers grasped Marie's boot and Faul quickly engulfed Marie's body like some arachnid ready to bind up its prey.

"Not so fast Princess," the lizard woman hissed. Their enmeshed bodies cartwheeled up through darkness, then meeting saltwater spray, the outer edges of the maelstrom caressed their death embrace. Faul's python arms clutched and crushed Marie. Marie fought to catch breath. Mesmo armor leapt to life and discharged a sputtering barrage of electricity. Faul laughed with glee and hugged Marie tighter. The charge ignited her passion to kill.

Without warning, a concussion of massive scale, rocketed through Marie's body. The steely surface of the castaway body of Khephri-Dio cracked the princess' body almost in two. Slamming, flailing appendages scraped against Marie's armor. Suddenly Marie was free of Faul, her body meeting churning waves. She struggled through the deep blue waters and then surfaced, lungs grasping hold of disparate bursts of air. Salt stung her mouth and eyes. The body of Khephri surged along the water top. Marie grasped at a slippery beetle leg, hoisted herself on the massive appendage.

"Marie!" Faul's voice screamed out above the waves which tore relentlessly at the fringes of Khepri and sprayed them with stinging pellets. Marie raced up the bug leg, grasping, arms straining desperately with every bit of length acquired. She grabbed each segmented panel and then heaved her body atop the belly of the scarab.

From the body of Khephri, the vista of the massive swirling ocean splayed out before Marie. Its immense form became walls of awful dim glowing waves that dwarfed even the massive body of Khephri-Dio. Marie flung her body down against the adrift beetle as a wall of water slammed down upon her. The massive burst of water raged and then subsided. Marie flicked away errant strands of hair plastered across her face. In the distance, high atop the back of the Khephri's head, the figure of Randt struggled to stay upright. The Sabre of Destiny glowed in his grip. The LUCY was sputtering the air at his side on practically extinguished foot jets.

"Randt!" Marie screamed. Her voice was caught and smothered by the raging waters. She shot a glance over her shoulder. Faul clamored along the bug back, eyes seething flames of yellow. Marie jolted. Faul leapt and clamped hold of Marie's legs. Her body slammed against the ground and Faul's hungry fingers tore at every part of Marie's body. Marie shot off a thunderous round of wrist gun bullets, point blank. Faul's body rocketed back across the surface of the scarab. Marie caught boots and raced toward Randt, crying out.

Suddenly the beetle was caught up upon a wave of water. Randt turned attention to her, startled, then relieved, he began yelling back at Marie. The head of Khephri swelled above her. Randt, caught up in the uplifting appendage, slid expertly down, side footed along the beetle back, immense speed captured him. "She's coming!" Dove shouted after Randt, sputtering a distance behind. Marie turned. Faul raced towards her. "Marie!" Randt screamed and flung the Sabre toward the princess.

Faul tackled Marie just as the princess' fingertips touched Sabre hilt. Grunting and denouncing any further smothering grip from the lizard woman, Marie turned heel and thrust the sabre's searing, electrified blade straight through Faul's abdomen. Shock contorted the Is'rondai's face. Marie screamed and kicked Faul's body free from the blade. Randt slid to Marie's side. He grabbed at her arm. "Are you okay?" Dove called hovering above them. Then Marie caught glimpse of a massive form rising high above the waves. It was Ba'al. A gargantuan spinning mouth of teeth whipped up and shredded white caps. Randt shot Marie a disheartened glance as the leviathan crashed down upon the beetle raft. Everything became a cataclysm of water, crushing steel and churning, screaming air that was suddenly doused by endless hungry fathoms.

Jet black unconsciousness swiftly took resolute hold of Marie.

~ PART IV ~

EPISODE 40.

On the Banks of the Seine.

"I thought I would find you here..." Sheng said. Marie was relieved to hear his voice—so relieved that her heart ached. She did not turn around to look at him. She was afraid. She peered out over dark waters, sun star flaring like a supernova casting her body gold. She was wrapped in a dress of billowy linen. It caressed her skin. Her belly was heavy with child. "You always come here when you want to think..." he continued.

"It's where I come," she murmured. It was a matter of fact. "...where I ran to when I was afraid, where I played, where I was taught, where I dreamed...everything...this place IS me. You remember when I brought you here for the first time?"

"We were cadets at the Academy. You wanted to bring me back to Titan, to meet your father..."

"We hiked all day in the grasslands around my father's estate. I told you about the willow tree. You wanted to see it, so I brought you here."

"You were right. It is a beautiful place—the grasslands. The riverside outside your father's estate. Brighter than the Tors of my home-

land. Here by the willow tree the river catches the light of the sun star just so..."

"You were a nice boy from a fine family. My father and my grandfather couldn't argue with that..."

"We were uncomfortably in love. Friends who didn't know we were in love. -well, I knew. I wanted you to be. You. To be in love with me..." Sheng stumbled over his words as he sometimes did when he was talking to her.

"Yes." Marie laughed.

"We both knew."

"Yes. We sat right here. Let the day settle in around us. 'At last,' you said, 'I fear you're going to be the death of me, you know? How many men have fallen for you now, Marie, one hundred and fifty-eight?' 'Nice, so specific,' I said. 'Someone's been keeping track—one thousand, apparently, now...one thousand and one.' I punched you in your shoulder. You just laughed. Your eyes consumed me. They were dazzling, thrilling kaleidoscopes, 'Not the boys that I wanted to...' I said at last. I thirsted for your touch. You put your hand over mine. I was elated. This was it. 'The death of you?!' I said sharply, then— 'What about me? I'm the one being pressured constantly. Everyone's looking at me and I just want to hide. My grandfather only talks of marriage—but I'm only just now graduating...' my voice trailed off; the rushing water ate my words. 'Marriage,' you said, pretending disgust. 'Horrendous...' you shot me a sly smile, then went on: 'I totally understand Princess, you have things you want to do with your life—but you're not the only one with dreams, Marie Antoinette. You want to be out there flying; I want to be a Commander of the Dauphin's Armadas.' (You thought I would be impressed.) 'Are you sure you want to be just a pilot?" you went on. 'I'll totally outrank you. You think you can handle that?' I gazed back at you, pondering the lines of your mouth. I was enraptured by them. 'I can handle anything...' I said. My eyes searched the raging dark waters of the Seine. I thought of my mother.

You brushed a strand of hair away from my eye. Called me into you. 'I'll be there for you always,' you said. This promise was strange and welcome to me. Nothing like any man had told me before. I remember the heat of your body in that moment. It was a dangerous proposition for a woman who wanted to live a life among the stars. But I kissed you anyway. I was satisfied. You were relieved. We loved exploring each other's bodies on the banks of the river that day. The lines of your bare torso and hips fascinated me like the far reaches of the solar system did. You finally got the courage to say you loved me—that you had from the moment we met. I knew those words had scratched impatiently in your throat for years. But you finally said them. It was what I wanted to hear. The prospect was both cathartic and excruciating."

"I hung on to your every kiss," Sheng responded then. "Every curve of your body, every dream you ever had. A forbidden moment by the water's edge...."

"That day we didn't care about laws or religion or what my father or grandfather would think—the only guiding force was the ceremonial lust within our hearts."

"We finally did get married, though," Sheng said.

"Yes...before God, we made ourselves one. We took vows."

"Yes," Sheng's voice was sad now.

"I came here to the river's edge the day that we fought. You were wondering why six years after we were married, still no children came. I took offense. I thought you wanted too much from me."

"Maybe I did..." said Sheng.

"I hated the distance that exploded between us that day. I had lied to myself so long. The idea that I was in control, but my secret actions were controlling me instead. I was fearful of you then. Of what you would do. I hated being afraid of my best friend."

"What is it, Marie?"

"I was addicted to your steadfast patience. Waiting in the wings. Many times you did so willingly, so I never really thought..."

"I knew being a mother wasn't really in your plan," said Sheng at last. "I was right, wasn't I?"

"I may have led you to believe that one day I wanted to be. But that day kept getting delayed. We had our lives. Our goals. Our dreams. We only shared fleeting moments here and there when we were both on leave. Those times were magical. We had our wonderful lives together and apart. You wanted more."

"It's only natural..." said Sheng.

"The day we fought I ran back here to the river's edge, but this place wasn't even my friend. I went back to my father's house. You had taken to my family chapel to pray. I peered quietly at you through the doorway. My communi-com vibrated. I was called back on another mission. I left you there at the feet of the Virgin and wrapped myself up in the cockpit of my ship. Titan retreated beyond contrails and clouds ate up the sparkling river below. Space welcomed me again as I knew it always would."

"We made up, though, Marie. We continued on as couples do..."

"Did we though?"

"What is it, Marie?"

"I had insurance Sheng. I did what I had to do. I made sure we never would have a child. I lied. I never told you it wasn't a possibility. I was so scared, but now by some miracle, this child is the only thing..." Marie heard a torrent of wind suddenly scour the grasslands at her back. "Sheng..." she murmured. Finally, she turned around to face her husband, but only empty fields and the rustling boughs of the willow tree met her searching gaze.

EPISODE 41.

Blood Hollows of Hout.

Luscinia's final words ran on repeat in Corvin's processors: *"Do as I say, now, do as I say. Magnus must be destroyed, if you fail, all of Hout will surely fall..."* The cataclysmic words became his mantra. Each precious word the nightingale had spoken returned valid tokens of action, courage, and valor within him. Corvin's new piezo heart, a gift from the priestess, now supercharged his every cell. He soared viciously through the blood red breeze in pursuit of the evil cyborg.

The blight had thrust itself through the substrata of the realm, creating a passageway several hundred meters wide. The spiraling red-light-doused channel was encumbered by a multitude of dark reaching arms. Corvin soared the troubled thoroughfare, swooping, dodging, and jetting. Pulsing lava clung to the recesses of the vast space and raged along crags and crevices. The environment was so hyper-crimson, Corvin had to engage red-cancelling ocular lenses just to see. The twisting, porous environment spun out around him in an insane kaleidoscope. He was dead locked on Magnus' electronic signature.

"Only several hundred meters now!" Corvin yelled out at the Aramen who kept pace beside him on wolfsdamsylfly back. The raven general took lead of the V-shaped formation. "He should be coming into view..."

The Aramen saluted and lashed wolfsdamsylfly reins. The creatures let out wicked howls.

"There he is!" Corvin cawed. A knife-shaped, black conveyance sliced through the ruddy air just ahead of them and disappeared quickly behind a massive number of spans.

The Aramen dug silver feet into wolfsdamsylfly sides. The beasts reared, roared, and shot ahead with amazingly intense speed. Corvin drew a power surge and raced ahead.

The air concussed around Magnus' speeder and slowed. The cyborg's thrusters were flooded. The Aramen took advantage of this and assailed him; the howling wolf headed beasts became raging banshees of vengeance around the vehicle. The Aramen aimed hands and fired. Explosions rocketed across the back of Magnus' black, spiny nosed conveyance. Magnus thrust downward.

The Aramen were not deterred. They directed their beasts after him. Corvin raced behind them. Suddenly some unseen electromagnetic shockwave, perhaps emitted from the vile hands of Magnus himself, yanked the Aramen free from wolfsdamsylfly saddle and bashed them together in the air beyond. Their bodies erupted into an orange-green fireball. Wolfsdamsylflies soared free.

Spanning structures cracked; smoldering debris rained down. Magnus' speeder evaded the collapse; smashing ahead, the vehicle charged out through the crimson mists, full throttle.

Only a few more leagues and he will be exiting out int the Tweelach swamp. Corvin was sure that Marie's complete obliteration was now Magnus' greatest obsession. Corvin feared for the princess and for the frail, dying realm of Hout. He had to stop the beast. It was now or never.

Corvin charged down the hyper-lit chamber with a blast of supersonic speed and touched down on the jet-black speeder. He fought buffeting winds. Latching on fast to the quickly moving conveyance, the raven general thrust his talons into glass, pulled open the speeder's canopy and ripped it from its hinges. Sparks erupted into the blood-red air. Corvin thrust the canopy aside. It fell off into the far crimson reaches of the hollow.

Shurikens immediately rang past Corvin's head and shattered through his wings; unfazed, the raven general took hold of the cyborg's hair and his claws hungrily searched for eye sockets to impale.

Magnus yanked himself away, thrusting fists in the direction of the raven, he pounded out more bracer bullets. Corvin's breast plate ate them. Alerts blasted the raven's vision; the cyborg's contorted face pulsed insane bloody red in its scope. Magnus let out an enraged howl. Corvin pulled at the beast harder. Magnus slammed his boot down into the throttle and yanked the yoke. The speeder turned, clattered, and spiraled frantically down the channel with enormous speed.

Corvin lost grip and caught wind. His wings flailed as he tried to maintain posture, clutch air, and pound it. He rallied and aimed himself for the speeder cockpit again. Racing toward the gnarled visage of the beast, he attacked the cyborg with full force and jerked the monster free from his seat, flinging him into the red-charged air.

Magnus ate crimson wind, body akimbo momentarily, he snarled and flung out magnetized claws, his body boomeranged back to Corvin. The cyborg caught hold and vice-gripped the raven general's leg with desperate ferocity. The other hand sealed them both in a death hold to the flashing speeder back. The conveyance, steady now, locked on to its destination once again and rocketed through the spinning cavern with immense speed.

Corvin punched Magnus in the skull with a mighty, quaking wallop. Pus spewed from the monster's mouth. Tumbling, Magnus fell back along the speeder top and rebounded. He raged at the raven; unsheathing his battle ax, he charged and let out a machine-breaking blow. Corvin quickly blocked the attack and leveled out a seismic punch into cyborg gut.

Magnus' body skittered across the back of the speeder again. Metal screamed against metal. Sparks erupted from beneath his steel cuirass. Corvin flung up wings and descended back upon the supine monster like some vengeful black angel. Screeching out a hateful caw, the raven fired off quick rounds of mechanical bullets. Magnus' magnetized hand sent Corvin's shots exploding off into the ruddy distance. The detonations railed against Corvin and sent him reeling.

A trio of wolf-fly-backed Aramen approached the speeder. They set silver palms against the cyborg and fired. To Corvin's glee, Magnus soon became engulfed in their white-hot fire spray. Magnus catapulted his body up against the raging inferno, induced magnetic charges and smashed Aramen bodies into the raven with the full force of his anger. He screamed in defiance.

Corvin desperately caught air, his wings beating rapidly in the super-charged atmosphere. He angrily aimed and rapidly emptied what remained of his bracer bullets into the body of Magnus' conveyance. The speeder detonated. Clattering, screaming steel shattered. All was doused in blazing vermilion.

Corvin slowed flight, beat the air, and watched thankfully as the burning speeder peeled out of the air and plummeted into the hungry red. The passage trembled as the conveyance hit ruddy earth. Corvin screeched in victory, but the victory was short-lived.

In the distance, reaching up through the orange atmosphere, Magnus' charred black form rose from the breath of the fiery wind. He had caught hold of a wolfsdamsylfly wing and mounted the bucking derelict beast. He bellowed a victorious "YAH!" followed by a merciless boot kick. The wolf headed fly bore the cyborg quickly into the distance.

Corvin flicked back burning air, spun round, and flung himself full-bodied toward the beast.

A gleeful gasp sputtered out from the cyborg, who turned in the saddle, aimed disembodied, hotwired Aramen arm and let loose an inferno that engulfed Corvin entirely.

Eating fire and doused in a rampage of screaming catastrophic alert processes, the consumed raven general crashed into the ruddy hollow wall. His pulverized body fell free of the reaching, angry blight arms and plummeted into the blood red lakes below.

EPISODE 42.

Maelstrom and the Leviathan; or, Belly of the Beast.

Marie felt awash in tears, as if endless crying suffocated her. She swam through layers of unconsciousness. Her heart ached for her husband. The man she had run away from was now the only person she was desperate for. Her legs and arms were useless, wound up in a relentless undertow. She cried out for Sheng, but realized he was only an elusive specter. The ghost of his lips lingered on hers. The distant realization that they were only mirages made Marie cry out. Suddenly she awoke. Her body was awash in sloshing, dim-lit brackish waters. Clanking oxidized steel surrounded her suffocatingly. The Sabre of Destiny lay at her side tossing to and fro in the shallow waves.

Gasping for breath, Marie flung wet hair out of her eyes and searched the environment she now found herself in. *How long have I been here?...Randt...Dove...* She grasped her throbbing head. A staticky, wavering wireframe remerged in her eyesight. Readouts showed her armor was still functioning. She still had a quarter of ammunition and 40% power. *Not a total loss.* She grabbed up the Sabre from the slogging brine and stood, wobbling. *Challenging, but doable.* She could not tell if her legs were failing or if it was the constant rhythmic motion of the chamber. *Maybe a little of both*, she realized.

Another thought occurred to her; she placed her hand on the barnacle encrusted metal wall. She could sense reaction there. Molecules communicated between the suit and the surface. Her mind screamed out—*engage!* The Mesmo-suit began analysis and soon a full picture of this interior world developed in her mind: passageways, avenues, chambers of mechanisms, generators, massive tubes, and wires. She was inside the leviathan. Nearest way out—a cavern of massive rotating teeth, or the ocular housing above. Marie would seek out the latter.

The pale blue light of the Sabre of Destiny and the infrared wire frame of Mesmo-vision guided her as Marie sloshed down a slippery tunnel amid spinning, foaming torrents of water. A distant, plaintive groaning echoed throughout the long expanse. She ushered her battered body forward along the dank watery floor, utilizing massive rust-eaten ribs of joints to propel her forward.

A quartet of chambers converged. Marie whipped around to figure out the path. Mesmo-vision told her the way. Down she went; the avenue led to cascading intestinal chambers and passageways, then suddenly up ahead—a blockage. A slick, massive turquoise body lay before her. *Khephri-Dio...* Marie skittered up over wings and legs. "Randt! Dove!" she cried out. She searched the dripping dark expanse frantically, but her search was cut short. Suddenly the air exploded behind her. Pain erupted in her back and she face-planted into the steel scarab body with full, bone jarring force. Mesmo-suit held; she spun around to face her assailant.

Awash in the dim, cold light of the passageway, Kitrank advanced to where she lay, gnashing mandibles at her threateningly. The steaming proton cannon in his grip whined, then flared; another charge ignited. He aimed the weapon directly at her and hissed gleefully. Marie skittered away, back pressed desperately against scarab surface. Marie braced for another blast, but none came. Some invisible force whipped the wasp man into the air, slammed his body against the ceiling. His weapon mis-fired and exploded. The cramped passage resounded ear-shatteringly. Kitrank thudded back to the ground and splashed into the slogging channel, a mass of twisted, twitching limbs.

A small orb hovered in the smoke-filled air. Marie realized who had saved her. "Randt!" Marie cried out. Quickly hands both human and small robot pulled Marie back to her feet. Relief flooded her entire being. Marie regarded her friends gratefully and then her gaze latched on to the murky distance. "We're inside it..." she said.

"I know, it swallowed us whole!" Dove's voice was morbidly gleeful.

Randt pocketed his orb. His breathing was raspy and labored. Concern flickered across Marie's face. "I'll be fine, I'll be fine," Randt grimaced. Marie nodded.

"I know the way," she said. "Further up ahead the central mechanism, then a passage to the head of the beast. The ocular—it's the only way out..."

To Marie's relief Randt was able to keep pace as they raced the top of Khephri and leapt back down into the sloshing chamber. The darkness became immense for a moment as they waded through the murky passage. Then a dim light appeared, a yawning mouth. At length they reached the outlet. Beyond the portal was a massive screeching, clanking cavity. Hissing steam erupted around the companions as they emerged from the portal. The expanse was a whirring, chugging cacophony. Twisting metal whipped the air above, a crank shaft of immense size clattered above their heads. Thrusting pistons tore up internal air. The temperature was almost unbearable.

"This way!" screamed Marie. Sweat already leapt from her pores. Beyond the ledge, gigantic rings of steel marched out into the distance. In between, mechanical pistons plunged deeply, then retracted. In the void below, a dark channel loomed. Marie sensed it was an immense barrel waiting to be filled with something lethal. *Going down there should be avoided at all cost.*

Marie analyzed the timing of the pounding metal cylinders, then catching the rhythm, she cried: "Jump!" Marie leapt as a gargantuan piston rose revealing the series of steady curved platforms ahead. Randt followed suit. Dove ignited the LUCY's foot jets and rocketed past just as another plunging metal cylinder slammed the air behind them.

They proceeded on momentarily, jumping arcs of steel and allowing pistons to fall and rise before proceeding on. The progress was steady and slow. They continued until only three more jumps remained. "Almost there," Marie said. Randt nodded. Marie jumped. Randt was about to leap when shots exploded at the master coder's feet. Randt staggered and fumbled thin air, his body lurched forward. The LUCY, foot boots aflame, grabbed him up and thrust him to the safety of another rib as a plummeting piston demolished space and lifted again. Marie leapt to the next rib. Alarmed, she turned. Kitrank charged the air behind. His rapid wasp wings slashed through the heated environ.

Marie cursed. Annoyed. She braced for another battle. Flinging herself against the pirate, shielding Randt, she slashed Sabre at the attack. Kitrank blocked with bracers. Electricity sizzled; metal melted. She smashed the pistols from his hands, with a flick of the Sabre. Kitrank thrust knee to Marie's abdomen, slamming her to ground. The Sabre of Destiny launched free of her grasp. Kitrank leapt, grabbed up Randt by the jacket and launched him aloft. Then, turning shiny black orb eyes upon Marie, he paced slowly towards the princess.

"No time t'wait for Magnus anymore," Kitrank hissed. Weaponless, he now sought to crush Marie entirely with the brute force of his myriad of arms. "You and me... this ends here."

Randt's feet flailed out above the channel below. His fingers grasped frantically at the ledge. Suddenly an immense noise rose within the chamber. It was the whining of incredible energy swelling. Marie froze, something very bad was being birthed within the leviathan's gut.

Kitrank flung his body up into the air. On rapid wings he aimed himself at the supine princess. Marie scurried back and thrust up her arms. A squeal shattered the air. More swelling static, a horrendous clatter and then the whole chamber ignited. Marie looked to the air preparing for Kitrank's wrath, but instead, a roaring painful howl punctuated the trilling-charged chamber. Wings separated from body, Kitrank fought the merciless wind. The incendiary breeze caught and flung free-flowing yellow Vespa blood. The LUCY hovered just overhead brandishing the Sabre of Destiny proudly. Dove cried out in victory. Kitrank, wingless, clattered over Marie's body and tumbled full force, uncontrollably along the ground and disappeared into the turbulent rocket glow beyond.

Randt cried out above the raging, thrusting fires that quaked the channel beneath his feet. Kitrank was consumed by the detonating air. Marie and the little bot raced to Randt and hauled him up again as the chamber became a seismic furor of exploding electrons; —they leapt across the final distance and thrust themselves into a small portal beyond.

The safety of an upward passage met them, and they became entangled in a mass of twisted wires. Shooting hot steam invaded the passage. "Upward!" Marie screamed. Randt and the LUCY rapidly followed as Marie tugged her body upward through the smoldering air. Grasping at swinging strands of chord, kicking feet, Mesmo boots finally magnetized and latched onto the wall. Encouraged, Marie fought upward, grasping at fistfuls of cables. She tugged Randt along. "I can manage!" he screamed back up at her. The LUCY rocketed past. Foot jets disappeared into the darkness above. At length they escaped the exploding electrified atmosphere shooting out from the belly of the leviathan beast.

"Almost there!" Dove cried back at them. Soon Marie and Randt reached the apex. Marie finally caught breath again. Her heart steadied. There was a haunting stillness here, an aquamarine enchantment. The battered companions had reached the elegant head-chamber of Ba'al which glittered with thousands of illuminated circuit boards. The components created abstract mosaics on the swooping walls. Ahead, a grand round window ringed with white light beckoned to them. Beyond the curved glass, Marie discerned fathoms and fathoms of churning ocean.

"The eye of the beast," Randt said. Marie nodded and touched the master coder thankfully on the shoulder. They stood in silence for a moment. They mourned for Quilp. Marie then strode to the glass portal and peered out into the endless blue. The little bot jetted to her side and handed her the Sabre of Destiny. Marie nodded and took the hilt gratefully. She reached back and let the Mesmo-suit sheath the Sabre upon her back.

"We've made it. Now what..." Marie murmured. Exhaustion set in. The churning waters outside hypnotized her.

"We're close," said Randt alarmed that Marie sounded directionless. "The central core is beyond the maelstrom and at the bottom of that channel lies the Temple of Saint."

"The processor...the key to all this..." Marie shot a glance back at Randt.

"Look!" Dove exclaimed. The small bot's nose was pressed against the window. "The gate. Down there!"

"That's it. That is the way." There was excitement in Randt's voice.

Marie peered through the churning waters. There it was—a massive round portal, shuttered. "It's closed," she said.

"What did the cypher say—destroy Ba'al's leading eye?"

"We're in it, how would we destroy it?" Marie told the bot. "Besides, it's keeping us alive. We won't survive out there in the waters. The maelstrom will crush us."

Momentary silence. Then Randt pointed pudgy, battered gloved finger in the air. "I have an idea," he said. "We don't open the gate. We crash through it."

Marie thought for a moment. Nodded. Then a smile spread across her lips. "Do you think you can hack into Ba'al, take control, and steer it?"

"I can do anything," Randt said proudly. "Dove, help me."

The two quickly went to work wiring in. Dove was able to utilize the LUCY to infiltrate systems, identify them and Randt worked in tandem to access the correct process and begin the coding. He acted rapidly with his coding bracer to create a burrowing program that would bash open security systems and allow him to access the navigation. This quickly done, Randt turned to creating a system slave. "He's mine," Randt said finally, after only a few moments of clicking away on his bracer.

Marie analyzed the physics of the task. She gauged that the thrusting power of the steel beast would be enough to breach the door and propel them downward. There was enough steel surrounding them to brace them against the cataclysmic collision. "We'll need to strap in," she said, "proceed."

Randt flooded steam power into the leviathan's engines. He directed the head to charge forthwith to the target. Quickly, the shuttered portal accelerated towards them. Grabbing hold of cascading wires, Marie, Randt and the LUCY lashed themselves to the interior. "Hit it!" Marie screamed.

A seismic blast quaked through the chamber. Steel clamored against steel, waters churned, iron shutters groaned and broke open. Randt charged another blast of energy, sending the leviathan body rattling down into the core shaft beyond. Blight infestation exploded against the window. The companions became weightless as the beast flung itself down leagues of endless passage. The unknown end sent a thrill of fear through Marie. "Brace yourself!" she shouted. Suddenly she felt her body consumed by turbulent upheaval. Horrific grinding and crushing steel mangling in upon itself wailed out amid sparks and flashing surges. Glass shattered, followed by catastrophic detonations—then silence and darkness.

EPISODE 43.

Hall of the Sapphire Lords.

Marie awoke to clamoring water. Twisted metal cradled her. Glittering orange and fuchsia light filtered up into the misty air; the distorted body of the leviathan receded up for fathoms into a yawning expanse. Tumbling water cascaded around it; frothy inlets and channels created by catastrophic destruction gave way to crashing falls. Peering over the edge of the destroyed face of the decommissioned sea monster, Marie discerned a cracked, gleaming sapphire platform and nothing but churning dreamy nebula clouds beyond.

"Randt? Dove!" Marie cried out.

A distant voice responded. "Over here! Down here! Stairs—passage to the temple! We're so close!" Randt's voice was incredulous and jubilant.

We survived! We actually survived! Marie was awash in victory. She hoisted herself up and managed to climb down contorted cables and crumpled steel. Her body was in pain. Every movement seemed an excruciating endeavor; however, becoming upright and walking again seemed to dull the ravaging soreness. *Walk it off...It will be better.*

She strode out gingerly to the edge of the platform. There, spiraling tendrils of Hout roots reached out elegantly among the clouds. They sprouted then turned from the massive entanglement above. Captured within their arms, some distance below, was a lantern-like structure ensnarled with feasting ruby-colored vines. It was the temple. Glinting gold and silver peeked from beneath the entanglement. Leading out from the structure, a sapphire span also covered in red blight, arched to the steps and pathways that caressed the edges of the massive roots of Hout.

There was a balustrade beyond the lip of the platform. Marie went over to it. Randt and the LUCY were already making their way down a vine ensnared sapphire stairwell. Here the blight was devoid of ebony exterior and only the angry pulsing core of pure ruby remained. Crashing rivulets of water turned to vermillion in the atmosphere below. The body of the maelstrom poured out into space. Ruddy rainbows flitted along the showering surfaces. Marie began climbing downward.

"Be careful of the path, it is mostly consumed. Bits come off underfoot," said Randt. "But look, the temple! The fabled hall that houses the Brain of Adelphi Saint. Hout's survival is mere leagues away!"

Randt struggled along the steps; the LUCY assisted him dutifully. Dove had already enticed the bot to create a thin layer of skin that was placed upon Randt's hip and arm wounds. Randt was not deterred, though. The promise of finally reaching their destination was too great an incentive to keep moving. His fervor elicited renewed energy within Marie.

Marie breathed deep. The air here was moist and teemed with electricity.

"Well...we made it Quilp..." Dove said in quiet reverence. Marie paused in her steps. Randt faltered.

"He was a wonderful creation," offered Marie at last.

"He was my best companion –for a long time..." Randt finally said, choking back emotion, "Maybe one of my best works. He served us well."

The steps turned sharply and became steep. It was a perilous scramble to navigate the plunging stones. They led down. Orange atmosphere surrounded them. The temple was obscured by billowing clouds. The sapphire stairs' downward thrust was dizzying. Pieces crumbled and gave way. Marie scrambled to grab blight vines. Randt shot a gaze to her. Marie quieted his concern with a reassuring nod. They continued.

At length Randt asked, "You think Magnus is far behind us?"

"The pirates seemed assured he was close," Marie responded. She glanced down at her communication bracelet. The lights were lit, but dimly. "I don't know. Corvin... You saw what happened in that chamber. Magnus won't stop until he gets complete vengeance. I fear that the conquest at Aramen was a suicide mission..."

"We *are* the last hope..." Dove said. Sudden thoughts flared bright across Marie's mind. *Will I ever see Titan again—or the river? My father...CA(RO)-LYN?* The thoughts haunted her. She couldn't get worry out of her brain. *Will I ever get the chance to set things right with Sheng? And the horror of what happened aboard my ship...when I return, IF I return, what will I return to? I will be a survivor amid endless mourning masses. The poor families...will I even survive this? Will I ever get the opportunity to be a mother? Maybe this child will be a comfort...a blessing...* More and more she clung desperately to the promise of the being growing inside her. The baby suddenly now became completely real. She pictured the child wrapped up, carefully, in her own arms, its bright new eyes staring up at her in wonder. She felt love.

The great sapphire bridge now spanned out ahead of them, piercing through the miasma of coral-colored clouds. Shimmering blue pavers, splattered with massive sprays of feasting red fungus, appeared both grotesque and beautiful to Marie

"The Brain is housed within the temple," said Randt. "The dark code had taken hold of it, rendering it functionless, perhaps. We need to assess it. Hack in, of course, and see what state it's in."

"I can search out the systems," said Dove.

"It has powerful capabilities. You could be consumed by its massive database, dear boy."

"I can do it." Dove said. "I found you, didn't I? I made it to Hout with only a simple string of code. I figured that out. Besides, I've tapped into systems of Hout—I see the framework, it's like an abstract painting -or hieroglyphic language, confusing to most, but I understand it. I know...I see the patterns and I can make it work for us."

Marie felt assured by Dove's words. They *could* do this.

Everything around seemed strangely serene. The nebula was massive, breathtaking, peaceful. It yawned out beneath the bridge. Marie was sure this sight was the most beautiful in the galaxy. Silver streams of water filtered down from above spraying them with reviving mists. "I don't see how this place exists..." murmured Marie.

"Almost impossible, totally impractical," Randt babbled smiling. He scratched his beard with thoughtful leather gloved fingers. "But Adelphi's experiment worked. That's the miracle. Sending out probes into time interdimensional allowed for a millennium to produce an immaculate world. It feeds on the elements of stars—hydrogen, helium...for power, carbon and oxygen, iron...nickel all things bountiful in intergalactic nebula to produce structures and then organizes them, combines them and imbues them with miraculous code."

"He *did* become a god," said Marie.

"Yes," said Randt. "He finally got the respect he craved, up here in the stars away from all those who wanted to steal from him, take him down, those that said that he was a madman—not bad for an outcast artist..."

"Respect in a greater sense. Respect in a world hidden from the rest of us."

"It was enough for him to create something completely without the promise of it ever being discovered."

"What does it matter if neo-humans know? The Houtans know...this is all they know..."

"This is their world; it must be restored for them and for Adelphi."

"Wrongs must be avenged. For them, for us, the Empire, my crew..."

The door to the temple soared before them in the mists. Draped with blight, the slender golden portal was a thankful sight. Randt and Marie heaved the heavy golden gate aside and entered. The inside of the temple was glorious, although infested. A grand hall of sparkling blue marched out before them, ringed in arcades of archways. Within each arc, a wide-open portal gave view to endless orange cumulus beyond. At the other end of the temple stood an apse which held three monolithic figures, kneeling, alien looking; Marie thought they referenced the Janid race, bowing over a tabernacle which held a silver pedestal and a vicious hungry ball of blight. The mass glowed an angry red.

"It's consumed..." Dove said.

Pulsing energy radiated out through the vines that descend in massive amounts from the soaring silver vault above. It spilled out along the floor and plunged out beyond the yawning windows.

"Let's peel it back," Randt told them. They quickly crossed the expanse. The blight was docile here. The creepers could easily be moved aside. The gnarled red arms felt like coagulated jelly. "Perhaps they're drunk on stardust, binging on copious amounts of life-giving elixir..." They neared the apse. Randt called forth his orb and cast it toward the engulfed Brain tabernacle. Punching in a code to his bracer, the orb at Randt's command conducted the blight ball to crack open. Layers of ruddy fungus immediately peeled away. What lay inside the infestation was disheartening.

"Is...is it decommissioned?" Marie said.

Adelphi's Brain was definitely compromised. The oval shaped relic was blackened, extinguished, not the miraculous gleaming, living probe that Randt had described. The machinery now seemed like a useless clump held in the arms of blue-black spans which reached from the fingertips of the sapphire lords that kneeled over it.

Randt climbed the steps of the tabernacle, closely followed by LUCY. Marie was afraid to get near the object. Something felt forbidden about it. She allowed Randt to do his work.

"It may be totally inoperable," said Randt examining the Brain. His voice echoed dishearteningly within the chamber. "There's an outlet..." he said at last. "Hopefully there is some power left within it, something that can induce enough charge to help us connect..."

"I can..." Dove said.

"Let me first," Randt told him. "Just a cursory look." He plugged in his coding bracer. A small screen on his wrist scrolled with diagnostic. Marie mounted the steps to the altar to get a closer look. "I think it's salvageable." Marie was relieved to hear those words. She was hopeful. "Just a little jerry rigging and then maybe..."

A violent concussion shredded the air nearby. Marie flung herself to the steps to avoid a spinning catastrophe and watched as the Brain exploded into pieces. Marie thrust up gauntlets against flinging debris. Sacred fragments crumbled, sparked, and tumbled. Randt was knocked clean from the tabernacle steps and the LUCY clattered to the floor. The whole temple heaved.

In the clearing air, Marie realized what had shattered the Brain of Adelphi Saint. It was a gargantuan battle ax. The massive weapon was now embedded in the bent knee of one of the kneeling sapphire lords. Some unseen force dislodged the ax and induced it to hurl back across the temple to the hand that had launched it in the first place. Marie tracked the ax to its source. There in the doorway, the hulking figure of Magnus eclipsed the glorious atmosphere outside. At his back a wolfsdamsylfly bayed and reared up in rage.

Marie's voice left her.

The entire temple moaned and shuttered. Suddenly a sonic eruption vibrated the entire expanse. Marie quickly flung herself behind a sapphire lord to evade the collapsing vault. Above the raging tumult, Marie heard her name ring out, mournful, angry, vengeful—her heart leapt and ravaged her chest; she was sure this was a cry of war.

Then the solemn task resonated within her and she knew, *it is time to face the beast.*

EPISODE 44.

Brain War.

Marie was sure the whole of Hout trembled. The temple spire tumbled in from above and exploded fragments of sapphire across the expansive floor. Orange atmosphere erupted inside the hall and silver rivulets of water poured in from above. Randt pulled the LUCY over to where Marie hid, back thrust up against the carved robe drapery of a massive sapphire guardian.

"You okay?"

Marie nodded. "We don't have much time...I must stand and face him. The Brain is demolished. How are we to save Hout now?"

Magnus' voice echoed above the tremors. "Marie!" I know you're there! Come out and face MEEEE!" the last word was an insane guttural scream. Magnus pounded his chest and bashed his battle ax into the ground.

"Wait a minute!" Marie gasped. "You said that all of the knowledge of Hout is in every element of Hout. It just has to be accessed..."

"But there has to be a host. Something that has processing capabilities. I can't just hook up thin air to the leads..." said Randt, grimacing, choking on particles of debris.

"MAAARRIEE!!" another curdling scream erupted from the beast's contorted lips followed by thunderous smashing of debris with battle ax blade.

"W...wait a minute...I...I know," Dove said. His voice mingled with the garbled underscore of the voice of LUCY.

Randt looked to the small bot, wide eyed, shock and knowing crossed his features. "I...I'm not sure..." the master coder said at last.

"I have too. It's the only way. You know it's the only way." The bot touched Randt's arm with a tiny copper hand. "WE agree," said Dove/LUCY.

Randt thought for a moment, worry and anguish soured his face. Then he nodded and said, "It may work, it *will* work," he looked to Marie. "Transferring processes, accessing the hidden programming that lies within. The bot functions –could function like the Brain—it only needs to know itself as the Brain of Adelphi."

"It must be done then," said Marie. She leveled her gaze at him and searched his eyes. The master coder knew this was their final hope. Marie delivered the last clear instruction: "Whatever happens, don't stop your work."

He nodded. "Marie..."

Marie didn't respond to Randt. She immediately turned and leapt out into the churning haze filled hall, yanking Sabre of Destiny from the scabbard on her back, she cried out at the monster in the distance. Thrusting electrified blade, Marie let out a slashing fury. Magnus turned and met her charge with his mighty battle ax.

Mesmo-suit pulsed and charged. It screamed. Inner processes roared to life. Energy flared throughout her body. The suit, recognizing the purpose of its manufacture was now to be fulfilled, utilized the final bits of piezo power to solidify the armor and turn Marie's body a shining, glimmering gold.

"There you are!" Magnus screeched. "Lovely princess...good princess...righteous princess..." Marie grunted. The battle ax clamored against her blade. She bowed against the thrust, rebounded then parried. Grunting, she met his rage; they slashed violently against each other. Magnus' rotting mouth curled up with intense glee. Red ocular drove into Marie's soul. His machinery hissed and mighty gears cranked out more rapid-fire thrusts. She met each barrage with expert swiftness and flung herself back, somersaulted, and kneeled, preparing to rail back at him again.

"Bow down to me..." he bellowed with merriment. She flung her body back at him and punched him into a massive bolder of sapphire. It exploded. Magnus slid across the floor and then rebounded, jumping, he met Marie again. They whipped out savage bouts of warfare.

"You're a coward!" Marie screamed. "You are stained with hate and dishonor! You use and kill innocents!"

He punched her to the earth. Sabre clattered out across the chamber floor. She shot him a horrified glance; he paced around her exhausted body, relishing all he had just done.

"So I am. Does that surprise you Princess? You *made* me. You caused this to happen. Am I any worse than you? Than the Queen of Cal'vary?" he gestured down at himself. "Witness the beauty of your work standing here before you...you taint. You maim, you destroy. You're a hypocrite."

"I never wanted you to be destroyed. Killan..."

"Don't say that name. NEVER SAY THAT NAME!" Magnus screamed. "You don't deserve to say it. You lost that right the day you denied me your hand. The day you married Sheng. The day you destroyed my kingdom. The day you watched as the

Queen of Cal'vary took the head from my body!" He leapt at her. She flung herself away.

Scrambling to where the Sabre lay, she thrust body toward the Sabre and felt the hilt come across her palm. She gave thanks. She rebounded and thrust. The electrified blade seared into a fleshy bit of arm exposed between Magnus' metal casing. Staticky blue erupted. No blood. Magnus was unfettered; he slammed her with the flat side of his ax, and she crashed across the room. Marie's body clamored over debris. She righted her body and peered back through the churning atmosphere to the cyborg.

"Here we are the King and Queen of war," Magnus said, tapping ax handle against his hand thoughtfully. "The husband and wife of treachery—the baby that *we* made is not growing there inside you—it's out here—in the open...it festers...and burns."

"For you, perhaps. My conscious is clean. I wanted you to stand trial for your crimes. It was out of my hands..."

"Was it?" he paused. "So naïve, you always were—or the most insidious, I could never tell. The princess of beauty and innocence—or perhaps the Queen of Lies!" His thunderous voice consumed Marie. He rampaged against her. Relentless ax hacks bent her to the ground. The Sabre of Destiny met each barrage and then Magnus pressed down upon her body with his massive form. He placed a tremoring claw over her mouth. "Shhhhh..." He said. "I will have what's mine..."

Marie's mind screamed. She shut her eyes against his probing gaze. She felt the massive handle of the battle ax pin against her abdomen, cyborg knee searched her thigh and claw trailed down from her mouth along her body. Hate and anger welled up within her. All she could do was grasp the handle of the Sabre with all her might. She was useless.

Suddenly the rancorous air of Magnus' breath erupted in pain. A bird-like cry flung out from behind the cyborg followed by a hurricane of battering concussions. Magnus yelled out and Marie was free. The princess scrambled over sapphire rocks and silver bits of heaven-rent architecture scattered along the floor. Finding a safe moment, she searched the orange air to seek out the identity of her rescuer. In the distance she saw him—the raven general had returned. Corvin's wings thrust back in vengeance as he bowed over the body of the beast hacking away at the cyborg with the blade of his black sword in relentless fervor. The beast clamored back, clashing, thrusting, the raven general and the cyborg became a rampaging entanglement of forms. Marie thrust her eyes over her shoulder. She searched the hazy distance. "Randt..."

In the tabernacle, Randt was feverishly at work. The LUCY was now connected to crystalline leads, secure, locked in. Randt gave the little bot a worried glance.

"You will do it, Poppa, I know you will," said Dove/LUCY.

"Yes, my boy...yes..." he was almost tearful. He finalized the connection. "You'll see it soon. You'll see it."

"Yes, Poppa...listen..." Dove's voice came through very clear. The boy's next words were measured and calm. "From the vantage of...Imperial Point of Orbit, right ascension 17h 37m 36.15s, declination -03 degrees, 14' 45.3", planet of Omhawk, the Overseer's Palace. Battery fields...find me Poppa.... Please." The bot's eyes dove into Randt's soul. Randt nodded and tears flowed freely from his eyes. Dove's voice faded.

"I'll come for you Dove! I *will* find you! I promise!"

Randt heard the raging war behind him. It induced him to act. Punching a final code into his bracer, the bot began to whirr and glow and then...

"I SEE!!!" LUCY's voice was a sigh of ecstasy. The bot, infused with massive amounts of energy became a white-hot light. Randt flung himself from the dais. New instructions flooded Dove's senses and the boy saw everything he needed to see; tapping in, he found the correct procedures and initiated the sacred codes of Adelphi Saint. Instructions of resurrection ignited and flooded back through every element of Hout. Dove felt intense honor and satisfaction wash through every neuron as the unending light of salvation consumed his awareness. At last, the boy disintegrated into the ether.

The bot's body quickly became the endless channel of Adelphi's mystical codes. The small mass of andromatron metal surged and glowed bright, even brighter. Randt shielded his eyes and scrambled to the far recesses of the chamber as the bot induced stardust from the nebula outside to be channeled into concealed chambers housed within the ancient guardians. Hout was soon consuming life-giving nutrients again.

Corvin let out a final gasp as Magnus hacked relentlessly into the raven general; screaming, Marie flung her Sabre into the cyborg's back. He thrust her aside with a battle tank arm and kicked away the mangled form of the raven with merciless glee. Tears ravaged Marie's eyes. She carelessly raged out again and clashed with the beast. Hurt welled up within her –emotions she had kept inside burst forth in swelling catharsis. Metal clanged, sparks rained out, electricity erupted, their bodies enmeshed in lightning and war. Light swelled from somewhere in the apse where the LUCY became the life-giver of Hout. Glittering radiance drenched them in starlight.

Magnus thrust his knee into Marie's abdomen and wrenched the Sabre free from her hands. He beat her with the hilt of it and pressed her to the earth. Flinging the ax boldly from his grasp, he took complete hold of the Sabre and turned the blade downward, pressing tip into Marie's abdomen. The thrusting, searing tip melted through armor and cloth. Marie screamed. Pain and fear contorted her face. The point of the electrified weapon stabbed down even further into her flesh under Magnus' crushing weight. She struggled against his powerful body.

"Allow me, dear Princess, to deny you of everything you ever cared for. I will extinguish the spark of life inside you, surely, and then, so too, will I extinguish the light of this wretched robot world for good!"

Marie's hands flung up to the blade. She tried to force it away. The Sabre ate through Mesmo-gauntlets, melted her hands, and ignited them into flames. Pain and horror erupted from her throat. Magnus' unrelenting gaze seared itself in her vision.

Somewhere in the distance she heard Randt scream; footsteps pounded across the hall. Marie peered up at Magnus; she recognized a glimmer of sorrow stitch across his human eye and then only hatred welled up within. The blade of the Sabre of Destiny impaled her. It rapidly made a catastrophe of the core of Marie's body. Awash in the firelight of her burning body, a hint of satisfaction crossed the monster's visage. Marie and Magnus locked eyes for one last tortuous moment and then Magnus' head suddenly launched free of his body. The monster's humongous form convulsed then collapsed. The ground heaved. Steam and sparks issued from the wound at the beast's neck.

Death stole quickly upon Marie, but not before the visage of Dr. Hannah Krane emerged through the churning, violent orange air. Battle ax in hand, the doctor glared down at Marie for a moment, then complete nothingness.

~ PART V ~

EPISODE 45.

Awakening.

The distant memory of roughhewn edges, cusp of cup pressed against her lips; the smell of moistened gold, water flowing into throat, body washed in coolness soothing the harsh sting of burnt and bubbling flesh...the hole in her very core made well...then nothing for a long, long time.

Faint bouts of consciousness. Far off voices veiled in the fog of dreaming. Caressing breezes. Light, billowing cloth flowing across her rapidly renewing flesh. The smell of rebirth tinged upon the air and, finally, one blessed Houtan cycle, Marie awoke.

The room around her was a hazy, splotchy myriad of twilit forms. It took a moment to focus; she felt like an infant first gaining the full power of sight. Things seemed fresh and new. She drew a breath, so deep, the air was the sweetest she had ever known. A peaceful rustling emanated from the window beyond her bed. The chamber was simple, small, compact. Distantly she felt her fingers and toes come back to life. She did not dare to move, not yet. Beyond the foot of her bed of convalescence, a small lead dresser sat. Upon it, to Marie's surprise and wonder, sat the missing Chalice of Doña Urraca. It looked different. Cracks marred its surface; between each fissure a welding of gold mended the pieces back together. It was an exquisite and perhaps divine golden repair. Marie then realized, with humble awe, that perhaps she was also remade in this way.

A wavering green hologram caught her attention. It hovered within the ribs of architecture which soared up to a darkened point above her bed. The womb-like vision buzzed quietly. A small peaceful form, a bowed down shape, a curling comma of flesh with undulating umbilical rolled delicately in the air above her. Small eyes appeared and then Marie distinguished the beating of a tiny heart. Marie's breath caught in her throat. Her baby was there in front of her, and sudden relief washed over her entire being.

Suddenly a commotion clanged out in the corner. Marie glanced to her side. A familiar figure buzzed back to life from a watchful hibernation. Blue ringed oculars and flashing black beak appeared beside her. Careful talons reached for her hands. "She awoke...you awoke..." it sputtered out in electronica.

"Corvin..." Marie murmured. She was surprised she could speak. Her throat felt like it was made of desert baked parchment chords. "Where am I?"

"Tweelach," Corvin said. She realized he was a mosaic of black, gold and silver.

"What happened to you?" Marie laughed. "Oh," she clasped her throbbing head, "now I remember."

"The trilobite did his best to repair me," Corvin sounded indignant. "But you're awake now..." something like joy radiated in his speech.

"How long have I been here?"

"Three and a half phases, by Imperial Time standards," a female voice resounded from the doorway.

Marie paused for a moment. She did not dare to speak. She did not dare to move. Dr. Hannah Krane strode into the room. The doctor was dressed in a body suit the color of deep forest shadows. Her hair was pulled back in the common severe style she liked—eyes, ice emerald, mirror like. Marie could not tell what the woman intended.

"Don't be afraid," she said at last. "I want no more to do with fear. Or anger."

Marie said nothing, but Hannah could sense the princess' anxious animosity.

"I know you don't believe me." The doctor strode toward the bed. "Why would you? I don't blame you. You *will* be fine though," Her eyes probed Marie's. The look of the doctor still annoyed her. Marie could tell she was looking for some sort of contrition. *I'm not sure I'm there yet, Hannah*, thought Marie. The doctor peered up at the ultrasound; she checked the readouts scrolling at the edges of the image. "Your baby will too..." Hannah murmured. Momentary silence, then, "Corvin and I have both been looking after you. Vitals are stable. Looks like you're about seven phases along..."

"The chalice..." said Marie.

"Yes. A thing of miracles. It saved both our lives..." She laughed.

"I thought it was stuff of legends. I know it is sacred to the people of Cal'vary and a holy legend of the church, but I never really believed..."

"It's real. I can't explain it. After all, who could resist immortality?" Hannah picked up the cup, inspected it. "Not me. The waters consumed from it *are* divine. I drank out of that cup as soon as I stole it from you...in the Orzos killing field..." The memory of the moments after the escape pod crash resounded in both of their minds. "I'm glad I did. Insurance. Insurance against *him*."

"You knew of its powers..." said Marie.

"Yes. Magnus knew it too–how else could he evade death? He stole the chalice from Cal'vary Keep for a reason."

"That's why the Queen wanted it back so desperately –and to keep it hidden. You were his accomplice all along..."

"Yes..." Hannah said. Then a thought occurred to the doctor, smiling, her voice became almost giddy. Marie soon realized it was probably painful sarcasm. "Having drunk from the Sacred Cup—will I become the most powerful woman in the universe? Will you? You have a better shot than me, of course, you always *did* have the upper hand, Marie Antoinette..." Her voice died on the air. Marie knew Hannah was struggling with her own emotions.

Extreme gratitude suddenly filled Marie. It unsettled her that she felt that way toward this woman, but she knew that without Hannah she and her baby would not be alive. "Hannah, I..."

"No. You don't get to apologize. I can't suffer that too," Hannah turned to gaze out the window. "Sheng loves you," she said. "He told you the truth. I was just a momentary lapse of judgement. I'm not even part of the equation any longer..." Marie considered her words. A pause, then turning back to Marie Hannah said: "Now *you* get to decide what happens."

Marie gazed up at the ultrasound. She became lost in the lines of her child.

Hannah pondered Marie's awe, then said quietly to the princess: "It's funny how some women want so very desperately to have a child—with all of their being, but never, ever can." Marie looked at the doctor. "And then there are those that will have a baby no matter if they really want one or not." Marie saw intense hurt well up within the doctor's gaze. "I wish you the best of luck Marie," the doctor said at last. "I'll check in on you again later if you don't mind..."

Marie did not say anything, only nodded. Hannah left the room.

Marie bathed in silence for a moment. She was comforted by Corvin's presence at her side. Finally, she said to him, "I can't stay in Hout."

"I know," he said. His blue-black hued oculars reflected her swaddled form.

"I feel strength returning rapidly."

"A few more Hout cycles then..."

"Where's Randt?" Marie asked.

"Gone." Corvin's processers whirred thoughtfully, "Things have changed." Marie set upright to listen, grimacing, she immediately regretted it. "Hout has been renewed," Corvin said. "Tweelach bustles again. The blight has turned itself green and has become life-giving. It now blooms everywhere. Instead of defiling our realm, it now pumps in new energy. Endless, bountiful streams of energy." Marie smiled. "The war machines in the Mech Mech village are being dismantled as we speak, new Houtans are being delivered to us every day. Hout is forever changed. We will learn to work together in a new way."

Marie nodded. "...And the Aramen, and the Beestjes..."

"The Aramen reclaimed their original coding as soon as Hout was renewed. The war ceased. Any of Magnus' pirate cohorts have been taken into custody. The Beestje village is in the midst of rebuilding. The Volgens that remain have taken up residence here in Tweelach."

"So, it worked," Marie laid back into her pillow relieved. "Randt went to find his grandson," Marie realized. She was happy for the coder. She was happy for Dove.

"Yes."

"He found a way out of here...I hope he can save his grandson..."

"We discovered several vessels that Magnus held in Aramen, ones that can traverse realms outside of Hout."

"Spaceships..." Marie told him, "ones that Magnus used to attack my vessel, no doubt."

"Nines and Randt left about seven Houtan cycles ago...they both wish you well."

Marie smiled and nodded. "Yeah..." A rising light from the window casement caught Marie's attention. The glinting light fascinated her. It was a strange incandescent. She sensed the swamp outside was now a blooming garden of wonder, that Volgens soared the renewed currents of air which caressed the bright-lit cavern expanses and that endless shades of green stretched off far into eternity.

Marie's eyes rested on the chalice framed in the window. Transposed over the sound of the gentle breeze from outside, panicked voices, screams and futile gun blasts swelled in her memory; retreating crew, ravaged bodies, the fiery decks of her starship and the strained voice of First Officer Blake ordering her to save the sacred relic in the last moments before she fled. "There's something I must do..."

EPISODE 46.

Blackout at the Overseer's Banquet.

Randt arrived at the overseer's palace dressed in a jet-black tux. He prayed that the still steaming taser holes which tattered the area just under the shoulder blade of the elegant black long coat would not be detected by anyone at the party. Randt was not above murder, nor stealing the clothes off a dead man in order to save his grandson. Nines, sans red robe, strode close to Randt's side.

The palace of the overseer was a grand ziggurat which swelled up from the vast orange desert plain and was set back along a massive stone-paved thoroughfare lined with towering gold-topped obelisks. The night was warm and clear. The midnight-colored sky of Omhawk was spattered with smears of rupturing Messier clusters. The courtyard outside was teeming with finely dressed humanoids and aliens alike.

Randt tipped a hat to the serpent guardian who checked invitations at the door. Randt showed the armored Charon the lifted code in his device. The guard eyed Nines suspiciously. Randt explained, in his most noble voice, that he was being accompanied to the event this evening by his esteemed robot courtier. The guardian checked the code against a master list, then annoyed, nodded them through.

"The stolen invite code worked," the Aramen commented quietly as they entered the massive earthen gate. His manner of speech was more assured and clearer now enhanced with advanced mechanics and coding by the master coder.

Randt nodded slightly to a group of elegantly dressed Charon Omhawks just inside the gates. The native spiney snake headed andromorphs were clad in colors of black, gold, and green. Randt quickly pushed his way through the crowd and down the earthen stairs.

"Lanthruk has proven his worth," Randt told Nines. The pirate had once worked for the overseer as a gun runner. Detained by the Volgens after Magnus was defeated, he paid for his freedom by giving over information about the palace on Omhawk, including access codes to the palace basement as well as a layout of the compound which included the way to the viro-energy battery fields.

Melodic symphonies played from the chambers below. Randt sought to avoid the central ball room and banquet hall at all costs. The last thing he wanted was to come face to face with one of the most reviled governors in the galaxy. "This way," Nines directed. They scurried down a passageway and then quickly to an elevator. Nodding, Nines punched in the codes. They launched down into the cool damp cavern below. Randt, nervous, fumbled for his flask and took a swig. Warm liquid quelled his jitters.

"It won't be easy..." Nines said.

"No," Randt choked back emotion. "It won't. But we will find away. There's a doctor in an outpost on Mars...I hope..."

Nines nodded. Randt thrust hands into his pocket. He made sure that the orb was there. He knew what the stakes were in releasing his daughter and grandson from the battery fields—not just the high probability of being caught by the overseer's guards and put to swift and certain death. "They aren't meant to be removed," he stammered almost trying to wrap his head around what he was about to see. "Never meant to be." He looked at Nines. Once a human is induced, committed to their pod, they're just not meant to be removed..."

"You've committed to this Randt. You made a promise," said Nines.

"I know...knowing now what he really faces, just makes it hard."

Nines continued. "Just below is the access door to the underground field. We will follow the plan."

Randt nodded. He fumbled with the orb in his pocket.

Nines reassured him. "The enhanced coding to the orb *will* work. We've already tested it. The synthetic skin will produce rapidly. The bodies will be properly encased. Then the orb will levitate them. We will attempt evade the palace guards through the back passages and back up to the surface where Lanthruk awaits with the ship."

Randt nodded rapidly, "Then on to Mars and hopefully, a cure..."

The elevator grounded; doors whooshed open. Massive lead portal stood closed at the other end of a shallow chamber beyond. Nines hacked in; the doors opened.

There in the dim green light, thousands of pods stretched off in the vacuous chamber in front of them. Randt's breath caught in his throat. "All these poor souls..." he murmured.

"We have to cut the power," said Nines ascetically. "We won't have much time after that. We have to find them quick." Randt nodded. Nines tapped in at an access point by the door and rattled off a code into the palace's systems. Somewhere, a *thooming* drain echoed through the chambers. Surveillance cameras whined to silence and darkness engulfed them.

Randt flicked on his brim light and searched frantically through the pod numbers. The numerals became frenzied and meaningless to him. He cursed himself, tried to find calm and then sense returned to his mind. Finally, he figured out the system grid, the correct row "P" and then racing down to the section which palace records said contained his daughter and grandson. *10124, 10125....10130...* His mind was a battering frenzy. *10150...no, no, no—back, back, back.* Randt's foggy mind raged.

Alert beacons doused the room in flashing crimson. Sirens screamed out. Nines clanged down the aisle between the pods after Randt. "They're coming!" he screamed.

"10135! —here! He's here! My boy!" Randt peered through the small window housed in the upper portion of the lead cylinder cradled in a myriad of wires. "My boy, my poor boy!" Transparent virus eaten eyelids undulated beneath the milky green surface, blackened orbs rolled sickeningly beneath. "*Here* he is...*here* he is. My boy. My boy!"

"I'm about to open the pod," Nines said, punching in numbers. "Best get ready to catch him. Put your mask on." Randt nodded, donning gas mask and gloves he quickly initiated the orb to produce a synthetic sack. With a final click, the pod lid hissed opened, and the jellied body of the boy tumbled out. Randt wrapped the naked body of his grandson in synthetics. He held to the lolling lifeless face and peered down at it.

The black orb eyes seemed to sense Randt was there, and Dove's wavering lips let out a frail, "Poppa."

Tears wracked Randt's body as he rocked the virulent young man in his arms. "Boy, my boy we found you," he said "finally! And we're going to get you well!"

EPISODE 47.

Cal'vary Keep.

"I know...I know what you're probably saying to yourself, Sheng. But listen. I was hurt. I was hurt and maybe I was unfair. Let's just put the past behind us. I must tell you...It happened. I got pregnant. It's what you wanted, right? To have a baby. For us—a future. We'll build a place by my father's estate. Maybe in that field just beyond the gardens of the Grand Trianon. It doesn't have to be big. Small. Small is good. We'll figure it out. I'm thankful now. Lucky to be alive...the crew of the *Marie Antoinette*...in the face of such tragedy. Alive. Anyway, I just wanted to let you know I want to try. I want to try. Let's make a go of it and see what happens. Who knows, maybe we'll be amazing parents. I don't know. But I'll be home soon. Don't worry. We'll talk. You'll see..." Marie finished the recording. She pressed [TRANSMIT] and prayed the transponder still worked. She expected it to take several hours, but then, suddenly, the red hued screen came back... [TRANSMISSION TERMINATED].

"Damn it!" Marie flung her communi-com at it. "The wiretap was good. I checked it!" she screamed. "It should have gone through...what's going on?" She sighed. "What a piece of junk..."

The ship was an ancient relic from some colonial community long lost to the annals of galactic history. She vaguely knew of the race of Proximin Aminths who lived near Rigel Kentaurus that had manufactured the ship. It was small, cramped, urn shaped. The interior was encrusted with golden knobs and dim lit recesses. The cockpit lay towards the center of the vessel. Marie tried to get comfortable in an orange vinyl upholstered seat that would have better suited a child. The fleeting expanse of the God's Eye Nebula spread out in a holo-screen around her.

Marie relied now on old-school navigation methods. Calculating arc seconds and parallaxes, she was finally able to enter in the coordinates to Cal'vary. "I just have to do this Sheng, for the crew of the *Antoinette*..." she murmured, eyeing the chalice peeking from the satchel at her feet. "Promises made, are promises kept." Punching in the data, she flicked on hyper-speed. 48 Imperial Hours and she would be entering the C-Infinity System.

***

Cal'vary was a planetoid, locked within the barycenter of the red giant, C-Infinity and Krainion its sister protostar. The three other planets, Magdalene, Purgatory and Genesis orbited in a figure eight manner around the two stars. Upon nearing the planet of the Celestial Knights Templar, otherwise known as the Cal'vary Guards, Marie's ship was immediately surrounded by four red cross-winged guard ships. The transponder was a whining radio-staticky mess, but still, thankfully, she was able to communicate. She explained she was there by orders of the Queen of Cal'vary and that she needed to speak with the keeper of the sacred treasury. Upon giving them her credentials, they agreed to let her land and enter the sanctuary upon completion of a retina scan and rapid genetic ID. She agreed.

Landing the ancient ship was a breeze. She donned a snow white flight jacket and exited the ship. White and red armored guards met her on the platform and ushered her to a glass enclosed chamber. As they quietly took her blood, she scanned the enclosure beyond. Layers of pink marble and steel structures dripping with wisteria marched off into the ruddy distance. Beyond, the terraced sides of the keep loomed. It was hewn in massive red stones, levels grown over with grasses and olive trees, sprays of lilacs and the very top, a tempietto silhouetted against the churning fiery sky.

Finally, she was granted approval to enter the keep. Guards led her to the lower levels of the enclave of buildings and down a great hallway to massive copper doors decorated with scenes of valor and conquest. She was met by the grand conservator, who wore red and gold vestments and the grounds chatelaine, dressed in a gown of black and silver. Marie offered words of greeting. They bowed as was their custom. Then she drew out her satchel and produced the chalice.

The grand conservator's eyes lighted, they were ghostly blue. "So, it is returned, its rightful home. And you..." she searched Marie curiously.

"Captain Marie Antoinette."

"The step-granddaughter of our queen," the conservator gasped. The pair bowed again, deeper this time, at the realization of who's presence they were in. "Please..."

The chatelaine inserted a key code into the massive portal. The door opened. They entered. The room inside contained a vast array of exquisite religious art, many, many things from the Templar Knight's crusades to Ancient Earth: artifacts, texts wonderous and mystic and archaic valuables beyond anyone's imagining.

Marie found great satisfaction to see the chalice placed in a specially hewn niche in a small tabernacle within the very center of the keep. It fit perfectly in the marble alcove. At the press of the button, a plasma shield enclosed it. The conservator looked to Marie and the chatelaine retreated to the shadows.

The conservator grabbed Marie's hands. "You must stay—we will prepare a place, a banquet..."

"I'm afraid I can't. I must get back to the *Maa'ta Karé Spaceport* and then onto pressing business back at the capital, I'm sure. Time is of the essence."

The conservator clapped her hands to her breast and bowed, a gesture of thanks and respect. "Very well then...your Highness."

Suddenly there was a commotion by the doors. A pair of Cal'vary guards filed into the room.

"Yes?" the conservator said.

"A Vatican ship has just arrived on platform 12," said one of the women Templars. "Cardinal Vesper. Here to request audience with Captain Marie Antoinette."

Marie looked confused. *Why would my grandfather send a Vatican ship?* She wondered. *Word must've already gotten back to them.* "Very well," she told the guard. *At least they know I'm alive.*

***

Marie was quickly escorted to the Vatican ship, *Votive III*, which was a golden, crown-shaped vessel decorated in fluted, swirling filigree. Amber colored windows punctuated the exterior. A flickering light emanated from inside. *It doesn't compare with the pope's ship, of course*, which was fabled for its magnificence, *but this conveyance is grand enough*, Marie supposed, *a definite quaint elegance of its own.*

Two senturions stood outside the gilded ramp amid exhaust sprays. Their blue armored bodies shone against the redness of the evening hour. Their visors sputtered green surveillance procedures. The Cal'vary guards nodded to Marie. Marie returned the gesture and mounted the gilded stairs, climbing into the interior.

She was met by Swiss Guard Valencourt. He was handsome and polite. He led her through the rococo interior to the smoky blessed chamber where a small alter stood glowing with twinkling light wells. A statue of the Immaculate Heart of Virgin Mary, hands outstretched in prayer, stood in a highly decorated grotto. In the middle of the room a small table sat along with two mahogany red velvet upholstered chairs. On the table were two cups of tea. An aging man dressed in a red cassock stood nearby. He had eyes of palest gray, ruddy features and low hanging jowls; white whisps of hair disappeared beneath his blood red galero. His voice was barely a whisper.

"So, it *is* Marie Antoinette," he said.

Marie nodded. "My grandfather must have sent you. I must apologize to him—I had duties to attend to. I know everyone must be worried. There's probably been a great uproar in the capital—if you thought I was dead...there are so many dead...my ship..."

Vesper motioned to the table. "Please sit." He offered her tea. She was growing impatient. "No," she said at last. "No tea for me. I won't sit either, I apologize if you think I'm rude, Your Eminence...but I must get back to the *Maa'ta Karé Spaceport.* You see my husband's there and..."

"Sheng," the old man looked amused.

"Yes. My husband Commander Brandon Sheng, he's stationed on the *Maa'ta Karé*. I'm sure with everything that happened there will be inquiries...inquests perhaps. The horrible fate of my ship. It makes me sick. He must be worried. I must go—I have my own conveyance."

"Sheng is no longer on the *Maa'ta Karé*," said Vesper. He took up cup and saucer, sipped, and pondered.

"Well...where is he?"

The cardinal sat silent for another moment. "How long do you think you've been away?" The abrupt question startled Marie.

"A few phases...maybe..." she stammered.

Vespers considered her words for a moment, then said, "For man his days are like the grass; as a flower of the field he flourishes. When the wind has passed it over, it is no more; and it acknowledges its place no longer..."

The cardinal's voice sickened her. Her hands went to her abdomen. She leveled her gaze at him and with eyes fierce, Marie clearly stated: "take me to my husband NOW!"

EPILOGUE.

In the Garden of the Grand Trianon.

Rolling marmalade-colored clouds swept up against an immense aquamarine sky. *Votive III* entered the atmosphere of Titan with little fanfare. The moon, one of the first in the Empire to be successfully terraformed to match the neo-human's abandoned home world of Ancient Earth, was a somber and welcome sight for Marie. She stood now; hands pressed against an amber window lost in the numbing cacophony of her mind. The outpost of New Paris, a few kilometers from Kraken Mare, retreated below. It was the city of her youth, achingly familiar, with its nouveau domes and cathedrals, public buildings, residences all hewn of mercury glass and patina metals. The river Seine, named in homage to the earthly river of ancient lore, flared a streak of white below as the Vatican ship quickly followed it out into the countryside.

Marie had faced the hours long journey from Cal'vary mostly alone. The ship was indeed well equipped with advanced hyperspace technology, but still the wait to reach Titan was excruciatingly long. At length, the grounds of Versailles came into view. The long C-shaped building and a smaller residence tucked in the woods behind, set amid terraces of gardens and fountains.

It had been home to the Dauphins of the early dynasties of the Empire before the capital was moved to New City on Europa.

Votive III touched down quietly in the fields north of the chateau. *Quite a distance* Marie thought. *Why so far away?*

Valencourt came to get her, and they met the cardinal in the fields by the ship's ramp. They then silently trudged through waist high grasses to where a manicured yard came to meet it. *This was an awkward way to enter,* thought Marie. The back of the west wing of the older part of the chateau met them broad-faced, windows shuttered against the brilliance of the sky. Rounding the corner of the Trianon, Marie met the upper balustrade of the garden. What she saw in the grounds below struck her dead still.

An elegant woman sat at the head of a white linen draped table. She was dressed in a robe anglaise of peach and blue frothing with lace and tulle. Pearls and diamonds dripped from her neck and ears. She gestured to their robot maid and tucked an errant strand of jet-black hair back beneath her flaxen-colored wig. It was massive, curling, woven, piled high with rosettes and sparkling rhinestones. The pudgy little hands of a well-dressed boy and a girl, aged around five Imperial Years, waited at the ready to be filled with cookies and cake. CA(RO)-LYN complied to the woman's demand. The robot's gold and tempered glass body gleamed in the sunlight as it delivered another tray of gourmet dessert to the finely set table. The long, brilliant rectangle was the picture of abundance crowded with silver trays of sandwiches, tea, cakes, champagne, and china—the most divine—decorated with a rose and ribbon pattern. Vases of the most radiant flowers overflowed, almost reaching the garden walk. Across from the elegant woman sat Commander Brandon Sheng. His hair was now dusted with gray at the temples, handsome lines sprouted from the corners of his merry eyes and smiling mouth. He let out a ringing laugh that filled the garden entire with a trill of jollity. Marie's white-haired father walked the garden in the distance rocking a baby contentedly in his arms.

"So, you see," said Cardinal Vesper.

Anger flared up within Marie, but she could not move. She wanted to scream out across the garden—make her presence known to Sheng, to her father to CA(RO)-LYN...everyone who ever mattered to her. But for some reason her voice was stuck dead in her throat. The pressure of this newly discovered reality was like a massive glass bell jar descending upon her seeking to suffocate all that remained. "Who is that woman?" Marie finally said at last. She felt as if her own body had been stolen from her along with everything she ever knew.

"She *is* you, my dear," Vespers said. "Your genetic equal in every way. Brought to maturation in rapid time by a process that is forbidden, but yet deemed a necessity."

"She's an illegal clone," said Marie. "My grandfather will have your head for this! The church could not approve of this!"

"For those who love God, all things work together for good, for those who are called according to his purpose. Sheng could not bear life without you."

"No...this is not..."

"Marie, there are bigger movements here. God has blessed this version of you, in his own way."

"No. She is not real!"

"There are forces moving in the Empire unseen in the shadows—quickly searching for daylight."

"You cannot condone this."

"...and she *is* beautiful, compliant, fertile. She gives the dynasty everything it requires and the people everything they need to see. Your grandfather was pleased, very pleased by this change in you."

"Liar! Hypocrite! Monster!" Marie screamed at the cardinal. "Sheng!" She cried out and fled down the stairs. Suddenly a blast of stinging energy ruptured through her back and doused her limbs in ice. Her arms and legs were struck numb. She fell. Thudded down steps. Limp. Hands grabbed her up.

In the garden beyond, merriment. Children played and Sheng and the clone danced, drenched in heavenly daylight.

Senturions joined Valencourt; they dragged Marie back up the stairs, across the lawn, through waving tall grasses back to the mouth of the waiting Vatican ship.

Marie's gaping eyes ate up the last bits of air and daylight before the darkness of the ship enveloped her. A distant voice, her own perhaps, cried out in hateful judgment: *this is what you wanted all along, Marie! This is exactly what you wanted!*

FIN.

LOOK FOR BOOK 2—

PEARL OF HEAVEN,

COMING SOON....

THANK YOU, Reader, first and foremost, for taking the time to consider this work. Mom, Dad, Daryn, Titus (watchdog and moral support system extraordinaire), Dr. V.L.S. & BIAM-for getting this infernal machine to work. David for reading and showing me that it *is* worth it. The tree.

www.ingramcontent.com/pod-product-compliance
Lightning Source LLC
Chambersburg PA
CBHW030810310726
48980CB00006B/448/J
* 9 7 8 0 5 7 8 9 0 1 8 1 7 *